# MIDNIGHT'S DOOR

# ROBERT F BARKER

# Other Robert F Barker Titles

## The DCI Jamie Carver Series

*Last Gasp (Worshipper Trilogy, Book #1)*
*Final Breath (Worshipper Trilogy, Book #2 )*
*Out Of Air (Worshipper Trilogy, Book #3)*
*Family Reunion*

## The Northern Noir Series

*Midnight's Door*

## DEDICATION AND ACKNOWLEDGEMENTS

This book is dedicated to all those who work 'on the door' and whose job it is to put themselves in the way of trouble, just so that others can enjoy a night out without having to worry about the dangers they may otherwise face. Their role demands patience, diplomacy, restraint - physical *and* mental - and an impressive grasp of human psychology. My gratitude goes to those with whom I had the pleasure to work with and to train, and who showed me that even thirty years policing doesn't teach you everything. For the difficult work you do and for your sheer professionalism, you have my utmost respect.

My thanks also to Nikki, Sue, Caroline and Geoff for your help and support in getting this book ready for publication, and to Steve, Kath, Raj and Daniel for your advice, expertise and professional knowledge in helping me produce a story which, hopefully, bears some relationship to the reality of what goes on, 'on the door'. Finally, my special thanks to my good friend and former colleague, Terry Oates, through whose work I first became acquainted with the likes of those such as Danny Norton, and whose experience of working with and training licensed Door Supervisors proved invaluable in helping me refine some of the details.

## Author Note

For many years, Mr Smith's nightclub at Warrington was renowned as Northern England's premier dance venue. Clubbers travelled from far and wide to enjoy the buzz and excitement generated by its heady mix of music, dance - and other pleasures. During this period, when the town's club scene was at its height, I worked as a Detective Inspector in charge of the local CID. We were always busy. Elements of the story that follows were inspired by incidents that occurred around those times. Some years ago, the iconic building that housed the club was destroyed in a fire. For the purposes of this story, it still stands.

## Prologue


The girl stands in the full glare of the car's headlights, like a stage performer under spotlights. She is crying constantly now, and the rough ground attacking her bare feet makes it ever harder to meet her tormentor's demands. All around is darkness. The nearest houses are those they passed just before he turned off the main road, a good half mile away. And though she can hear, clearly, the music coming from the car, she knows it is not so loud as will carry that far. Even if it were, the residents are probably used to their peace being shattered by those who make use of long, lonely lanes at night. Couples. Adulterers. Doggers.

Cold now in the flimsy black dress that is fine for clubbing but not the open-air in late-autumn, she winces as something sharp digs into the sole of her foot, the left one this time. Again she wishes she had kept her shoes on instead of discarding them for fear of breaking an ankle. Even if she could, she does not need to look to know that her soles are cut and bleeding. But despite the pain, she does not break from her task. She dare not. Since she began, she has stopped, twice, to try to plead with him. Each time her reward was a stinging blow, first to her buttocks, then the back of her thighs. And though she cannot see what he wields in his hand, the bite as it lands and the swishing noise it makes as it flies through the air tells her it must be long, and thin. Both times she felt it she let out a scream, which itself was painful. He must have crushed something, bone or cartilage, when he first turned on her, gripping her throat like a vice as he finally revealed why he had brought her here. As well as the strikes to her backside, the interruptions bring on further tirades, renewed demands that she do as he tells her, '-And stop that snivelling.'

By now, black rivulets of mascara on her cheeks and chest mark the flow of her tears. They are driven not just by pain. It has taken a while, but she now realises the full horror of her predicament. And for all that she is hurting in several places, she knows now they are just the beginning. Barring a miracle, worse is to come. Far worse.

Like all her friends, she has been party to the debates concerning what, exactly, the so-called Club-Killer does to his victims. Speculation has ranged between brutal rape followed by strangulation, to bloody imaginings involving the sorts of methods favoured by the type the media revel in labelling a 'Ripper.' No one knows for certain of course. So far the police have been selective in the details they have released. The result is that in the safety of the clubs, or at home, at work, there are some who delight in dreaming up and giving voice to tortures of the most appalling kind imaginable. Right now the girl wishes she had never listened to any of them, and does her best to focus on the one means through which she hopes she may still avoid the fate she dare not even think about.

At the beginning, he said that if she does well, he

may spare her. The part of her that is still capable of rational thought knows this is a lie. Having revealed himself, he will not, could not let her live - whatever promises she makes about not going to the police. But right now, most of her brain is not operating rationally. Right now it is ready to latch onto anything that holds out hope, however slim, she may come out of this alive.

The trouble is that, while the particular piece of music coming from the car is one of her favourites, she is finding it impossible to respond the way he is demanding. Sure, on a club night, on the dance-floor, she only needs to hear the piece's distinctive opening riffs and she is into it. Within seconds, the sensuous gyrations and provocative thrusts she practises at home in front of the mirror are in perfect syncopation with the music's seductive rhythms, its intoxicating, driving beat. When she is in that place, others stop to watch.

But right now, pain and the fear that is threatening to turn her legs to jelly make it impossible to reproduce the fluidity of movement that, on a club night, draws admiring comments. Instead, her movements are jerky, uncoordinated. The rushing noise in her ears is making it difficult to even hear, never mind pick up on, the music's rhythms.

Lifting a hand to shield her eyes from the headlights' glare, she tries pleading with him once more.

'I, I can't,' she whimpers. 'It- It *hurts*. My feet-'

'Yes, you, CAN.'

His snarling response is accompanied by yet another strike - to her lower back this time. Again she screams as pain she can only liken to being branded with a red-hot iron ripples through her. Desperate to avoid further punishment, she draws a gasping breath, and renews her

3

efforts to keep up with the music. But she is aware that the longer the torture goes on, the harder it is becoming to control her movements, making it ever more unlikely she will meet his demands. In which case, what?

As if reading her thoughts, he snaps at her. 'Come on. You can do better than that. I've seen it, remember? You do it for THEM don't you? Well now you can do it for ME. Come on. DO IT.'

Head spinning, the girl flexes her arms and gyrates in a way she hopes is a passable imitation of her usual performance. She does not need what happens next to tell her it is not.

She feels his hand, balling in her long hair. Without warning he pulls her head back, exposing her throat to the stars. In the dark she had not even seen him slip round behind her. Crying out in agony, she staggers back, going with the pull. Fearing what may be coming next, her instincts are to remain on her feet, whatever happens. On the ground she will be helpless, even more at his mercy.

'PLEASE,' she cries. 'DON'T.'

Then she feels him, right next to her, pushing in close. His rasping breath is on her cheek, bristly stubble rubbing against the smoothness of her skin. She is aware of a musky-sweet smell. It comes from his aftershave. She has smelled it before.

In a voice that is quieter, almost a whisper now, he says, 'You're just a fucking whore, aren't you? What are you?'

Her first instinct - survival - is to agree with him. 'I-I'm a fucking whore.'

'That's right. I bet you get off thinking about men's cocks, growing as they watch you. That's what does it for you, isn't it? Thinking about men's cocks. Growing. I'm right, aren't I? TELL ME I'M RIGHT.'

'OWW.' She cries again as his grip on her hair tightens. But some vestige of pride still remains. 'NO. I'm not like that. I just like to dance.'

'Yeah, I know. Especially when you know you're surrounded by cocks. You like cock don't you? Well here, like THIS.'

Grabbing her flailing wrist with his free hand, he yanks it back and down. She gasps as she feels him, right next to her.

'TAKE IT, BITCH,' he yells in her ear. 'You know you want to.'

Trembling with fear, fighting against the gag reflex that just the thought of touching him brings on, she dare not resist as he guides her hand to him.

'That's it. Harder. SQUEEZE it.'

Sobbing now, close to collapse, she does as instructed as his hand wraps itself round her wrist and forces her to engage with him in the way he craves. There is a flurry of movement as his body writhes in her grasp. As he pulls even harder on her hair, she feels the warm spillage on her fingers, the back of her hand. At the same time he lets out a groan.

'Uunngghh.'

But in that moment, his reflex response causes his grip on her hair to loosen. Just for a second, he lets go altogether. In that second she sees her chance, the only one she may have. She takes it. Springing forward, she tries to force her aching legs, her torn feet, to carry her away somewhere, anywhere, into the surrounding dark.

She manages only a few short metres before something soft - a scarf? - loops round her neck and yanks her backwards, pulling her off her feet. She lands, hard, on her back in the dirt, the force of it spilling the air from her lungs. Before she can replenish it he is on top of her, crossing his hands in front of her face and pulling the two ends of the garotte in opposite directions, constricting her arteries and windpipe. Her mouth opens and closes repeatedly, but in vain. Astride her, and with the car's headlights behind, he is silhouetted against the night sky. Black spots begin to flash across her vision. Some memory tells her they are the first signs of oxygen starvation.

But even as she feels her strength draining away, his grip on her changes. Clamping the ends of the scarf in one hand he lifts up the other so she can see what is there. A knife, like ones she has seen in films and on television but never in real life, flashes before her eyes. She tries to scream but the constriction round her throat renders it silent.

With his full weight on top of her, she can only watch, helpless, as he swaps his grip on the knife's handle so it now points down, rather than up. At the same time he winds the garotte round his wrist, twisting the material so it tightens further round her throat.

As her eyes began to flutter and the blade plunges downward, her last thought is how she now knows the answer to the debates about what he does.

They were *all* right.

# CHAPTER 1

*Saturday. Late Evening*

In the four years I've been running the door at Midnight's, I've only ever been late for work once. Sod's law, it was the night all the stuff that had been brewing for months kicked off.

By 'stuff' I mean the problems with the Russians, the attacks on the girls, the thing with Vicki. Especially the thing with Vicki. And by 'late', I mean really late. It was close to half-eleven when I finally pulled onto the car park at the back that used to belong to a carpet warehouse but since they went bust is now up for grabs.

I've gone over what happened that night many times since, and still can't say if my being late made any difference. But I can't help thinking that if I had been there from the start then maybe, just maybe, things may have turned out differently. At the very least I'd know who to blame for what happened after - me.

The reason I was late was because I'd stayed too long visiting my Dad at Stoke and got stuck coming back up the M6 Northbound when a lorry-fire turned it into a car park. And I only stayed at Dad's because he was in a bad state when I got there and it took longer than I expected to settle him before I could get away. At one stage I was thinking I might have to stay, but he eventually calmed down enough that I was happy to leave him.

I only mention all this because it was while I was sitting in the fast lane going nowhere that I got the call from Thailand. And while it wasn't directly relevant to what happened that night, it would play its part later.

The call came from Stevie B, and if I said it came out of the blue, it would be an understatement. Two-and-a-half years to return a phone call has to be something of a record.

It started with a voice I recognised saying, 'Is that you Danny?'

'Who's this?' I learned long ago never to let on until I know who it is. But I was already placing the heavy scouse accent.

'It's Stevie, Danny, Stevie B.'

'I thought you were in Thailand?'

'I am. That's where I'm ringing from. How you doin'? How's the team?'

I didn't answer straight away because I was trying to remember whether the tariff I was on included free calls from abroad, or if the call was costing me. Eventually I said, 'I hope you're ringing to tell me you've got that hundred you owe me?'

'Better than that, Danny. Guess what I'm looking at. Right now.'

Stuck on the M6, with Eric, my number two, ringing me every quarter hour to update me on the Agnes situation, I wasn't in the best of moods for guessing games.

'A beautiful sunset? A lady-boy? A wok? Stevie, you're six thousand miles away and I haven't seen you or your dumb-nuts mate, Shane, since you both buggered off to Thailand with my hundred quid. How the hell do I know what you're looking at?'

'It's Ged Reilly, Danny.'

Right then it was as well I wasn't going anywhere because I locked up. I gripped the wheel so hard my wrists hurt. A thousand thoughts invaded my not-so-large brain. All I could say was, 'Ged Reilly?'

'Honest to God, Danny. He's right here in front of us, trussed up like a turkey ready for the oven. What do you want us to do with him? You want us to-'

'WHOA STEVIE, you-' For a second I couldn't get the words out. I'm like that sometimes. I get tongue-tied when I'm flustered. Not like my Uncle Kevin. I never saw Uncle Kevin lost for words. Not even the night my Aunty Betty stuck a knife in his ribs. 'You bloody bitch,' Uncle Kevin said. 'That was a new shirt. And it was from Next.' Then he fell down and we didn't see him again for two months, or Aunty Betty for six.

One of the things that's different about my line of work is that to do it properly you have to make people believe that you're not just hard, but sufficiently borderline-psycho that punters won't want to mess with you. The trouble is, people you think would know better actually fall for it. People like Stevie B and his mate, Shane, who if he ever took up acting, would be a shoo-in for Lennie in that great Steinbeck novel, Of Mice and Men.

Eventually I said, 'You're on a mobile, Stevie. Keep your mouth shut while I think.'

Only I couldn't. Not in the time available. What do you say to someone you wouldn't trust to wire a three-pin plug, who's six thousand miles away but tells you he's found the bastard that for the last seven years you've been telling everyone you'll put six feet under if you ever get your hands on him? When I think of Stevie B, the word 'initiative' isn't the first that springs to mind. Nor Shane.

'What's he-' I started again. 'How'd you find him?'

'He was in this bar in the middle of Phuket. The Golden Dragon it was called. Me and Shane was looking for some good quality-'

'STEVIE.'

'Oh, yeah, right. Well, he was just sitting at the bar with this right-fit Thai girl.' Stevie paused. 'Least, I *think* it was a girl. Anyways, I recognised the fat bastard soon as I saw him. We just walked up to him and I says, "Aye-up Ged. Fancy seeing you here." Then Shane bottled him from behind, just in case he had a shiv on him. Which he did. Down the back of his pants. You should have seen the look on his face, Danny, when he saw me. It was like, 'Aw, fuck.' So we just carried him out and brought him back here.'

I sucked air. 'Where's 'here'?'

'Our place. We've got a room next to a nice little knocking shop right on the beach. You can see the sea and every-'

'Your place?' Not sure I'd heard right.

'We needed to take him somewhere. Where else could we take him?'

I shook my head. *What a pair of screw-ups.* 'Stevie?'

'Yeah Danny?'

'I'm going to hang up now. Don't call me back. If anyone ever asks, you rang to tell me you're sending me the hundred quid, right?'

'Oh, okay. But what do you want us to do with-'

10

''Bye Stevie.' I rang off.

We still weren't moving. I stared ahead. Somewhere amongst all the brake-lights I caught glimpses of blue flashes. I thought about Ged Reilly. More to the point, I thought about Ricky Mason.

Last I heard, Ricky was taxiing. This was about three years ago and at that time Sharon, Ricky's child-bride, was well on with their fourth. I knew things weren't going too well with them so I bunged him a couple of ton via a mutual friend, just to help cover some of the bills. I remember how sad it made me feel. Me and Ricky grew up at the same boxing gym, Joe Ryan's in Bewsey. Ricky was always a better boxer than me. A lot better. After Joe took me aside one day and had a quiet word in my ear, I moved on to other things. But Ricky stayed with it under Joe's management. He was setting himself up nicely and was hitting all the right notes, until an old 'friend' of Joe by the name of Ged Reilly decided Ricky was just the sort of investment opportunity some of his Liverpool 'business acquaintances' were looking for. Unfortunately I was in Germany at the time doing personal protection for a poncy finance guy who I later learned was taking the bungs for some Euro-MP. I like to think that if I hadn't been, I'd have seen it all coming and warned Ricky off. I'm still not sure why Joe didn't. Joe was like a father to us. I don't like to think about that too much. For a while it looked like everything was going great. Ricky thought he was being groomed for the big fights and was doing alright for himself. He met Sharon and when she turned seventeen they got married. They had their first two. He was still improving. The future looked rosy.

It was the night before his first tilt at a national title

he found out the truth. Months later, Ricky told me about it. The call came from Ged Reilly.

'You go down in the third and stay down.'

'You can fuck right off,' was Ricky's response.

'Listen to what I'm saying,' Ged said, and repeated the instruction.

Ricky told him where to go again. He went on to win on points. I don't think Ricky ever appreciated how lucky he was to get away with it - sort of. By all accounts there was hell to pay. Ged nearly copped for it himself, but somehow managed to convince his 'investors' it was all a mistake, that Ricky was young and had 'misunderstood things.' Whatever, they decided to give Ricky a second chance. When the same thing happened and he won again, the writing was on the wall.

They came for Ricky when he was celebrating with his mates at Havana-Fiesta's on Bridge Street. There were over a dozen of them, all imports from Liverpool brought in specially. They met, weirdly enough, at what was then Mr Smith's but is of course now Midnight's, and hazed their way up the main street to Havana's. They were all in black and wearing balaclavas. By the time Ricky saw them coming it was too late. Four grabbed him and held him down while two did the business and the others formed a circle, warding Ricky's mates off with baseball bats and blades. The one with the Stanley knife did his back, legs and the tendons behind his knees. In all, he needed three hundred and twenty-four stitches. What the other guy did was worse. He lump-hammered Ricky's hands. A doctor at the General was heard to say that when he picked one up, it rattled like a maraca. Back then Jamie Carver was only a Detective Sergeant, but I know the police did their best. They got the names of the crew no trouble, ran an early-morning swoop and pulled them all in. But no one said a word and they all had witnesses prepared to swear that on the night in question, they were all at a rugby-do at the Royal Oak in Wavertree that lasted into the early hours.

By the time I heard what had happened and got back from Germany it was too late. The CPS had already dropped the case and despite me turning up three hostesses from the club willing to testify they saw the crew meet there, it cut no ice. And whilst I managed to get all their names – me and Jamie Carver were at school together– Ricky found out and begged me not to do anything. By then he knew his boxing days were over, and that if I got involved it would end with someone dead and someone else – me most likely - doing life. He wasn't bothered for himself, but by then Sharon was expecting her third. She had already had to put up with the phone calls. And their cat nailed to the back gate.

But I did turn up something no one else had. Ged Reilly was in Warrington the night they got Ricky. Around the time the crew-leader at Mr Smith's took the call telling him where Ricky was, Ged was seen leaving Havana's, on his mobile. I went looking for Ged but by a pure fluke - for him - missed him. Next thing, Ged's done a vanishing act any magician would have been proud of. As far as I knew, no one had seen or heard of him since - until I got the call from Stevie B.

Some good did come out of what happened back then I suppose. But for me, not poor old Ricky. To this day, the word around Warrington is that when I went looking for Ged, I found him.

I thought about what to do.

I thought about ringing Stevie B back.

I was still thinking about it when the traffic started to move.

We moved a mile. Two miles. Speed picked up. The blue lights had gone.

I rang Eric.

'Twenty minutes,' I said.

## CHAPTER 2

As I pulled onto the car park I pressed re-dial. Eric answered at once.

'Back door,' I said.

'Winston's on his way,' Eric said, then hung up. Things were obviously happening. By then it was over forty minutes since I'd rung to say I'd be there in twenty. After a couple of miles the motorway had bunched up again and we'd crawled a while more.

I spotted an empty disabled bay close to the back door. I floored the pedal and roared up to it then hit the brakes and yanked the wheel right so the truck skidded the last few yards and came to rest with the nearside wheels up against the kerb. I was pleased. The last time I'd tried it, the back end had ended up in the flower bed.

Jumping out, I grabbed my jacket off the back seat, then jogged over to the rear fire-exit, shrugging into it as I went. The door opened just as I got there. Light spilled out, but not much. Winston Ajero is six-four and built like the proverbial brick s***house. All I could see was a dark silhouette. But then all of Winston is dark, and his uniform - suit, shirt, tie - is black. The way his rasta-braids stood out against the light behind, reminded me of the last holiday I took with Caroline in Majorca. Palm trees against the sunset.

As he stepped aside to let me pass, he handed me a clip-on tie.

'Thanks Win,' I said.

'S'okay boss.' As always, 'boss' came out, 'baaaz.' When he's working, Winston likes to play up his Jamaican roots. Off-duty, you wouldn't tell him from any other Manc.

As I headed inside I called back, 'How're we doing?' Behind me I heard Winston rattling the fire-exit's push-bar, making sure it was locked.

'They're in the office, baaz,' he drawled. Winston has a habit of answering some other question to the one you've asked. Then he added, 'An' dat guy Charnley's been in again. Sniffin' roun'.'

'Right.' I filed it away for later. Dave Charnley and I used to work together. Now he runs his own door company. But not the one that has the contract for Midnight's. That's mine.

The corridor curved to the right, following the contour of the outer wall. Built in the sixties, Midnight's was originally a cinema. As I hurried along I could feel as much as hear the music coming through the wall on my right. By now the floor would be bouncing. At the front door, the corridor joins with the lobby, but I peeled off before, heading for the office. I could check the door later. Besides, I already knew what I would find. The previous week we'd agreed with the Police they would make their appeal and hand out flyers tonight. One-by-one they were getting round all the clubs. But I needed to sort the Agnes thing out before I got involved in anything else.

In the office, I found Eric, Vicki and Mr Midnight himself, Frank Johnson, crowded around the CCTV.

Behind them, arms folded and looking serious, was Tony Chapman. Tony manages the place on Frank's behalf. Least, that's what he's supposed to do. As I came in they all looked round.

'About time,' Frank said.

To say he looked stressed, would be another understatement. Midnight's owner, I always thought Frank looked like he would be more at home running a carpet warehouse, than a nightclub. Thinning grey hair, wire-rimmed glasses, business suit that would stand a good press. Crumpled-incompetence I call it. That said, I've no reason to believe carpet warehouse managers are particularly incompetent. And to be fair, Frank owned three night clubs around the Northwest all of which were doing okay thank you very much, despite the recession. As is her way, Vicki didn't acknowledge me but went straight back to the monitor. Tony stayed with his arms folded, looking stoic. I think he practises it. Only Eric moved, stepping aside to let me in.

Eric Pritchard and me go way back. His dad and my dad were best mates. He's been my number two ever since we started up. A hard-bitten scouser, he taught me everything I know about door-work, having learned the trade first in the city, then later in the pubs around Huyton and Kirkby during the time the Wallaces and Rathbones were at each others' throats. He was on the door of The Laughing Cavalier in Huyton the night Jimmy Wallace got his legs blown off. He once told me that when the car pulled up, he recognised Deggsy Rathbone just before he pulled his balaclava down. But he never said a word to any one. 'Not my business,' he said.

Taking Eric's spot, I found myself next to Vicki. She

was wearing her usual perfume. At this distance, its scent was pretty intoxicating. I tried to play it casual, making out I was focused, like a Security Guy should be.

I said, 'What've we got?' But the only thing in my mind at that moment was that I'd never been so close to Vicki as I was right then. The screen was angled slightly away from me. The way the strip light overhead was reflecting, I didn't have the best view, or so I told myself. I went, 'Tch,' and leaned to my right so my arm pressed up against hers. She didn't move and her gaze stayed rooted on the screen. I had no idea what that meant, but my imagination ran riot. I'm a real dick when it comes to women like Vicki.

Vicki Lamont is Midnight's resident, VIP Hostess. Young Miranda helps her out now and again, but she's not a patch on Vicki. Vicki is amazing. She has this gorgeous mid-brown hair that falls in waves across her face in a way that gets men going and always reminds me of Kim Basinger in LA Confidential, one of my favourite films. Thin around the waist and with a face that wouldn't be out of place on the front of one of those women's glossy magazines, she still has a girly look about her, though she won't see thirty again. A club like Midnight's needs a VIP Hostess who's classy and has certain qualities. Vicki ticks all the boxes and more besides. She takes her job seriously and is good at it. Say what you like about Frank Johnson, he has some excellent contacts and manages to book some good VIP Guests. Most of the time they're soap stars or one of those celebs who've appeared on some singing/dancing reality programme, but now and again he gets a real Pop Singer. Rick Astley is a regular, naturally, though he's getting on a bit now. Most of them are okay. They know their star will only shine so long, so they don't want to fuck it up. Others are real arseholes, out to boost their ego by showing they can still get people to run around after them while they act like spoiled kids. That's when Vicki comes into her own. I've seen her use humour, diplomacy, patience, and anger to get them to perform the way they're being paid to. I've seen her play coy, daft, flirty and downright seductive which, naturally, upsets me. But at the end of the day she sticks to her job description and doesn't do add-ons – 'favours' - like some hostesses I've known. Some of the team call her, 'Ronseal' - *Does exactly what it says on the tin.* Seeing as she comes from Widnes and her dad was a rugby prop-forward, she's pretty remarkable. I've only ever seen her struggling once. It was a Saturday night and I was walking past the Green Room when I heard a commotion inside. I won't say who the guest was but suffice to say that back then his name was 'household'. He'd had one Number One and has had a couple more since. The noise I heard was something between a scream and an angry shout. I stopped dead. It was followed by what sounded like some sort of scuffle and then I heard Vicki, giving a very clear, 'Get *OFF.*' Other than escorting them to and from the dias in the main dance floor, we're not supposed to have anything to do with the guests. I knocked on the door.

'Vicki?' I said. 'Can you spare a minute?'

There was more scuffling, then urgent whispers which I couldn't make out despite trying. A moment later Vicki opened the door, just a few inches. She sometimes wears a blouse and skirt, which can look professional while still being sexy as hell. On this occasion her blouse had come undone so she was showing more cleavage than when I'd seen her earlier. A stray lock of hair was hanging across her face. She was breathing heavily.

'What is it, Danny?'

'I need a word, if you don't mind?'

She gave me a long look. It was the first time I ever noticed how green her eyes were. I wasn't sure if what I saw in them at that moment was relief, annoyance or shame.

'Just a moment.' She shut the door.

There were more whispers. What sounded like another brief scuffle, followed by a sharp slap. I'd had enough and was about to go in when the door opened again and she came out. She closed it, firmly, behind her. Her face was red. She looked close to tears. She took a deep breath, composing herself.

'Everything alright in there?' I was desperate not to embarrass her.

She seemed to think about it. She didn't ask what I'd called her out to speak about but simply said, 'Would you mind the door a minute?' I like to remember there was a pleading look in her face, but I've probably imagined that bit.

'No problem.'

She disappeared down the corridor towards the Ladies. I thought about nipping in and having a quiet word with me-laddo, but opted not to. The embarrassment factor again. Hers mainly, but the club's also.

When she returned, five minutes later, you'd never have known. She was all together, hair put right, relaxed. And her usual distant self.

letting the Russian take a long-lease on the Ten to Midnight Suite. We'd talked about it several times. But at the end of the day, how Frank runs his club is nothing to do with me. My job is simply to advise on how to make sure everything runs smoothly. Besides, what he was getting off Yashin for exclusive use of the suite every night equated almost to a full night's takings. And Frank isn't so moral as he would pass up on a return like that. I could see he was waiting for the, 'Told you so's.' He would get them. But not yet.

I turned to find Vicki, ready and waiting. She looked beautiful. Worried, but beautiful. 'Are you up for going in with me?'

She didn't hesitate. 'Yes.'

I could have kissed her.

But Frank was uneasy. He turned to Vicki. 'What about Jack? Shouldn't you be seeing to him?'

He meant Jack Carpenter, the night's VIP Guest DJ. The only thing I knew about him was that since joining the cast of some teenage-college soap set somewhere south of the River Mersey, the viewing figures had rocketed.

Vicki waved Frank's concern away. 'Miranda's with him so he's happy. This is more important.'

*Good for you,* I thought. Up to then I'd always imagined Vicki doing exactly as Frank wanted. But I could tell he still wasn't happy.

'What are you going to do?'

I couldn't help noticing that Tony-the-Manager was staying out of it, saying nothing and just watching what was going on. I often wonder what he gets paid for

'Exactly what Eric was going to do an hour ago,' I said. 'Before you stopped him and told him to wait for me. Get Agnes and Bernadette out of there.'

'But you know the agreement, Danny. It's a private party. I'm not sure-'

I rounded on him. 'Whatever your agreement with that Russian prick is, it doesn't extend to kidnap, or anything between assault and rape.' I was a fair bit sharper with him than I'd intended, but it had the desired effect.

His face paled and he threw a wary glance at Tony. 'Come on, Danny. That's a bit-'

'Don't tell me I'm being dramatic. If you don't believe me, the police are in the lobby. Go and ask that DCI Carver. Those are two vulnerable girls up there. Ask him about the law on consent. And while I've got the contract for the door, I'm in charge of safety and security. That includes the clientele.' I pinned him with a look. 'Have I got the contract, Frank?' He stared back at me. He knew what I was getting at. That I knew that Charnley had been in. Something else for another time.

After a couple of seconds he looked away. 'Yes,' he said.

I turned to Eric. He was already wired for sound, the mic button showing on his shirt. 'Tell Eve to meet us in the lobby.' He nodded, and turned away. As he spoke into his shirt, I went back to Frank. 'Maybe you'd like to go upstairs and have a coffee? It might be more relaxing than watching?' I nodded at the screen.

He hesitated then started to rise. 'Right.' He didn't look too well.

Ready to go, I turned to find Vicki staring at me. It was a look I'd never seen before. 'You okay?' I said.

She gave a little nod. And I swear to God, there was almost a smile there when she said, 'Definitely.'

# CHAPTER 3

Eve was waiting when we reached the lobby. The look on her face, I could tell Eric had already told her what we were about.

Eve Mai-Ling is A-Team as well. She's tall for a Vietnamese, about five-eight. Dark and willowy, she wears her jet-black hair short. She lives with a red-haired Irish girl called Colleen, who I've met. I once heard someone describe Colleen as, 'Junoesque.' I'm not sure what that means exactly, but it somehow seems to fit. I don't know what their interests are and I don't care, but Eve is into martial arts and I've always suspected she quite enjoys the rough stuff. That's not to say she isn't professional. I've never seen her come even close to losing control. Just the opposite. I once saw her deal with two lads from Wigan who were kicking off in the queue and weren't for doing what she was telling them. They were both beefy and I was ready to lend a hand any time she needed me. She didn't.

I took a few seconds to fill Eve in, then we all trooped up the stairs. As we turned the corner into the top corridor, Alexei saw us coming. His hand went to his mouth and he talked into it. Then he squared round to face us in classic doorman stance, legs apart, hands clasped across his front .

'Good evening, Mr Norton. How are you?' His accent was a bit like the bloke in the old, 'Wadivar Wodka, from Varrington' advert a few years back.

'Not bad Alexei. We're just going to have a word with your boss.' As I made to step round him, his hand came up to press against my chest. I could have reacted, but I didn't.

'I am sorry, Mr Norton. This is a private function. I must first speak with Mr Yashin.'

I looked down at his hand, then lifted my gaze so our eyes met. After a couple of seconds he looked past me, checking out the others behind. He must have seen sense because the next thing, he took his hand away and stepped aside. I took out my pass key, unlocked the door and went in. The others followed.

As we came in, music was playing. The first thing I saw was Bergin and his mate coming at me in a way I would describe as 'purposeful.' They had obviously got Alexei's message. Their shirts were open to the waist and Bergin's pupils were dilated in the way I've seen many times. At the extremes of my vision, I was conscious of several men and women dotted around the room, all in various states of excitement. But whatever they'd been doing just before we came in, they weren't doing it now. Alexei's message had seen to that. I decided not to waste time pissing about but to send a message of my own. I took a step forward to meet Bergin head-on and pipped him, just the once, in the middle of his face. There was a nice-sounding crunch, his nose exploded and he went down like a sack of potatoes. Eric was about to do the same with his mate, but he had the sense to do a quick reverse. Everyone froze. The music stopped.

Down the far end of the room, near the dance floor, Yashin was on one of the sofas. Sasha, the blonder of his two floosies. next to him. His shirt was fastened but not his belt or the top button of his trousers. A glass coffee table in the middle of the room was suspiciously empty. Rainbow smears of wet showed under the lights. Someone had recently run a damp cloth over it. Next to it was a guy carrying a bar towel in one hand, various bits and pieces in the other. I thought about what a forensic examination of the towel would show.

I didn't have to look for Agnes and Bernadette. They were on the dance floor, in their knickers and bras. I couldn't tell if their confused looks were due to the music having stopped or something else. Floosie Number 2, Misha, the darker one, was between them. She was holding up their dresses like she'd been about to help them back into them. Vicki and Eve went straight over, snatched them out of Misha's hands and started helping the girls dress. At this point Yashin stood up. There wasn't a trace of any embarrassment and he kept his eyes square on me as he did up his button and fastened his belt. Then he wandered down to meet me and Eric. Behind me, a couple of his men were helping Bergin to his feet. He was groaning and slurring Russian. The only word I could make out was, 'bastard.'

Yashin played it straight. 'What is going on, Mr Norton? Why are you here? Where is Mr Johnson?' Nothing about what I'd done to Bergin.

I decided that if I said any of the things that I wanted to say right then, it would cause more problems for others than myself. So all I said was, 'These young ladies shouldn't be here. We're taking them back downstairs.'

For a second Yashin looked like he was thinking about arguing. His first thought was probably around why, considering how much he was paying for the room, couldn't he do as he pleased? Deep down I was hoping he would, when I would have happily put him right about a few things. But he must have realised which way the wind was blowing as all he said was, 'I'm sorry, I did not know that. I understood they were two of your dancers.' As he turned back to the dance floor, Vicki straightened up from dressing Agnes and gave him a look that I swear, if she'd given it me, I'd have dropped dead.

He clicked fingers at his women. 'Sasha. Misha. Do not just stand there. Help Miss Lamont.'

The two women jumped to it, but Vicki made a 'stop' sign. 'We can manage, thank you.'

Along with Eve, she guided Agnes and Bernadette off the floor and to the door. As she passed by me she whispered. 'Thanks.' It was all I needed. I closed on Yashin until we were nose to nose. It helps sometimes when you want to make a point.

'This was a mistake,' I said. He didn't flinch. I didn't expect him to. But I saw the ice form in his eyes as he stared me out. Right then I knew that from now on and until things were resolved, I would have to watch my back. I turned to the door. The women were gone. Eric was eyeing one the Russians like he was daring him to have a go. 'Eric,' I said. After several seconds he nodded, then backed off into the corridor. I followed him, closed the door.

Outside, we faced each other. There wasn't a trace of humour in Eric's face as he sang the words, 'There's going to be trouble.' I twitched an eyebrow. Only then did he let out a wide grin. 'But it was fun. Can we do it again sometime?'

I caught up with the women down in the store room that also doubles as a first aid suite. Vicki and Eve were talking to the girls who were responding in the semi-robotic way that, for them, is normal. I nodded Vicki to step outside.

'How are they?'

'They seem okay. They say they were just dancing. Neither of them is saying anything about anyone interfering with them in any way.'

'So how did they end up half-naked?'

'They said everyone was talking about how hot it was, then someone told them they could take their clothes off if they wanted to.'

'Really?'

Vicki gave a shrug. 'That's their story. To be honest, knowing how they both are, it could be right.'

I shook my head. The Russians weren't daft. 'Any sign that they were given anything?'

'Not that I can tell and they say not. I think we got there just in time. The way everyone was when we first went in, I suspect things were about to go a stage further.'

'My impression also.' I gave her a sideways grimace. 'Police?'

She batted it straight back. 'You're in charge of security.' But then she eased a little and added, 'If it makes you feel any better, I can't see there's anything to be gained. The girls are okay and they aren't making any complaints.'

I nodded, glad I didn't have to worry about her

thinking I was after brushing anything under the carpet. 'Can I leave them with you? Something else I've got to do.'

'No problem. I'll arrange a taxi and see them home. What's next?'

'The police appeal.'

Her mouth made an exaggerated, 'O' shape. I fought against the obvious image until it went away.

About to leave, I stopped at the door. 'What happened upstairs. Will that cause you problems?' I was conscious that while Yashin wasn't a 'guest' as such, he was still classed as VIP

She barely thought about it. 'Don't worry about me. I can handle him.'

Heading to the lobby, I worked myself into a muddle trying to work out if she'd simply meant to reassure me there was no need for me to worry, or whether she didn't like the idea of me worrying about her.

Sheesh.

# CHAPTER 4

When I got to the lobby the police were there in force - no pun intended. A man and a woman dressed in the high-vis jackets that pass for uniforms these days were handing out flyers, two more outside doing the same. Now and again they would stop a group and talk to them. Winston was there along with Golman Gurung and Chris Banks, the last two members of the A-Team. They and a couple of my rota guys were mingling to make sure everyone behaved themselves. Frank had said that the last thing he wanted was the sort of nonsense that could lead to a headline along the lines of 'Drunken Clubbers Obstruct Murder Cops.'

Gol is an ex-Gurkha soldier. He's short, stocky, solid as a concrete block and older than he looks. His son is still serving in the regiment - Afghanistan I believe, though Gol is never too sure. Chris is the newest member of the team, though he's still on his probation period. A Manchester lad and part-time fireman, I'd elevated him off the rota three months before after seeing the way he handled running the door at Charmaine's, Frank's Runcorn club, while the regular Team Leader was recovering in hospital. Chris is okay but there'd been a couple of incidents recently which had left me wondering if he's still sometimes a bit too quick with his fists. Restraint is the quality that marks A-Team from the normal rota.

I looked around for the DCI in charge, Carver, and spotted him next to his not bad looking DS, a girl called Jess, over by the cloakroom. A six footer like me and dressed smartly in suit and tie, Jamie Carver always looks like an advert for M&S. But the way he was standing, with his arms folded and watching everyone as they came in, he might as well have been wearing a uniform. Most of the punters weren't bothered, but the odd one or two, probably those with something to hide, eyed the pair warily. They weren't exactly keeping low-key, but then it wasn't like it was some undercover operation.

I crossed to them and went through the pleasantries. When I said, 'Alright love? to Jess, she glared and made a point of calling me, 'Mr Norton.'

Jess and I had met several times since the murders started. She's nice; friendly, quick-witted, but easy to wind up. I've already mentioned I was at school with Jamie Carver. Come to think of it, quite a few I went to school with ended up in the police. Back then, I suppose it was either one way, or the other.

'Any progress?' I said.

Carver rocked a hand. 'Some sightings but no break-throughs. Maybe tonight.'

'You still doing the appeal?'

'That's why we're here. When's best?'

'Soon as you're ready. They're still coming in but if you leave it much longer those who are in now will be too far gone to listen.'

'Will they anyway?'

'Don't worry, we'll be on the floor making sure.'

Jess leaned round her boss to give me a look. 'You seem pretty sure of yourself.'

'In my business, you've got to be, love.'

She gave me another look, but this time through half-closed eyes. She was beginning to cotton on.

Carver checked his watch. 'Let's make it fifteen minutes.'

I told him I'd let Frank know. I needed to tell him how it had gone with Yashin anyway. As I was about to leave Carver said, 'Everything okay upstairs? Do you need us for anything?'

I looked at him. *How the-*? 'It's sorted. And thanks, but no thanks.'

'Is Agnes okay?'

*Jesus.* 'She's fine. Nothing happened.'

'Good.'

Coming away, my thoughts were around who the blabbermouth was.

I found Frank upstairs in the Early Hours Coffee Bar. When I filled him in on what had happened with Yashin he looked worried. I couldn't not say anything, so I went for it.

'I know it's none of my business, but you do know what you're doing with this guy don't you? I told you before he's bad news. This thing with Agnes could have been nasty. If something had happened and the Guardian found out, you can imagine what they'd have made of it.' He nodded, glumly.

The Warrington Guardian has been waging war on the town's nightclub scene for years. Every week they publish photographs of blood and vomit on the streets and never fail to give full coverage to the assault cases when they come up in court. The on-line edition is even worse. That said, the local council keeps quiet on the subject. They know what the scene does for the town's economy.

Eventually, Frank looked up from his coffee. 'I understand your concerns, Danny, but-'

I waited, but then had to give him a nudge. 'But what?'

'It's complicated. It's not just about what he's paying for the room.'

'You mean he's setting up to buy you out?'

Frank paled. 'Where did you hear that?'

'Come on Frank, it's obvious. This is the biggest club in the Northwest outside Manchester. Why else would someone like Yashin be showing so much interest?'

He became flustered and for a few seconds looked like he was going to avoid answering, then he said. 'It's not what you think. And I'd appreciate you not spreading any rumours.'

I showed him my palms. 'I never comment on my client's business. It's your Club.'

He nodded, but stayed silent. Time to change the subject.

'One thing I will ask. And I'd appreciate an honest answer.'

'What's that?'

'What did Charnley want?'

His face showed he wasn't expecting it but he recovered quickly. 'Nothing in particular. He just called in.'

'Frank, Dave Charnley doesn't call on his mother unless he thinks there's something in it for him.'

'No need to be paranoid, Danny. You know what he's

like. He likes to think he's keeping well in. He's just full of bull.'

I gave him a long look. 'If you're not happy with the service you're getting from DoorSecure Frank, I'd like to think you'd speak with me about it before speaking to the likes of Charnley.'

'No Danny. Honestly, there isn't a problem. Like I say he's just doing the rounds.'

'Well I'd appreciate it if you'd remember that when my guys see you entertaining our main business rival, it makes them a little unsettled, if you know what I mean?'

'Of course. Sorry Danny. I'll bear it in mind in future.'

'Thanks.'

'Are the police doing the appeal?'

I checked my watch. 'Five minutes. I'd better get down there.'

'One other thing.'

'Yes?'

Tony's going to do some staff checks later. Thought I'd let you know.'

'No problem,' I said. Everyone who works at Midnight's, including my guys, signs to say they agree to be searched at the end of a shift. It includes bags, lockers, etc. I've always thought it's a good idea. Helps keep the place clean.

'You know where I am if you need me,' Frank said.

As I headed for the dance floor I wondered what it would take to get the club's owner to show himself in front of the clientele, if the possibility of them being murdered wasn't enough.

# CHAPTER 5

Two sets of double doors, fifteen yards apart, lead from the lobby into the club proper. Both open onto a short stretch of wall that curves away left and right. The walls' main purpose is to stop people seeing into the club from the lobby, or even outside. But they also act as an effective sound buffer so that it isn't until you round the wall that the full impact hits you. I've probably made the short walk from the relative quiet of the lobby into the main dance area more times than anyone. But I've still never quite got used to the assault on the senses you experience as you turn to find yourself looking out over the main dance floor. These days clubs are all about creating mood and atmosphere through noise, and light. And I've nothing but respect for the techies who know how to set things up so that the lights, music and amplification are always in harmony wherever you are around the dance area. Nevertheless I sometimes think about the similarity between what the techies do in terms of manipulating people's senses, and the dealers and pushers we work so hard to keep out of the place. The longer I work in a club environment, the more I'm sure there's an interesting thesis waiting to be written by some bright researcher on the subject. At the end of the day they are

two minutes before, everyone had been in full flow, the change in mood was remarkable. Some of the girls especially were really taking it all in, looking scared and anxious. A few - guys as well as girls - were actually crying, probably because they knew one or more of the victims. Carver didn't try to dramatise anything. He didn't need to. The facts spoke for themselves. When you're out clubbing and someone tells you that when you leave there is a chance you might meet someone who will take you off somewhere and kill you, it focuses the mind. He didn't say too much about how the girls were actually killed, but it was no secret they were all strangled. Other than that, the police hadn't released further details. There were rumours of course. They ranged from suggestions – always from a, 'reliable source', naturally - that the killings followed in the bloody tradition of The Ripper – Jack or Yorkshire, take your pick - to speculation that the bodies were arranged in ways that hinted at some bizarre religious-style ritual. As Carver explained, the biggest puzzle for the police was how the killer lured the victims away. Clubs have always warned about the dangers of women accepting lifts from people they don't know, unlicensed mini-cabs, that sort of thing. Inevitably, it had led to speculation that the victims must have known their killer, though Carver emphasised it was just that, speculation. He ended by asking anyone with information to speak to one of the officers who would be around the club the rest of the night. When he thanked everyone for listening and told them to enjoy the rest of their night, some of them actually gave him a round of applause.

He handed back to Mickey who surprised me by immediately following up with an earnest, 'Thank you

Officer. On behalf of everyone here at Midnight's we all wish you well with your investigation. Let's hope you catch the bastard soon.' Then he was back in character. 'Right everyone, let's get the party going again with one you can rock your socks off to.' Tapping his laptop screen he yelled, 'It's... ENIGMA.' By the time we got to the top of the stairs, Mickey was already flailing about like nothing had happened. He's a real pro is Mickey.

At the bottom of the stairs some kids were already lining up, waiting to speak to Carver and Jess. Over by the doorway that leads to the Green Room I could see Vicki loitering so I left them to it and went and joined her. Her face told me she'd been listening to the appeal.

'How awful.' she said. 'Did you know that they'd all visited Midnight's sometime?'

'Doesn't surprise me. Sonia Carter was a regular some while back. I think she danced on the podium a couple of times. Everyone visits Midnight's some time or other. Even if it's just to compare us with somewhere else.'

She gave a little shiver. It made her look vulnerable and just about pierced my heart. 'I hope they catch him soon,' she said.

'Echo that.'

I waited, not sure if she wanted to tell me something. But when she spoke it was to say, 'Can you send someone to fetch us in ten minutes? Jack's just on the phone.'

I nodded. The guest DJ usually takes the half-hour slot after midnight. It was now quarter past. 'What's he like?' I said.

She thought about it. 'Not too bad, if a bit flash.

Fancies himself too much, but then they all do. Too much money of course. And he's young.' She gave a wry smile. 'About ten, I'd say.'

I smiled back but tried not to laugh in case she thought I was simply humouring her. Vicki doesn't often talk about her VIPs, but when she does it's usually something that tickles the hell out of me. But she was right about him looking young. Because I was late I'd missed him arriving, but I'd seen his picture on the posters. If he'd turned up unannounced and without ID, he wouldn't get in. I remembered to ask about Agnes. She pulled a face and pointed behind me. I turned to see a small knot of people in a circle, clapping and waving their arms. Agnes was in the middle, doing her thing. I turned back to Vicki. 'I thought you were sending her home?'

'I tried to, but she started to get upset and said she hadn't finished dancing. I couldn't force her so I had to let her stay.'

'Fair enough. She's an adult.'

'I know but I don't like her still being here after what happened. Have you spoken with Frank about what was going on upstairs?'

'Yes, but it might help if you said something to him as well. All I get is pound signs in his eyes.'

'I will.' She turned to go back to her guest. 'See you later.'

As I watched her sashaying her way back to the Green Room, I found myself wondering if she'd ever done any modelling. Then, snapping myself out of it I headed off on my rounds.

## CHAPTER 6

The Man Who Likes To Watch is doing just that. He is not concerned that others may see him watching, after all, he is hardly alone. Hiding in plain sight, as they call it. He is pleased to see that the girl to whom he has been giving most of his attention recently seems to have lost none of her artistry. As good as ever, he thinks, if not better. It is clear now that she is special, unique in fact. It is that uniqueness that appeals to him. Just for a moment, he allows himself the luxury of imagining the pleasure she will bring him, but then returns, swiftly, to the present. It would not do to lose himself too much. Whilst people may understand him being distracted, it would be foolish to draw attention to himself. Right now he exists, 'below the radar' as far as the police are concerned. At least, that is what the evidence of the last half-hour would suggest.

It was interesting but strange listening to the detective. It isn't often people hear their work being discussed in front of so many people. In fact there were a couple of occasions where he'd had to fight against the egotism that made him want to jump up and shout out, 'IT'S ME. I'M HERE.' Its all well and good being proud of your achievements, but there is such a thing as going too far.

He isn't sure if he has learned anything new amongst what the detective said. But he was reassured to learn that, as far as they are prepared to say in public at least, they seem no nearer to catching him than they were six months ago. Not that he considers himself lucky in this regard. Since the beginning, he has invested time and effort in avoiding the pitfalls his research shows are most often the undoing of many in his line of business - unexpected witnesses, last-minute changes to the plan, CCTV, leaving evidence through which the police may identify him, and so on. And while the DNA thing is something he has thought about a lot, even it does not worry him too much. For one thing, he has no police record, so will not show up on any database. But the precautions he takes after - moving the body, removing and getting rid of contaminated clothing, the antiseptic wipes - all help to ensure that the chances the police may connect him directly with the crime are minimised. Even if they do find a connection, the circumstances surrounding his contact with the victims means he will always have a ready 'story' that will explain things - at least as far as any court is concerned.

Earlier, he had wondered if the police's presence might mean he ought to postpone his current plans, that it may prove too dangerous. But on reflection he thinks all will be well. Having acquainted himself, previously, with the girl's homeward journey, he sees no reason why the police should be a problem. Their focus tonight is on the club. Come three o'clock in the morning they will either be in their beds or back in their Arpley Street bolthole, drinking tea and scoffing biscuits, or whatever it is they do when the rest of the town is asleep.

Not that he will be asleep. Far from it. By then, if all

goes to plan, he will be enjoying the performance he has been looking forward to, probably more than any of the others.

*God, look at her. She is so beautiful, her movements so sublime.*

Suddenly he realises that as he has been watching, his hand has dropped, instinctively, to his crotch and he returns it, quickly, to a more appropriate place.

He chides himself, 'Tch.'

He knows there are times, when he watches, when he is like a prepubescent schoolboy, playing with himself while wondering why he finds the female teacher so fascinating. It is something he knows he must guard against. It is as well that the place where he spends most of his time is one where he is not likely to be observed too long or too often. Hiding in plain sight, indeed.

Pulling himself away from what, for him, is the night's main attraction, he turns his attention elsewhere. The night is still young and there is much still to occupy him. After all, come tomorrow he will be needing a fresh target for his affections. But for the time being he is happy to let the music, the buzz and the dance, wash over him.

He loves it here.

# CHAPTER 7

The rest of the night was the usual mixed bag. Backing the team up when a shout goes up over the radio, though things are usually all over by the time I get there. Helping remove those so far gone they need to be shown the door. Checking that everyone who has a job to do is doing it properly. The only event of note was when a group of lads on a night out from Burnley fell out with some of the locals. It kicked off on the dance floor about one o'clock. When we arrived there were a dozen or so in a ruck, throwing kicks and punches at each other. You can always spot the leaders in such situations so Winston and I grabbed one and dragged him away. He was a big lad – Lancashire farmer's son type - but once we got him near the door leading to the lobby and he got a good look at who had hold of him, he seemed to quieten down.

Winston paused at the door. Looking back at the dance floor we could see Eric and Chris still pulling bodies out and reeling them away 'You okay here, baaz?' he said.

I nodded. 'Go.'

As Winston returned to help the others I guided farmer-boy towards the main entrance. He must have realised it was now only one-on-one and thought this was his chance. Coming-to suddenly, he wrenched himself from my grasp and rounded on me, fists up and clenched. The look in his eyes told me what to expect. As he swung at me he shouted, 'AND YOU CAN FUCK OFF AS WELL YOU- AARGH.'

Self-defence is all about staying calm, and speed. Stay calm, read what is happening, respond fast and you can deal with most things, including knives. Apart from making people unpredictable, alcohol always acts in your favour as it slows them down. In this particular case, a drunken farmer's lad wasn't much of a contest. He telegraphed the punch so much I could have had a brew while thinking about which way to take it. I went for the most simple and caught his fist about a foot away from my face, then twisted it round and to his left so he had to go with it until his arm was up his back. I grabbed his shoulder and pulled him up and back, hence the, 'AARGH.' Then I took him out and put him across the threshold. As I let him go he turned on me again, but he resisted whatever impulse was driving him to make the biggest mistake he would have made in a long time and settled for giving me his hardest, *if I was sober...* glare. Around us, several yellow-jacketed police officers looked on.

'Sorry about that, mate,' I said. 'What's your name?'

'Yer what?' He spoke with the East Lancashire drawl that always makes me think of the old ditty, 'Burnley born, Burnley bred. Strong in brawn, soft in t'head.' It works just as well with Blackburn, Bacup or any other Northern town beginning with 'B'.

'My name's Danny.' I put out my hand. 'What's yours?'

By instinct, his hand came out to take mine. 'Er,

Alan.'

'Okay, then Alan. You've had a good night so let's leave it there. Your mates'll be out soon so you won't have to wait long. Got any cash?' He fished in his trouser pockets, pulled out a twenty. 'There you go.' I pointed round the corner, towards the car park. 'The hogey wagon's round there. Go and get yourself a burger and you'll be fine, okay?'

'Uhh-' He looked bemused but couldn't think of a reason to argue. 'Raaghhht.'

As I watched him wander away, one of the police sidled up to me. 'You should be a psychologist, Danny.'

I smiled. 'Tell me about it.'

'That's our Danny, officer,' a voice came from behind. 'The gift of the gab.'

We both turned to see a man who looked like he could be grandfather to most of those inside, grinning at us like a Cheshire cat. Dressed in a blue velvet jacket over a black shirt with a flared collar, white shoestring tie, purple drain pipe trousers and blue suede shoes, the speaker was puffing on an emaciated roll-up pinched, stylistically, between the thumb and middle finger of his left hand. As I recognised him and nodded an acknowledgement, he lifted it to his lips and drew on it so hard his face looked like it might implode.

Another club regular, Elvis Presley-Kershaw - as his deed poll-changed name implies - is a throw-back to the fifties era of teddy boys and greasers, DA hairstyles. I've never got round to checking his actual age on his membership record, but while his creased features and the way he presents himself gives the impression he could be from that era, I'm pretty sure he can't be much beyond his mid-forties. A builder I know who is

approaching his fifties once told me he remembers Elvis
– which is his real first name, he only had to add the
'Presley' - coming up behind him in High School.
However old he is, Elvis wears the title, 'Oldest
Swinger In Town,' like it was made for him. A club
regular since long before I took over, he has a reputation
for liking the ladies. Certainly he never misses a chance
to introduce himself to any visiting the club for the first
time, drawing on a catalogue of chat-up lines that range
from the arcane, 'Not seen you here before,' through the
tired, 'Julie? That was my mother's name,' to the
inspired, 'My magic watch says you aren't wearing
knickers,' the usual retort being, 'Well it's wrong. I am,'
thus triggering the clincher, 'Ahh, but it's running an
hour fast.' Among regulars and staff, opinions about
Elvis divide about equally between those who think he's
a creep and can't stand him, others who regard him as
'harmless fun' and a surprising number who seem to
find him genuinely fascinating and are happy to buy
into the Grease/John Travolta fantasy he evokes. One
thing's for sure. He's one of the best jivers I've ever
seen. When Elvis gets into his Rock-Around-The-Clock
routine, even those who say he makes them squirm stop
to watch.

'Hey Elvis,' I said. 'How's it going?'

'Okay. A few live ones in tonight. I'm just taking a
break.'

'So I see.'

As the policeman wandered off – most of them have
little time for Elvis – he flicked his cigarette away and
gave me what I guessed was supposed to his 'serious'
face. 'Bad business with these girls.'

'That's putting it mildly.' I turned to go back inside.

'I tell you, there're some right weird characters hang around clubs these days.'

I glanced back, regarding the colourful figure. 'You're not wrong there.'

'Capital punishment, that's the answer. It's the only thing that's good for people like that.'

I nodded, but said nothing. It was one of the few topics my Dad could still raise himself to argue about – not that you could engage with it in any meaningful way. Dad's capacity to take on board others' views has drained the last few years. All I do now is tut in the appropriate places, nod, and say things like, 'Too right,' when expected.

'I bet you'd sort him out if you ever got your hands on him, Danny.'

I stopped. 'What makes you say that?'

He seemed surprised by the question. 'Well, you know. You being…'

'What?'

'You know... Someone who…'

'What?'

There was a long pause before he eventually said, '…Can take care of himself.'

I gave him a long stare. 'It'll be golden-oldie time soon Elvis.' Before he begins to wind things up, Mickey always throws on some classics, sometimes even sixties stuff.

Elvis grabbed at his escape route. 'Better get back to it then, hadn't I? Don't want to keep the ladies waiting.'

I stepped aside as he shuffled past, rubbing his hands together, vigorously, to get rid of the night cold. Either that or he was relishing whatever he thought he might be onto before the night was over.

I gave it a minute, then followed.

The rest of the night was pretty routine, the odd flare up, young women puking in the toilets, a couple of lads caught in the gents trying to do a line on the top of the toilet cistern before they realised we spray it with WD40 at the start of the night. Winston and Chris chucked them out and flushed their supply down the pan. Apart from the Agnes thing, it was more or less a normal Saturday night.

It was closing time when things turned to rat shit.

# CHAPTER 8

The music stops at two on a Sunday morning. By half-past everyone's usually gone, apart from those left hanging around because they've lost their purse/phone/keys/wallet/boyfriend and need help. Or they're so far gone it takes them half-an-hour to realise the music has stopped and the night is over. By three, the team have done their rounds and reported their findings to me and the cleaners are in. That particular night, Eve handed in a bag of wraps she'd found behind one of the sinks in the downstairs back toilets - evidence of a botched deal. It never ceases to amaze me just how many we find, which goes to show how much the pushers are making in a night if they can afford to abandon them. Don't get me wrong. By most clubs' standards Midnight's is pretty clean. We work hard to keep it that way. But in a place this size, you can never stop it one hundred percent. I logged Eve's find and was putting it in the safe for handing to the Drug Squad on Monday morning when they do their rounds when I got the call from Frank to come to the staff room where the lockers are. I remembered him mentioning about Tony doing locker searches. I can't explain why, but straight away my gut knotted up.

Frank and Tony were there. So was Winston. Soon as

I walked through the door he was on me. He looked like he was about to explode.

'It's a fuckin' set-up, Baaz. They're fuckin' wit me.' He pointed to the table where a sports bag carrying the Nike logo, and which I recognised as Winston's, lay open and emptied. Set aside from the toilet bag, spare socks, boxers, gels, and the rest of his stuff, was a clear plastic pouch containing white powder.

*Shit.*

I turned to where Frank and Tony were standing looking suitably apologetic, sad even. In Frank's case I believed it. Tony is just a two-faced twat. It was him who spoke.

'Frank's a witness Danny. And Winston was present when we searched his locker. He nodded at the pouch. 'That was in his bag.'

I looked across at Winston and read his mind. There was only one thing on it - strangling Tony. I could guess why.

Winston had been with DoorSecure for over three years. It's no secret that some of his brothers have been done for drugs - one for dealing in Manchester - but I also knew Winston wasn't into it. A keen body-builder, he'd no doubt pumped steroids in his time, but there's no way he'd ever do C, or E, or any of the other recreational shit you come across in clubs these days. Straight away I was remembering Charnley's visit to the locker room earlier that evening. But I knew I couldn't stop what was going to happen.

I turned back to Frank. 'You know Winston as well as I do. This isn't right.'

He spread his hands. 'It was in his bag.'

About to say something I'd later regret, I clamped

my mouth shut.

Tony chipped in. 'You know the rules, Danny.' He paused before adding, 'So does Winston.'

It was too much for Winston. Luckily I was ready and stepped between them as Winston went for him shouting, 'YO FUCKIN' BENT BASTARD. Why yo stichin' me up for?'

Tony retreated to the wall as I acted as a barrier. It was all I could do to hold him. 'WINSTON. CALM DOWN.'

It took me several shouts to get through to him, and I was glad I was there else Carver and his team might have had another death on their hands. Eventually Winston quietened enough so it was safe to let him go, though he kept up his mutterings. For a guy who looks like a lummox, Winston's sharp as a knife. He knew as well as I did what was going on. But right then the only evidence of anything was the sachet. I took a deep breath. I knew what Frank was waiting for. I had no choice.

'Take your stuff and go home, Winston. You're off the door.' As I said it I kept an eye on Tony. But he knew enough not to let the slightest hint of a smirk show, which was as well.

'Dis is BULLSHIT, baaz. You know it is.'

I stood square to him. Just me and him. 'Go home. I'll speak to you later on this morning.'

Winston is one of those who is big enough and good enough at what he does to never have to show anger. But right now he was, outright, unmitigated anger. I was glad I wasn't the cause of it. It made me admire even more that in three years on the door, he's never hurt anyone, not seriously, I mean.

He kettled for another ten seconds before letting the pressure go.

'FUCK.'

Grabbing his kit, he paused only to give Tony one last, hate-filled look, then stormed out.

The silence lasted a while longer before Frank said, 'I'm sorry Danny.'

'Me too,' I said. I stared across at Tony. He knew what I was thinking. So did Frank.

'Tony was just doing his job,' Frank said. 'I don't want any backlash from this.'

There was nothing I could say apart from, 'I'll do my best to make sure there isn't.' Then I waited while Tony realised he needed to be elsewhere.

'I'll go and see if we're ready to lock up,' he said.

After he'd gone, I turned to Frank. 'This has not been a good night,' I said. 'Things have happened that will have consequences.' I didn't mean it as any sort of threat, just my assessment.

'If that's the case then it's your job to make sure the club doesn't suffer.'

I almost snorted, but managed not to. Right then I couldn't have cared if the place got petrol-bombed. 'I guess that's what you pay me for.'

We let another silence draw a line under it – for tonight at least. Finally Frank said, 'The team did a good job tonight. Thank them for me will you?'

'Right.'

I went in search of the guys.

Eric and Golman were in the lobby. The others had already gone. I could see from their faces they knew something had happened.

'What's up with Winston?' Eric said.

'You've seen him?'

'He just left. I've never seen him like that. What happened?' I told them. No point in keeping it secret. Eric's response was as I expected. 'I don't believe it.' I nodded. He read my lack of reaction. 'What's going on?'

'I'm not sure yet.'

'So what are you going to do about it?'

'I've done it. He's off the Door.'

Eric stared at me. 'Fuck off.' Eventually he realised I wasn't kidding. 'Jesus, Danny. This is bad. The team won't like it.'

'I know, but I had no choice. Make sure they know that when they ring you.'

'How do you know they'll ring me?'

I gave him a look. 'It's time we called it a night.'

I'm usually the last to leave with Frank, about three-thirty. Tonight was no exception. Setting the alarm, half my mind was on Winston, the other on Vicki. I hadn't seen her since seeing her talking with Frank, not long before the thing with Winston happened. As usual, I felt a little disappointed she hadn't sought me out to say something about the night's events. But that's her all over.

My disappointment wasn't to last long.

## CHAPTER 9

As I stepped out the back door I was alert for signs of Russians lurking in shadows. It would have been a stupid move on their part of course, and I was pretty certain that when it happened it would be well away from the club. But I learned long ago not to take chances.

There were no Russians, but I did hear raised voices. A couple arguing isn't exactly a rare event after chucking-out time so I didn't pay it much regard to begin with. They usually quieten down and bugger off when they see it's me. It was only when I came out onto the car park and recognised one of the voices as Vicki's that I took an interest.

She was standing next to her red Honda soft-top. The door was open and the interior light was on, like she'd been about to get into it. Next to it was a tidy looking Beemer, its owner leaning across the Honda's roof, giving it loud. I'd never met Vicki's husband, Vincent, in person but I knew him by sight and reputation. He runs a car dealership in the town and is known for putting himself about a bit. What little I knew of him had always made me wonder how they'd got together, though that could have been jealousy. I'd heard rumours recently they were having trouble.

As I headed for where I'd parked, I heard him shout. 'Just for ONCE, will you do as your FUCKING TOLD? GET IN THE FUCKING CAR. We need to talk about it.'

I gathered he meant his car rather than hers. Glancing over I could see she was upset. I diverted towards them.

'You're drunk, Vinny,' I heard her say. 'And I'm not going anywhere with you when you're like this. We've said all there is to say. Go home. I'll ring you tomorrow.'

His response was to bang his fist on the Honda's top so hard I was surprised he didn't go through it. 'FUCK tomorrow. I want to talk to you NOW. TONIGHT. Just, GET IN THE FUCKING CAR.'

I approached from her left, his right. 'Everything okay here you two?'

She spun round. The sodium street lights lining that side of the car park rendered everything in grey-scale, nonetheless I saw her face darken with the blush. Before she could answer, Vincent turned his attention to me.

'What the fuck's it to do with you?' Then he said to her, 'Who's this? Another of your boyfriends?'

I showed him my hands. 'I'm not looking to interfere. I just-'

'Well fuck off and you won't.'

I looked at him, then her. Her lips moved but no words came out.

I said to her, 'Would you like me to take you back inside?'

'HEY, WANKER. She's MY fucking wife. If you want to talk to her, you speak to me first, right?'

He was starting to get on my nerves. 'Is that so?'

'YES, it FUCKING is.' He came out from between the cars. The way he was thrusting his chest out I could see where things were heading. But I wasn't about to do anything she wouldn't want me to.

She finally found her voice. Stepping quickly forward she put herself between us. 'I'm sorry Danny, I don't think you've met my husband, Vincent. Vincent this is *Danny Norton.*' She said my name like it should mean something. She did it again when she said, 'You've heard me talk about *Danny Norton*, Vincent? He *runs the club's door?*'

Fascinated to hear she even knew I existed away from the club, my first instinct was to want to focus on what that could mean, pull it apart, analyse it. But before I even had a chance to park it for another time, something must have clicked with Vincent because everything about him changed, just like that. In the act of squaring up to me, he suddenly froze, before almost shrinking in front of us. He was still staring at me, but the fire in his eyes was suddenly gone.

'Uhh… Danny Norton? Oh yeah. Uhh... I've heard of you.'

He backed off a couple of steps, switching glances between her and me. It was almost as if he was expecting I might pull a gun and shoot him. I waited and watched, saying nothing. He retreated between the cars. Apparently satisfied I wasn't about to rush him, he turned his attention on her again, but not like before. 'We need to talk, sometime.' He checked me out again before finishing off with, 'I'll ring you. Tomorrow. Or Monday.'

He threw one last glance at me, made as if he was about to say something, but thought better of it. Wise move. Opening the door, he slid into the driver's seat. A moment later I stepped aside as he reversed out. I saw him checking his mirrors so he could keep me in view. He gave Vicki one last withering look, another glance in my direction, then put his foot down. He swung left off the car park onto Arpley Street, and away.

I turned to her. Her eyes were tight shut. I could see she was struggling with how to handle it, what to say, what to do. I gave her a moment. We both started speaking together.

'Are you al-'

'I'm sorry about-'

We stopped. Smiled, weakly, at each other. She shook her head, still a bit tearful. I could see she was conflicted.

I said, 'Are you going to be okay?' I had no idea what was going through her head.

She took a deep breath, as if she was about to confess something. 'Vincent and I split up a few weeks ago.'

'Oh.' *What do you say?*

'I've been staying with a friend.'

'Uh-huh.'

'He knows where she lives.'

*Ah.*

'If I go there now he'll be round. Either now or later.'

'Right.'

'He'll make trouble.'

I nodded.

She turned to face me full on. Whatever she was thinking, her face was entirely blank as she said, 'I don't know what to do.'

## CHAPTER 10

Bravery is a funny thing. To my mind, people confuse it with heroism. For me, heroism is where someone does something amazing, like rushing into a blazing building to rescue someone or diving into icy water to save a drowning man. Or a soldier who takes out a machine gun nest on his own to save his unit. The trouble is that while such acts may be heroic, they aren't necessarily brave. Sometimes people do things on the spur of the moment, without thinking. They act on instinct because to them, it's the right thing to do in the circumstances. And because they don't have time to think about it, they're not scared.

Bravery on the other hand, is when someone does something, *despite* being scared.

I remember a young Welsh lad, Owen Jones, who came to work for us. He seemed okay on interview, but his first night on the door – a busy night at Midnights and we were short of staff - I knew it wasn't for him. He looked the part, but soon as someone squared up to him, I could tell he was shitting himself. Some lads are like that. They think they can handle confrontation. They're okay with someone next to them. But the first time they come up against someone who means business, they bottle it. Only Owen didn't bottle it. He did what he had to do, though I could see his legs shaking, hear the crack in his voice. I realised at once and told him he could go home right after. But because we were short, he insisted on staying. He stayed right through the night. I knew he was hating it and scared to death, but he stayed nevertheless. Now that was brave. Last I heard, he was working in insurance.

The reason I mention all this is because people think I'm brave when they see me do what I do on the door. They actually say things like, 'That was brave.' Or they ask, 'Weren't you scared?' But what I do when I'm working doesn't involve being brave. I'm just doing what I'm trained to do. I'm never scared, so I never have to be brave.

Vicki, on the other hand, scares me to death.

Which is why, when she turned to me that night and said, 'I don't know what to do,' what I did next was, by my reckoning, the bravest thing I'd done in a long time. And it was how I came to be driving home at half-four in the morning trying to remember if I'd left anything embarrassing lying around. The scary bit was worrying she might burst out laughing, or respond with something like, 'Are you out of your fucking mind?' or be so outraged she'd say, 'How DARE you?' when I said to her, 'You can come and stay at mine if you like?'

It was big relief when, after thinking about it a moment, she simply said, 'Is it far?'

I live in an end town-house in a quiet close on a newish development a few miles outside Warrington in an area called Whitely. It used to be just a small village but it's expanded a lot over recent years. I bought it with Caroline a few years ago, but after she left she sold her interest to me. It's got three bedrooms, which is handy, and more space inside than you'd think looking at it from the outside. It's nothing special, but it does me.

By the time we got there, I was less worried about something lying around. I'd remembered that Jean, who does a bit of cleaning for me now and again, had changed her day this week from Friday to Saturday. She'd have been in while I was at Dad's. When I came through the door, everything looked fine. The whiskey bottles were gone, tumblers washed and upside down on the drainer. Clothes either in the washer or hung up and put away.

As I went around putting lights on, Vicki looked the place over. The downstairs is all open-plan. Diner-kitchen, living area, bathroom off.

'This is nice,' she said. She sounded almost surprised. I wasn't sure how to respond so I said nothing.

I came back to her in the middle of the room. We stood there for several seconds while I tried to think of the right questions to ask. My first thought had been, *Are you ready for bed*? Duhh.

She cocked her head at me, frowned. 'Well?'

I panicked. 'WHAT?'

'Aren't you going to ask me if I want something?'

'Like…?'

She rolled her eyes. 'Like… a drink maybe? Maybe… something to eat?'

I snapped out of it. 'A drink. Yeah. Would you like a drink?'

'That's a good idea.'

'Or food maybe? Are you hungry?'

She stared at me, shook her head. The frown again. She stepped towards me, looking deep into my face, seemed to realise something. 'You don't, do you?' The surprise again.

'Don't what?

'Do this.'

'This what'?'

'Bring women home.'

I felt myself turning red. 'Er. No. Not often.'

She seemed to find that amusing. 'When was the last time?'

I couldn't believe she'd asked me. Like a moron, I repeated, 'The last time? Er- well, it was, er-'

'Never mind. Let's try something else. What are the sleeping arrangements?'

'Sleeping arrangements?'

She raised her eyes to the ceiling. 'Jesus, Danny. You're never like this at the club. Where. Am. I. Sleeping?'

'*Sleeping*. Right. Of course.' Daft as it sounds, I'd never given it a thought. I started to. My sister, Laura, had used the second bedroom about three weeks before. I tried to remember if Jean would have changed the bed.

I must have been taking longer than I thought as she broke in to say, 'Okay. One step at a time. How many bedrooms are there?'

'Three.'

'How many beds?'

'Two.' Her face said, *Why only two*? 'The third's my gym.'

'Right. Your bedroom is…?'

'The front one.'

'Okay, so shall I have the other?'

'If you're alright with that?'

She shook her head again. 'What do you usually do

when you get in on Sunday morning?'

'I dunno. Couple of drinks. Sometimes a bit of breakfast. Check out the football. Bed.'

'Sounds great. Any Vodka?'

'Yes.'

'Lemonade?'

'There's some Sprite.'

'That'll do. I'll have vodka and Sprite. And ice if you've got it. What do you normally eat?'

'I sometimes make myself an omelette.'

'That'll be fine too. Do you have anything I can change into?'

I thought about it. 'There'll be some of Laura's stuff in the second bedroom.'

'Laura?'

'My sister. She's in London. She visits now and again.'

'Housecoat by any chance?'

'There's a robe behind the door.'

'That's my boy. Shower?'

'In the bathroom.' *Where else you pillock?* 'It's a Power shower. Just pull the cord first.'

'Right. You do breakfast and I'll sort myself out, how about that?'

'Sounds good to me.'

'Okay.' She headed up the stairs. Near the top, she stopped and poked her head down again, looking at me through the stair rails. I was still standing in the middle of the room. Putting a hand through the railings, she pointed round the corner.

I looked at the wall, then back at her. 'What?'

'Kitchen?'

I finally realised. 'Oh. Right.'

I went to make breakfast.

## CHAPTER 11

I was busy with the eggs when she reappeared, showered and wrapped up in Laura's robe. Her drink was ready and waiting on the worktop. She picked it up and started to mooch around. I kept my head down and tried not to think about all the films I'd seen where, the morning after, the girl floats about the guy's place wearing someone else's clothes. As I brought the plates to the table I realised she was checking out the middle book shelf.

'What's all this?'

'It's, erm…'

She leaned in for a closer look.

'Is this Open University stuff?'

'Yeah. I, erm.-'

The look in her face as she rounded on me, she might have found my porn collection.

'You're doing an O.U. course?'

'What's wrong with that?'

'Nothing at all. It's just that-' She turned back to the shelf. 'What're you studying?'

Before I could answer she picked up one of the Unit Guides. 'English Literature?' And there was more than a touch of amazement in her voice when she said, 'You're doing an O.U. Degree Course in English

Literature?'

I felt myself bristle - the first natural thing I'd done since we'd arrived. 'Why shouldn't I do a degree in English Literature? Lots of people do.'

'Yes, but not-' She put the guide down and came back to the table. 'I'd just never have figured you for the studying kind. And definitely not Literature.'

'Right. So what would you expect? The History of Martial Arts Movies perhaps?' I have to admit, I was playing up the Being Indignant, thing.

She met my gaze head on. 'I wouldn't have expected anything. But let's be honest, bouncing and degree courses don't exactly go together, do they?'

I could have kept it up a bit longer, but at the end of the day we both knew she was bang on. I shrugged. 'You're right. They don't.' I turned my attention to my plate. 'And it's Door Supervising these days, not bouncing.'

We ate in silence. As I concentrated on the eggs, I could feel her gaze on me.

'I'm sorry,' she said.

I looked up. Her expression was one I'd never seen before. A bit serious, yet also somehow sad. 'What for?'

'If I've offended you. I actually think it's great you're doing a degree.'

I nodded. 'Don't worry. Most people think bouncers are brainless idiots. It goes with the territory.'

What she did right then nearly sent me into orbit. Reaching across the table, she laid her hand on my arm, held my gaze and said. 'I've never seen you as a brainless idiot, Danny.' And I knew she meant it, one hundred percent.

We talked through the rest of breakfast. She had a

71

couple more Vodkas, I stayed on beers. I didn't dare open a whiskey bottle. She seemed genuinely interested in my course and why I was doing it. When I explained I'd left school without any qualifications – I left out the reasons why – but had always loved reading and books and wanted to understand more about the subject, she seemed genuinely impressed.

'So who are your favourite authors?'

I had to think about it. Nobody had ever asked me before. 'Graham Greene isn't bad. At the moment we're doing Steinbeck, who's *really* good. But if I had to plump for someone, I guess it'd have to be Hemingway. You've heard of him? For Whom The Bell Tolls? The Old Man And The Sea?'

It was her turn to do the pretend-hurt thing. 'Unlike some people, I did actually come away from school with qualifications.' I was glad she was relaxed enough to joke about it. 'But Hemingway was American wasn't he? I thought you're doing English Literature?'

'Yes, well, the English part is actually a bit figurative.'

'Ah. Figurative. Yes, I see.'

I stopped eating to look at her. Her face was all innocence. After a pause that lasted several seconds, we both burst out laughing.

By the time we recovered I felt relaxed enough to try a little exploring.

'It's none of my business, and if you don't want to talk about it that's fine. But you and… Vincent?'

It opened a flood gate. Over the next quarter hour or so I got her life story, or most of it. She'd left home at seventeen to share a flat with a friend while finishing her A levels. She hinted at problems she'd had with her

Dad when she was young, but didn't elaborate beyond the fact he was an, 'Arsehole'. She was about to start Uni when she got pregnant by a boyfriend who joined the army the moment he heard. She dropped her studies in favour of a job in marketing. Her plan was to bring baby up on her own with help from her Mum, but she miscarried twelve weeks before he was due. She was about to go back to University when she got offered what she thought would be a plum PR job working for one of the big hotel chains. But the travelling didn't suit her and she soon got fed up with lonely hotel rooms and having to ward off passes by trainee managers – boys and girls – who thought they were God's gift. She returned to Warrington and a so-so marketing job and was given some work to do for Vincent's dealership. He'd just made his first million. Over the space of six weeks he romanced her off her feet with flowers, weekends away and promises to help her start up her own business, which to be fair, he later did. Until that moment I didn't know Vicki also had a day job, running her own PR and Marketing company from home.

'It's not what you would call full-time work, but it keeps me busy enough and gets me out of the house when I need to.'

After the hands life had dealt her so far, it all sounded pretty good, so when he proposed to her on top of the Eiffel Tower she accepted, though against her better instincts. 'I only ever did half a job convincing myself I loved him.' They married a month later. She knew within a week she'd made a mistake. Vincent was a control freak who didn't want a wife so much as a trophy he could show off at all the Round Table dinners he saw as important to helping him network. He also had a tendency to be heavy-handed if he'd had a few drinks and she didn't bend to his will. It took her a further two years to finally accept that as far as Vincent was concerned, marriage is not a good enough reason to stop playing around. By then she was bursting to break out of the prison he was making for her, and working from home wasn't helping. She'd always had a thing for nightclubs - 'Not the drink or the drugs or anything. Just the whole atmosphere you get in a big nightclub.' Her mother was an old friend of Frank Johnson's first wife. When she heard he'd bought the old Mr Smith's and was looking for a new VIP Hostess, she went to see him. He offered her the job on the spot, and at close to twice the pay rate she'd been expecting. At first Vincent was furious and she fully expected it would see the marriage off, but being old fashioned about these things, she tried to convince him – and herself – it would be good for them. Turned out she was wrong again. She loved the job but over the two years she'd worked at Midnight's, Vincent had grown more and more resentful. 'Because he can't keep his penis in his pants, he assumes I can't resist banging the VIPs. The last few months I've given up even trying to convince him otherwise.' She'd known for the last year he was seeing some girl called 'Candy,' but chose not to make a big thing of it. It was obvious where things were heading and she was happy to let things take their course. Three weeks ago, things had come to a head when she arrived home to find him smashed and Candy hiding in the en-suite bathroom. She decided it was time to call it a day and packed her bags and moved in with a friend. 'He's been trying to get me to come back since. Which was what you saw tonight.'

74

Having listened to it all, all I could do was shake my head. What sort of prick would play around when he's married to someone like Vicki? Though she hadn't made a big thing of it, the thought that he'd been prone to laying a hand on her from time to time made me feel like getting in my car, driving to their big house in Appleton, kicking the front door in, dragging him out of bed and beating him to a pulp.

We stared across the table. In the space of half an hour we'd learned more about each other than in all the time we'd worked together. Something between us changed that morning, though at that moment I had no idea what. What I did know was we had shared more than I'd ever dreamed possible.

By now it was getting on six o'clock. Light was filtering through the curtains. We cleared the dishes away and as she begin to run the kitchen tap I said, 'Leave them and get yourself off to bed. You'll want to use the bathroom first.'

She gave a wry smile. 'Okay.' She headed for the stairs. As she brushed past me in the kitchen I was disappointed when she avoided my gaze. But she stopped at the bottom of the stairs and turned. 'G'night Danny, and thanks.'

I just nodded. I watched until she disappeared. I gave her a few minutes and followed. Her bedroom light was off. I went straight to bed.

I've no idea how long I lay there, thinking about her lying the other side of the wall. My heart was pounding. I was thinking about how little sleep I was going to get, when the bedroom door opened. She stood there framed in the doorway for what seemed forever. And it was light enough that I could see she was naked. I'd stopped breathing. Stepping inside she closed the door then came straight across to the bed, lifted the duvet and slipped in next to me. She said nothing and didn't hesitate but pulled me to her and kissed me long and hard. The events of the next hour are amongst the most memorable of my life up to that point, alongside the Jury's 'Not Guilty' verdict, and the day my mum died.

It was the theme tune from Star Wars that woke me. My ringtone. I remembered at once and stretched my arm out, but felt only empty sheet next to me. I sat up. She was gone. The clock read 12.35. I answered the phone. It was Frank.

'I'm at the club Danny. I need you to come in, as well as those of your team who were working last night.'

'What's happened?' My gut was already tightening.

'Agnes didn't make it home last night. The police are here. She's missing.'

# CHAPTER 12

*Sunday*

When I got there some of the bar and front of house staff had already arrived, others coming through the door. In the foyer, a woman police officer with a clipboard was checking names before directing people to the upstairs coffee bar to wait to be interviewed. Tony-The-Manager was buzzing around, trying to make it look like he was doing something important. I headed straight for the main office where I found Frank talking with Jamie Carver. Vicki was over in the corner, giving a statement to DS Jess. When Frank rang, he'd told me he'd already spoken to Vicki. As I came in she glanced up, gave me nothing and went straight back to Jess. Eric was on the computer, compiling all the video clips from the night before in which Agnes appeared. Eric lives just round the corner from the club. I'd rung him and the rest of the guys as I was getting dressed and on my way in. The only one I hadn't been able to raise was Winston. I imagined him either crashed out after hitting something, or not wanting to talk to me yet.

I said to Carver, 'Any more news?' He shook his head. The look in his face wasn't reassuring. 'You've spoken to Bernadette?' I said.

He nodded. 'They rode a taxi home together. Bernadette dropped Agnes off at the end of her street before carrying on. Agnes's mother calls in at eight every Sunday morning to check on her. There was no sign Agnes had come home so she rang Bernadette. We've traced the taxi driver and he's in the clear. Right now we're working on the assumption that someone picked her up after the taxi dropped her off.'

'Agnes would never break her routine,' I said. 'Someone's got to have taken her.'

'Maybe,' Carver said. 'We're not ruling anything out.' He said it so calmly that, for a second, I lost it.

'There's no bloody 'maybe' about it. Someone's taken her. Why the fuck are you all standing around when you should be out looking for her?'

Everyone stopped what they were doing to look at me. I felt like an idiot.

Carver gave me a straight look. 'We're doing everything we need to be doing, Danny. What we need right now is information. If you want to do something practical go and speak to the staff. Make sure they know that if they've got any thoughts or theories then whatever their opinion of the police, they need to be telling us.'

I got the message. 'Right.'

Before I went, I shot another glance at Vicki. She didn't look up.

Upstairs in the coffee bar, I spent a bit of time doing what Carver had asked. Most of the staff are okay with the police but there are always a few – usually the new ones – who think they are the enemy. I did my best to put them right. Among them was the DJ, Mickey

Midnight. He was distraught and being comforted by a couple of the girls. When I was finished saying my piece I took him to one side.

'You alright Mickey?'

He nodded, wiping away tears. 'I just want them to find her, Danny. I can't bear the thought of some bastard hurting her.'

'We all feel the same. Let's just hang in there.'

'But why her Danny? She was so innocent, so sweet. Why would someone want to take her?'

'One, we don't know anyone has taken her yet, so let's not be writing her off. Two, whoever's doing these things isn't normal. He doesn't think like you or me. To him she's just another girl.'

He shook his head. 'But that's just it. She wasn't just another girl. I can't get this picture of her out of my mind. On the floor, doing her stuff to the Adagio. God, she was so gifted.'

This time I didn't bother trying to put him right about talking of her in the past tense. Truth be told, I was having to work at not doing the same myself.

Down in the staff room I found Eric, Eve, Golman and Chris in conference. As I came in it all went quiet and they stood up.

'You need to go upstairs,' I told them. 'The police want statements off everyone who was working last night.'

Eric nodded. 'We know. We were just talking.'

'About what?' Though I knew already.

'Winston.'

'What about him?' I knew that as well.

Eric looked at the rest, confirming his election as spokesman. 'We don't think it's right you've taken him off the door.'

'It's not, but right now I've no option. If I hadn't, Frank would have had an excuse to take the door off us and give it to someone else. And you all know who that would be.'

Chris was first to challenge. 'And we all know who set him up. Eve says Charnley was in here earlier on last night. On his own.'

I turned to her. 'Is that right?'

She nodded. 'I thought he was hanging around to see you. I didn't think anything of it at the time, but now I'm sure he was up to something. He could have waited for you in the office or out front. And he didn't stay long after I saw him.'

It was good intelligence, but not enough to change anything. 'Being sure and having evidence isn't the same thing.'

Eric squared himself. 'The team's looking for you to back them Danny. Like you've always said. We all stick together.'

I had no trouble reading what he was trying to tell me. Unless I gave them good reason not to, they were ready to walk. And though I didn't like it, it was reassuring to know they were prepared to go out on a limb for a mate. Sermon time.

'Listen. I don't like taking Winston off the door any more than you do. And for what it's worth I agree with you. He was stitched. If I thought for one minute the stuff was his, he wouldn't just be off the door, he'd be out of a job. But I have to run things according to the contract and the contract says that anyone found in possession has to be removed from the site, immediately. If I hadn't done it, then believe me we wouldn't still be here. I don't intend to leave it at that and I'm aiming to have Winston back here as soon as I can. But I need to let things settle for a couple of days. I know how you all feel. But right now I need you all to stick with me, keep your heads down and get on with the job. If we don't, Frank will use it as an excuse to void the contract and we'll all suffer.'

It was a measure of their anger that even the ever-respectful Golman, who usually prefers to listen, wanted to have his say. 'But how can Mr Johnson treat you, and us, like that after all we've done for him? If it wasn't for us, he'd be closed down by now.'

'You're right Gol. But there's things going on I'm not clear on yet. I'm not sure it's all Frank's doing. I think he's under pressure.'

'To do what?'

'Take the door off us.'

'Pressure from who?'

'I'm not sure about that yet either. Yashin, maybe.'

Eric bridled. 'That Russian twat. I knew he was bad news. He's setting us up so he can take control of the door.'

Eve nodded. 'Control the door, control the drugs.'

'Exactly,' I said. 'And I don't know about you, but I'm not about to let that happen.'

They all looked at each other, exchanging nods, silently giving Eric his mandate. He turned to face me.

'Okay Danny. We'll go with it, for now. But the sooner you get Winston back here the better.'

'Soon as I can. I promise.' As they all nodded their acceptance, they relaxed and the mood in the room lightened. 'Now you need to get upstairs and tell the police anything you know that might help them find

Agnes.'

They all trooped out, Eric bringing up the rear. I called to him as he was about to leave and he hung back.

'Thanks.'

He threw me a wink. 'This is why you need to pay me more.'

I waited to make sure they'd gone, then let out a relieved sigh.

Ten minutes later I was passing through the lobby when Vicki came down the stairs. I stuck to the business.

'You finished with the police?'

She nodded. 'They wanted to know what went on with the Russians last night. I think some of Yashin's men may be getting knocks on their doors before the day is over. Maybe Yashin himself.'

'It's nice to think of them being grilled. But I'll be surprised if they're anything to do with Agnes going missing.'

'So will I, but at least it'll make them think twice about pulling another stunt like the one they pulled last night. Have you given a statement?'

'I'm about to.' I remembered what I'd been thinking about before Vicki appeared.

'The girls who have all been attacked.'

'What about them?'

'What do you know about them?'

'Not much. I knew Sonia of course, and I met Naomi once, but I didn't know the others.'

'You said last night they'd all visited Midnight's. Who told you that?'

'I heard the front of house girls talking. Between

them they probably knew all of them. Why are you asking?'

'Hmm, just thinking about something someone mentioned. No matter. I'll speak with the girls myself.'

There was an awkward silence. She broke it.

'I'm sorry about this morning.'

'There's no need. I'm not-'

'No, I should explain why-'

'You don't owe me any explanations.'

'Maybe not, but I want to anyway, if you'll listen.'

I shut up.

'Last night- This morning, was- I woke up confused. It wasn't what I expected. You weren't... how I expected.' My face must have said, *Really*? 'You were...'

'Normal?'

'I was going to say... nice.'

'Ah. Fooled you there then.'

'Don't mock me Danny. I'm trying to get my head round things.'

'I'm not sure what it is you're trying to say.'

'I'm trying to say that in the time I've known you, all I've ever seen is Danny Norton, The Hardest Man In Warrington. But this morning you were... different.'

'In a good way I hope?'

She gave me a long look before she said, 'Yes.'

'So where does that leave, you?' I'd nearly said 'us'.

'I'm not sure. That's what I'm trying to get my head around. It's why I left early. I needed room to think.'

'And have you?'

'Not enough. Frank called as I was coming away from yours. I've not had much time since.'

'So where are you going now?'

83

'I'm going to see Vincent. We need to sort things out.'

I wasn't sure what she meant by that and wasn't about to ask. I'd had enough of making myself look daft. But I hoped it didn't mean she was looking to patch things up with him.

She gave me one last look. 'Thanks again for last night.' Unsure which part she was thanking me for I just nodded, then worried in case I reminded her of a nodding dog on a car's back parcel shelf. After she left, I made my way upstairs. Jess was already there, looking for me.

'I need a statement off you about last night.'

'I'm all yours.'

I was with her over an hour. The times we'd met before there'd been a fair bit of mutual mickey-taking but this time she was all business. I didn't ask her directly what she thought had happened to Agnes but the way she kept focusing on what seemed to me like the most minor details, I got the impression she wasn't expecting it would stay a missing person enquiry much longer.

By the time we finished, I'd about had enough and was ready to get away. I had things to do. But I needed to speak with the girls first. Tony had opened the Dusk-'til-Dawn bar and I found those who hadn't gone home yet sat on stools in a circle, sipping vodkas and Cokes and swapping gossip. It's a sad aspect of human nature that when something bad happens, people revel in it. Even before they know the facts, they like to imagine, to develop theories. Which is exactly what they were doing. I picked up on a couple as I approached.

'I heard she was seen leaving the club with some Russian guy.'

'My mum told me she heard a load of sirens this morning. She reckons her neighbour said something about hearing a scream about three o'clock this morning.'

They almost seemed to be enjoying it which I didn't like at all, but I didn't say anything. Abi, one of the cloakroom girls, saw me coming and pulled a stool round.

'I'll bet Gladiator'll know.' Gladiator is one of my nicknames. I'm told there are others. 'Park your bum, chuck. What're the police saying?'

I played dumb while I waited to get to what I was interested in. Eventually I said, 'I suppose that between you, you'll have known all the girls?'

'We was just saying that,' Abi said, a bit too enthusiastically 'We all knew Sonia.'

'And me and Lisa knew Naomi.'

'And she knows- Sorry, knew Claire.'

'And of course we all know Agnes.'

Ignoring the last I said, 'What were Claire and Naomi like?'

As they queued up to tell me what they knew, I sat quietly and listened, letting them paint the picture I was looking for. After five minutes I'd heard enough.

I said, 'I know its big news, but perhaps its best not to talk about all this too much just yet, eh? Agnes is still only a missing person, remember?' Checking faces, I saw guilty looks being exchanged. 'Maybe it's time you all got off home. The police are nearly finished here and we'll be needing to close up.' They got the message.

The party spoiled, they slid from their perches,

downed drinks and reached for bags. As they trooped off they bade sad farewells to each other, and me. 'See you, Danny,' Abi said. She gave me a hug and stretched up to kiss my cheek. 'Sorry if we were being bitches.'

One of the bar girls, Laurie, made a point of coming over all emotional as she copied Abi's hug, only it lasted a while longer than it needed to. I was careful not to respond. A couple of weeks before, Eric had told me he'd heard a couple of the girls talking about Laurie being a bit of a stalker-type.

Returning to the office, I found Frank talking with Tony. There was no sign on Carver. We'd all had enough by then and none of us had much to say. I left them to lock up and headed for my car. Before starting the engine I rang my business partner, Mike Nelson.

'What's happening?' Mike said. 'I'm hearing a girl's gone missing from the club.' In the background I could hear men's voices, dry laughter. It was around three. I imagined him somewhere around the sixteenth tee.

'Not *from* the club. On her way home somewhere.'

'Are *we* okay?'

By 'we' I knew he meant the business. Mike doesn't like us to be tainted.

'As far as the missing girl is concerned, yes.'

'I sense a 'but.'

'There's some other stuff I need to fill you in on. You in the office tomorrow?'

'First thing, as always.'

'I'll see you there.'

'Whassup Danny? Sure you don't want to tell me now?'

For a split-second I thought about it. 'It'll wait.'

'If you're sure.'

'I'm sure.' I rang off. Truth be told, I probably didn't need to ring Mike at all. It wasn't like there was anything he could do. But I was having to run round on what should have been my one day off, so why not let him experience a bit of what it's like? It's not like it happens often.

Mike is my partner in DoorSecure Ltd. The business is split between us, fifty-fifty. Least that's what Mike tells me. He handles what he calls, 'The Business Half' of things - finance, accounts, taxes, contracts, paperwork, filing. Me, I handle the 'People' half. Recruitment, training, operations, management, supervision and maintaining site cover - which is the bastard - as well as drumming up new business and making sure that we run our sites the way they're supposed to be run. The fact that my side seems to be a twenty-four-seven responsibility while Mike manages to do what he does in the couple of the hours each weekday he isn't at Warrington Golf Club practising his swing and trying to reduce his handicap, is something I've never got my head round. But then, Mike's never worked in Security. His background is I.T. He still runs his own software company from home. It's small, but probably doubles his income along with what he makes with me. How we got together and came to start up a door security business is a long story. Suffice to say I don't let Mike near any of our doors. Ever. Apart from anything, he'd piss his pants soon as some half-cut gob-shite looked at him. Like most over-forties, Mike's long forgotten what the inside of a night club looks and sounds like. Now he wouldn't tell between someone who's had a couple of drinks, is a bit loud and boisterous but prepared to do as he's told once things have been explained to him properly, and one who's high on something and unstable as sweating nitroglycerine. At three in the morning, when it's all kicking off and me and the rest of my team are practising our Physical Intervention skills, I'm happier knowing that Mike is safely tucked up in bed, dreaming of winning the next Captain's Cup rather than trying to pretend that because he's co-owner of a door security company, he knows anything about supervising doors.

I stopped at the garage Spar on the way home to get some supplies. I'm not sure why or what I was expecting. I don't usually shop on a weekend. It was close to seven by the time I walked in the front door. Normally Sunday evenings, I'd try and catch up on my course work. I was two weeks late with my latest module essay – *'Discuss the relationship between narrative style and moral judgement in Joseph Conrad's Heart of Darkness'* – so I thought I should give it another go. I pulled my work folder off the shelf - Vicki's nosing had stopped short before she found it, thank God - and laid it all out on the kitchen table. For the next half hour I tried to force my mind to stay focused on the question, thumbing through the novel and trying to remember what I'd been thinking when I made the notes in the accompanying work-book. It was no good. So much had happened the past twenty four hours, every time I laid one intruding train of thought to rest, another rose to take its place. Eventually I slammed the folder shut and put it back on the shelf. As I did, the thought came it was the first time since starting the course that I'd really felt like I was struggling. It brought on a sudden panic that I may not finish it after all. I went and opened a new bottle of JD.

I'd just sat down, glass in hand, and grabbed the TV remote when my mobile rang. I recognised Carver's number.

'I thought you'd want to know.' Even before he said it, the flatness in his tone told me what I didn't want to hear. 'We've found Agnes. She's dead.'

'Ahh, Christ.' I stayed quiet a few moments, letting it settle. 'Was she- Is it… like the others?'

There was the briefest hesitation, then, 'Yes.'

'Can you say where?'

'Grappenhall. Just off the canal tow path.'

I knew the area and pictured it. Grappenhall is a couple of miles or so from the town centre.

I tried fishing for more information, but apart from telling me no one had been arrested, Carver was guarded.

'Can't say too much yet. We're doing the scene now. I'll be able to give you more tomorrow.'

I asked if her family had been told. They had. 'This is crap,' I said, conscious of the understatement but unable to think of anything that would do the remotest justice to the circumstances.

Carver must have felt the same. 'I'll call you again tomorrow. I just thought I ought to let you know now. We're going to have come and do the club again.'

'Right. We're open again on Tuesday. Student night.'

'I know. I've already spoken with Frank.'

He was about to ring off when I remembered. 'Are you working on any connection between the girls?' There was a pause.

'We know they were all into clubbing, obviously. Why?'

'Do you know they were all dancers?'

89

'Isn't that what clubbers do?'

'Yes but they were more than just clubbers. They were all show dancers. They'd all either danced on podiums or were known as terrific dancers, like Agnes. People liked to watch them dance.' The silence on the other end stretched until I said, 'You still there?'

'Leave that one with me. Have you mentioned it to anyone else?'

'Not directly.'

'Do me a favour and keep it to yourself for now.'

I said I would. He rang off.

Afterwards I sat there, staring at my mobile and thinking about Agnes. I was there quite a while. When the phone suddenly jumped into life again, I did the same.

It was Laura. I'd forgotten I was supposed to ring and tell her how Dad was.

'Sorry, it's been a busy weekend.'

She snorted. 'Yeah. Right.'

I didn't rise to it and didn't try to explain. My high-flying sister isn't hot on empathy.

'So? How was he?'

'Not too good when I got there, but he bucked up and was okay by the time I left.'

'How was his breathing? Any worse?'

'Hard to say. He's okay sitting down but soon as he starts to do anything, it just brings on the wheezing.'

'Is he using the oxygen cylinder?'

'He didn't while I was there.'

I heard her tut. 'You should make him use it. It's what it's there for.'

All I said was, 'Hmm.'

'What does, "Hmm" mean?'

'It means you know what he's like. And if you think you can do better than me getting him to do what he doesn't want to do, then get your arse on the train and come up here.'

'That's not fair, Danny. I work as well you know. And that includes most of the weekend.'

I shook my head. Considering she spent her first ten years working around here, Laura has no idea. Listening to her sometimes, you'd think Canary Wharf is the only place people work these days.

'I wasn't having a go Sis. I was just saying. The older he gets the more stubborn he is.'

'Have you tried mentioning care to him again yet?'

'No. The way he was last time I don't want him getting upset like that again for a while.'

'Well he's going to have to accept it eventually. When we spoke with his Doctor he said if we ring Social Services they'll-'

'I know what the Doctor said. And I will ring them when it's time to do so. For the time being he's doing okay, considering.'

She hesitated 'Was he- Was he… clean?'

I looked at the ceiling. 'If you mean, did he have shitty toilet paper hanging out of his pants then the answer's "no".

'No need to be crude, Daniel. I'm just concerned to know he's alright.'

*Daniel?* Not for the first time, the thought came my sister was turning into our mother. *And there's a response I could give to that as well.* But all I said was, 'I know, Sis. We both are.' That's the trouble with older sisters. They always think they know better.

We talked a while longer but I could tell she was just

going through the motions. She made me promise to call in on Dad again mid-week and let her know. It's amazing how caring people can be when they're a couple of hundred miles away.

After she hung up I drained my glass, went back to the kitchen, refilled it and was about to try again with the TV remote when the phone rang again. The screen showed 'Vicki'. My heart skipped.

'Have you heard?' she said. She was crying.

'Just.'

'Could I- Would you mind if I came round?'

''Course not. Where are you?'

'I've just left Vincent's.'

The fifteen minutes it took her to arrive felt like an hour. When I opened the door she stood on the step for a second looking like she was trying to hold it all together, before the dam burst and she just fell through the door and into my arms.

'Oh, Danny. Poor Agnes.'

I guided her to the sofa and went and got her a vodka and me another whiskey. Then I sat next to her and put my arm round her. She responded by nestling into my chest as the tears flowed. The sobbing came and went in waves as the wet patch on my shirt grew. We stayed like that for a long time, sipping drinks and holding each other. At one point I wondered whether to distract her by asking about how things had gone with Vincent, but decided against. Eventually she became still in my arms and I realised she was asleep.

Two hours later I came awake with a start. When I remembered the weight on my chest was her, I had the best feeling I'd had since when things were good between me and Caroline. Then I remembered why she was there and the euphoria vanished, replaced by a profound feeling of guilt.

Eventually we roused ourselves enough to take a sandwich supper which she had with some wine while I popped a Bud. We had little to say and by eleven we were both ready for bed, worn out by the day's events. We said our goodnights on the landing. There were no hugs or kisses, though as she turned to enter her bedroom her hand sought out mine and squeezed it. It did for me.

I lay awake for ages. But there was no repeat of what had happened that morning, not that I was either looking for, or expecting it. Sometimes things happen that change everything. Agnes's murder was one of them.

# CHAPTER 13

*Monday*

I woke at half-six expecting to find Vicki had done another runner. Her bedroom door was open, but unlike the previous day her bed was unmade. I found her at the kitchen table nursing a mug of tea. I was glad my shopping had included fresh milk.

'The kettle's just boiled,' she said as I came in. 'I couldn't find a teapot so I made it in the mug.'

'I haven't got one. Teapot I mean.'

She gave me a sad look. Her eyes were puffy and her face drawn. She was clutching the remains of a tissue. A mother seeing her daughter the way she looked would tell her she looked awful. But to me, the way she was right then, full of sadness over Agnes and showing the sort of vulnerability I'd never seen before, she was more beautiful than ever.

'Would you like some breakfast?' I said.

'Toast'll be fine. If you've got any bread?'

'I have.' Another tick for Sunday shopping.

I made toast and coffee, and joined her at the table. Sleep must have strengthened my resolve as I asked her straight off, 'How did it go with Vincent yesterday?'

She took her time before answering.

'He knows now we're finished.' My heart leaped. 'But he didn't like it and it wasn't easy.' She paused to look across the table at me. 'If I'm honest I'm a little worried how he's going to react. He- He doesn't take rejection well.'

'Did he touch you?'

'No. And I didn't hang around long enough for him to think about it. But I know what he's like.'

'If he ever tries anything and you need someone, fast, you've got my number.'

'Thanks, Danny. Hopefully, that'll never happen and he'll get over it. And he's still got Candy he can turn to.'

'True.' I didn't comment further. It wasn't my place.

She made an effort to lift herself. 'Right now I've got more urgent things to think about than Vincent.'

'Such as?'

'Such as finding a place to stay. I'm now officially homeless remember?'

'I thought you're staying with your friend?'

'I am, but that was only temporary. I think she's getting a bit fed up sharing a house with someone who comes home at four in the morning most nights and sleeps through the day at weekends.'

I thought I could see where she was going and didn't hesitate. 'Hey, it's fine. Feel free to stay as long as you like. The room is-' I stopped as she shook her head, in the way I was becoming used to when she thought I was being thick.

'I'm not talking about staying here. Much as I enjoyed yesterday, and for all sorts of reasons, not least of which is I don't want trouble between you and

Vincent, I don't think it's a good idea for us to be sharing a house together right now. Even if I was only a lodger.'

'Sorry. Right. Of course not.' As she gave me another of those looks I couldn't fathom, I realised she was the only person I'd met in a long while who I kept getting wrong.

'I was going to ask if your connections extend to anyone who might have property to rent out? A small flat or something?'

I reached for my mobile. The week before I'd bumped into Harry Shankley in the Brigadoon. A developer-builder, Harry had just finished some flats in Sankey and was talking about looking for tenants. It was just gone seven, but I've helped Harry out on jobs a few times and knew he likes to be up and out early. I made the call and got him en-route to a site. As Vicki listened to me laying it all on to Harry about this real good friend who was in a bit of a fix and needed somewhere quick but could only afford a sensible rent while she sorted things out, her eyes widened. When I handed her the phone so she could speak with Harry herself, she beamed me a big, 'Thanks.' Five minutes later she was fixed up with a furnished apartment she could move into straight away while she decided whether to take it permanently. Conscious I was amassing brownie points, I tried to play it cool when she leaned forward and planted a kiss on my cheek.

'Thanks Danny.' She followed it with a giggle.

'Now what's up?'

She shook her head so her hair fell across her face in a way I really liked. 'You keep reminding me of The Godfather. Everyone jumps when you ask for a favour.'

I feigned offence. 'Harry's just a good mate, that's all. He could have said "no".'

She smiled. 'Yeah. Of course.'

The way it was going, I was tempted to stay and see how things might develop. But I decided it was time for other things. I got up from the table. She looked surprised.

'Are you going somewhere?'

'There's some stuff I need to sort out.'

'Stuff?'

'I run a business, remember?'

'Oh.'

I imagined that I saw disappointment in her face. 'Did you want me for something?'

She was hesitant. 'I was thinking your truck would've been useful to help me move my stuff. My car's only-'

'No problem. Give me the morning then I'll come and give you a lift. You'll need me to show you where the flat is anyway.'

She turned suddenly serious. 'You really are different to what people say, aren't you?'

As I mounted the stairs to get ready I wondered which particular stories about me she'd heard.

I was into work for eight, having given Vicki the spare house key in case she needed it. She was in the shower when I left and didn't reply when I shouted up a, 'See you later.' On the way in, I wondered if it was because she was wary about it all seeming a bit too cosy.

DoorSecure's offices – all two of them – are above a row of shops in Flixton, a mainly residential area half a mile from Warrington Town Centre. They're nothing grand but the rent's okay, and depending on which direction you come from, morning traffic's not too bad. The front door is plain and painted mid-blue. We re-paint it each year. In the middle, at eye-level, is a square white sign with blue lettering that Mike designed on his computer. It says simply, 'DoorSecure Ltd.' and a voicemail number in case we're out. There are two locks, one a 5-lever mortice lock - the best you can buy - the other an electronic swipe-lock for which there are only three cards in existence. Through the door, the hall and walls are cream emulsion and the stairs are carpeted in a heavy-duty commercial cord. I think the look is a bit stark, but Mike reckons it shows we are efficient and business-like. I leave these things to him. At the top of the stairs you turn right into the larger of the two offices. It contains two IKEA desks, one for me and one for Mike. We both have leather swivel chairs - also IKEA - though for some reason Mike's is bigger than mine. Mike's desk gets a fair bit of use, but mine's still like new. The corner next to the window is laid out as a bit of a conference area, with a round table that doesn't quite match the desks, and six chrome-steel framed chairs with maroon, cushioned seats. We got them off a mate of mine when his business went bust last year. There's an adjoining office, where Julia works and where we keep all the paperwork, office equipment and filing cabinets. There's another desk, not as big as mine and Mike's, which is kept free for when Julia arranges work-experience - usually one of her nephews or nieces - to give her a lift.

As I came in, Mike was already at his desk, working on spreadsheets. He's another who likes his early starts. Apart from the depths of winter, it means he can finish in time to get some holes in without feeling too guilty.

He swivelled his chair round towards me. 'Heavy night?'

'Not the way you're thinking.'

From the adjoining office, Julia's singsong echoed through. 'Morning Danny. Coffee?' Julia's our admin clerk. Actually she's more than an admin clerk. She runs things.

'Yes please Jules. 'Morning.'

As I flopped down into my chair Mike said, 'So tell me what's doing.'

I hesitated. *Where to start?*

I decided on what he already knew. Agnes. I finished that bit with Carver mentioning about the police coming into the club again on Tuesday.

'Frank won't like that. Footfalls are down in all the clubs since these girls started getting themselves killed. This is the second one from Midnight's. It's going to hit him hard. And if it hits him hard, it hits us as well.'

I heaved a sigh. Mike's mind only works one way, and that's business. I said, 'So we better hope the police catch the bastard sooner rather than later.'

'You know lots of people,' Mike said. 'Don't any of them have an idea about who would do this sort of thing?'

As Jules set my mug down on the cardboard coaster on my desk we exchanged glances. The way her eyebrows went up I knew what she was thinking. Mike doesn't always live in the real world.

'We're not talking about someone dealing drugs or doing-over post offices here, Mike. This is a psycho who's pulling girls off the street and doing God knows what to them. If I knew anyone who might know something, don't you think I'd have told the police by now?'

'What about that weirdo who used to do the rounds of the clubs? What was his name, Wer... Worsesomething?'

'Colin Worsley'

'That's him. Didn't you once tell me he likes to rough women up?'

'He's already inside. That business with the Chinese girl last year, remember?'

'Oh yeah. The champagne bottle thing.'

As Julia returned to her office she gave a loud, 'Tch.'

'So what's this bloke into then? I hear he cuts them up quite badly. Is that right?'

'Jesus, Mike, how the hell do I know?'

'I thought you and the cop in charge are best mates?'

'We're not mates. We know each other, that's all. He doesn't confide in me or anything.'

Mike must have sensed my growing frustration as he dropped the subject. 'So what else?'

'Get ready. You'll love this.'

I told him about our run-in with the Russians. Charnley's visit. The stuff found in Winston's locker and me taking him off the door. As I laid it all out, Julia wandered back in and perched on the end of my desk, listening. When I outlined my suspicions about Charnley being snug with Yashin and trying to set us up so Frank would have to take the contract off us, Mike's face grew dark. When I'd finished he was quiet for a while before he said, 'The Midnight's contract is the biggest we've got.'

'I know.'

'If we lose it, we could be in trouble.'

'I know.'

Julia switched a wary look between us. With two lads at university and her girl due to start in September, her interest in the business was at least as great as ours.

'What about the Russian? Will there be trouble between you?'

'Probably.'

Mike shook his head. 'So what are you going to do?'

I almost laughed. Mike's got a gift for seeing certain problems as *mine* as opposed to *ours*. 'I'm going to fight fire with fire.'

'I don't like the sound of that. What're you planning?'

I tapped the side of my nose. 'You'll have to wait and see.'

'Nothing stupid, I hope?'

As I rose to leave I said, 'Would I?'

His answer was a worried look.


Outside I took out my phone, brought up 'Jasper' in my contacts, and hit dial.

It rang out long enough for me to think about hanging up when a voice said, 'D?'

'Hi Jasper. Can you talk?'

'Always time for you buddy. And I'm not driving.'

'Who's doing pick-ups this morning?'

'Chaz, I think. Why?'

A picture of Charlie Knight in his usual builder's labourer attire formed. Heavily built and with hands like spades, he's the most unlikely drug squad officer I've ever met. 'I've got a slight problem.'

'Fuck. I knew it.' His tone changed as I imagined him turning to his partner, Gary. 'It's that Norton twat. Didn't I say that he'd be onto us after that Liverpool lot?' He was referring to a bust they'd made on the car park behind the club the month previous. My part only involved a phone call. He came back. 'Go on, I'm listening.'

'There's a package in our safe.'

'What's in it?'

'I'm assuming it's C.

'And?'

'I could do with borrowing it back.'

'For how long?'

'Until this afternoon.'

'When do you need it?'

I checked my watch. 'Noon?'

'Okay. Next question. Why?'

I smiled to myself. 'Funny you should ask.'

# CHAPTER 14

The Abbeywood Development on the outskirts of Winwick is one of those housing estates that might have been designed to confuse postmen and delivery drivers. The houses are arranged in angular closes and crescents with names like 'Cedar' and 'Laurel', all running off a ring road that circles the whole estate. Behind the houses are parking areas where there's usually at least one jacked-up car with its bonnet off waiting for a new engine. Hedge-lined walkways meander through the estate in all directions. If you didn't know the layout and set out to walk to the shops in the centre, you could walk in circles for hours.

As it happened, I'd called in at Winston's a few months before and remembered he lived in the first turning left after you came onto the estate. Cypress, it was called. I parked outside his back gate which was tall and solid-looking. I recalled he had a German Shepherd – 'King' - which he keeps in the yard, so I followed the path round to the front. I'd barely rung the bell when, through the frosted glass panels in the front door, I saw Abigail approaching up the hall. When she opened the door and saw me she put her head on one side and gave me a look that said, 'You've got a nerve.'

Abigail is the most striking African woman I've ever

met. Glossy black skin, almond-shaped eyes, high cheekbones. When I first met her – the night she turned up at the club not long after she and Winston got together - I totally believed it when someone told me she was the daughter of some African tribal king. My Dad would say she has, 'Regal bearing,'

Right now she was carrying little Jasmine on her hip and hefted her round into a more comfortable position before hitting me with, 'What yo' wantin' yo' come here fo'?'

'I need to see Winston, Abi.'

'Why? He don' work fo' yo' no mo'.'

'Yes he does. I haven't sacked him.'

'He says you took him off the door.'

'I did, but only Midnight's. That's why I need to see him.'

Her hesitation showed the first chink in her defiance. If there was still a chance their income wasn't going to be as affected as she'd imagined, she needed to be careful about abusing me as much as she'd been about to. Not that it would change anything if she did.

Eventually she said, 'He's in back,' and stepped aside. As I passed her to make my way down the hall, it was like walking past an open fridge.

As I neared the back room I could hear voices, deep and low, like rumbling thunder. Someone was saying, '- just enough so he won't fuck wit you like dat again.'

As I came through into the living area, Winston turned, saw me and shot out of the leather armchair that, like the matching sofa, was way too big for the room but had to be to accommodate him. In less than a second his face changed through surprise, to guilt, to the same defiant suspicion I'd seen in Abigail. Opposite him,

104

nestled in the sofa like twin Jabba The Hutts, were Gabriel and Anthony, two of his brothers. As they recognised me a wary look passed between them. Though there were only four of us in the room, it was way crowded.

Overcoming his surprise, Winston squared up to me. 'What you doin' here Danny?'

'We need to speak,' I said.

He shot a look at his brothers. 'You should have rung first.'

'I did. Several times. You aren't answering.'

He shrugged it off. 'So, what is it?'

'I know you're pissed about last night but I want you to know this isn't over yet. You're still on the books and I'm going to get you back at Midnight's as soon as I can.'

'How you goin' to do that?'

'I'm not sure yet, but let's just say there are things going on that need to be sorted out.'

'What things?'

'Things like Charnley, the Russians, whatever it is they're trying to do with Frank.'

At mention of Charnley, Winston's face twisted into a snarl.

'That fuckin' mother set me up. You know I don't do that drugs shit.' He shot an apologetic look at his brothers.

'Which is why I'm here to tell you not to do whatever you and your brothers-' I turned to give them an acknowledging nod. '-were just talking about doing, and give me some time to work things out.' I was in no doubt they'd been talking about 'sorting' Charnley in a way that, for the brothers at least, would be no more than what they did, day in, day out, anyway.

Winston turned to them. They were sat forward on the edge of the sofa, almost on their haunches, listening carefully to my pitch. The way they were looking at me, eyes no more than slits in puffy faces, they could have been trying to work out whether I'd be best grilled, roasted or fried.

It would be wrong to say that the relationship between me and Winston's brothers is based on mutual respect. I don't respect anyone who makes a living fucking up other people's lives – not even those who deserve to have their lives fucked up. But I know enough about the several businesses they are involved in – none the remotest way legal – to respect that they stick to their turf and have never tried to take advantage of the fact that their baby brother works the door at the biggest night-club in the North West. For their part, I guess they know enough about the way I run things that, on the few occasions we've met, they've always adopted a weird formality, calling me, 'Mr Norton' rather than Danny, like everyone else does. It was as if they were grateful for me giving Winston a job and vouching for him for his Security Licence, so that at least one member of the clan was living a life that was, for the most part, clean. That said, they also knew that if they ever tried anything at Midnight's, there'd be trouble between us.

Turning his gaze from me, Gabriel, the oldest of the pair, gave Winston a look that read, 'Do you believe him?'

Winston looked between us, weighing things.

'Listen to him, big man.' Abigail's voice sounded behind us.

I turned to see her leaning on the door jamb, still cradling baby Jasmine. She'd obviously been listening and right now the look she was giving her 'big man' wasn't a million miles from the one she'd given me when she opened the door. She continued.

'I don't want you doin' no shit that might end up wit' you inside and me havin' to bring this one up on my own.' She nodded at the package she was carrying before turning, pointedly, to her brothers-in-law and adding, 'No disrespec''.

The brothers-in-laws nodded, slowly. They didn't seek to argue against her. I wouldn't argue with Abi either, if I knew her mind was set.

She and Winston exchanged a long look. For all the closeness with his blood-family, I knew that as far as Winston was concerned, Abigail and Jasmine took precedence. It was why he was still managing to live a life free from the sort of trouble his brothers' business brings from time to time. And he didn't bother looking for their permission when he put a big hand out to me and said, 'I'm relying on you, Danny. Don't let me down.'

'I won't,' I said.

## CHAPTER 15

I'd arranged to meet Vicki at her friend's house in Winwick around one-ish. On the way there, I stopped off in a lay-by on the A49 for the meet I'd arranged during my little chat with Jasper that morning. It went well.

After loading Vicki's stuff into my truck – there wasn't that much – I took her to Sankey where we met Harry. He handed her the keys to the flat and showed her round. It was a first-floor, straight-up-the-stairs-through-the-front-door affair. Clean, modern, comfortable, two bedrooms, well appointed kitchen. Though she played it cool like she does at work, I could tell she was made up. After helping her carry her stuff up, Harry and I came away and left her to settle in. On the car park I offered him a fifty for his trouble.

'No need for that Danny. Thanks to you I'm pulling rent I wouldn't have got if I'd had to wait for the agency to find a tenant.'

'Even so,' I said, pushing the note into my shirt pocket. 'I'm grateful and I wouldn't want anyone getting the wrong idea about you doing me a favour.'

'What's that mean?'

'Never mind. You and Diane go out and have a Chinese on me.'

'If you insist. By the way…'

'What?'

'You and her.' He thumped up at the flat. 'Are you…'

'No.'

'Not even-?'

'No.'

Returning to my truck I made a point of not looking back to see Harry's leery smirk. And as I drove off I knew that by the time I called in at The Brigadoon later for my Monday-night pint, the word would be out about me and some 'posh bird.'

It was still a couple of hours before my next planned call-in, so I attended to some business. We had a couple of prospective new contracts in the pipeline - pubs and clubs around the Warrington area – and I made some PR visits to keep them sweet. If Midnight's contract did go tits up, we'd need any new business that was going.

I was between sites when Carver rang and we talked about what he had on Agnes's murder, which was basically nothing. They'd worked out she'd been driven to where her body was found, but so far they couldn't even say if she was killed there or somewhere else and her body dumped. It was an isolated spot and there were no witnesses – just like the other killings. He was interested in my 'dancer' theory.

'Run it past me again. This thing about them all being good dancers.'

I went over it again, telling him about the girls I'd spoken to and how they'd all described how the victims weren't just good dancers, but exceptional, as in Pop Video standard. Naomi and Sonia had even auditioned for some TV talent show and got through to the first round of judging before managing to get chucked off after Sonia got pissed one night and was caught slagging off one of the female judges.

'You think it might be something?' I said.

'Every serial killer uses some means to select their victims. It's never random, even if it looks that way. This guy's thing could be dancers.'

I thought about it. 'If it's right, then he'd have picked them out after seeing them dancing in the clubs.'

'Most likely.'

'How often would he have watched them do you reckon?'

'Impossible to say. So far the killings have been weeks apart. All the victims frequented clubs two or three nights a week. If he's a regular as well then he may have watched them several times, working himself up, planning it.'

'Jesus. We've probably seen him, and not realised it.'

'Very possible.'

'So what line are you taking?'

'We need to speak to other girls who are known to be exceptional dancers. They might have some ideas. They may even have spotted someone in the crowd taking more than normal interest.'

'Am I okay to pass that around?'

'By all means.'

I didn't mention the stuff with the Drug Squad. I didn't think he'd want to know.

Dave Charnley operates from a pair of bolted-together portacabins next to a plumber's merchant's on a small industrial site in Padgate. Like our offices, they're nothing to brag about but they do the job. One of the cabins serves as Charnley's office, with a small toilet-cum-kitchen off. The other is his 'Control' and staff office where his number two, a local lad by the name of Ian, works along with a couple of girls. Between them, they do about half of what Julie does for us on her own. I parked up next to Charnley's Range Rover and went inside. As I came in, Charnley was just finishing up with a couple of shady-looking but smartly-dressed guys. They didn't look to me like the normal sort who run pubs and clubs around our area. Their gruff farewells as Charnely ushered them out – he made a point of not introducing them to me - marked them as foreign, possibly east European. It sometimes seems like they're the only people interested in investing in the sort of places that need door supervisors these days. As they left, I caught their suspicious glances and shifty gazes enough that I would remember them if I came across them again.

As they drove off the car park, Charnley turned to me, a wide but insincere smile creasing his weather-tanned features. He's another golfer.

'Long-time no-see, Captain. What brings you here?'

'You tell me. I heard you were in the other night. I assumed you were looking for me so I thought I'd drop in while I was passing.' Caught off-guard, I could almost hear the cogs whirring as he thought about what excuse to dream up.

'The other night.. er, you mean Saturday?' I nodded. He cast his gaze about his office. 'That was just- I was, er-' He pinched the top of his nose. Something came to him. 'That's right. I just wanted to check if you'd heard anymore about what's happening with this new licensing authority thing?'

Months before, the Government had announced yet another review of the Security Industry Licensing arrangements. This time it was in light of some Sunday newspaper-led exposé about companies getting round the licensing regulations and employing illegal immigrants as security at sports stadiums. Since the original announcement it had gone quiet, but when I'd looked at it at the time it was obvious that any changes would impact more on the industry's big players rather than small-fry like us. Charnley would have done the same and come to the same conclusion. Nevertheless I played along, letting him have my thoughts while he feigned interest. For a few minutes it was a real double-act between us. Eventually Charnley had had enough and changed the subject.

'It's a bloody bad situation over these girls. I hear this last one was from Midnight's?' I nodded, glumly, no longer acting. Then he said, 'Any thoughts?' and I saw my chance.

'A few, but first, what does someone have to do to get offered a brew round here?'

Happy he'd managed to divert me away from the subject of his sabotaging visit, Charnley snapped into action. 'I was just going to ask. He grabbed at the two mugs on the desk near to where his two most recent visitors had been sitting. 'Still the same?'

I nodded. 'Black. No sugar.'

As he disappeared through the door into the kitchen, he called back. 'Make yourself comfortable.'

Along the wall where I'd been leaning was a bank of four grey steel filing cabinets, just like the ones in our office. And like ours they'd seen better days. I was pretty sure that if I checked out their contents I would find they would be pretty much the same as well. One cabinet would contain staff files, another folders relating to sites, clients and contracts. The third would be jammed with all the regulatory crap security firms have to comply with these days and the fourth would be full of 'miscellaneous'. There're only so many ways you can run a security business. A set of keys hung from the lock in the top right-hand corner of the fourth cabinet, the one nearest Charnley's desk. I reached into my inside jacket pocket and fished for the package I'd 'reclaimed' on my way to Vicki's.

When Charnley returned with the coffees, I was in one of the chairs vacated by his visitors. I'd checked my watch a few seconds before and knew it was close to four thirty. For no other reason than to fill time I said. 'Who were the suits?' and nodded in the direction where his visitors had disappeared. Charnley must have thought about it while making the coffees because he barely hesitated. 'They're a couple of Poles. They're looking at taking over a pub in Salford but want someone from outside the area to run the door.'

I nodded. It was plausible, just. 'Which one?'

Charnley looked blank. 'Which one what?'

'Which pub? You said they're taking one over.'

'Oh, it was, er-' He became flustered again. Dave was never a good liar. 'They didn't actually say. It's all a bit sensitive until the deal's done apparently.'

I nodded like I believed him. But you don't talk door-security business, even in principle, without knowing the location.

'So what about these murders?' he said, eager it seemed for inside dope. 'What're the police saying?'

I shrugged as I downed my coffee. 'Not much. In fact I don't think they have much. They're checking everyone out of course, but so far they seem to be fishing in the dark.' I gave it a few seconds. 'You heard anything?'

His looked up, sharply. 'Me? Why should I hear anything?'

'You've got doors. I assume your guys hear the same goss as mine.'

He relaxed again. 'I guess so. But no, no one's come up with anything worth passing on that I've heard.'

'Me neither.' Outside I heard a car pulling onto the car park. I checked my watch again. Bang on four thirty. I finished my coffee and stood up. 'I'd better be going.' Outside, two car doors banged. Charnley craned to look through the window for sight of who it was. 'Nice seeing you again, Dave.' I lingered in the doorway. Two men in jeans and casual jackets were heading for the door having parked their nondescript Nissan next to mine. I turned back to Charnley. 'By the way.'

'What?'

'Next time you want to call in on one of my sites, ask me first.'

He pulled a smart-ass face. 'I'll try to remember that, Danny.'

I gave him a blank look back. 'Oh, I think you'll remember it alright. Dave.' I followed it up by looking, pointedly, at the fourth filing cabinet. The keys were now out of the lock and resting on top. His eyes narrowed as he spotted them, but before he could say anything, I stepped out to let in the pair from the Nissan. I didn't let on other than to nod as I stepped round them. ''Afternoon gents.' They both nodded back and went into the office.

I hung back long enough to hear one of them say, 'Dave Charnley?'

'Who are you?' Charnley said.

'I'm DS Pritchard and this is DC Walker. We're with the Drug Squad.'

I imagined Dave's face losing some of its colour. 'What do you want?'

'This is a Search Warrant under the Misuse of Drugs. To search your offices.'

'WHAT?'

I turned and leaned out so that I could see back into the office and Charnley could see me. He was staring at Jasper and Gary, mouth hanging slightly open. I waited long enough for him to see me then threw him a wink and a nod. He stared at me. I heard the cogs starting up again. He looked at the filing cabinet. The penny dropped just as one of the officers said to him, 'Are there any illegal substances on the premises?'

Torn between giving Jasper his attention and throwing me a look of pure hate and anger, his face was a picture. At this point it was time I went, so I headed for my truck.

Just about to shut the door, a shout erupted from Charnley's office.

'I'LL FUCKING HAVE YOU, NORTON, YOU BASTARD.'

# CHAPTER 16

*Monday evening*

It was past seven in the evening and I was making my way to the Brig for my Monday session when I got the call I'd been waiting on since coming away from Charnley's.

'Hellfire, Jasper, you've taken your time. Was there a problem?'

'Not really. He just had a lot to say for himself and we had to listen. I think it's fair to say he'll think twice before trying to set up one of your team again.'

The thought of Charnley trying - desperately, I liked to think - to negotiate his way out of a possession charge, brought the first smile I'd managed in over twenty four hours. 'So what happened?'

'We put him on police bail to come back in a month. We'll wait a while before cancelling it. Just to keep him on his toes.'

I allowed myself a self-satisfied nod. 'Serve the sneaky bastard right. By the way, did you manage to check out what was in the bag?'

'We did, and it's good quality stuff. Any idea where it came from?'

'My guess would be the Russian, but to be fair, it could have come from anywhere. Charnley knows as many people as I do.'

'Let me know if you hear anymore. If someone's got easy access to stuff this good then we need to know about it.'

'Will do.'

'And Danny?'

'What?'

'He's really got it in for you now. You'd better watch your back.'

After he hung up I was in two minds. On the one hand, I was glad to have got one back on Charnley. On the other, I was mindful of Jasper's warning. The way things were going, I was going to have to start walking backwards.


Apart from the 'regulars' – which includes myself and a disparate gang of ne'er-do-wells I hesitate to call mates – Monday nights at the Brigadoon are usually pretty quiet. Which was why as I pulled into the car park shortly after nine that evening I had no trouble clocking the white transit van with the tinted windows. It was in the middle of the single line of cars that were parked up against the low chains that separate the car park from the pavement at the front of the pub. Even as I passed in front to take the spot at the end, I glimpsed movement behind the windscreen, as if someone – or more than one - had just woken up. By the time I parked up and walked back along the line, heading for the pub's front door, all was quiet again. But a quick glance confirmed my first impressions. Behind the darkened glass two motionless figures were following my progress. I had an impression of at least one other in the back, leaning between the gap to see what I looked like. From what I could make out, they were wearing dark clothing and woollen hats, probably the balaclava-type that pull down to hide the face.

Inside, I headed over to the pool table where a group of four, one of which was Harry the builder, were quaffing pints and chalking cues.

As I approached, it came as no surprise to me when someone chimed, 'Aye up, here's Romeo now.' It was followed quickly by, 'It's Danny Norton, the man who moves women…' completed, in excellent timing, by, '- to fucking tears.' Cue raucous laughter. Harry hadn't let me down.

Wading through them towards the bar, I snatched the cue out of young Pete Williams' grasp and brandished it, growling, 'If there's anyone else thinks he's a fucking comedian then let's see if he's as funny with this up his arse.'

It drew further quips and smart comments, though I thought it best not to rise to any of it.

For the next hour or so I managed to push the events of the past forty-eight hours to the back of my mind as the conventions of a Monday evening – mutual piss taking and putting the world to rights - took over. I was glad when their early interest in Agnes's murder waned as they realised there was little insider knowledge that I was able or willing to share, and talk returned to the quality of the ale, football, and occasionally, musings on my love-life. Despite what had happened the other night between Vicki and me, I was desperate not to start any rumours flowing. Now and again I checked the car park through the window. The white transit never moved.

Near to finishing the second of my regulation two pints, I turned to Pete Williams. Pete's a motor mechanic and the youngest of our Monday-nighters.

'Is that your Astra out front?'

'Yeah, why?'

'Do me a favour. Whizz out and get something from your glovebox. While you're there check out the white transit parked next to it then come back and tell me what you see.'

Pete gave me a puzzled look but didn't ask questions. 'Okay.'

A couple of minutes later he returned. 'There're a couple of guys in the front trying to make like they're not there. I thought I heard more in the back but when I went to mess about in my boot it all went quiet. What's the score Danny?'

'Not sure yet, but thanks.' I put my cue in the rack and downed what was left of my pint.

'That's me done guys. See you later.'

Harry checked his watch, made a show of being surprised. 'It's not half-ten yet.'

'Yeah but he's on a promise don't forget.' This from Paul Cosgrove, another old school-mate.

I made a point of ignoring them and left to the inevitable chorus of, 'We-know-where-you're-go-ing.'

I didn't look at the van as I returned to my truck, but as I started the engine I noticed it give a little rock, as if someone in the back was settling back into their seats. I pulled off and turned right towards the car park entrance but as I passed the transit's bonnet I stamped on the brake and jumped out. I was figuring that the last thing they would be expecting would be a confrontation outside the pub so I went for the surprise element. As I headed for the driver's door I saw the shocked looks in the faces of the two in front. I reached for the door handle but the driver reacted just in time to press down the 'lock' button. For a couple of seconds I stood at the side of the van, giving the driver my best, *What-the-fuck-are-you-up-to?* stare, while he stared back, mouth half open, trying to work out what their best play was. My betting was their instructions were to wait until I was somewhere isolated before making their move. A pub car park in the middle of town didn't fit. Too much CCTV.

I returned to my truck on the passenger side, rummaged behind the seat where the toolbox was and found what I was looking for. Closing the door I came back round the front of my truck, heading for the van driver's window. But he must have seen the wheel brace in my hand and realised what I was going to do as the engine suddenly sparked into life. I managed another two steps before it took off backwards, bursting through the chains slung between the fence posts and bouncing first onto the pavement, then down onto the roadway. A red Toyota heading for Stockton Heath just managed to swerve out of the way in time and let off a searing horn-blast. I stood and watched, wheel brace dangling from my hand as the driver floored the accelerator and took off back towards the town centre. The last I saw of them was the driver's raised middle finger which I read as, 'Until next time.'

As the van disappeared from view, I rang Eric.

'I'm at the Brig. I've just been staked out by some guys in a white transit. They may belong to the Russian.'

'Did they try anything?'

'Not this time, but I need you to give the team a heads up, just in case they're working to a list.'

'Will do. Do you need any back-up?'

'Nah. They skipped when they realised they'd been clocked. I don't think they'll be back, not for me at any rate, which is why the others need to know.'

'Gotcha.'

I rang off and headed home.

The last noteworthy event of the day occurred as I was slouched on the sofa doing some late night channel surfing while nursing a JD and telling myself I should listen to the voice in my head telling me it was bedtime. A click from my mobile announced the arrival of a text. It was from Vicki and read, 'Settled in nicely. Thanks for everything. x.' I spent ten minutes pondering on what, 'everything', covered and the significance, if any, of the 'x'. I then spent another quarter of an hour trying to dream up a casual-seeming reply that would also make clear I was open to further contact, if that was what she wanted, but without sounding desperate. Eventually I realised my writing skills weren't up to the task so I settled for a simple, 'No probs,' then agonised another couple of minutes over whether to return her, 'x'. I decided against, imagining I was playing hard to get.

As I climbed the stairs I remembered to take with me the pick-axe handle that I'd dug out of the under-stairs cupboard when I'd arrived home, and where I keep all the stuff that doesn't have a natural home. I leaned it against the bedside cabinet while I got undressed and as I switched off the light, thoughts already drifting to Vicki, I reached out and touched it, just to make sure it was in easy reach.

# CHAPTER 17

The Man Who Likes To Watch is doing so again. But instead of live action he is doing so now through the medium of video, blue-toothed from the camera direct onto the big screen TV in front of which he spends so much of his time. As he watches, he is amazed how well the piece of equipment he bought recently for less than a hundred pounds off Amazon has captured the event, particularly considering how dark it was. He thinks back over all the jerky footage he has downloaded in his time. Considering that much of it was produced by so-called 'professionals', a good proportion of it is barely watchable. But here, seeing the way the device has performed, the way it has captured her movements, her facial expressions, he thinks his work must bear favourable comparison with a good many of the sort of hand-held camera productions that are currently popular and which the younger generation flock to cinemas to see.

He has reached the part where she is in the final stages of her performance, before he moved in to bring things to their climax, as it were. And he is acutely aware of the dissatisfaction that has been growing as he has watched. A feeling that something is lacking somewhere. He thinks he knows what it is.

In the end she was even more different to the others than he'd anticipated. Looking back, he isn't sure now if she understood what was happening to her, more to the point what was about to happen. Right from the start she had shown none of the resistance the others showed to his requests, even going so far as to ask questions such as , 'Like this? Is this alright?' It had annoyed him, slightly, at the time. It was annoying him even more now. If it was conversation he was after, he'd have rung a fucking chat line.

For the first time he realises how important the fear factor is to his projects. That without it the whole thing loses its edge, like a champagne bottle left open and from which all the bubbles have escaped. Sure, she was a great mover, possibly the best he has had. But without her awareness of what was looming, he may just as well have been watching one of those soft porn flicks some satellite channels show late at night.

*Where's the fucking bite?*

His enjoyment ruined by the sudden realisation of the recording's inadequacy, he picks up the device and switches it off. Immediately he is frustrated that he has not been able to relive the pleasure of the event the way he has done previously - even if his mobile phone video capability was not a patch on his new device. That ability is vitally important. It is what sustains him during those periods when the intensity of police activity dictates that he curtails his activities and bides his time while he seeks out new talent. Periods like right now. In the past they have stretched as long as several weeks. How will he manage so long when the product of his latest venture is not up to the task? True, he still has the records of his past achievements. But good as they are - Naomi was particularly memorable and well worth the occasional reminder - he knows they can only go so far in providing the regular dose of satisfaction that now seems to lie at the heart of his addiction. When all said and done, it is the NEW that drives him. Like a cocaine addict, the next hit is always the one that will do it for him. After that he will think about how to wean himself off. But if the latest 'new' is not up to the task, where does that leave him? Even if he had another already fixed in his sights - which he does not - he wouldn't dare to contemplate another performance so soon. It would go against all his principles about careful planning and not rushing things. It could, he knows, be disastrous. But with his latest venture proving such a dud - he is already thinking that he will probably never now watch it again - how will he manage over the coming weeks? Where will he find what he needs to feed his addiction while he lays the groundwork for his next project - a process that can sometimes takes weeks?

It is a worry. One that is already giving rise to the pain between his eyes that, if not avoided, will incapacitate him for a couple of days or more. Such an outcome, particularly at this time when the police are alert for any sign of disruption to people's routines, could draw unwarranted attention - and that would never do.

Knowing he must find something, anything, that will divert him from the course on which he is presently headed, he picks up his laptop off the floor beside his chair and navigates to the hidden folder where he stores his oh-so-precious data. Running the cursor down the list of files, he stops when it reaches the one labelled,

'Naomi'. He hesitates, closing his eyes and breathing deeply while he prepares himself. A few seconds later, he clicks on it.

## CHAPTER 18

*Tuesday*

The next day I decided to go down to Stoke and see Dad again. I usually visit on a Saturday, but truth be told, I was looking to take my mind off things.

I got there about eleven. As I came through the gate, I glimpsed someone turning away from next door's window. I was halfway up Dad's path when the front door opened and Alison appeared on the doorstep.

'Hi Danny.'

Alison Henderson and her husband, Ken, have lived next door to Dad for about eight years. Alison works part-time as a nurse and is a good neighbour. She's rung me a couple of time when she's been concerned about him or thinks he may be struggling. A fair-looking woman for her age - somewhere around fifty - Alison is one of those older women who still takes pride in her appearance. The last time I saw her, her hair was dark. Today I couldn't help notice it was a much lighter shade. Not quite blond, but heading there.

'Hey Alison,' I said. 'How's things?'

'Okay thanks, Danny. We don't usually see you in the week. Is he alright?'

'As far as I know. Just a flying visit, that's all.'

She seemed to hesitate. 'I, er- Could I have a word with you before you go, if you can spare a minute?'

'No problem.' As I put my key in the lock, my thought was, *what's he been up to now?*

Dad was in the back kitchen. Though I'd rung to let him know I was coming, he still seemed surprised to see me.

'You on you're own, our Danny?' The family habit is to put an 'our', before someone's name. It extends to close family friends as well.

I looked over my shoulder. 'I'm always on my own, Dad. Who are you expecting?'

'I wasn't sure if your sister was coming with you. She said she might.'

'Our Laura? You've spoken with her?'

'She rang yesterday. We had a nice long chat. She said she was going to come up and see us. That's why I thought you were coming here.'

I started. My sister works in what she never fails to let me know is a Pressure Job in one of those glass towers in Canary Wharf. She'd last visited about three weeks before. I measure her trips in three-month intervals. Nowadays she talks about coming 'Up-North' the same way some southerners do.

'I think you must have misheard her Dad. I don't think she's coming up just yet.'

'No? That's a shame. I can't remember the last time she was here. Do you and her ever ring each other?'

'I spoke to her yesterday as well. She wasn't talking about coming up.'

'Ah well. Cup of tea?'

As he filled the kettle, I noticed he was holding it at

an odd angle.

'What've you done to your arm?'

'Eh? What? As he put the kettle on the stand he winced. 'Oh, it's nothing.'

'Here, let me see.'

Moving him closer to the window, I took his left arm and pulled his shirt sleeve back. The area above and below the elbow was a mass of blue-purple. The elbow itself was skinned and red raw, seeping pus.

'What the hell?' I pulled his shirt out of his trousers and checked beneath. His rib cage on that side matched his arm. 'Bloody Hell Dad, what happened? Did you fall?'

'Fall? Me? Nah. I just woke up one morning and it was like this. It's nothing.'

'It's not, 'nothing', Dad. It looks really nasty. That didn't happen in bed. You've fallen, haven't you? What did you do?'

He started to become agitated. 'Nothing, I tell you.' He pulled away, at the same time stuffing his shirt back into his pants, hiding his injuries. 'Don't fuss. You're acting like your Mother.'

'I'm not fussing Dad, but those bruises need looking at. You may have cracked a rib. Is it very painful?' I reached out to take another look at his arm but he snatched it away, at the same time wincing in pain and sucking air through gritted teeth.

'It's a bit sore, is all. It'll be alright.'

I waited until I had his attention. 'Dad. Tell me what happened.'

He looked up at me, sheepishly at first. Then a glassiness came into his eyes and in a voice that trembled slightly he said, 'I don't know. I can't

129

remember,'

I finished making the brew, then we sat in the lounge and talked a bit. Football, the weather, his garden. I didn't press him on his accident, but I watched him like a hawk. The main thing was he seemed to be breathing okay - the oxygen cylinder was next to his chair but right now he seem to be managing without it - but his arm and side were clearly hurting. All the time I was weighing whether it was worth the argument and the state he would get in if I mentioned taking him to A&E.

After pulling apart the latest Liverpool signing - one good thing, he still pours over the sports pages - and lamenting the direction the club was heading under its new management, he turned towards me in his seat. 'How's the boxing going then? Won any fights recently?'

I stared at him. It had been years since we last mentioned boxing. 'I don't box any more, Dad. I run a security business, remember?'

He looked at me for long seconds before saying, 'Oh yes. Of course. That's right. I remember now.' But his face gave the lie to it.

I made us beans on toast with cheese on top for lunch - another family tradition - which we ate at the kitchen table. He seemed more comfortable sitting upright. It was obvious that the longer I was there, the brighter he was becoming, less forgetful. When we'd eaten I managed to get him to let me take another look at his side. After a bit of prodding and pushing I decided there was probably no point taking him to hospital. He was on tablets for his blood pressure as it was. But I got the first aid box out from under the kitchen sink and put a dressing on his elbow. As I wound the bandage above and below, it reminded me that I needed to check when my first aid qualification runs out. The week before, Mike had mentioned we had a Security Licensing Audit coming up in a couple of months.

Eventually, after a bit more chat - 'The Bloody Government,' this time - I got up to leave.

'Just rest up for the next few days. Remember you're not as young as you used to be. And tell me if that elbow locks up. If it gets infected you'll end up in hospital and you won't like that.'

He gave a bored look. 'Right.'

We're a lot alike, my Dad and me.

As always, the front door closed behind me when I was still only half-way down the path. I smiled. No change there then. As I went out the gate, I remembered Alison and made a U turn through hers.

The door opened as I reached the step. Alison stood there, smiling. She'd changed out of her jeans and trainers and was now in a smart pink skirt, cream top and white stilettos. Perfume wafted through the door.

'Come in, Danny.'

She guided me through to the living room, sat me down on the couch.

'Can I get you a drink? Tea, coffee, something stronger?'

'No, thanks. Just had one.' I smiled and checked my watch. 'I can't stop long. Work this evening. You know how it is.'

The smile stayed but behind it I thought she looked a little disappointed as she sat down next to me, but not so close as to give me any reason to be concerned. The only times I'd been inside Alison's it was always the weekend, when Ken was there. Right now, he wasn't. As I waited for her to tell me why she'd called me in I thought the house seemed unnaturally quiet. I waited some more. Eventually I said, 'Ken not around?'

She shook her head, slowly. 'He's never around weekdays.' She said it like I might want to make a note of it. I just nodded, and swallowed.

She took a deep breath, like it was the start of a serious conversation. 'So. How's your dad doing?'

I thought that maybe she'd called me in to tell me about his fall, but when I told her about his injuries, she looked shocked.

'Oh my goodness. Is he alright?'

'He will be, so long as he takes it easy the next few days.'

She leaned across, patted my knee. 'Don't worry Danny. I'll keep a close eye on him.' Her hand lingered a second or so longer than I thought it needed to, before she drew it back.

'Thanks,' I said.

For the next few minutes we talked about Dad, what he'd been up to recently. I was glad to hear he was keeping up his morning walks, but concerned when she said she thought his 'down' days seemed to be becoming more frequent. When I showed it, she slipped into Florence Nightingale mode. 'There's nothing you can do about it, Danny. It's called old age. And loneliness.' Her tone dropped half an octave as she added, 'Everyone gets lonely, sometime, Danny, you know?'

I nodded, 'True,' and left it there. Nevertheless I appreciated her homely common sense and was grateful Dad had a neighbour willing to keep an eye on him. I said so. She edged closer.

'You don't have to thank me. That's what neighbours are for.'

'I know. Even so, it helps to know there's someone he can turn to if he needs to.' I was beginning to feel warmer than when I'd arrived. I wondered if she'd turned up the central heating.

She said nothing, but sat there, smiling sweetly. I started to feel uneasy.

'So. Was there something you wanted to speak to me about?'

At that point I was pretty sure I saw something flash in her eyes, but all she said was, 'I just thought I'd check how he is, that's all. Besides, we don't always get a chance to speak when you call at weekends-'

'No, I-'

'When Ken's here.'

It stopped the conversation. We looked at each other. Her face was neutral. My move. I stood up. She rose with me.

'Well I guess I'd better be off. It was nice talking to you again, Alison and thanks again for looking aft-'

The words cut off as her mouth suddenly clamped itself against mine, her tongue probing for an opening. Instinctively, I stepped back, hands coming up defensively, only to position them nicely to receive the substantial chest now thrusting towards me.

'Alison- I-'

Leaning away from her, I leaned too far and toppled back onto the couch. She came with me, falling on top, hands already grabbing at my belt buckle.

I tried again. 'Alison. I can't-' The mouth again.

At that moment I could easily have escaped her. All I had to do was grab her by the arms and I could have swung her off me and onto the floor. It wasn't like she was that big a  woman, though as Dad and I had once

133

joked, *there's meat there- and in all the right places*. But it would have meant being heavier-handed with her than right then I was ready to be. The last thing I wanted was to hurt her, physically or emotionally. Nor was it the case that I didn't find her attractive. If I'm honest, I've always had a thing for slightly older women, and part of me was wanting to respond - fuck it, WAS responding - in the way most men would who find themselves in that position. But I knew enough about getting involved with married women to know how dangerous it is. Oh sure, at the club I've been groped by married women hundreds if not thousands of times. Every second Thursday is Grab-a-Granny night. And there've been times when I've enjoyed it. Not that I'd say anymore on that score. But there's a difference between a woman whose had a few drinks and is up for a bit of fun during a night out with, 'the girls,' and one who is looking for someone to provide what she's maybe not getting off her husband, and whose house you know you've got to walk past every week. And then, of course, there was Vicki.

After several seconds, the lack of any enthusiastic response on my part - despite what was going on between my legs - must have told her something. Suddenly she stopped groping and trying to get her tongue down my throat. Still on top, she levered herself up so she was looking down on me, hair spilling around her face. At first all I could see was a puzzled look, like she might be trying to work out if I was gay. But something - the bulge in my pants probably - must have told her that was not the case because the look in her eyes changed to something else.

In one quick movement she clambered off me and started straightening her skirt and the top I must have pulled round during the struggle. I sat up.

'I'm sorry, Alison, I-'

'Don't bother,' she snapped. 'It's my fault for being stupid.' But she said it in a way that made it sound like she thought it was anything but her fault, in which case it could only be mine. I tried to think back to previous times we'd met. I didn't think I'd ever come on to her. Then again I'd always considered her a good-looking woman. And there had been the odd bit of banter over the fence as I walked up the garden path on occasion. 'That's a nice top you've got on there Alison. Is it new?'

*Oh, God.*

'I think I'd better go,' I said, quietly.

'Yes,' she said. 'You'd better. Before my HUSBAND gets home.'

As I headed for my truck, walking faster than normal, I thought on how, at my age I ought to understand more about how the female mind works.


I was halfway up the M6, still thinking on how I'd handle the next time Alison and I, 'bumped into each other,' when my phone rang. It was Eric.

'Gol's just rung. He said a white van was hanging round the back of his house earlier on. Two guys in it. Looked liked they were scouting. He's worried how they've got his address. When he's not there, Margarita's on her own.'

'Is it there now?'

'No. It took off before he got a good look at it.'

'Okay. The others know?'

'Yep. I told them to stay on their toes.'

'Good.'

'I don't like this Danny. If something's going to

135

happen I'd rather we be the ones who take the initiative. Know what I mean?'

'I know exactly what you mean. We'll talk about it tonight.'

'Okay. Keep your eyes peeled. If they've got Gol's address they've probably got all of us.' He rang off.

The rest of the way home, my mind kept busy pondering on the fact they had our addresses. The only place we keep them is the office. We've always been pretty tight on not leaving personal details at places we work, for obvious reasons. After thinking through possibilities, I found myself going down a route I didn't much like. So much for having a run out to take my mind off things. I tried to break out of it by turning my mind to what that evening would bring. Then I remembered what night it was. Tuesday.

At least it stopped me thinking about my next meeting with Alison the rest of the way home.

# CHAPTER 19

*Tuesday night*

In most clubs, Tuesday night is the week's low point. Too close to the weekend just past, and too far from the one coming to entice the usual crowd out. Which is why clubs all over the country designate Tuesdays as 'Students Night.' By slashing the prices on drinks and entry, they aim to pull in those for whom normal clubbing is too expensive. Non-students aren't barred of course, but to qualify for the discounts, punters have to show Student ID - though even that is optional in some places.

When I first started in the door business – having never done college - I assumed student nights would be a doddle. My reasoning was that kids with limited funds and studying earnestly for degrees to please their paying parents wouldn't be anything like as difficult to handle as the week enders. I was wrong. Students are worse. Much worse.

First, you can forget the limited funds thing. There's a lot gets written and said about levels of student debt. All I can say is, any breakdown of student spending must show up the fact that 'social activities' accounts for at least as much, if not more than, 'education' and 'living expenses'. Besides, student loans apart, Mums particularly seem to have no limits when it comes to making sure their little Bradley or Alice has enough extra pocket money so they can feed themselves properly while they're away from home, working hard and missing their parents. Yeah, right. It's rare you see obese students these days. And if you do, take it from me, it's more to do with alcohol than burgers.

Secondly, most students are of an age where they are yet to fully understand the effects alcohol, not to mention other substances, has on their still-developing bodies. Which means the potential for over-indulging is far worse than other nights. I don't know what Ambulance Service figures show, but I suspect that those who do the duty-rosters have to take account of the fact that on Tuesdays, the paramedics sometimes have to work long and hard just to talk some kid who doesn't realise how badly he or she needs treatment to get into the ambulance. Unlike a Saturday-nighter who's just been bottled, has blood streaming from a head wound, but isn't so drunk they don't have the sense to know they need a few stitches.

True, there's less hard violence on student nights. Something to do maybe with students being more laid back than those who have to earn a living in the real world. They don't get so wound up when someone has a go at chatting up their girl/boy friend. And while I'm not daft enough to think they have less interest in other 'recreational' substances, the reality is that most aren't willing to blow good drinking money on the sort of stuff that the dealers try to peddle to those with a regular income. Which means the dealers are less active, and we don't have to spend as much time looking out for them as we do other nights.

It all means that, on Tuesdays, our number-one objective is simply to make sure we get them all out through the door safely at the end of the night. However, this still calls for every bit as much of the attention and effort my team puts in on a weekend night, and more. Eve, naturally takes the lead when it comes to dealing with the girls. And while I know she loves her work, I've heard her say she hates Tuesdays. I suspect it's something to do with the fact she spends half the night in the Ladies toilet.

But this particular Tuesday was different. For a start it was relatively quiet. By now the murders were hanging over the club scene - the whole town in fact - like a shroud. It came as no surprise therefore that as eleven o'clock came and went – the usual time when people start to spill out of the pubs to make their way to their club of choice for the rest of the night – I didn't need to check footfalls to see that numbers were well down. By midnight, the club was about half as full as normal.

The other factor, of course, was the police presence. Carver and his team of uniforms and detectives – including a very brusque DS Jess – had turned up around nine. They were loaded down with Witness Appeal Notices, statement forms and clip boards. I grabbed a look at one of the forms. It was basically a pro-forma enabling the witness to choose from a menu of options and it looked like it had been put together by someone well-tuned to police-speak.

'I am/am not a frequent visitor to Midnight's Night Club.'

'I attended/did not attend Midnight's on ……………..(Insert date).'

'I was/was not personally acquainted with Agnes Moorecroft,' etc.

It was only on reading the last that I realised I hadn't even known Agnes's last name. It made me feel guilty, though I wasn't sure why.

A while later I was in the office when Carver and Jess met with Frank and they talked about being around again on the coming Friday and Saturday. 'This isn't the crowd that was in over the weekend,' Carver said. 'They're the ones we need to get to.'

Frank had no choice but to agree, 'Of course. Anything we can do to help.' As I listened to his sympathetic promises of cooperation, I imagined the calculator in Frank's head working out the hit he was already taking following Agnes's death and which was set to continue until such time as the police caught someone.

I hadn't seen Vicki yet so I went off in search. I found her just about to enter the Green Room. She was carrying a tray of drinks.

'How you doing?' I asked. I meant generally, as in the flat, and maybe other things if she wanted to mention them. But I was disappointed when either by mistake or design she interpreted it like I was talking about work.

She nodded through the door. 'Just a couple of the lads from Freeway tonight Danny. They're going to do a guest DJ slot.' I nodded. Freeway were a local boy-band. They were doing alright around the North West but the jury was still out as to whether they were worth a break-out into the big time. Vicki continued. 'They're

140

no trouble, but I think they'll be disappointed with the turn-out.'

'They're not the only ones.'

She gave me a half-smile and my soul lit up. 'Don't worry,' she said. 'I owe you one for the flat. If the club scene folds I promise I'll get my Uncle Joe to fix you up with a job.'

I gave her my best suspicious look. 'And what does Uncle Joe do?'

'He paints houses.'

'Great.'

She flashed me a last mischievous look – enough to see me through the rest of the night – and disappeared through the door to continue with her babysitting duties. I headed back to the lobby to see if there were any signs of numbers improving. They weren't. By now we had about the usual number of non-students in, but it was the youngsters themselves who'd gone AWOL. I imagined mums and dads flooding the phone networks advising their little darlings, 'Don't go anywhere near any clubs until the police have caught someone. Especially that Midnight's place.'

Towards midnight, Mickey-the-DJ introduced Carver just as he had the previous Saturday. Carver did a re-run of the appeal he'd made then, but referring specifically to Agnes's abduction and murder, obviously. This time the audience listened in glum silence. My team didn't have to respond to any incidents of people not paying proper attention.

When they had finished and I had played my part by making sure Tony-the-Manager fixed Carver and all his team with drinks – not a request for a drop of alcohol between them – I made my rounds, starting with the main dance floor. I can honestly say I'd never seen Mickey-the-DJ working so hard for so little effect. Even with the reduced numbers, there were enough they could have filled the floor, if they'd wanted to. Clearly they didn't. It reminded me of one of those African Serengeti watering holes you see on wildlife programmes where some smart zebra has twigged there are lions lurking in the long grass. No one was venturing near. I found Eric loitering around the edge, arms folded, bored as I'd ever seen him.

'I've never seen the floor so deserted,' I said.

'You see,' Eric said, like it had been a long-running argument. 'Students do have a serious side after all.' He turned and nodded in the direction of one of the bars and I followed his indication. 'At least the bar takings should be up. They may not be dancing, but sure as hell they're drinking.'

He was right. Along the bar, a queue of lads waited to be served. Turning back I saw that around the floor those tables that were occupied were strewn with glasses. Groups of boys and girls were leaning over, shouting across to each other so they could make themselves heard over the music and Mickey's increasingly desperate pleas to 'Get onto the floor and shake those asses.' No prizes for guessing what they were talking about, I thought.

I shook my head. 'Frank won't like it. If it keeps up, it's going to put people off coming even more.'

Across the room, I saw Vicki arrive with her young charges and begin to shepherd them up to the podium. I sensed something embarrassing about to happen and decided I might be needed elsewhere.

I spent the next hour seeing Carver and DS Jess and

the rest of their team off the premises and touching base with the team. Before they left, Carver told me they had got little from their visit. A lad had come forward with a tale about a friend of his who had been in on Saturday night and had talked of seeing a young girl who may have fitted Agnes's description on her way home in the early hours of Sunday morning in the company of an older man. It was all pretty vague and needed following up and, unusually for him, Carver didn't let himself sound too hopeful. It made me wonder what sort of pressure he and his team were coming under.

I headed back to the main dance floor. As I came through the door and looked down on the floor I was surprised to see people actually dancing. In fact the place was almost jumping like a regular Tuesday. Eric was still where I'd left him and I made my way across.

'Okay,' I shouted in his ear. 'What did you spike their drinks with?'

He smiled and shook his head. 'Nowt to do with me.' He cocked his head towards where a group was gathered in a semi-circle around one of the lower podiums. They were all clapping and slamming as they followed the gyrations of a dancer I couldn't see properly through the throng.

'Check it out,' Eric said, a strange smile growing.

Intrigued, I made my way round to where I could get a better view through a gap in the mass of cavorting bodies. A girl I didn't recognise as any of our regular dancers was going through a series of full-on rolls, whirls and struts that was as energetic and - no denying it - slinky-sexy, as anything I'd seen in a long while. My view was still being blocked by bodies so I moved further round. As I got closer I saw she was tossing and whipping her hair in a way I'd last seen someone do in a Manchester pole-dancing club. 'Hell,' I thought. 'Who's this?' By now Mickey was back in charge – I could see no sign of Vicki's young guest DJs - and his laser light-show was turned up to max. As I tried to focus in on the girl on the podium it was like trying to make out someone's face through a strobe-light. Every now and then I caught a flash of face that seemed a little familiar, but each time I tried to catch it, it disappeared again, lost in the flashing lights or because she'd turned away.

Later I would remember how realisation crept up on me in stages.

She actually looks a bit like-

Hang on, is that-?

It can't be-

Holy *shit*, it IS..

It's VICKI.'

As it finally hit home that the body I'd been admiring and which had succeeded in waking the club up and working a good part of it into a frenzy, belonged to the young woman I'd shared a bed with a few nights before, I must have resembled nothing as much as a goldfish. Eventually I realised someone was standing just off my right shoulder. I turned. It was Eric. The strange smile I now understood was still there.

'Not bad, eh?' he said.

I nodded, dumbly, still too surprised by what I was seeing to voice my thoughts. In fact at that moment so many thoughts and feelings were coursing through me I wasn't sure what to make of it. Part of me was still struggling to accept the truth of my own eyes.

It was Vicki. Cool, calm, professional VIP Hostess, Vicki. Vicki, who doesn't let herself go, (not in public at least, I thought, remembering another place altogether), and who in my memory has never, ever, been seen on the dance floor. Vicki who's now shaking it like she was born to dance the podium.

Then there was also a whole other set of thoughts. Not as clearly defined as the others, they revolved around feelings I can only describe as broadly negative. Some of it was discomfort, arising from the fact that the woman I'd long ago placed on my own pedestal was now cavorting on a public one - and for the delectation of a bunch of people who not only didn't know her, but who were probably harbouring thoughts that were even more salacious than some of those I'd allowed myself on occasion. Also, there was an undefined feeling of apprehension, bound up with the knowledge that the women who had been murdered were all known for their ability to dance, exactly the way she was now doing.

I turned to Eric, 'What made her..' I let the question tail off, still distracted by her performance.

'Frank was having a go at Mickey, blaming him for not getting everyone going. She said she was going to help out. I thought she meant by going up top and winding the kids up. But she went straight up onto the podium and, well, you can see for yourself. I never knew she had it in her. Did you?'

Not sure if there was something hidden in his innocent sounding question I turned to him, but his face was on Vicki. I'm getting paranoid, I thought. 'No,' I answered. 'I didn't.'

I had a look round. Eric and I weren't the only passive watchers. Around the floor there was another half-circle made up of mainly men who had drifted over to take a look at a sight they might never see again. As my gaze roamed the crowd I forced myself to relax. Where's the harm, I thought? Besides, I've no rights when it comes to what she does. And if she's doing it with the best interests of the club at heart, well good for her. But even as I tried to steer my negative thoughts away, my gaze fell on a familiar figure.

I'd seen Elvis round and about a few times through the evening. My last sighting had been in the upper bar where he was trying hard – doomed to failure I'd judged – to chat up a well-endowed woman by the name of Gloria Pearce. Gloria is one of a group of not-so-young-anymore mothers - all former clubbers - who show up a couple of times a month to let off steam and pretend they are still single. But right now Elvis was on his own. He was standing away from the rest of the onlookers, pint in hand, staring at Vicki and drinking in her performance. Only there was something about Elvis's stare that, to me, put it in a different category to the others. Most were watching with smiles on their faces. The smiles may have been lustful – which is par for the course - but they were still smiles. Or they were nodding their heads in time with the music in a way that suggested that while they may not have been joining in bodily, mentally they were right there with her.

But Elvis wasn't smiling. Nor was he nodding in time with the music. Instead he was just standing there, staring at Vicki with an intensity that made me uncomfortable, like he was harbouring thoughts a lot darker than just admiring a beautiful young woman letting herself go on the dance floor.

Right then a shiver ran up my spine and a shudder of something – revulsion? – rippled through me. It was brought on by the memory of something Carver had said when he left an hour or so before. A report of a possible sighting of Agnes the night she was killed - in the company of an older man.

# CHAPTER 20

What a revelation, thinks The Man Who Likes to Watch. And how opportune. Only last night he'd got himself all worked up, stressing about how he would get through the next weeks with no new project in development and nothing to show for his latest apart from memories, and even those were now tainted. Then, right out of the blue, appears the answer to his problems. Who'd have thought?

Of course he'd always been aware that Vicki Lamont was gifted in the looks department. You only had to see her to know that as far as appearance goes, she can hold her own against anyone, particularly the sort who like to show off what God gave them and with whom you don't need to get into a conversation to appreciate. But ever since he'd first come across her, soon after he started coming to the club, watching her going about her business, he'd always seen her as distant. A bit up herself. A stuck up bitch in fact, not to put too fine a point on it.

But right now, he was seeing her in a whole different light. Not only was she talented at what she was doing, it was clear that she knew, exactly, the effect she was having on all those watching - and he means, *all*. Which, for all her snooty ways, makes her no different to the others and, therefore, most suitable for his purpose.

The only issue is time. She doesn't usually show herself this way, and for all he knows it may be some time before she does so again. In which case, when that time comes, he may have to move fast. No dragging things out for a few weeks like he has done in the past, enjoying the watching, building up to it, slowly.

No, he is decided on the matter. When Miss Vicki Lamont chooses, if she chooses, to display her talents again, he will make sure he works to a shorter, tighter deadline.

But that isn't a problem. Like many creative types, he enjoys a challenge, and he is nothing if not flexible.

## CHAPTER 21

By the time Mickey's dance-medley ended and Vicki stepped down off the back of the podium, I was feeling distinctly uneasy. During its last few minutes, I hadn't been able to stop myself looking to see if Elvis was still drooling. He was, right to the end. Worse, his semi-catatonic staring set me off wondering about others in the crowd. A kind of paranoia crept into me as I began to think that several of the smiles I'd previously noted, masked dark, possibly dangerous, thoughts. Even so, my gaze kept returning to Elvis. As everyone showed their admiration for Vicki's impromptu performance by clapping and cheering, I watched as he gave her one last, long look, drained his pint glass then turned away to slink off towards the bar. It was all I could do to stop myself following after, dragging him to some dark corner and getting him to tell me exactly what he'd been thinking during his silent vigil.

'She's worth her weight in gold, that one.'

It was Frank's voice and I turned to find him standing off my right shoulder. Like Eric beside me as well as everyone else, I'd been so wrapped up in what was happening I hadn't noticed he'd joined us.

'Dead right,' Eric agreed.

Still distracted by thoughts about Elvis, Vicki,

everything, all I could muster was a pensive, 'Mmm.'

'Is that it?' Eric said. 'Nothing else to say?'

I dragged myself back to the here and now. 'About what?' I said.

He looked at me like I was a moron. 'Er, weren't you just here? I'm talking about that.' He thumbed towards the now empty podium, as if a shadow of her still lingered.

'Oh that,' I said. 'Yeah. She was good.'

'Good?' Eric said. 'Fuck me Danny, she was frigging brilliant.' He turned to Frank. 'You need to get her on the podium more often. She's a knockout.'

'NO,' I said, too quick and loud. They both looked at me sharply so I tried again. 'What I mean is, I don't think that's a good idea.'

But Frank was ready to run with it. 'No, I think Eric's right. I'll have a word with her, see what she says.'

A sudden panic welled within me and I just managed to stop myself grabbing Frank by his lapels. 'Vicki's not a podium dancer. That was a one-off. I think you should leave it at that.'

Frank gave me a dismissive look. 'That's not for you to say, Danny. I actually think she'd be-'

'FRANK.' He jumped and had to lean back as I brought my face close to his. 'Believe me on this one. Vicki is not to do that again. Ever. Right?'

He blinked, several times before swallowing. As he stared up at me I saw the fear that had entered his face. He tried to speak. 'I- I-,' Couldn't get the words out.

Suddenly, I felt pressure on my bicep and realised it was Eric's hand. He drew me back, breaking whatever it was had me in its grip. 'Take it easy, Danny. I think

Frank's got the message.'

As if to confirm it, Frank nodded, still not sure what to say. I knew right then that I'd overreacted. Badly. Worse, I'd done damage. What I should have done next was apologise to Frank. Explain some of my reasoning. I should have shared my theory that the killer may be targeting dancers. I should have explained that my outburst was simply aimed at making sure we didn't expose someone else to potential danger. But I knew I couldn't do it without revealing some of what had happened between me and Vicki the past few days. I wasn't ready for that and didn't think she was either. What I did was look away towards the lobby and front entrance, as if something had grabbed my attention.

'Something I need to do,' I said, and left them all to stare at my retreating back. I'd gone only a few paces when Vicki veered in from my right. She'd obviously seen us talking and come across to join us.

'Hi Danny. What did you think of-'

I showed her my palm saying, 'Can't stop. Catch you later.' Like a frightened teenager bailing out of a fight I let my legs carry me away, feeling like I'd just done more damage. But I just managed to catch her words as she turned to Eric and Frank.

'What's up with Danny?'


For the next hour I busied myself in ways I thought would stop me bumping into Vicki and Frank. I visited Golman and Eve at the front door and hung around there until I got the sense that my ludicrous small talk about how quiet it was tonight, asking after Gol's family and how Colleen was doing with the new job I'd heard about, was beginning to freak them out. From there I went upstairs and wasted several more minutes checking out the Private Suites. They were all empty. Even Yashin doesn't hold court on Tuesdays. And having been thoroughly cleaned out and re-stocked since Saturday, there was nothing that really needed checking on. I headed back downstairs and made my way round the rear fire doors, checking the alarms, making a point of looking to see that the sensors on the doors were all aligned with those on the frames and were working as they should. I'd just checked that the rear fire door's crash-bar was engaging properly when it shut - we'd been having trouble with it the past couple of weeks - when I turned back to head towards the lobby. It was getting towards closing time and the exodus would begin soon. Vicki was standing there, waiting for me to come back along the corridor. There was no reason for her to be there and I realised she must have come looking for me. As it happened, she'd found me in what, at that moment, was the quietest part of the building.

I made my way along the corridor towards her – there were no other exits and nowhere else to go - wondering what the hell I was going to say, knowing I should apologise for giving her the brush-off earlier, but feeling like something I couldn't identify was stopping me from doing so. I was already feeling myself beginning to redden. Thankfully, she spoke first.

'Is everything alright?'

I barely glanced at her as I passed by, walking half a pace faster than normal so she had to turn and do a skip to catch up with me. 'No probs,' I said as she scurried along beside me 'Why do you ask?'

'I don't know,' she said. It wasn't easy for her in heels while looking for eye-contact. 'I just get the feeling you're not happy about something.'

'What's not to be happy about?' I said, keeping up the pace. We were closing on the split in the corridor that leads to the lobby one way, the main office the other. 'Our girls are getting murdered. Takings are down. The Russians are fixing for trouble and on top of that the place is like a morgue. Or at least it was until you decided to show everyone what you've got.' To this day, I have no idea where the last sentence came from, or how and why it seemed to spit itself out.

Her reaction was instant. 'WHOAAA.' She grabbed my arm just above the elbow and yanked to try and get me to stop. I could have ignored it – Vicki's strength isn't in her arms – but somewhere deep down a voice was yelling at me to stop acting like a dick-head. I stopped so suddenly she had to totter on her heels to balance herself.

'Just what does that remark mean?'

'What remark?' I said, all innocence.

'Me "showing everyone what I've got."' What's that all about?'

'I don't know what you're talking about. I was just saying everyone was miserable until you got up on the podium.'

'That's not how it sounded. What's wrong with me getting up on the podium?'

I tried shrugging it away. 'Nothing at all. Who's saying there was anything wrong with it?'

'Well according to Frank and Eric, you for starters. They said you were well-pissed about something when I finished.'

'That was nothing to do with you dancing.'

'Wasn't it?' Her gaze locked with mine. I felt her

burrowing deep into what lay behind the blank expression I was doing my best to maintain.

'No.' I said it as if the idea I was pissed-off was ridiculous.

'So what was it then?'

'What was what?'

'What was it you were pissed about?'

I wafted a hand. 'I don't know.' I made to turn away. 'I'm sorry I need to-' But she grabbed my arm again, harder this time.

'Right now the only thing you *need* to do is talk to me,' I turned back to her. Her beautiful green eyes burned into mine. There was glassiness in them. I wasn't sure if it was reflections from the yellow up-lighters strung along the corridor wall, or something else. Inside my chest, it felt like something was melting. I swallowed.

'What do we need to talk about?' I was conscious that very soon one of my team would be coming along to open the doors I'd just checked to let the punters out. The other side of the wall I could hear the famous Coldplay track I can never remember the title to, and which usually marks Mickey heading for the big close-down.

She raised her arms then dropped them, like she was frustrated. 'This whole situation. Me on the podium. *Us.* Everything. Anything.' Without warning she actually punched me in the chest. There wasn't much force in it but her spindly knuckles stung. 'Dammit, Danny. Talk to me.'

I looked at her. I knew exactly what she wanted me to say. She wanted me to admit that, Yes, I had hated seeing her dancing on the podium. That I didn't like to see her exhibiting herself to a bunch of drunken idiots who couldn't tell the difference between a girl who gets off showing her body in public, and a beautiful, intelligent young woman who can move as well if not better than any podium dancer I've ever seen and who, while she would normally only perform in private for someone she cares about, her commitment to her job – and the Club – is such that she will do what she thinks she needs to do to pull things up when it's needed. I also knew she wanted me to say something about her and me. Something that would show her that since last Sunday morning, the thought had occurred that maybe, just maybe, there was a connection there worth exploring - as she had been thinking. Okay Agnes's murder and the problems with the Russians and the door meant that the time probably wasn't ideal to be embarking on a new relationship. And true, I had helped her out with her flat. But that was just Good Old Danny being Good Old Danny. What she wanted to hear – what I *knew* she wanted to hear - was that it wasn't just a case of me being 'Good old Danny' but wanting to do something that would draw us closer than just colleagues helping each other out through some temporary difficulties. I had no idea how I knew that all this was what she wanted me to say, or that she wanted to hear. It wasn't like I'd been giving it all a whole lot of deliberate thought the last few days, at least I didn't think I had. But somehow, as we stood there looking at each other in the corridor that was now deserted but would soon be jammed with punters, I felt closer to her than ever before. Closer even than on the Sunday morning when she came in to my room and slipped under the duvet next to me. So close that I could sense the thoughts and feelings coursing through her. They were the same thoughts and feelings that I had been having since Sunday morning, but without ever realising it.

Norton, I thought. You're a fucking idiot.

I took a breath, opened my mouth to speak.

Disappointment flooded her features as she looked at something over my shoulder. Behind me, a voice said. 'Am I interrupting something?'

I turned to see Chris standing at the open door to the lobby. As I'd been expecting, he was on his way to open the fire doors in readiness for let-out but had stopped on seeing us. Somewhere in the back of my mind I wondered what sort of rumours it would give rise to.

'S'alright Chris,' I said. 'You carry on.' I turned back to her. She was waiting, expectantly. Hopeful. I thought about what to say. Like I've said before, I'm not always the quickest when it comes to words. I needed time. And besides my mind was still full of things that had come to me as I'd watched Elvis, watching her. I'd even wondered about calling Carver and mentioning it to him.

What I ought to have said was, 'I understand what you're saying, Vicki, and yes, I'd like to talk, about all these things, others as well.' I should have reached out, stroked her cheek, maybe pushed back the lock of hair that had fallen across her face in a way that, now I focused on it, gave me a funny feeling inside. I should have smiled at her in a way that would have said, 'Don't worry, we'll sort it all out.' At least it would have given her the reassurance that I was certain she was looking for at that moment.

I did none of those things.

Like the idiot I am, I said to her. 'I need to close up. I'll catch you later. When it's quiet.' Even as I turned away, having already caught the first sign of the angry/crestfallen look that my stupid, hollow, empty words had already triggered, two others took up residence in my tiny brain.

Big Mistake.

## CHAPTER 22

Over the space of the next thirty minutes, I must have run on auto pilot as I went through the motions of closing down and wrapping up. The only thing I was aware of was the growing feeling that not only was I a tosser, I was completely out of order for not giving her something back. Something that would let her know what I was really thinking and feeling. It's all well and good playing the Hard Man, but sometimes you need to show you're human too. By two-thirty, with most of the punters having already spilled out onto Bridge Street, getting ready to join in inflicting on the town centre the drunken, spewing mayhem that always follows 'Student Night,' I knew exactly what I needed to do. I just hoped it wasn't too late. I went looking for her.

I tried the office first. She wasn't there. I checked the Dusk 'Til Dawn bar where I knew she sometimes likes to take a late latte, while taking stock of the night's events. Not there either. I tried the Green Room, but it was empty. In the staff room, Eve was stowing her stuff and signing off. I asked if she had seen Vicki.

'She left half-an-hour ago. I let her out the side door. I've got her mobile number if you need it?'

'S'okay,' I said.

I made my way up to the Early Hours Coffee bar. It

would be quiet there. The staff had just finished putting the chairs up on the big, square tables for the cleaners to come in. I pulled one down and settled in a far corner. I took out my mobile and dialled her number. It went straight to voicemail, which meant her phone was either switched off, or she was talking to someone. I waited a few minutes then tried again. Voicemail again. This time I waited for the beep.

'It's me. I just want to say I'm sorry. I was way out of order. I'd like to speak, if you don't mind speaking to me. Ring me back?' I waited another five minutes, just in case and tried a third time. Still voicemail. I went back downstairs.

In the office Eric was talking with Frank. 'Where've you been?' he said as I came in. 'We thought you'd bunked off early.'

'Just a couple of things I needed to sort out. How's everything?'

'No probs,' Eric said. Then he added. 'I'll cover lock-up if you want to get off?' I think I'd heard him make that offer once in four years. I turned to him. He was looking at me strangely. Like he knew something. Everything, even. Unlike the last time he offered, I nodded. 'Okay. Thanks.'

As I left the staff room and headed for the back door and car park, Eric appeared again beside me.

'How long?' he said.

'How long what?'

'You and Vicki.'

I stopped, gave him a look.

'Oh come on,' he said. 'I'm not as bleedin' thick as you like to make out.'

I managed a half-smile. 'Less than a week.'

He whistled through the gap in his bottom teeth. 'And problems already? Doesn't look good.' He paused. 'It's you I take it?'

Christ, I thought. He knows me better than I do. I nodded.

'Thought so. Want some advice?'

'No, but I assume it's coming anyway.'

'Sort it out. She's worth it.'

I nodded again, said nothing.

I left him at the door and stepped out onto the car park. I'd gone less than a dozen paces when I saw it. Her red Honda sports. Near to where she usually parked it. I came to a dead stop. 'What the-?'

I turned back to the club. Eric had already closed the door. I stood there, thinking. Eve had said Vicki had left over half-an-hour ago. There was nowhere else she could go this time of night. I went over to the car. It was locked. I ran through the possibilities. There weren't many.

Breakdown. But she would have come back into the club. Chris is a car mechanic, as are half the bar staff.

Someone offered her a lift. But why accept? And if she knew her car was going to be there all night she'd have come back and told someone. Either Eric or I would have heard.

That was as far as I got before the memory that had been stirring since I first saw her car in its usual spot thrust its way to the surface. It was an image of Elvis, staring at her as she danced, what I now remembered as a leering, sinister look on his face.

A bomb went off in my stomach.

I turned and ran back to the club. I had to go round to the front where Chris had just shut the doors. Seeing me, he opened them again.

'What's up Boss?'

'You haven't seen Vicki come back in?'

'No.'

I headed to the office. Frank was there. I asked him the same question.

'No. Something wrong?'

'Her car's still on the car park. She's not there.'

He looked puzzled, but not alarmed. 'Strange. Why would-'

I cut him off. 'Where's Eric?'

'Doing the rounds I guess. What do you-' But I didn't hear the rest as I was already out the door.

I found Eric at the D-D bar, about to take a pint. He jumped up off the stool as he saw me approaching across the empty dance floor.

'What's up?'

I told him about her car then added, 'Do you know where Elvis lives?'

'Elvis? What's he got to-?'

'Do you know where he lives?'

'Sankey, I think. Greta would know.' Greta runs the cloakrooms. Has done for years. She knows everything about everyone. 'I've got her number if you need it.'

'I've got it.' He didn't ask how I had Greta's number and I didn't say. 'Do me a favour. Ring the police. Get hold of Jamie Carver. Tell him Vicki is missing. Tell him Elvis likes dancers.' I headed for the door.

'Elvis like dancers? What the fuck? Where are you going?'

'To find Elvis.'

'What the fuck's going on Danny? What's it all got to do with Elvis, and why the big panic?'

'I think Elvis has taken Vicki.'

## CHAPTER 23

Out on the car park, I stood by her car and tried her mobile one last time. Still voicemail. Not good. In the short time I'd been with her, I'd seen enough to know that like most young women these days, her phone was her third hand. I brought up Greta's number. As I rang it, I checked the time. Three fifteen. She would be arriving home about now. Longford isn't far. It rang four, five, six times.

'Danny?'

I didn't want her to get any wrong ideas so I just said, 'I need your help Greta. Do you know where Elvis lives?'

She didn't, other than it was somewhere in Sankey. But she knew someone who did. I asked her to find out and ring me back. She started to ask, 'Why do you need-?' but I just told her it was urgent and cut her off. I was probably gruffer than I needed to be but hey, WTF.

By the time she rang me back I was already half-way to Sankey. 'Twelve Lunts Drive,' she said. I thanked her and rang off. I knew where it was. A former council estate, on the Widnes side.

Ten minutes later, I pulled up on the other side of the street and twenty yards down from a pair of three-bed semis with big front gardens enclosed within low picket-type fences with hedges behind. Number twelve was the one on the left. I got out and headed towards it. As I neared, I saw the house had the sort of run-down look that often marks a man living alone. The front garden was untidy and overgrown, unlike the one next door which had a nice lawn with neatly kept borders. Dull net curtains that looked like they hadn't been washed for months if not years hung at the downstairs windows. An old Ford Focus was parked up in the drive. I didn't know if Elvis drove or even owned a car, but I assumed the killer had to have one. But what drew my eye was the orange glow in the upstairs bedroom window. Behind the red curtains that hung like a pair of nailed-up blankets, a light was on. One of the transom windows was open.

I stopped at the front gate and strained my ears. From far away, the rumble and clatter of Widnes's twenty-four-seven chemical plants echoed through the night. I shut it out and concentrated on the small opening. Then I heard it. A sound like a sharp smack or slap followed immediately by a woman's squeal of pain, then a man's voice. At first I couldn't make the words out, but the last few were clear. '…and you're a *dirty fucking whore*. WHAT ARE YOU?' An image of Vicki, threatened, terrified, crying, came to me. It was enough.

I felt for the gate latch, pushed through and ran down the path to the front door. It was one of the typical old council house front doors, plain wood with a four-panel of bubble glass about eighteen inches square at head height. There was a brass knocker on the letter box and a bell-press mounted on the left hand door frame, but they were never going to come into play. As I neared the door another smack sounded through the window above me, followed by another yelp of pain, louder this time. I didn't slow but simply leaped in the air with my right foot leading and aiming a good three foot beyond the door. It gave easily, bursting open and crashing back on its hinges against the right hand wall. Council door locks were never any good.

The stairs were right in front of me, coats and jackets hanging on hooks attached to the wall on my right. As I entered into the hall I was aware of the sort of musty-stale smell I had come across many times and had begun to notice during my last couple of visits to Dad's. I took the stairs three at a time. As I reached the top and turned left round the newel post I caught a glimpse of Elvis's bollock-naked figure just before he slammed shut the front bedroom door. Cries and shouts came from within. The door was hardly a barrier but I didn't kick it like the front door just in case she was somewhere close. I grabbed the handle. Someone was leaning against it. I put my shoulder to it but kept hold of the handle and burst it open with enough force to send Elvis sprawling across the floor where he banged up against the radiator under the front window.

As he landed, I saw the terror in his face, then it changed as he lifted his head and saw me. 'D-Danny? What the fuck-?'

Ignoring him, I looked right to where the double bed faced the window, hoping to God I wasn't going to see something that would stay with me the rest of my life. I did, but not in any way I was even half-expecting.

Gloria Pearce was lying face down on the bed in a spread-eagled position. She was naked. Black ties ran from her wrists and ankles to the corners of the bed. What looked like one of her stockings was tied between

166

her lips as a gag. Her backside was raised up in the air by the several pillows under her stomach and legs. She was under the bedroom light so I had no trouble spotting the rose-red glow on both her arse-cheeks. As I came through into the room, she looked round over her shoulder and up at me. At first the look of terror mirrored Elvis's, but as she recognised me it changed to surprise, then something else. We stared at each other, my mouth hanging open. She didn't pull at the bonds tying her to the bed and she wasn't exactly shouting or screaming for help, just staring up at me. I turned to where Elvis was picking himself up, nursing the bang on the back of his head and a sore shoulder. He was looking at me with a mix of fear and bemusement. Then his mouth opened and his face changed, like he'd just worked something out.

'Awe, fuck. *You and Gloria?* Honest to God, Danny. If I'd known, I'd never have-'

He stopped talking as I showed him my palm. I needed to think. My head was spinning, all my expectations upended. I looked down at Gloria again. She still wasn't struggling, but just lying there, like she was waiting for something to happen.

I have an image in my brain of what I must have looked like as I stood there in the middle of the room that night, looking from Gloria to Elvis and back again, trying to make sense of the scene I'd burst in on. Neither of them were saying anything now, both waiting for me to make a move. A muffled murmur from the bed drew me back there. Gloria was looking back at me over her shoulder and wearing an expression I couldn't read, until I noticed the way she was moving her bum from side to side and realised she was grinding herself into the cushions between her legs. That was when I saw the black leather paddle – like a square table-tennis bat – lying on the bed between her legs. Elvis must have dropped it there when he jumped across to the bedroom door to see what the earthquake below was and saw some madman racing up the stairs. Finally, I twigged.

I've never been into SM or any of that sort of stuff. That's not to say I wouldn't oblige a woman if she wanted me to 'push the boundaries' as the saying goes, so long as they were within reason. But I'm not a saint and I'm as partial as the next man to a bit of porn so long as it doesn't involve kids or animals. That night, I think it took me so long to realise what was going on because, (a), you don't imagine people like Elvis and Gloria having much interest in anything after a night out in the club beyond either a quick shag in the back of a car or a blow-job round the side of the club, and (b) a spanking session is the last thing you expect to come across in a former council house bedroom at four am in the morning, especially one as dismal as Elvis's. It's fair to say that my impressions of Gloria changed that night.

As it all sank in, I checked out Elvis again. His hands were up in front of him, in a defensive posture. He was shaking. He's going to piss himself any moment, I thought.

'W-what you, g-going to d-do, Danny.'

I checked out Gloria again. She was okay, the fear all gone now, replaced by a glazed, dreamy expression. She mumbled something through the gag. I couldn't hear it clearly but it sounded something like, 'Yeahhh, whatcha gonna do, *Danny*?'

*Jesus Christ.*

I turned to Elvis. Held my hands up in a 'peace'

gesture. 'Sorry, Elvis. I made a mistake.' I turned to the door.

'WHAT?' I heard Elvis call. 'A MISTAKE? What do you mean a mistake? It's fuckin' four o'clock in the fuckin' morning.'

But I was already at the top of the stairs. The only thing on my mind right then was getting out of the place and thinking it all through again. Vicki was still missing. There was no way I was going to even try to explain to Elvis - or Gloria - how or why I'd come to interrupt their little bondage session. I left the house to the sound of Elvis's strident complaints about me bursting into his house - 'AND WHAT ABOUT MY FUCKIN' FRONT DOOR?' - and Gloria's muffled shrieks - possibly of disappointment.

As I got back into my truck and started it up I saw Elvis at his front door - still butt-naked and framed in the light from the hall. He was waving his arms about like he was upset about something. I pulled away and didn't look back. I stopped at the entrance to the estate, well out of sight of Elvis's house and pulled out my mobile. I rang Eric.

'Carver should be here in the next five minutes, he said. 'He says not to do anything until he gets here.'

'Too late,' I said.

'What have you done?' There was a note of doom in Eric's voice.

'I'll tell you later. But I was wrong. It wasn't Elvis.'

'You found him?'

'Yeah. I found him. Tell Carver I'm on my way back.'

## CHAPTER 24

Before I returned to the club I stopped off at Vicki's flat, just in case. It was in darkness and there was no response to my urgent banging on the door, just as my intuition led me to expect. By the time I got back to Midnight's I was experiencing the nearest thing I'd ever had to a panic attack. My heart was pounding, my hands were wet on the steering wheel and I was gulping air like I couldn't get enough into my lungs. The only thing I could think about was Vicki. Where was she? What had happened to her?

Inside, I found that no one had left since I'd gone looking for Elvis. Frank, Tony and Eric were in the main office, going over things with Carver. Jess and a couple of CID were there as well. Jess was taking notes. Carver turned to me as I came in.

'What made you think it was Elvis?'

'Doesn't matter. I was wrong.'

He gave me a scrutinising stare. 'Definitely?'

'Definitely.'

'And you've checked her flat?'

I nodded. 'No sign of her. She wasn't there.'

'You're sure?'

'I'm sure.'

For several seconds Carver looked at me like he was

weighing whether he needed to check what I was telling him. He must have decided he didn't. He turned to Jess and his detectives and started issuing instructions. They were to speak to all the staff who were still there and find out the exact time Vicki had left. He told Tony to come up with a full list of staff who'd been on duty that night. One of the DCs was to start contacting those that had already gone home. Carver turned to me. 'Your team know a lot of the punters.' I nodded. 'Get them to start ringing round. We're looking for anyone who saw her leave the club.'

'Right.' I was grateful that his brain was working because I doubted that I was capable of anything beyond shouting Vicki's name over and over. I met with my team in the staff room, gave them their instructions. As they took out their phones and began punching numbers, Chris said, 'Do we really think something's happened to her?'

Before I could do or say anything Eric grabbed him and steered him away, muttering something in his ear. The only words I could make out were, 'daft,' and, 'cunt..'

I left them to it and went to report back to Carver.

'Good,' he said, when I told him the guys were ringing round. I waited as he seemed to think about something. When he turned to me and put a hand on my shoulder I looked up in surprise. 'We're doing everything we can, Danny. It's good we're on it early. We'll find her.'

I didn't try to answer him. I'm not sure I could if I'd wanted to. I swallowed. I looked across at DS Jess, She was looking at me in a way I'd never seen before. I think they call it a 'pained expression.' I nodded.

The next couple of hours were among the worst I've ever experienced. There was nothing I could do but sit and wait as people made phone calls and took calls back. Each time a phone rang my heart leaped, only to sink back again when whoever took the call showed no sign of excitement or relief. Myself, I was in no shape to make calls so I gave out the numbers I had of people I thought might be worth contacting to others, Eric and Jess mainly. I had the impression they both knew what I was going through, though neither said anything.

Some time after five, as the phones began to fall silent, Jess pulled me to one side. 'We're going back to the nick. Jamie's called a six o'clock briefing to start a full-scale search operation. There's nothing more we can do here. I suggest you go home and try and get some sleep.'

I started at her. 'You must be fucking joking.' Her reply was a straight look and I realised. I'd never sworn in her presence before. 'Sorry.'

She gave a wan smile. 'Listen Danny, I can only imagine what you're going through, but I'm serious about you getting some sleep. We may need you later today and it would help if you're able to stay awake.'

'Need me? What for?'

'Your local knowledge. You know the area, the clubs, the punters.' She hesitated. 'You know her.'

I wasn't sure if she meant it, or was using it as an excuse to get me to go home. Whichever, there was enough sense left in my by-then exhausted brain to realise that if there was the slightest chance I could be of some use in helping to find her, then I needed to get some rest, even if it was only a couple of hours. 'Okay,' I said.

'Want me to drive you?'

It was then I realised that the last hour people had begun treating me like I was the parent of a missing child. Suddenly I was grateful for Jess's get-out. I needed to be away from there. I shook my head. 'I'm good.'

I had a last few words with Frank, Carver, my team and a couple of others, then left. As I walked out the door I was conscious of the silences and sad looks that followed my leaving. I'm not ashamed to say that as I drove home, I had to fight not to break into tears.

When I got home I went straight to the kitchen cupboard and pulled down an unopened bottle of JD. About to twist the cap off, I hesitated. Standing over the kitchen table, I held the bottle in front of me and looked at it, long and hard. Then I put it back in the cupboard, switched off the light and went to bed.

## CHAPTER 25

*Wednesday*

I never expected to sleep, but I must have done because the next thing I knew my phone was buzzing on the bedside table next to my ear. I didn't look to see who it was but just snatched at it. 'YES?'

There was a short silence then a man's voice said, 'Danny?'

'Who's this?'

'It's Alan, Danny. Alan Brannigan?'

I remembered the name. A local lad, Alan was the son of a family we'd lived close to in Longford when my mum was still alive. He'd used to be a regular on student nights but had started to graduate up to weekends the last few months. Still half asleep I couldn't remember if I'd seen him in the club the night before.

'Wassup Alan?' Any other time I'd have asked how he'd got my number. Right now it didn't matter.

'A mate of mine's just rung me. He said something about that right-fit-piece who works in Midnight's being missing. He says you're looking for her.'

'Vicki. Her name's Vicki. She's the VIP Hostess.'

'That's the one.'

'So why are you ringing Alan?' I checked the clock on my phone. It read 09:17.

'Well, it's just that.. I don't know whether it's relevant or not but...'

'Just tell me.' Firmer this time.

'Well me and some of my mates... We was coming past the club last night in a taxi. We was on our way back from a party in Widnes.' He stopped.

'And?'

'Well I'm not a hundred percent certain it was her, but I think I saw her, just by the car park at the back of Midnight's.'

'What time are we talking about?'

'It must have been around one. Maybe a little later.'

Close enough. 'What makes you think it was her?'

'Are you joking? She's fit as a butcher's dog. I turned round when I saw her. She's always worth a look.'

I bit back the words that were about to come. 'What was she doing when you saw her?'

'Well as we come down Arpley Street from Widnes, there was this car. It was stopped on Arpley Street right by the car park, pointing back towards Widnes. As we came towards them she was leaning down, like she was talking to the driver through the passenger window.' He stopped again, like he thought he needed permission to continue.

'What happened then?'

'Well as we passed, I saw the driver get out and start to walk round the front of the car towards her.'

'Then what?'

'Well that was when I thought I recognised her. I was in the back seat so I turned round to see what was going off.' He stopped again.

*JESUS.* 'And?'

'And that's when I saw him hit her.'

It was like an electric shock, right to my heart. Already racing harder than the night before, it seemed to stop for a moment before carrying on, even harder. 'HIT her?'

'Across the face. Like a right good slap.'

I started sweating. 'What happened then?'

'Dunno. Just after I saw him hit her, we turned into Bridge Foot and we lost them.'

'So what did you do?'

'Do? Nuffin'. We carried on home.'

'You didn't think to turn round and go back?' I was conscious my voice was getting louder.

'Go back? What for?'

'Jesus Christ, Alan. You've just seen a girl being attacked and you carry on home? Haven't you heard that women are being murdered on their way home from clubs in town right now?'

'Hey, it was nothing like that, Danny. It wasn't like he was some fuckin' murderer or anything. It was more like a couple having a barnie. You know, your normal boyfriend-girlfriend stuff, that's all.'

'Why d'you say that?'

'The way she was talking to him in the car. I just got the impression she knew him.'

'I repeat, why?'

'I dunno. Just the way she... I just got the impression she knew him, that's all.'

By now my mind was whirring. I rubbed my hand roughly over my face, trying to bring myself fully awake so I could work out what to ask, what to do next.

Then the obvious came to me. 'The driver?'

'What about him?'

'Did you get a good look at him?'

'Not really. It was her we was all looking at.'

*FUCKING-* 'So you can't say if you knew him or had seen him before?'

'Nah. Like I says, we weren't really looking at him.'

I waited some more, still thinking.

'What about the car? Did you see the car?'

'Yeah, like I said, it was parked on Arpley Street, next to the car park.'

'THE MAKE, YOU PRICK. I mean, did you clock the make? The colour?'

'Alright Danny, take it easy. Fuck me, I've rung to try and help. Don't bite my fucking head off.'

I took a breath. 'Sorry Alan. It's been a long night. The make, the colour. Could you say what-'

'Oh yeah, we saw the car. We all said, like he was obviously some rich twat. He'd have to be to pull a bird like her, wouldn't he?'

I waited, but only a second. 'So? What sort of car was it?'

'One of those right smart types of Beemer.'

As he said it, I swear my pounding heart almost stopped again. Everything seemed to slow down.

'A beemer? What colour?'

'Black, I think. Maybe dark blue.'

At that moment my grip on my phone tightened so much I was surprised it didn't snap in two.

I swallowed and took a deep breath.

'A Beemer,' I repeated. 'A smart one you said. Possibly black. Is that right?'

'That's it. If I had to guess I'd say it was a six series.'

I froze.
A black BMW. Six series.
Vincent.

# CHAPTER 26

It goes without saying that I know now what I should have done at that point. I should have rung Carver and told him what Alan told me. I should have told him what I knew about Vicki and Vincent then left him to sort it out. It also goes without saying that in view of what happened, I wish to God I had. I can give lots of reasons why I didn't.

While you could fit what I know about police procedure on the back of a postage stamp, one thing I do know is that the police response to a situation isn't always as snappy as people like to think it will be. Warrants, permissions, authorities, the need for clarity. I've known situations where they've all meant that by the time the police get their act together, the bird, as the saying goes, has flown. My particular experience in this area was the night I got twitchy about some seriously-scary dealing going on in the club and rang them to report it. This was in the early days, not long after I took over the contract and before I knew better. I made the call just after midnight. By the time a van full of police and a token representative DC from the drug squad turned up, it was close to three. The dealers had long gone and the buyers had dispersed into the town. 'We needed to check it all out and get a squad together,' was the DC's excuse. I've heard similar stories since.

I knew where Vincent lived. I could be there in fifteen minutes. If I rang the police, even Carver himself, I could see a couple of hours disappearing before anyone rang the doorbell. Two hours is a long time when someone's in trouble.

Also, if the bloke Alan had seen *was* Vincent, then the way I saw it, Vicki's going missing was more than likely nothing to do with the murders at all. Vincent was a prick, and a nasty one at that. But there was no way I'd tag him as a serial killer. In which case what was the point of getting the police involved? If I'm scrupulously honest - and assuming Alan had his facts right - the way my mind was working at that time, I probably preferred not to involve the police, as I'll mention shortly. It was also probably fair to say that at that moment my mind was operating at the level of a five year old. Worry, fear, lack of sleep. Take your pick or all three together, I wasn't exactly thinking things through rationally.

Maybe I didn't want to think rationally. Because at the end of the day, for all the excuses I might come up with, there was probably one overriding reason why I didn't ring Carver. It was a reason based on emotion. And that emotion wasn't fear, but something else. I wish to God I'd seen it at the time.

Fully awake now, I dragged on jeans and a tee-shirt and headed out.

Vincent's house was along the main road that runs through Appleton village. Bordering open countryside, all the houses along that stretch have long front gardens that fall in landscaped tiers - rockeries, ponds, exotic shrubbery - to the road below. Most of the drives had been re-done in block-paving long ago. Long and twisting, they run up from the gateways in sweeping turns to finish in turning circles outside the front doors. Only a few of the houses along that stretch are gated. I've always suspected that their owners like to be able to show off their good fortune to the envious M6-avoiding commuters who use the village as a rat-run each morning and evening. I must say that the first time I ever drove past Vincent's - the evening I just happened to find myself in the area where the club's new VIP hostess lived - I was surprised to see how open it was to access. In my experience, car dealers like Vincent are renowned for falling out with the sort of people whose first response to settling a dispute isn't always a letter from a solicitor. Then again, the open fields that I knew ran at the back of the houses meant that making the houses fully secure would involve spending thousands on fences, lights and alarms. Even then, all someone determined to gain entry needed to do would be to wander through a neighbour's garden and hop over a wall.

The sun was shining and it was a beautiful morning when I pulled up at the bottom of Vincent's drive. As I got out, birds were singing in the trees. At least I assume they were. Contemplating the beauty of the English countryside on a sunny day wasn't exactly what I was there for. I checked the house out from the road. The driveway was empty, which didn't really mean anything. A double garage was built onto the left hand side of the house and facing in to make an 'L' shape. The doors were closed. None of the windows had curtains drawn across which might have indicated an occupied room. Everything seemed peaceful, idyllic even. It wasn't how I was feeling. I started up the drive.

The house was finished in white stone-paint with the sort of black fascia-boarding that's supposed to lend houses a 'period' feel, though which period is always lost on me. It had the look of an expensive, well-kept property. I remember thinking that if I ever won the lottery, it was the sort of house I might go for.

I stopped outside the front door. There were still no sounds, apart from the birds. I looked about me, at what I could see through the trees of the houses either side, back down to the road. There wasn't a soul in sight. I decided to investigate before seeking entry. I headed towards the garage side of the house.

Walking round the side and back of the garage I found a small window. Looking through I could see the black Beemer. Next to it was a Ford Mondeo. The fact the cars were there still didn't mean anything either. Vincent had access to any number of cars. But my instinct was that being the sort of character he was, Vincent would use the Beemer if he was out and about working around town. And Wednesday is, after all, the middle of the working week. I carried on round, down the side of the house and came out into the back garden. As I expected it was lush and looked-after, with a manicured lawn surrounded by borders with flowers and bushes. A row of trees screened the house and garden from the fields at the back which rolled away to give a nice view over Warrington town, nestled on the plain below. Over to the right, was a wide patio area with a huge conservatory. Along the back of the house there were sets of patio doors and windows, all shut.

I started along the back, keeping close to the wall. The first window I came to was the kitchen. It was empty so I carried on. The next window was a double

French window into what looked like the main living area. Sumptuous-looking beige and tan leather sofas and chairs were arranged around a wood and glass coffee table that was littered with glossy magazines. A huge - and I mean, huge - plasma TV stood in the corner. Not that any of it registered with me at the time. Because I found myself staring at a bare-chested Vincent, dressed only in trousers and standing in the middle of the room. Vicki was cowering in the corner of the big sofa as he loomed over her, shouting and gesticulating at her. She was still wearing the blouse and skirt from the night before.

She saw me first. Her mouth dropped open and she sat bolt upright. Vincent stopped his shouting to turn to see what had grabbed her attention. Seeing me, he froze. I don't know who was more surprised, them or me.

Through the double glazing I just heard Vicki shout,' DANNY?' at the same time Vincent yelled, 'WHAT THE FUCK?'

I didn't say anything. I was too busy focusing on the red, soon-to-be-blue-black, welt that was already spreading across the right side of Vicki's face.

I felt myself going.

'DANNY,' Vicki called out again, though what the message was I wasn't sure and in any case it didn't matter.

Vincent immediately rounded on her and screamed, 'SHUT THE FUCK UP, BITCH,' before turning back to me. 'GET OFF MY FUCKING PROPERTY. I'M CALLING THE FUCKING POLICE.' Bending down, he picked up a mobile and brandished it, theatrically, as if he was about to start punching numbers. If it was meant as some sort of scare tactic or he imagined it would lend weight to his words, he was hopelessly misguided.

For the first time since seeing them I moved. Stepping forward I reached out to try the handle to the French windows. They were locked. I called out, 'Open the door, Vincent,'

'FUCK OFF.'

By now I was conscious Vicki was becoming even more agitated. She was crying and sitting forward on the edge of the sofa as she looked, terrified, from me to Vincent and back again. She was imploring him to do something but I couldn't make out what. I thought she might be telling him to get out of the house and run. I think she was already beginning to see what was likely to happen. For his part, Vincent looked like he was trying to figure out what his best play was, shouting at Vicki to keep quiet while also trying to keep an eye on me.

Behind me and across the patio, a set of solid-looking wooden garden chairs were arranged around a square table. I went over and picked up one of the chairs. It was even heavier than it looked. Good. Returning to the French window, I hefted it at shoulder level. Both Vicki and Vincent's eyes opened wide as they realised what I intended.

'NO DANNY,' Vicki shouted, but to no avail, as they say. Vincent's mouth opened like he was about to say something but as I heaved the chair at the window he turned and legged it out of the room while Vicki turned away to bury herself in the sofa's cushions. I doubt that the explosion of glass shattering and wood splintering could have been louder if I'd driven a car through. Even before all the shards from what was left of the top half of the window had stopped falling I was through and crossing to where Vicki was lifting her head and beginning to sit up, though hesitantly, as if she half-expected the rest of the house might fall down.

I reached out to take the hand she was stretching towards me. 'Are you-' I began. Our fingers never got to touch as Vincent came roaring back into the room. He was wielding a length of four-by-four above and behind his head and screaming at the top of his voice, 'FUCK YOU, NORTON.' He gave it one wild swing which missed me by a mile as I took a step back and leaned out of the way. But it was only by the grace of God and a couple of inches that it missed taking Vicki's head off. There wasn't a snowball's chance in hell he was ever going to get a second chance.

The next thing I remember, something was pulling at my right arm as I tried to move it forward. At the same time, somewhere far away, someone was calling my name. I remember feeling irritated by it, the way you do when a fly keeps landing on your arm and you flick it away, only for it to land again a few seconds later. And like the fly response I tried flicking whatever it was away by jerking my arm back, sharply. My elbow connected with something and there was a scream. It was a woman's scream. I turned in time to see Vicki falling to the floor amidst the broken glass and wood, holding the side of her jaw where I'd caught her. It was the other side of her face to the one showing the welt.

'VICKI.'

Two quick strides took me to her. Kneeling down, I took her hand and with the other tried to lift her round the shoulders into a sitting position. She was dazed and mumbling, still pressing a hand to her jaw.

'I- I'm sorry. Are you okay?' My stomach was turning somersaults at the thought I'd hurt her. She nodded, and mumbled something I couldn't make out. 'What? Here let me help you. Can you get up?'

It was then I noticed she seemed to be resisting my help, like she was trying to shake loose from my grip. She mumbled something again.

'I can't hear you. What are you saying?'

She removed her hand and looked up at me. 'Ambulance... Call an ambulance.'

She was breathless and it seemed like it was all she could manage just to get the words out. I must have really caught her one. I looked her over. I could see some red staining on the arm of her blouse, near to where I'd taken hold of her, but I couldn't see she was bleeding from anywhere. 'Where are you hurt? I think you're okay. Let's just get you up off the floor.'

I reached for her again but she jerked away and there was something like anger mixed with fear in her eyes as she shouted, 'LEAVE ME. Just call the ambulance. DO IT.'

Her reaction stung me. I was confused by her reluctance to let me help her.

'Hey, you're okay. I don't think you'll need an ambulance.'

She shook her head and lifted the hand off her jaw again, at the same time wincing with pain. She lifted her arm. Her hand was shaking as she pointed at something behind me. 'Not for ME. For HIM.'

I turned to see what she was pointing at.

Vincent was on the floor beyond the sofa. He was on his back, lying still and with his head turned to the side towards me. His face was a mass of blood, some of it already soaking into the plush carpet. I stared at him, blinking, for several seconds, like I was trying to make sense of what I was seeing. The last time I'd seen him he was trying to recover for a second swing at me with the pole. But I knew right then what had happened. I looked down at my hands, to confirm it. They were covered in blood, the knuckles grazed and raw.

After all this time, it had happened again.

## CHAPTER 27

According to the psychologist-lady I began seeing shortly after my ninth birthday, the first 'documented' episode arising from my condition occurred when I was four. It happened, apparently, at the play-group me and my cousin, Howard, used to attend. One of the other boys, a lad a bit bigger and older than me, wanted to play with the big yellow Tonka Truck Howard and I were using to build our M6 extension. He just came over to where we were playing, pushed Howard over, grabbed the truck from under my nose and made off with it. I didn't cry or anything but just went straight for him. According to the account in the play-group incident book, it took two staff and another mum to drag me off, one staff member holding onto him, the other me, while the mum had to pinch the back of my hand, hard, in order to get me to let go of his hair. After much brouhaha - the worst of which for me was my Dad not believing me when I denied knowing anything about it - things settled down and eventually they let me back into play-group.

Nothing else of any *real* note happened after until I was in the second year of primary school. This time we were playing 'ball-tick' and a lad threw the ball at me way too hard, deliberately I thought, and caught me square on the nose. By this time I'd learned what fists were for and was making good use of them when one of the male teachers picked me up and carried me to the staff toilet, which was about the only place he felt I might not do further harm to someone or myself. When afterwards I again denied any knowledge, my Mum and Dad began to worry. Since play-group there'd been a couple of minor incidents - one involving my sister, Laura - which had set them thinking, but it wasn't until the school headmistress began asking questions of the, *'Has-he-ever-done-anything-like-this-before?'* variety, that they began to wonder if something might be wrong. Again, the enquiry came up with nothing other than a recommendation that staff should keep an eye on me and report any incidents. When, eighteen months later, I blanked out again with the result that a boy in my class who had been winding me up for a long time ended up in hospital needing stitches to a cut lip and torn ear, the balloon really went up. I remember at the time wondering what all the fuss was about. I was still only eight. I had this vague notion that I might be ill with something. But seeing as how I didn't feel ill, my attitude to the monthly counselling sessions that began just after my ninth birthday was, I seem to recall, reasonably positive. This may have had something to do with the fact that once a month I had an extra day off school. Also, the psychologist, whose office was in Chester, was a nice lady with big, funny spectacles and grey frizzy hair and smelled of fresh-baked scones. Mary Oakley her name was. She spoke quietly and kindly, which was a bit different from what I was used to at home. She had this huge sweet-jar on her desk which was always well-stocked with lemon sherberts, lollipops and packets of Love Hearts, Refreshers and pastilles. It wasn't until many years later I twigged that her invitation to, 'Help yourself, but you're only allowed one go,' was a test to see how long it took us to figure out the best way of getting as much out of the jar as we could in one 'dip' without our hand getting stuck.

I can't remember much at all about the sessions themselves. There were questions of course and I recall being shown lots of pictures and asked what I felt about little stories she told me, but I forget the details. I was also put through various tests, including some sort of brain scan which, for a lad of nine, was pretty scary. The end result was that Mary declared there was nothing wrong with me, physically or mentally, other than I appeared to suffer from a condition which she described, in a way my Mum and Dad could understand, as a sort of, "Lone Ranger Complex". According to her, my 'episodes' were triggered when I encountered a situation in which my brain perceived that someone was behaving 'badly' towards me or someone close to me - bullying being typical - and was therefore deserving of some sort of punishment. This would have been okay, perhaps even praiseworthy, were it not for the fact that - and this is the ironic bit - I also had a deep-rooted abhorrence of violence - where from God only knows - so that my brain switched off when I was actually meting out the 'punishment.' This meant I didn't know when to stop, hence the need for third-party intervention on such occasions.

After another incident at school when the threat of exclusion loomed, my Dad hit on an idea. He'd done some boxing in the army and knew Joe Ryan from his school days. He signed me up at Joe's gym. Despite my dislike of violence, I took to it at once. I can only put this down to the fact that Joe's philosophy was based upon his view that boxing is nothing to do with violence. In Joe's book, boxing is an art form that just happens to involve the application of certain physical skills, allied with extreme self-control and used against an opponent to best him in a sporting contest where he is attempting to use the same skills against you. Joe likened boxing to chess, only with blood, and pain. I'm sure now it was Joe's training that sorted my problem out, at least while I was boxing. Joe's method left no room for loss of self-control. If Joe ever saw signs of one of us losing our temper, he would stop the fight/training and send the 'offender' home. 'The boxer who loses his temper will always lose the match,' Joe used to say. He always used, 'match', rather than 'fight'. And the likes of me and Ricky Mason believed it, one hundred percent.

From the day I began to box and right through my schooling I never had another episode, which I can only put down to Joe's training. When, on Joe's advice, I gave up chasing boxing as a serious career option, I came away thinking my 'condition' had been cured. For several years that seemed to be the case. I was wrong.

I was twenty two and had been working doors for a couple of years when the event I now have to live with for the rest of my life happened. It was a Saturday night and I was on the door of The Red Dragon in Woolton. Up to then, I'd never had a problem, despite being in plenty of situations where people tried to have a go at me, or one of my mates. Around half-ten, a local lad by the name of Kevin Campbell turned up with his girlfriend, Kathy. I already knew both of them, though separately. Kevin had trained at Joe's along with me and Ricky, only he didn't last as long, while I knew Kathy from when I'd helped out at the Odeon Cinema in Sankey where she worked as an attendant. Kevin was a nice-enough lad but was prone to turning nasty after too much ale. This particular night he was already well-oiled when he showed up at the door, too much so for me to allow him in and I told him so. Once he realised I was serious and that despite knowing each other, I wasn't going to budge, he began to turn. Kathy saw it and started trying to talk him into coming away, but he wasn't for listening. I knew Kevin was handy with his fists so I kept a close eye on him and made sure my oppo - who that night just happened to be Dave Charnley - was on hand to back me up. When Kevin threw his first punch I was ready. With his arm up his back, Dave and I had him under control and as I began to talk him down, I thought he was listening. Kathy was becoming a bit hysterical by then, which is par for girls who can see their boyfriends either ending up getting a good hiding, or in the back of a police van before the night's out. Once Kevin had quietened down, I checked he was okay and let him go. He even shook my hand and apologised. As he let Kathy start to walk him away I thought it was all over and turned to talk to Dave. I never did find out who it was who shouted, but I turned in time to see the blade in Kevin's hand as it flashed towards my face. I just managed to take a step back but it was close enough that I felt it zip past my nose. My first response was instinctive. This wasn't boxing. Knives are life and death stuff. I'd learned that much in the time I'd worked doors. I hit him once in the face, hard. He went down but to my surprise got up again straight away. Drink and other substances can have that effect. Straight off I could see that at that moment he was on another planet. Before I could do anything Kathy jumped in between us to try and stop him. He lashed out, hit her full in the face and sent her sprawling backwards into my arms. I still had hold of her when he came at me again and I had no option but to take the hit. He caught me with an upper-cut to the jaw and I felt a dull pain in my upper right arm where he got me with the knife. That was it.

The next thing I knew, I was on the ground with Dave Charnley and four other doormen on top of me. By then someone had already called the ambulance for Kevin. The police arrived just as the ambulance did. I spent that night in a police cell, worrying about him. I'd managed to get a look at him as they put him in the ambulance. He didn't look good. It wasn't. He was in intensive care for three days. They nearly lost him twice, but got him back with those electric-paddle things.

I was charged with GBH - Grievous Bodily Harm - with intent - which is about as close to attempted murder as you can get. The CPS case was based upon the fact that what I did to Kevin went way beyond any reasonable notion of self defence. Several witnesses testified that I carried on beating Kevin long after he gave up resisting and went limp. Luckily for me, the lottery that is Legal Aid drew me Maurice Etherington as my defence barrister at the Crown Court. Maurice also handled prosecutions now and again and at that time was one of the most respected briefs on the Chester and North Wales circuit. He knew straight off that the self-defence case the CPS was gearing up to counter

193

would never play, so he dug deeper. He called Mary Oakley, the psychologist from years before to give evidence on my behalf. She was retired by then but she remembered me and still had all her records. She was able to show that my attack on Kevin was not planned or deliberate, but a symptom of the condition for which she'd treated me years before. Further, under questioning from Maurice, Mary stated that because I'd 'blanked out', I couldn't form the intent necessary for the charge to stick. The Judge, Sir Robin David, agreed and instructed the jury to return a not guilty verdict. Even so, waiting for them to come back as instructed was the most nerve-racking hour of my entire life. There were no celebrations however and there never will be. One simple reason. The injuries Kevin suffered to his face and body healed in a few weeks. An Odontologist from Rodney Street, - Liverpool's equivalent of Harley Street - gave him a new set of teeth. But there was little the doctors could do about the injuries to his brain. They never healed, not completely at any rate. I'm told they never will. It's hard to celebrate when you know you've turned someone into half the person they used to be. Kevin's not entirely ruined. He still manages to work, as a street cleaner for the council. He lives with his Mum in her ex-council house in Longford. He can look after himself, more or less, but the chances of him ever meeting someone and entering into any sort of relationship are, I guess, pretty remote. Kevin's mum, Sally, is an amazing woman. After the trial she came up to me, shook my hand and told me she knew it wasn't my fault and that she bore me no grudge. She'd seen her son grow up and knew what he was like. I see her and Kevin regularly. About once a month, which is about the same as I see my Dad. I call in for a brew and a chat and to see how Kevin is. He doesn't bare me a grudge either, which is pretty strange when you think about it. It's usually around tea time when I call, by when Kevin is finished work and at home, watching TV re-runs of Only Fools and Horses or Star Trek. I stay for an hour or so, which is about as long as I can manage. I always come away thinking, 'I did that.'

Now, as I looked across the glass and splinter-strewn carpet to where Vincent, lay stretched out on the floor, my thoughts turned to Kevin.

'Oh please God. *Please* not again.'

## CHAPTER 28

From somewhere I could hear my name being called, but at that moment all I could focus on was Vincent. A vision came to me of him sitting in front of a television, watching Only Fools and Horses.

A hand crossed in front of me, grabbed my right cheek and pulled me round. Another clamped itself to my other cheek and I found myself staring into Vicki's anxious face.

'DANNY,' she yelled. 'Snap out of it.' She squeezed my cheeks together, trying to get me to pay attention.

I blinked once, twice, then nodded.

'Are you okay?' she said. I nodded again.

I squeezed my eyes tight shut, trying to purge the thoughts that had brought on my paralysis. Suddenly my brain kicked in and I realised everything was backwards. I'd come here to find her and, hopefully, help her. To make everything right. Only the reverse had happened, and now it was her having to help me. Pulling back, out of her grasp, I looked up at the ceiling, and drew air into my lungs. It was a long, cleansing breath. When I looked at her again, her face was full of worry, and fear. I knew what I had to do.

'Where's the phone?' I said.

She made a, *Thank God* expression, then pointed

across the room. 'On the bookshelf.'

Raising myself up, I crossed to it. As I went, glass crunched into the carpet beneath my feet and my gaze kept straying to Vincent. From a standing position I had a better view of his face - *Jesus Christ* - but at least I could see and hear he was breathing.

I picked up the phone, punched 999, pressed the green call button and lifted it to my ear.

'WAIT.'

I turned to her. She was still sitting amidst the debris, but waving her hand, furiously, at me to stop.

'What?'

'Hang up.'

'Why? I thought-'

'Just do it.'

I hit the red button.

'Give it to me.'

'What for? What's wrong?'

As I lowered the phone, she leaned forward and grabbed it out of my hand. She re-dialled and lifted it to her ear. She looked up at me.

'I've just remembered. They record nine-nine-nine calls.'

I opened my mouth to ask why that mattered, then realised.

Considering what she'd been through I was amazed how together she was. As she began talking to the emergency operator, sense began returning to my brain. Crossing to Vincent I crouched beside him. Although he was breathing, it was rattly, laboured. Reaching under, I turned him so he was in the recovery position, airway clear, leg bent, arm raised to level with his head to open his chest, just like they teach us on the Door

197

Supervisor's Course. As I tended to him, I listened to the phone conversation. She kept it short and simple. There'd been some trouble at home. There'd been a fight. Her husband was badly injured - facial injuries - and needed an ambulance. 'Yes, he's breathing but unconscious.... Yes, I've already put him in the recovery position.' When asked she gave the address, then rang off. She'd said nothing about anyone else being involved.

'How is he?' she said, more calm than I imagined she'd be.

I looked him over again before turning to her. 'He needs treatment, but he's breathing okay.'

'Thank God.'

I stood up, went across to her and helped her into one of the chairs. She sat there for a while, on the edge of the seat, looking across at Vincent as she got her breath back. Every now and then she lifted a hand to her forehead, the way someone does who is trying to get their head round a difficult situation. Eventually I couldn't wait.

'Vicki,' I said. She turned her face up to me. 'I'm sorry. I didn't mean to-' Unable to finish what I wanted to say I gestured towards Vincent.

'What?' she said. 'Didn't mean to what?'

'This,' I said. I spluttered a bit more then got it out. 'Hurt him. I didn't mean to hurt him like this.'

She gave me a disbelieving look, then said, 'No. It seems you never do.'

I wasn't sure what she meant, but the way she said it, flat, matter-of-factly, it frightened me. I looked at her then back at Vincent. I couldn't think of anything to say so I settled for, 'The ambulance shouldn't be long. I think he'll be okay.'

She stretched her head back, looking up at the ceiling, then nodded.

'Are you okay?' I said. 'Did he hurt you?'

She lifted her hand to her cheek, running her fingers over the bruise. 'Not as much as you did him.'

I winced at that. 'We thought you'd been-' Again I stopped myself. Now was probably not the right time to explain how we'd all feared she'd been abducted, possibly murdered. Besides, it would probably sound like an excuse.

I crouched down at the side of the chair, looking from her to Vincent and back again, plucking up courage. 'There's something about me you need to know. Something I need to tell you.'

She shook her head. 'Not now Danny.'

'But it's important. You see, I'm not normally-'

She waited. 'What? You're not normally what? Violent?' She snorted. 'Is that what you were going to say? That you don't actually like beating people to a pulp, like I just saw you do?'

I looked at her, mouth open. Surely she didn't believe I'd enjoyed doing what I'd done to Vincent? I shook my head. 'You've got to believe me. It's not how it looks.'

She snorted again, almost a laugh. 'Sooo.. what? You just decided that Vincent needed his face rearranging, even though he'd given up resisting and was begging for you to stop?'

*Holy Christ.* I hung my head. 'It wasn't me.'

'WHAT?'

'I mean, it *was* me. Of course it was me. But not like you think.' I shook my head, realising it sounded like nonsense.

She sat up. 'You've got a problem, Danny. You need help.' I was about to break in, to tell her that I've had help, that for years I'd been fine, but her hand came up so I stopped and she carried on talking. ' But right now you've got to go. Before the ambulance gets here.'

'Go? Why? I need to explain-'

She got to her feet. 'Explain what? That you beat a man unconscious then continued to hit him when he was just lying there? Don't be stupid. You need to get out of here, fast.'

I could hardly believe what she was saying. 'You're telling me to run away?'

'I'm telling you if you stay here the ambulance people will call the police and they'll arrest you. You've seen it at the club a hundred times.'

I stared at her, then back at Vincent, trying to work out what was best. 'It'll happen anyway. Vincent will tell them it was me.'

'You don't know that. Besides, I don't think Vincent will be saying anything for a while.'

Now I was really confused. 'But you've just said. I beat up, could have killed, your husband. Don't you want the police to arrest me?'

She stood up. I could see tears forming. 'Right now I don't know what I want. There were times last night, if I'd got hold of a knife, I'd have killed him myself.' She looked down at him. 'You shouldn't have done what you did Danny. It was wrong. But, God help me, I'm glad the bastard got something that will make him think twice before he ever lays a hand on me again.' She turned back to me. We stood there, looking at each other.

'What will you tell them?' I said.

200

'I don't know yet. I'll think of something.'

'The police are looking for you. We reported you missing. We all thought-'

'Ahh.' Realisation showed in her face. 'You thought I'd been taken, like the other girls.'

'Yes.'

'Well you were half-right.'

'But the police will want to know who did this to him.'

She nodded. 'They won't get it from me.'

I shook my head. 'They're not daft. Even if Vincent says nothing, they'll put it together.'

'Maybe, but they've still got to prove it. Show me your hands.'

'What?'

She reached out and grabbed them, turned them in hers, examining them. 'Go home. Get cleaned up. Get rid of your clothes. Burn them if necessary. Before the police speak to you do some building work or something. Anything that could cause cuts and grazes to your hands.' I looked at her, shocked. 'Go to the bathroom, now, and wash your hands, thoroughly. You don't want his blood on your steering wheel.'

'Jesus Christ, Vicki. I-'

'DO IT.' I jumped. 'The ambulance will be here any minute.'

I gave her one last look, then ran to the kitchen.

When I returned a few minutes later there were smears of Vincent's blood on her face, hands, clothes. Her blouse was torn and hanging off her. Her tights were ripped. There was also blood on the piece of four-by-four Vincent had brought in.

'My God,' I said.

She gave me an even look, then rubbed her jaw and cheek. 'At least I don't need to ask you to hit me.'

I shook my head in disbelief. 'How do you know about this stuff?'

'I watch CSI. Now, GO.'

I thought about going over to her, taking her in my arms, holding her close, kissing her. But I didn't. Instead I turned and went out through the hole where the window used to be.

As I ran back to my truck I remember thinking, how the hell will she explain that?

# CHAPTER 29

It was sometime in the early afternoon when Jamie Carver rang to tell me Vicki had been found. I was sitting on the sofa at home, staring into an empty glass. I'd come straight back there from Vincent's. When I arrived I put everything I'd been wearing in a plastic bag which I'd stuffed up in the loft-space until I could get rid of it properly, then took a long shower. Afterwards, I'd gone straight for the bottle but stopped after the one glass, the one that was still in my hand.

Since then I'd been sitting there, replaying the morning's events over and over in my mind. Each time I ran it, I veered between elation, and terror. Elation, that Vicki was okay. That she wasn't lying on some canal towpath somewhere and had come to no serious harm. Terror over the discovery that my condition was still there, and active. That for all that I'd run my business the past few years with no sign of a problem, the potential was still there in me for another Kevin Campbell. Hell, for all I knew, Vincent could already *be* another Kevin Campbell. Each time I thought about it I squirmed, mentally and physically. At the same time I kept wondering what was going to happen. I kept expecting to see blue lights outside, the police walking up the front path. The knock on my door. Some cop saying, '*Danny Norton, I am arresting you for...*', what? When I'd last seen him, Vincent appeared to be holding his own. But I'd seen and heard enough to know about bleeding on the brain, haemorrhages, heart attacks, the switches that can, without warning, turn life to death. During that period, waiting to see what would happen, I think I was as close as I ever came to losing it.

Now, as I listened to Carver telling me about how Vicki was fine, that it was her husband who had dragged her off to his house where she'd been all night, and that she was now at the station making a statement, the only words I could get out were, 'Right,' interspersed with the odd, 'Thank God.'

As Carver finished telling me about Vicki I said, 'What about Vincent? Where's he?'

'He's in hospital.'

'Hospital? How come?'

There was a long pause, which made me wonder what Carver was making of the conversation. Eventually he said, 'He's got severe facial injuries.'

'Facial injuires?' I said, conscious that I needed to stop repeating his words. 'How come?'

'That's the strange thing. Vicki says she did it, when he tried to have a go at her.'

I swallowed and tried not to ask the question that was uppermost in my mind, but couldn't stop myself. 'Do you believe her?'

Another pause. 'I'm not sure yet. Any other time I'd have said she wasn't capable of it. But then again, I'm beginning to see now what you see in her.'

'What do you mean?'

'I mean I wouldn't want to be the one who gets on the wrong side of her.'

I started and looked at the phone. Was he talking about the same Vicki?

'Are you coming down to the nick?'

'What for? Why do you want to see me?'

'We don't want to see you, but I thought you might want to come and see her, now that we've found her safe and sound and all.' I grimaced at my own guilty stupidity. He continued. 'I thought you may want to run her home. On the other hand, if you don't-'

'No, I do. Of course I do. I'll come straight down. Right now.' I grimaced again.

'Okay. See you soon.'

As I ended the call I fell back into the sofa with a long groan and sat there for a full minute, massaging my throbbing temples. Then I got up, grabbed my jacket from the hook by the door, my car keys and opened the front door.

My sister, Laura, was on the doorstep, about to insert her key in the lock. At the bottom of the path, a taxi was pulling away. For a moment we stood there staring at each other. A younger man I'd never seen before was loitering behind her. He was clean shaven. City-boy type.

'Laura?' I said through my surprise. 'What are you doing here?'

She gave me an exasperated look. 'Go on, tell me he didn't tell you I was coming.'

My brain raced. 'He did say something. I thought he was confused.'

'And my voice message? The one I left yesterday?' I must have given her a blank look because all she said was, 'Fuck, Danny. How you ever manage to run a business is beyond me.' She turned to the youth behind her. 'Grant, this is my dozy brother, Danny. Danny this is Grant.' I ignored the hand he offered to say, 'What are you doing here? Why have you come now?'

'To help you out with Dad, what do you think? Like we discussed on the phone, it's about time we got him into a home, and there's no time like the present. I take it you're not too busy to give some of your time to thinking about your ailing father's welfare?'

How I managed to not reach out with both hands, grab her round the throat and throttle the life out of her right there on my door step, is something I've never worked out.

## CHAPTER 30

To me, Warrington Police Station is a scary place. An ancient, red-brick Victorian-Gothic pile, it has the air of some old museum, a bit like a smaller version of the Natural History Museum in London which I visited once with Caroline. On the fringe of the town centre and less than a stone's throw from Midnight's, its tiled corridors are wide and echoing, with concrete pillars spaced, almost randomly it seems, here and there. The rooms are either huge with high ceilings, or small, cramped and strangely shaped. You can't help wondering if whoever designed it got the measurements wrong and kept finding odd spaces that needed to be put to some good use, so they put a door on and called it an office.

I've experienced its charms first-hand several times. Once as a kid when old Sergeant McIntyre pulled some of us in for robbing stationery from WH Smiths. While waiting for our mums and dads to arrive, he showed us the inside of a cell. We were terrified. If you've ever seen any of those 'Saw' films from a few years back, then you've got some idea. Years later I would spend three days in one on remand, after the Kevin Campbell incident. To say that experience left a lasting impression would be an under-statement. I still don't know whether my resolve to never again lose it the way I did with Kevin, (and so much for that!), was more due to my stay in the cells, or the realisation I'd nearly killed somebody. I was glad when I heard the cells were no longer to be used as such. A few years back they built a state-of-the-art, out-of-town, 'Custody Centre.' Human Rights probably had something to do with it. The last few years I've been to the nick a couple of times, but for legit reasons. One was a community meeting the police called to talk about the problems of town-centre violence. Another was a training session for Door Supervisors run by the Town Centre Inspector. Jamie Carver himself had an input.

Now, as I waited in the draughty public foyer waiting for whoever the elderly volunteer receptionist had rung to come and get me, I shivered at the memory of my extended stay. The walls, bare brick topped with old black and white marble tile, were every bit as cold and stark as I remembered. A huge, blue-felt notice board was covered in colourful posters proclaiming the local police's commitment to providing the Community with, 'Excellent Customer Service' - whatever happened to simply locking up thieves and villains? - and notices about a forthcoming series of Community Meetings to be held in libraries, schools and, in one case, a scout hut. The board was fixed to the wall behind the row of blue, steel-mesh chairs. As I sat there I wondered how many 'business' callers ever bothered to read it. All the time I was conscious that somewhere within the station's bowels, Vicki was telling her story. I wished to God I knew what it was.

Eventually the door that led into the station opened. Jess poked her head round. 'Come through,' she said.

She looked shattered. By now it was getting on for four in the afternoon and she'd have been on for fourteen hours with only a couple of hours sleep the night before.

'How's it going?' I said, as I joined her in the corridor.

'Okay,' she said, though I thought the look she gave me was a little strange.

She didn't say anything as I followed her down the main corridor, through a narrow, twisting passage then up some stairs. I had the vague notion we were heading towards the CID Offices where I'd once met with Carver.

As much to break the silence, I said, 'How is she?'

She said, 'As you'd expect, I guess,' which told me nothing.

At the top of the stairs we passed a big office full of bustle with detectives talking into telephones and shouting across to one another. I caught a glimpse of computers, piles of papers and white boards. I've only ever seen a Murder Control Room on the TV but I guessed that was what it was. A bit further on, Jess showed me into a room that was empty apart from a square table and four chairs set against the back wall under the window.

'We'll be right with you,' she said.

I took a chair, and waited. The window looked out across a couple of low grey-slate roofs beyond which was the police station yard. I could see the tops of several cars and vans which, from here, looked like they were parked all higgledy-piggledy. As I stared out, I remember thinking that something felt wrong - apart from Vicki's abduction by Vincent and the fact that people were being murdered. Jess had seemed unusually restrained, like she didn't want to say too much.

Eventually she returned along with Jamie Carver and another man I'd never seen before. As they sat down, Carver introduced him as, 'DCI Welbeck,' but didn't say anything about why he was there, which made me uneasy. DCI meant he was equal with Carver.

Before he began, Carver looked up at me, paused and took a breath. Something was definitely going on.

'Vicki is just finishing giving us her statement,' he said. 'She won't be long.' I nodded. As I waited for him to continue I could feel Welbeck's stare. He had pushed his chair back, signalling he was to play no part in the discussion but was simply an observer. That I had no idea what he was observing, or why, made me uneasy.

'While we're waiting, there're a few questions we'd like to ask, if that's okay?'

'Shoot,' I said, trying to seem relaxed about it.

'When did you last see Vicki's husband, Vincent?'

'I saw him on Saturday night, on the club car park with Vicki. They were having an argument.' Smart-arse-like, I thought that as a statement, it was true.

'Did you get involved?'

'Only to ask if everything was alright.'

'This argument, did it get physical?'

'Not while I was there.'

'Did you and he have 'words'?'

'If you mean did we have a go at each other, then the answer's 'No'.'

'Where did you go after you left the club this morning?'

'Home.'

'Anywhere else?'

'No.' You can only go one place at once.

210

A glance passed between him and Jess. I had the feeling they were skirting the issue. I wondered again what Welbeck's role in it all was.

'You and Vicki.'

'What about us?'

'Are you an item?'

'Define 'Item'.'

Carver gave me a narrow look. I read it as, *Don't piss me about*.

'Are the two of you you in a relationship?'

'Not really.'

'What does that mean?'

'She stayed at mine on Saturday night because she was worried about what Vincent might do. Then again Sunday night after Agnes's murder.'

'You like her, don't you?'

'She's a lovely girl.'

'And you've known her a long time.'

'I've known lots of women a long time, so what?'

'You feel protective towards her.'

'I guess so.'

'And you wouldn't like to see her get hurt, would you?'

'Of course not.'

'How far would you go to protect her?'

'How do you mean?'

'If you thought someone was hurting her. What would you do?'

'Whatever I needed to do to stop it. Wouldn't anyone?'

'Would you beat someone up?'

'Only as far as necessary.'

'Reasonable force, you mean.'

I nodded at the prompt. His input to the Door Supervisor course had been around how the law allows the use of Reasonable Force to defend yourself, or someone else. What constitutes 'reasonable' had led to a lot of debate. Carver continued.

'You know Vincent is in hospital?'

'So you said when you rang.'

'Do you know how he got there?'

'I presume in an ambulance?'

The narrow look again. Jess decided she needed to look at the floor. Welbeck's head was tilted back, taking it all in. Carver nodded at the table in front of me.

'Your knuckles are skinned. How did that happen?'

I flexed my hands out, showing the grazes. 'I was helping a mate with some building work. We were heaving bricks around.'

Carver folded his arms, gave me a long look. 'Building work.' I nodded. 'You run a security business. Why would you be doing building work?'

'His labourer rang in sick. He needed help to finish a job.'

'So he asked you?'

'We're good mates. I've done it before.'

'Building work,' he repeated, like it was the lowest form of work going.

'I help lots of mates with lots of things.'

'Who's the builder?'

'Harry Shankley.'

'And he'll confirm this I suppose?'

'Of course.'

He nodded.

I decided to push. 'What's all this about?' Why all the questions? I thought I was here to pick Vicki up?'

Another long look. From Jess as well. 'Vincent's quite badly injured.'

'And?'

'Vicki's telling us she was responsible.'

I pushed my bottom lip out. 'And you don't believe her?'

'He's twice her size.'

'So you think someone else was involved?'

'It's... a possibility.'

'Someone like, me?'

'We're not accusing anyone. We're keeping an open mind.'

*Yeah, right.* 'What does Vincent say?'

'Right now he's not saying anything.'

'Because he can't, or won't?'

'Probably both.'

I nodded, waiting.

Carver leaned on the desk, clasped his hands in front. 'Is there anything you're not telling us, Danny?'

'About what?'

'About anything that happened this morning. After you left the club. Before I rang you.'

'I went to bed. I slept.'

His head lowered into a glower. I had the feeling that but for Welbeck, the conversation would be very different. He changed the subject.

'I'm hearing there's trouble brewing at Midnight's.'

'What sort of trouble?'

'Around the door. And with this Russian, Yashin.'

'There's always some sort of trouble around clubs, you know that.'

'What do you know about Yashin?'

'Only what I hear.'

'What have you heard?'

'He's into different things.'

'Like?'

I gave a shrug. 'Girls. Drugs. The usual stuff his sort are into.'

'By girls, you mean sex trafficking?'

'Possibly.'

'I assume Frank Johnson is aware of all this?'

'You'd have to ask him.'

'Is Yashin after someone else taking over the door?'

'I think so.'

'Will he succeed?'

'Not if I have anything to do with it.'

'But will you, have anything to do with it, I mean?'

'Again, you'll have to ask Frank that.'

He gave a long sigh, leaned back and pinned me with a look. 'I've got a lot on my plate right now, Danny. With these murders and everything.'

'I can imagine.'

'What I don't need, is trouble in the town. Of any kind.'

'I'm not intending to start any.'

'No, you never do.'

'What do you mean by that?'

He pulled a face. 'You know what I mean.' Then he added. 'That said, I'd be interested to know about any developments involving Yashin.'

'You would?'

'He's bad news, Danny. We don't need the likes of him around, and nor do you. Morris was bad enough, but Yashin is ten times worse.'

He was talking about Jackie Morris. A gangster-type from Manchester a few years back, he was now doing a long stretch in Strangeways for dealing and attempted murder. He and his bunch had been at the heart of the last war over the town's clubs' doors. Towards the end it had all got nasty. A local doorman got stabbed and died. A Manchester lad called Vernon Springfield copped for it. He never said a word throughout his arrest and trial, but everyone knew he was one of Morris's team. It was in the aftermath of it all that I picked up the Midnight's' contract.

I said, 'What rates are you paying snouts these days?'

He looked at me sideways. 'Don't be a smart-arse. Just keep me informed, right?' He didn't wait for an answer but stood up. Welbeck lingered in his seat, giving me one last look before following. 'I'll see if Vicki's ready,' Carver said.

He and Welbeck left leaving me alone with Jess. I turned to her. 'What was all that about?'

She gave me an admonishing look. 'Don't play us for idiots, Danny.'

'I wouldn't dream of it.'

'You're a nice guy. I like you. You seem reasonably straight, and you've been helpful over these murders. But if you stray too far from the path, we'll deal with you the same as anyone else.'

I gave a her a square look. 'Fair enough.'

The door opened and Carver showed Vicki in. As well as looking like she had been in a car crash, I could see she was out on her feet.

'Can we leave her with you?' Carver said.

I checked with Vicki, just in case she had any objections. She didn't. I nodded, 'Yes.'

'I'll show you out,' Jess said.

Vicki sat quietly in the passenger seat with her head down as we pulled away from the police station. I waited until we were well away before I said, 'How are you feeling? Those bruises are coming out. Do you need anything?'

She shook her head. 'They got the police surgeon to look me over. He's given me some pain killers.' She lapsed into silence again.

I debated whether to ask, but knew I had to. 'What.. did you tell them.'

Her answer was a long sigh. I waited. Eventually she said, 'Don't worry. I didn't point the finger at you.'

'I wouldn't have minded if you had. And I wouldn't have blamed you either.'

She shook her head again. From behind the curtain of hair, I heard her sniff back tears.

'Hey,' I said, trying to sound reassuring. 'It'll be alright. Vincent will be okay. We'll be okay.'

She gave a half-hearted, snorty laugh and shook her head again.

'What?' I said.

'I'm not bothered about Vincent. I'm not bothered about us. I'm not bothered about anything any more.'

I felt her words like a kick in the gut. 'Don't say that. You're tired. You've been through a bad experience, that's all.'

She turned to face me in her seat. 'You think so?' Suddenly she seemed fully awake. 'You think all I need is a good night's sleep, a couple of day's quiet then everything will be okay again? I'll come back to your place after work. We'll shag. You'll do us a nice breakfast. Is that what you're expecting?'

I was stunned by the way she said it, the venom in

her voice. Thirty six hours ago she'd sent me a thank you text. With a kiss even. I couldn't understand how it had all turned so quickly. 'I'm not expecting anything. I just want to know you're okay.'

'Well I am. Don't worry. I've had enough of men looking after me. I'll take care of myself in future.'

I nearly said, *Like you did last night?* but managed not to.

'What I meant was, I just want you to know that I'm here if you need me.'

'I'll bear that in mind...   for when I need someone putting in hospital.'

It was the most painful cut. I think she must have realised as she suddenly said, 'Stop the car.' We were passing a block of shops. I pulled over. 'I need some things. You can let me out here.'

'That's okay. I'll wait.'

'No. I can walk from here.'

'We're still a mile from your flat.'

'The walk'll do me good. It'll clear my head.'

'You're not fit. Let me drive you home. I don't mind.'

She turned to face me again. 'Danny, just leave me here. I don't want you to drive me home.'

I opened my mouth to argue, but could see I'd be wasting my time. I bit my lip. She got out. She was about to shut the door when she stopped, turned back to me.

'Thank you for coming looking for me.' Then she slammed the door and started walking towards the shops.

I read it as she was closing her account.

## CHAPTER 31

On my way home, I called in at the office. Julia was still there but Mike had already left to go somewhere, I could guess where. Julia had heard about Vicki going missing but when she asked me about it I just said, 'She turned up back at home. She was with her husband.' Julia must have read my tone because she left it there.

I mooched around for half an hour, shifting paper from one tray to another. But it was no good. As I rose and threw everything back into the tray on which Julia had typed a neat label saying, 'Pending,' I called to her, 'Don't hang around, Jules. I'll be at home.'

'Are you okay?' She said it like she'd been storing the question up.

'Fine.' I said.

I headed home.

When I got there, Laura was on her laptop. As I passed behind her to hang my jacket up I cast a glance at the screen. It showed a page from a website. I recognised the name of a nursing home in Stockton Heath. It was the same one our Aunty Betty went to. Young Grant was busy in the kitchen. Smells of a rich pasta sauce wafted.

'He cooks?' I said, out of his hearing.

'Someone has to.'

My sister's never been big on domesticity. Ever since she first had a place of her own, she's had a cleaner.

'Did you ring Dad?' I said.

She nodded. 'I told him we'd come and see him tomorrow morning.'

I pulled a face. 'I'm not sure... There's some stuff I'm involved in right now that-'

'Don't tell me you're too busy, Danny. These may be our father's last few years. The least you can do is give up some time to ensuring he enjoys them.'

It prompted a discussion that probably got a bit more heated than it needed to. At some stage Grant disappeared upstairs, I'm not sure when exactly. I tried making the point that with a bit of regular checking up, Dad was still quite capable of looking after himself - for a while more at least. She argued that it was only a matter of time, maybe less than a year, before he would need full-time care. It was better that we got him to agree to move in somewhere early, so he would feel he was part of the decision and had time to adjust, rather than it all happens suddenly, when he gets to the point where he can no longer cope, or something 'bad' happens. I have to admit I could see her point, but I still felt inclined to let him enjoy at least a few more months of independence.

Eventually she said, 'I don't understand your objection. If it's about the cost then I'm happy to-'

'Whoa. Who mentioned anything about cost?'

'Well, no one, but we both know residential care is expensive and it isn't like he's sitting on bank-loads of money, is it?'

'No, but..' I wasn't sure where she was going with the subject. 'I'm not even thinking about the cost.'

'That's the trouble, with you little brother. You don't think ahead. We need to be thinking now about the practicalities. The property market isn't exactly booming is it?'

My brow furrowed. 'What's the property market got to do with anything?'

She looked at me as if I was being stupid. 'The house? We'll have to decide what to do with it. Don't tell me you've never thought about it?'

I looked at her stunned. 'No. I can't say I have.'

'Well you need to. Unless you've got some pot of gold stashed away to pay for his care?'

'You know I haven't.'

'And neither have I.'

'So you think he should sell the house?'

'Not necessarily.'

'What do you mean, not necessarily?'

'It just so happens that Grant is a Solicitor. He specialises in property law. According to him-'

Finally the penny dropped. I tipped my head back.

'Ahh, fuck,' I said.

She stopped. 'What?'

'That's what all this is about.'

'What do you mean?'

'You know what I mean. You wanted him to put the house in trust twelve months ago. So we could rent it out. We decided against, remember?'

'No, you decided against. I thought it was a good idea then. It's an even better idea now.'

'Why is it a better idea now?'

'Because he'll be ready to go into care soon anyway. Grant reckons that the way the rental market is right now, if we get the house put in trust to us, then when we come to rent it we'll get a better-'

I raised a hand. 'Stop.' I gave her a long look.

'What?'

'Tell me you're not looking to put Dad in care because some pretty-boy city lawyer has convinced you that the finances will work out better if we do it now?'

'I'm not. And don't call him a pretty-boy lawyer. He 's one of the best legal brains in the firm. But it just so happens that when I asked him about it he said-'

'LAURA.' She jumped as I banged my fist on the table. 'He's our father. It's what's best for him that matters, not what's best for us.'

'You don't need to tell me that Danny. Who is it spent three months looking after him after mum died?'

I rolled my eyes. 'You did. But then as I recall, you were between jobs at the time.'

She bristled. 'And you think I wouldn't have been there if I had been working? That I wouldn't have asked for compassionate leave?'

At that point I was tempted to point out how there'd been no mention of compassionate leave those last weeks when Mum started to go downhill quickly and Dad had to look after her more or less on his own, with me running them back and forth to the hospital every couple of days. But I said nothing and just shook my head. It was a circular argument, one we'd had before.

At the end of the day there's a fundamental difference between my sister and I. Laura's job means she sees the world in terms of pounds and pence. Right now she was seeing Dad's house as an investment for the future. It's value, therefore, needed to be preserved. Me, I didn't give a toss about the house, or its future value. All I saw on my weekly visits was a lonely old man whose main pleasures in life came from memories. He and Mum had some good times after they took the decision to up sticks from Warrington and move into the nice semi with a big garden that Gran left to Mum when she died. The memories were rooted in the bric-a-brac Mum used to bring back from their trips abroad, the garden she loved tending, the family photographs that hang on every wall and which are a constant reminder of their life together. They would all disappear the day he moved into a care home. But it had been a long day. I wasn't sure I was up for another bout of arguing.

'Tell you what,' I said. 'Let's wait until you've seen him. Then we'll talk about options.'

'So that'll be tomorrow, then?'

I sighed. 'Like I said, I'm not sure-' My phone rang. It was Eric.

Before I could say anything he said, 'I'm coming back from B&Q in Winwick. There's a van tailing me. Only it's blue, not white. It was there on the way out as well. It's four or five up I'd say, I can't be sure. When I stopped at the garage to fill up it waited down the road.'

I snatched up my jacket again. 'Where are you?'

'Right now I'm going round in circles on the Padgate estate. I don't want to go home in case they make their move there. The kids are having their tea.'

As I headed for the door, my brain was racing. Since my encounter at the Brigadoon two nights before, I'd been half-expecting something. But the timing could hardly have been worse.

'Where are you going?' Laura said. I could hear the frustration in her voice. She'd obviously spent the afternoon rehearsing all her arguments

'To even some odds,' I said, over my shoulder.

'But Grant's done us a Spag Bol. It's his speciality.'

Clever, I thought. Spag Bol has always been one of my favourites.

'Keep me some,' I shouted as I ran out the door.

# CHAPTER 32

'Eric?' I said into the phone as I left the house. 'You still there?'

'Yes.'

'Drive round for another ten minutes, then head for the new stadium site behind Morrisons. I'll be waiting.'

'Are we going to sort these fuckers out, or what?'

'I guess we'll have to.'

'Cracker. It's about time.'

'Don't try anything while on you're own.'

'I won't. Just make sure you're there when I get there.'

'I will be.'

As I pulled away to head back into town, I brought up Gol's number on the car phone. It took half a dozen rings for him to answer. Gol's never got his head around voicemail.

'Hello Boss?'

'Where are you?'

'At home. We're about to-'

'Meet me at the new stadium site in nine minutes. Eric's got a vanload on his tail.'

'Right.' He hung up. The good thing about Gurkhas. They never question.

My big fear was I'd get snarled in traffic. The site of

the town's new sports stadium was this side of the town centre on the old Greenall's site behind Morrison's Supermarket. Speed limits aside, it was easily reachable in ten minutes, but a jam through Stockton Heath could fuck everything up. As it happened, I sailed through and got to the site with a minute and a half to spare. It was all locked up, as I knew it would be. Work finished at six. I parked up against the blue hoarding perimeter fence next to the main gate. Eric would see me the moment he turned into the access road. I reached round into the back and pulled out the pick-axe handle that since Monday had become my travelling companion. Thirty seconds later, Gol's silver Toyota pulled up next to me. I dropped my window.

'You ready?'

He reached into the passenger foot-well and showed me what looked like the handle of a baseball bat.

'How many?' he said, through the toothy grin I'd seen many times before. He wears it when he knows he's about to call upon some of the skills he learned over fifteen years' army service in places as far apart as Northern Ireland and Afghanistan.

'Five, maybe?' I said. 'Possibly six?'

'Good,' he said, meaning the odds. The three of us together had faced a lot worse in our time.

We got out and stood between the cars, waiting. A minute passed. Then another. Then another.

'He should be here by now,' I said, checking my watch.

Even as I spoke, my phone rang, showing Eric's name. I just managed to catch his garbled shout of , '-ACKERS... BRID-,' before it cut off.

'Shit,' I said. already turning back to my truck.

'Where?' Gol shouted across.

'Ackers Road Bridge.'

Then I was back in the truck, spinning wheels on gravel as I made a quick reverse and took off.

Less than a mile from the stadium site where we'd been waiting, Ackers Road forms the 'T' across the end of Ellesmere Road, a long, straight road that runs parallel to the Manchester Ship Canal. Part of the leafy suburbia that is Stockton Heath, Ellesmere is made narrow by the parked cars that line the side where the garage-less houses overlook the canal. It was pure luck there were no kids playing in the road that evening, or dog walkers crossing to use the canal towpath.

Even before I got to the junction, I could see a line of cars backed up along Ackers Road, the bridge itself out of sight round to the right. In front of me, where Ellesmere joined with Ackers, half a dozen cars were also waiting in line, going nowhere.

Pulling up behind the one at the back, I grabbed my stave and jumped out. As I pressed the 'lock' button on the fob, I was conscious of Gol pulling up behind me. I ran to the junction and round the corner. The line of cars stopped about ten metres short of the crest of the bridge where it was all happening. Some of the cars' doors were open with drivers and passengers looking on and pointing in horror at what was happening in front of them, though none were looking to get involved. Eric's old Mondeo was facing towards me. It was embedded in the green metal rails on the bridge's nearside. The blue van, showing the damage to the front where it had rammed Eric from behind to send him into the railings, was now stationary in the middle of the bridge, blocking traffic in both directions. One man was behind the wheel, another - the lookout - standing next to the open passenger door, checking the approaches. The other four were laying into Eric, who was on the floor, with staves, feet and fists. They were all wearing full-face balaclavas. As I ran towards them, I read what had happened.

Having realised Eric was onto them - his driving in circles would have told them - they'd also have realised he'd most likely called for back-up. Knowing they needed to make their move before the cavalry arrived, they'd decided the bridge was as good a place as any. Easily defendable and with escape routes in both directions they'd rammed him into the railings, knowing that if he crashed straight through into the ship canal below it would just save time and trouble. Eric had had time for one last phone call before they'd either pulled him from the car or he'd tried to leg it. Only Eric isn't built for running.

I was still about twenty yards away when the look-out saw me coming, shouted and pointed. I couldn't make out what he said but I heard enough to recognise it wasn't English. The group stopped what they were doing to Eric to turn and look. There were more shouts - Russian, I thought - as two of them peeled off to come and meet me, joined by the look-out. They were all carrying staves of one sort or another. I couldn't tell at that stage if they were iron or wood, but I hoped they were iron. Being heavier, iron bars are less manoeuvrable and therefore easier to avoid. And if a big guy catches you with a stave, believe me, it makes not a lot of difference whether it's iron or wood.

As we closed halfway down the bridge, I saw there was another attacker I hadn't seen before. He was writing on the floor, right next to and almost under Eric's car. He was holding his right leg and yelling blue murder. Catching him out of the corner of my eye I had the impression his leg was bent at the knee in a direction that didn't look right. Eric's favourite move in a tight spot is a knee-kick. At least he'd managed to give one of them something to remember him by before they put him down.

We were about five yards away when, as I expected, the three coming at me stopped. The usual thing in such confrontations is that there is a stand-off - however brief - during which the respective parties weigh each other up, dance around a bit then select the tactic/opponent they are going to go for first. But I'd already decided I wasn't going to play that game. Apart from the fact that the two on the bridge were still giving it to Eric, good-style, the three facing me were all masked, which meant that there was no point in trying to weigh who was the weakest / the leader and should therefore be given priority / least attention.

It only took them a second to realise that I wasn't going to stop, but added to that second was the time they lost taking their sticks behind them in search of the momentum they needed for a swing when they realised their mistake. Mine was already behind me and coming forward and round when I moved to within a yard of them. It connected with the one on the right on his forearm as he bought it up to protect his head. I heard a 'snap' and he screamed and dropped his stick. As the others reacted I let my momentum take me in a three-hundred-and-sixty-degree pirouette so I came straight round with a second swing that caught the middle guy on his left side under the arm. It also put me in the right position to block the swing coming in from the third guy on my left. There was a dull crack as the two sticks clashed - wood on wood. By now Gol was coming up right behind me. Behind the third guy's hood, I could see his gaze flicking between us, taking in the danger, trying to work out what his best option was now that one of his mates had a broken arm and the other was still gasping for breath and holding his side. I made his decision for him, turning away to leave him for Gol as I carried on towards the bridge. By now the two on top of Eric had realised - or been warned by a shout from the driver - that all was not going to plan, as they turned round to meet me. This time their sticks were raised and ready as they came at me so I had no choice but to adopt a different tactic. Swinging my stick round my head as I ran forward, I launched it at them, full force, so they had no choice but to lift theirs to protect themselves, at the same time ducking and half turning away, as you do, instinctively, when a twirling stick that could take your head off comes at you. There was a rat-a-tat clatter as my stick crashed into theirs, before bouncing away, harmlessly. But by then I was in amongst them, close enough to plant a fist in the middle of the hood worn by the one on my left as he brought himself upright, followed immediately by me scraping my right shoe down the shin of the other as he was preparing to bring his stick down on top of my head. The first one staggered back, stick flailing the air and there was a howl of pain from the second - the shin scrape is one of the most effective 'distractions' I know. Off-balance, his stick went whistling past my right ear and shoulder to hit the ground beside me. The jarring impact of the stick hitting the road was enough to wrench it from his grasp and he staggered back realising he was not only hurting, but now defenceless. A shout from Gol, behind, made me turn just in time to duck away from the stick that was coming towards my head, aimed at me by the driver who had obviously decided his mates were now coming off worst and needed help. Even so it caught me a glancing blow on my left shoulder and an explosion of pain ripped through me. But by now Gol was nearly with me. Ten yards back, the man I'd left to him was also now writhing on the floor. God knows what Gol had done to him, but the guy didn't seem to know whether to hold his arm, his leg, his head, or all three. The driver was in the act of delving in the van for another stick and had it half out when I reached him. Stepping up close, I head-butted him straight on where his nose would be. Again, there was a satisfying crunch and he turned away, doubling up, hands to his face.

Turning to check the others, I saw that those still on their feet were hanging back, reluctant to engage us now that that they'd lost the initiative and some of their number were now in need of medical help. I pointed to the one whose shin I'd scraped.

'You'd better pick your mates up and fuck off. Now.' He moved to comply, though slowly. 'And you can tell your boss he can expect a visit from me.'

Satisfied it was over, I nodded to Gol - he still had hold of one, bat raised and ready - indicating he should watch and make sure there were no parting gestures while I turned my attention to Eric. As I jogged over to where he lay, he turned himself over onto his back. Bending to him, I guessed his turning over must have been some sort of reflex action because he was completely out of it. His face was a mess, his mouth a bloody black hole with gaps where some of his teeth should have been. *Bloody Hell*, I thought, *Just like Vincent*. In the distance, I could hear the woo-woo wail of sirens, but they were police rather than ambulance. I remembered what Carver had said earlier about not wanting trouble. Right, I thought. No need for him to find any. Checking Eric over as best as I could, I worked out he was just about moveable. I turned to see what was happening behind me. The gang were helping each other back into the van, the one with the shattered knee being carried, bodily, through the sliding side door by two others. There would be no further trouble from them.

I shouted to Gol. 'Give me a hand, Gol. We need to go.'

Together, we lifted Eric to a standing position - he's no lightweight - then, one under each arm, we half-carried half-dragged him past the line of dumbstruck motorists back to my truck.

# CHAPTER 33

It was around eleven when I came away from the hospital leaving Eric with his wife, Sally, and his eldest lad, George. By then the scan results had come back showing no sign of anything untoward around Eric's brain and skull, which was remarkable given the kicking he'd received. His main problems were concussion and a broken bone in his wrist. Lucky really. It could have been a lot worse. And it reinforced the fact that the attack was meant more as a warning rather than any real attempt to take him out. As far as I was concerned it didn't matter. A line had been crossed. Where it would stop, God alone knew.

Most of my time at the hospital had been taken up with batting off the questions from the two uniform police officers who turned up looking for Eric. After finding nothing at the bridge apart from Eric's car embedded in the railings and blood spills, they were on the ball enough to think to check round the hospitals. While I was talking to one, his mate rang around other A&Es but none reported any admissions involving Russian types. I kept my story as short as I could get away with. Gol and I had responded to a shout for help from a friend and we'd defended ourselves. That was about it, and it seemed to bear with what a couple of witnesses at the bridge had said. It was obvious the cops realised there was more to it, but as no one was yet making any formal complaint, they didn't show too much interest in following it up.

While I was there, I went up to the ward where Vincent was and spoke to a nurse who told me he was awake and 'comfortable', which made me feel a little better. I didn't drop by his bed for a chat.

Up to when I left the hospital, there'd been no sign of Carver or Jess, but I knew it was only a matter of time before word of what had happened got back to them. I guessed he wouldn't be best pleased.

When I arrived home, Laura was about to go to bed. Like with the police I batted off her enquiries about where I'd been and what had happened to my shoulder. It was bruising up nicely by then and every time I moved it, pain lanced through and into my neck. But something in my manner must have told her that I was not in the mood for conversation - on any subject - and she loped off to bed, frustrated she hadn't yet managed to get to where she wanted to be regarding Dad. Before I followed her I rang my partner, Mike, and brought him up to date with what was happening, though like with the police, I kept it all brief.

As I slid into my own bed I could hear Laura and Grant having words next door. I guess bickering families and gang wars hadn't featured in whatever picture Laura had painted to get him to accompany her, 'Up North'. I'd already pegged Grant as one of those city-types who believes the world ends at Watford. I didn't try to listen in, and despite everything that had happened the past twenty-four hours and which I could have spent all night thinking about, I must have fallen asleep almost at once. I think some instinct was probably telling me to get some sleep while I could because things could be about to change. Which they were.

I woke to the sound of heavy banging downstairs which, after a few seconds, I realised was someone at the front door. My phone's screen read 06.02. I knew at once who it was. The thuds were too heavy for Vicki, the Russians wouldn't have knocked, and any of my guys would have rung first. There's only one other group of people I know who are in the habit of making early morning visits.

As I trooped downstairs, shouting to Laura to stay in bed and, 'It's alright,' - which it clearly wasn't - images of Vincent, injured or even dead Russians, and a comatose Eric vied to occupy top spot on the list of most-likelies. There was no way I could have guessed how far out they all were.

When I opened the door I was surprised to see Carver hanging back, well behind the man doing the knocking, as if he were there only to observe. Uniforms hovered, the way they do when they are there, 'just in case.' In the backdrop I counted at least three cars that weren't usually parked in the close. As my gaze re-focused on the man on the step and I remembered him as Carver's mate, DCI Welbeck, alarm bells rang. Whatever was going on, it didn't look good.

'Danny Norton?' Welbeck said.

'Don't be a dick,' I said. 'It was only yesterday.'

Over Welbeck's shoulder, Carver looked exasperated and shook his head by way of a warning. But Welbeck must have been watching re-runs of The Bill because he stayed in role.

'Daniel Norton, I am arresting you for the murder of… You do not have to say anything...'

It was one of those moments when the words are so far away from what you expect they fail to register first time. Bad enough that my gut had sunk like a stone as soon as I heard the word 'murder', my brain wasn't quick enough to recognise the name and began to re-run those I'd been half-expecting. It wasn't Vincent Lamont, and nor was it anything that sounded in any way foreign. As Welbeck stepped forward to take hold of my arm and another officer came round behind me, cuffs in hand, I checked myself. By now Laura was halfway downstairs calling out, 'Danny? Are you alright? What do they want?'

'Hang on,' I said, trying to keep Welbeck in sight as the officer fitted the cuffs. 'Say that again. Who is it I'm supposed to have murdered?'

Welbeck gave me a look like he thought I might be pissing about, but played it by the book. And this time I heard it clear as a bell when he said, 'You heard me. Gerard Reilly.'

For several seconds all I could do was stare at him. My first thoughts were around Stevie B and Shane, and what they had done to Ged after finding him in the Golden Dragon. But then I realised, something was badly off.

'You're making a big mistake somewhere. Ged Reilly is in Thailand, least he was last Saturday.'

Welbeck gave me a look that was almost pitying, like he'd been expecting something a bit less desperate. He shook his head.

'Right now, Ged Reilly's remains are in the mortuary at Warrington General. They've been there since we found them in a shallow grave out at Winwick, where it seems they've been lying since he went missing several years ago.'

# CHAPTER 34

*Thursday*

On the face of it, the Interview Room in the new Custody Suite looks pretty much the same as the one I remembered at the police station. Table, chairs, recording equipment, bare walls. But the atmosphere was completely different. Somehow its pristine newness lent it a formality that was missing from the old one. Last time it had come as no great surprise when the detective in the case had leaned across, paused the tape and said, 'Okay. Off the record. Tell me what happened.' But now, as I listened to Welbeck going through his list of prepared questions, I knew that the chances of something similar happening were zilch. Not that it would have helped. Half an hour into the interview I was still playing it ultra-cautious. In particular I was trying to get my head round how Ged Reilly's decomposed body had, according to Welbeck, been discovered buried in some woods out at Winwick, when five days before, he'd been with Stevie B and Shane in Thailand. From what I'd heard about the police in Thailand, I wasn't keen to point any fingers in that direction until I'd figured out what the fuck was going on.

'Well?' Welbeck said. 'Are you going to give any answer?'

I lifted my head and blinked at him. 'Sorry. What was the question?'

Welbeck threw me an exasperated look - not the first since the interview had begun - before sharing it with the slight, balding man sitting on my left.

Peter Francis is someone else I went to school with. He and his professional and personal partner, Bernie Stokes, run Francis and Stokes Solicitors. They've got a good reputation as about the best practicing criminal law solicitors in Warrington. Peter represented me the last time I was arrested. Carver, sitting well back behind Welbeck and taking no part in the interview, turned away in his chair to rub at his forehead.

Welbeck gave a sigh, then said, 'My question was, if, like you say, you've not seen Ged Reilly for over ten years, how can you be so sure the body we've found can't be his?'

I stared at him quite a long time. I was thinking on what to say, while also resisting the temptation to turn to Peter. I didn't want to give the impression we had discussed anything we weren't prepared to share with the police. So far we'd played it that Peter knew nothing and was simply there to protect my rights. What I hadn't figured out yet was Stevie B and Shane's parts in it all. If the body was Ged Reilly's, then who was it they'd grabbed in Thailand, and what had they done to him? On the other hand, if Reilly was in Thailand, then whose was the body, and how had my old mobile come to be in the grave with it?

I had to say something so I said, 'I'm sorry, but all I can say right now is, I know nothing about any body and in any case, I'm pretty sure it can't be Ged Reilly.'

Welbeck gave me a straight look. 'That suggests two things to me. One, you're stalling to give yourself more time to come up with a believable story. The second is that even if the body isn't Ged Reilly, it belongs to someone else you killed and Reilly's body is yet to be found.'

I was about to tell him what I thought of his theory when I felt Peter's hand on my arm. 'Just a moment Chief Inspector. As I said before, that still suggests that you are treating the fact that my client's mobile phone was found with the body as proof that he was involved in its burial, as well as being responsible for the victim's death. And as I pointed out earlier, one does not necessarily follow the other. My client has already stated, quite clearly, that around that time his mobile phone went missing and he reported it as either lost or stolen. If you check the phone company records I am sure they will be able to verify that fact.'

'And as I also said earlier, even if they do, he could have reported his phone missing because he realised afterwards where he might have dropped it and then concocted a story about losing it to cover himself.'

'Bollocks,' I said, then felt Peter's hand again.

'You can answer, 'bollocks' to as many of my questions as you like,' Welbeck said. 'But it doesn't alter the fact that we have statements from people confirming they remember you looking for Ged in the days before he disappeared, *and* threatening violence to him.'

'Too bloody right I was. After what he did to Ricky Mason, I'd have-' This time Peter's squeeze was stronger.

'I think what my client means to say is, that he does

not deny that was the case, but again, he repeats, for the record, that he never found Mr Reilly at that time, and has never seen him since.'

Now it was Welbeck's turn to stare. His eyes locked with mine and I had no trouble reading the thought that lay behind them. *Liar.*

After the interview I spent another two hours alone in my cell, staring at the murky-beige walls. while Welbeck, 'checked out some facts.' What those facts were he didn't say. I spent some of the time wondering about whose names were on the statements he'd referred to and thinking about how it's times like this you find out who your real friends are.

It was late afternoon when they granted me police bail. As we left the station, the word Peter used was 'impasse.' Seeing my look, he explained. As of that moment, the only things identifying the body as Ged Reilly were the driving licence and cards in the wallet found in the back pocket of his trousers. A DNA test couldn't be done because as yet, there were no samples of Ged's DNA available for comparison. Ged had no children and so far the police hadn't been able to trace any other surviving family. On the other hand according to Peter, and despite Welbeck's attempts to make much of it, my mobile phone being found with the body didn't amount to much either. It was circumstantial evidence and that was all. I'd reported it lost around that time. Anyone could have taken it and dropped it in the grave. The only trouble was, I hadn't come up with a single name of who that someone might be, or who - if not Ged - the body belonged to.

As Peter dropped me off at the office and I was about

to get out, I turned to him. 'You've not actually said.'

'Said what?'

'Whether you believe me.'

'He gave me a straight look. 'You've been around long enough to know the score Danny. It's not my job to believe or disbelieve you. My job is to represent you.'

I gave a slow nod. 'Thanks for the vote of confidence.'

He shrugged his narrow shoulders. 'Nothing personal. I answered the question the same way I do with all my clients.'

'Right.'

About to drive off he stopped, wound the passenger window down. "One thing.'

I came back to the car. 'What's that?'

'It might just help your case if you could remember where you were and who you were with when you lost your mobile.'

'I'll give it some thought.'

'Do.'

I watched as he drove away. And as I turned away to go upstairs and see Mike my thought was, *That's the bloody trouble.*

## CHAPTER 35

Mike was waiting in the office and jumped up when I walked in.

'Thank fuck. What's going on?' Julie came through as well, a concerned look on her face.

I told him the story, or as much of it as I felt I could at that time.

When I finished he said, 'So they don't even know if it's Ged's body?'

'They're saying it is, but without DNA they can't prove it.'

'Let's hope it stays that way.'

I looked at him. 'Why? What difference does it make who's body it is?'

Realising his mistake, he waffled. 'Right, well- What I meant was- It would be easier all round if the whole thing just dies a death, which it will, hopefully, if they can't prove it's Ged.'

'Apart from the whole town will know I was arrested for killing him. And we all know how mud sticks.'

He gave a dismissive wave. 'I wouldn't worry about that. Everyone already thinks-' He stopped as Julie winced. Mike could never be a diplomat.

I looked at him, shook my head. 'Thanks Mike. Nice to know I can rely on your support.'

As the crimson began to spread up his face, I pulled out my mobile. Peter had brought it with him when he picked me up, along with some other stuff. I had voicemails and texts. The first few were from the team before they'd have heard about my arrest, wanting to know about Eric and what the plan was. Then there were more from them after my arrest and offering help with anything I needed when I was released. There were other messages as well. One was from a worried-sounding Frank Johnson asking me to get in touch as soon as I was, 'out.'

I turned to Mike, who was still looking sheepish. 'Have you spoken to Frank?'

He nodded. 'He rang this morning asking what it was all about. I told him you'd see him tonight, assuming you were released.'

'Good.'

'I take it you are aware that this could raise a problem with the contract?'

'Yes Mike, I know that.'

A clause in the contract allowed for it to be voided if any part of the company or its employees became implicated in criminal activity. The clause is standard in the business and is supposed to protect the club-owner. I supposed that criminal activity might just include murder.

'Would Frank invoke it?' Mike said.

I thought about it. 'He wouldn't have before. But with Yashin hovering- Who knows?'

'Perhaps I'd better talk with Isaac.'

'Perhaps you better had.'

Isaac Meyer is the solicitor we turn to for legal advice when we need it. I returned to my messages.

There was one from Vicki. I turned away while I listened to it. At least her tone was different from the last time we spoke.

'I've just heard about Eric. I'm sorry. Let me know if there's anything I can do. For Sally or anything. 'Bye.' It wasn't much, but it was her and it was the best thing I'd heard all day. I rang her back. She answered after two rings.

'They're keeping Eric in for observations,' I said. 'I think Sally's okay but I'll let you know.'

'Okay.'

'I hesitated before continuing. 'I looked in on Vincent while I was at the hospital. He seems to be recovering.'

'Yes, I saw him this morning.'

'Right.'

'He's not saying anything to the police about what happened.'

'Okay.'

'It's his decision.'

'Fair enough.'

There was a longish pause then she said, 'I heard about you being arrested. Was it to do with Vincent?'

'No, something else.'

There was another pause while she waited to see if was going to explain further. When I didn't she said, 'Are you in trouble?'

'A bit. But I'm working on it.'

'Will you be in tonight?'

'Yes.'

'Okay. See you then.'

'Right.'

She rang off.

I sat a while, thinking, before I took the next

message. It was fairly cryptic. A man whose voice I didn't recognise and who didn't give his name said, 'I'm ringing on behalf of an old school mate of your's. He says he'll meet you at six o'clock. The usual place.' He rang off. I checked my watch. It was already five-thirty.

The last message made me sit up. It was from Stevie B, in Thailand. 'Need to speak Danny. It's urgent. Ring me back when you get this.'

I put my phone away and stood up. Mike looked up, surprised.

'Where are you going?'

'Things to do. Places to go. People to see.' I headed for the door.

'Hang on a minute. Don't you think we should talk about-'

'No.'

'But we need to decide-'

'You deal with it.' At the door I stopped, turned. 'One thing you can do.

'What?'

'Roster half-a-dozen extra tonight, just in case.'

'You mean at Midnight's?'

'No. The OAP's Bingo Hall. And put Winston back on.'

'I thought you banned him?'

'I've just un-banned him.'

As I descended the stairs I heard Mike's plaintive voice calling after me, 'DANNYYY…?'


The 'usual place' referred to by the man who left the message was the big Tesco's car park in Bewsey. On the way there I made two phone calls. First I tried ringing Stevie B back on the number he'd called me on from

245

Thailand. There was no reply. Next I rang Laura.

'Where are you?' she said. 'I rang the police station but they said you'd been released.'

'I have. I'm working. Sorting some things out.'

'Are you coming home?'

'Not until after the club closes.'

There was pause. 'So you're not coming to see Dad?'

'Not today.'

'Tomorrow?'

'I don't know. Maybe. I can't say.'

'What are you mixed up in Danny? Do you need a good lawyer?'

I hoped to God she didn't mean Canary Wharf Boy. 'Already got one.'

Another pause. 'Are you going to be okay?'

'Course I am. You know me. I always come out on top.'

'I'm serious Danny.'

'So am I. Listen Sis, I gotta go. Someone's trying to ring me. I'll see you later.'

When I got to Tesco's, Carver was already there. His car was nose-up against the wall in the far corner where there are usually a few cars but it's not too busy. We've met there before, when there's been stuff we need to talk about. I parked next to him, got out and jumped in the passenger seat.

'You bastard,' I said. 'You could have given me a 'heads up' when we spoke yesterday.'

He was ready for it. 'No, I couldn't. If I'd told you what was going on you'd have been expecting it and Welbeck would have known. He may come across as stiff, but believe me, he's switched on.'

I couldn't disagree with the reasoning, so I dropped

it.

'So what's the score?'

'The body turned up four days ago. When we realised it might be Ged Reilly your name came up and I had to take myself out of it. People know we know each other and you're involved with us with these murders. Conflict of interest and all that.'

'So what happens now? Where does it leave me?'

'Depends.'

'On what?'

'On whether you killed him.'

I glared at him. 'Don't you start.'

He gave a half-smile. 'Okay, let's assume you didn't. In that case there shouldn't be any evidence to support a charge and your bail will get cancelled.'

'How long will that take?'

He pulled a, *how long is a piece of string* sort of face. 'Could be several weeks. Welbeck's a good investigator and he's thorough. He'd want to be sure before letting you off the hook.'

'Am I on a hook?'

'Like I said, depends on-'

'Yeah, I know. Whether I killed Ged.' After a moment I said, 'Your mate seems pretty keen on pinning it on me. Why's that?'

'He doesn't like doormen. He was at Stockport during all that trouble at the Alambra. He reckons it was the lack of cooperation from the guys on the door stopped him getting convictions.'

I nodded. The attack on the Alambra Club's door one Saturday night has gone down in Doorstaff legend as, 'The Night Of The Alambro'. I must have heard about ten different versions over the years.

I said, 'How did you come to find the body?'

'We got an anonymous tip-off telling us where it was buried.'

'Phone-call?'

'Letter.'

I thought on it. 'Good timing, don't you think?'

'How do you mean?'

'Think about it. Here's Yashin manoeuvring to take over the door, and here's me standing in the way of it happening. Suddenly I'm up to my neck in murder charges and, potentially, out of the equation.'

Carver shook his head. 'That only works if you get convicted. If you didn't do it, it'll take more than your mobile in a grave to make that happen.'

'It may not need a conviction.'

'Why's that?'

I told him about the void-clause.

'So Frank could drop you for another company anyway?'

'Possibly. We're looking into the legalities as we speak.'

He stared at the wall in front of us, rubbing his chin. 'Who would know where the body was buried?' I gave him a pointed look and waited for the penny to drop. Eventually he said. 'Right. Whoever killed him.'

'Thank you.'

He thought some more. 'I still can't see a connection. Let's just say that you getting pulled in on a murder charge is part of an attempt by Yashin, or whoever, to get you off the door. How could Yashin know anything about a buried body, or Ged Reilly being killed and that he could use that way? Yashin was in Russia ten years ago.'

'That's what's worrying me,' I said. 'I can't see the connection either.'

Carver fell silent again. When I'd had enough of it I said, 'What're you thinking?'

He shot me a distracted glance, thought some more, then said, 'I'm thinking about what would happen if Yashin did get a foothold in the club scene, particularly if he also had control of the doors. You remember what it was like around here ten years ago. The drug problem was out of control. The clubs were full of it. There was open dealing in the street. Christ, it was even rife in the schools. And we had all the shit that comes with it. Violence, beatings, petrol bombs, knifings. Not to mention the Bowling Club shoot out.' I nodded at his mention of yet another infamous entry in the annals of Warrington's Crime History. 'Okay, there're still plenty of problems, but they're nothing like as bad as they were. It's taken a lot of work by a lot of people to turn things around. But if Yashin starts to build a base, it'll undo everything we've done and we'll end up back at square one. Worse even.' He shook his head. I could see from his face his concern was genuine.

We both thought some more.

I said, 'Maybe we need a plan.'

'To clear you of suspicion of murder you mean?'

I rocked a hand. 'More than that, I think.'

'How much more?'

'As much as we need to stop Yashin.'

He shot me a wary look. 'You're talking to a cop, remember.'

I gave him my most level stare so he would know what I was thinking. Jamie Carver had a reputation for being as 'straight' as straight cops come. But I knew him well enough to know there'd been occasions in his career when the rules of his trade had clashed with what was best for the public. On those times the public tended to come out on top.

I began to talk.

We were there another thirty minutes.

## CHAPTER 36

After my meeting with Carver, I headed to the club. I wanted to get there early so I'd have time to think about what I was going to do with the extra staff I'd asked Mike to arrange. I wasn't certain there was going to be trouble, but after the incident on the bridge I wasn't going to leave anything to chance. The hospital was on the way so I dropped by to see how Eric was doing. He was awake, hurting in lots of places, but a mile better than the last time I'd seen him. He asked about his attackers and almost managed a smile when I described some of what Gol and I had managed to inflict on them. As I was leaving, I told him not to waste time getting better. The way things were going, I would be needing him, and soon.

He put on a cheesed-off face. 'Aren't you supposed to say things like , "Don't rush back", and, "Only when you feel up to it"?'

I gave him my best WTF look. 'In case you've forgotten. Midnight's ain't no charity shop.'

I got to the club just as Tony-the-Manager was opening up. His face showed surprise as he all-but ran up to me the moment I came through the front doors.

'What's going on Danny? I've heard all sorts of rumours.'

'Don't believe 'em,' I said as I waltzed past. Tony was the last person in the world I felt obliged to update. The only times he ever showed interest in my side of things was when there was scandal or the shit was about to hit the fan. Blow him, I thought. For now, he can stew with the rest of them.

I'd just worked out my plan, ready to brief the team when I heard Frank had arrived. I gave him a few minutes then went to see him in his office. He threw Tony out, shut the door and asked me to sit down.

Before my bum even hit the seat he said, 'What's all this about you being arrested for murder?'

'Suspicion of murder,' I corrected. I'm not usually one for splitting hairs but in this case it felt right.

'Are they charging you?'

'No.'

'Will they?'

'Unlikely. Seeing as how I didn't do it, now that you ask.'

He ignored the last and continued. 'It wouldn't look good for the club if you were charged.'

'I know.'

'Our licence is due up for renewal in the next few months.'

'I know.'

'When will you know if they intend to charge you or not?'

'Like I said, that's not likely to happen.'

'Yeah, I heard you. But when will you know?'

I wasn't sure whether to be offended or impressed. I hadn't seen Frank so focused in a long time. Then again, it was his livelihood we were talking about. 'It could be a few weeks.'

'That's cutting it fine, Danny. I can't apply for a licence renewal with my door security being run by a murder suspect.'

'I understand, and I've spoken with Mike about the contract. I know where you're going with this.'

'Don't get me wrong, Danny. You've done a great job since you took the door. But I have to put my business first. And it takes time to find good door companies.'

By now our gazes were locked on each other, the subject under discussion important to us both.

'What would help you feel reassured about the matter?'

'Nothing, while you've got a murder charge hanging over you.'

'But if I tell you that'll all go away. How long can you give us?'

'I'm not sure I can answer that. It's not just-'

He squirmed in his seat as he said it. I thought I knew why. I said, 'Can we talk straight?'

'Haven't we always?'

It was my turn to ignore it. 'I asked you the other night about the contract, and you said it's still mine.'

'Yes, but that was before-'

'Apart from what's happened, were you being honest?'

'What do you mean? Why wouldn't I be honest?'

For a second I debated whether to push. Then I thought, *What have I got to lose*? 'Is Yashin putting the screw on you?'

He began to redden. 'Yashin? What makes you think-'

'Frank, we're supposed to be talking straight. Is he putting the screw on you, yes or no?'

He closed his eyes, let out a sigh. 'Yes.'

'Tell me.'

'He's threatened that if I don't sell out to him, Midnight's will burn. So will Charmaine's, and Dexie's.'

I nodded, not surprised. 'What've you said to him?'

'At first I tried holding out, hoping he was bluffing. But-' His head dropped.

'What's happened?'

'Last Thursday, my youngest, Lily, came home from school scared out of her wits. On her way home a couple in a black Mercedes SUV stopped her to ask directions. Afterwards they followed her the rest of the way. She said they spoke with Russian accents. From her description they sounded like one of Yashin's men and the blond bimbo... What's her name?'

'Sasha.'

'That's her. I tell you Danny, it scared the shit out of me. Since I got into the club business I've had the odd threat and bits of trouble here and there. But no one's ever threatened my family before. I've run clubs for fifteen years and I've met some people, but none of them hold a candle to Yashin. He makes Morris look like an amateur.'

I nodded. It wasn't far from what Carver had said. But I still needed more.

'Tell me about Charnley. What's he up to?'

Frank looked even more sheepish. 'He approached me a few weeks ago. He said I'd be needing a new door outfit in the coming months and that he would give me a good rate. I tried telling him I was quite happy and there wasn't a problem but he kept saying, 'Not yet, but there will be.' Not long after, Yashin made me his first offer.'

'Is it a fair one?' Though I knew the answer.

He gave a sort of snorting sneer. 'Let's put it this way. It isn't one I'd normally be inclined to accept. Not until last week at any rate.'

'Before Yashin, were you looking to sell?'

'Not particularly. Okay, things are hard, with the recession and all, but we're holding our own compared to a lot of clubs. I was hoping to ride it out until things picked up. But now-'

Suddenly, like a deck of cards, he collapsed. His head went down and I saw the veneer he wears as Mr Midnight disappear. In the space of a single second he was the carpet warehouse salesman I sometimes saw him as, and a scared one at that. When he lifted his head to look at me, his face was etched with worry. He appealed to me.

'What can I do Danny?'

I looked at the ceiling. *Jesus*. 'Why didn't you tell me what was going on, Frank? You pay me to look after your security for fuck's sake.'

The sheepish look again. 'I'm sorry. I should have done. It was just that- I felt like I was trapped, that if I'd said something to you he'd have carried out his threat and firebombed the place.'

'And you think I'd let that happen?'

He shrugged. 'How could you stop him?'

I shook my head. 'Christ, Frank. How the hell did you ever get into this business? More to the point, how have you managed to stay in it this long? Haven't you ever heard of fighting fire with fire?' Then I added, 'Okay, bad choice of words but you know what I mean.'

He looked sad. 'Yes I have, and I know that's what you're trying to do now. But look what's happened to Eric. That's what comes of fighting fire with fire.'

I gave him a long look. 'For someone whose been around so long, you've got a lot to learn Frank.'

'How do you mean?'

'Eric wasn't the result of fighting fire with fire. Eric was just an early spark. We haven't even begun to fight yet.'

He stared at me. 'Are you planning something?'

I took a deep breath. 'I was thinking I might have to. Listening to you, I'm certain of it.'

'So what are you going to do?'

'Better you don't know.'

'But what do I tell Yashin?'

I thought about it. 'What's your timescale?'

'He's looking for me to accept his offer by the end of this month.'

'Two weeks. That's not a lot of time.'

'To do what?'

'Whatever it takes.'

He shook his head. 'I don't know, Danny. What if-'

'Leave it with me Frank. When it comes to threats, especially when they involve kids, I'm right at home.'

'But-'

'But nothing. This is my department. And one other thing.'

'What?'

'I'm putting Winston back on the door. As of tonight.'

He looked like he was about to question it so I said, 'There's a reason.'

He nodded. 'Okay.'

## CHAPTER 37

I was on my way to meet with my team when I bumped into Vicki coming along the corridor. She'd just come in and was on her way to check the Green Room. Looking her brightest best again in one of those sexy-but-smart jersey dresses that show off every curve, you'd never have known what she'd been through. The mark on her cheek was disguised under her make-up so you'd have had to know it was there to see it. And for all the words we'd had over Vincent, as she slowed down to speak to me, my heart beat a little faster.

'How are you?' she said. She seemed genuinely concerned.

'I'm okay.' I thought it appropriate so I asked ' How's Vincent?'

'Coming along. They're talking about letting him out tomorrow.'

'I'm glad to hear it.'

'Are you?' For a moment I thought she was going to start on me again but then I saw what I thought was a bit of a teasing look which gave me hope.

I pinned her with a look. 'Whatever you may think of me, I don't like hurting people.'

The way she regarded me, eyes narrowed, I felt like I was in front of some X-ray machine. She shook her head.

'What?' I said. 'Don't you believe me?'

A wan smile. 'I want to Danny, but- It's just-'

'What?'

She checked around. We were still alone. 'When I was young, my father- He-' I waited. 'He-'

'You don't have to tell me,' I said.

She wafted a hand. *Another time.* She changed tack. 'Anyway, then I made the mistake of marrying a man who likes violence.' I nodded, letting her tell it at her pace. 'When I came to work here and first met you, I used to think you were another who liked violence. Then over the weekend I thought, hoped, I might be wrong.' I waited, knowing now where it was going. 'The other day, when I saw what you did to Vincent-' I winced inside. 'I thought my first impressions were right after all. And now-'

I couldn't stop myself. 'Now, what?'

'Now I don't know what to think.' She gave me the look again. 'You're a strange guy Danny. People say you're not what you seem.'

I wanted to ask, which people? How do I seem? But I managed to keep my mouth shut.

She gave another head-shake. 'I guess there's only one way to find out.'

'What's that?'

What she did next nearly sent me into orbit. Stretching up on tip-toe she closed her eyes, put her lips to mine and kept them there. It wasn't so much a kiss, as a contact. It was like she was saying, 'Now what are you going to do?' I was so surprised, so scared of doing the wrong thing, I did the only thing I could. Nothing.

After a few seconds her eyes opened. Our lips were

still touching. I felt like a rabbit caught in headlights. I felt her lips move as her look changed to a puzzled frown. She dropped back onto her heels, stared up at me.

I had to say something so I said, 'Did that tell you anything?'

'Not really.'

I nodded, though I'm not sure why. 'I'd like to talk to you sometime, if you'll listen.'

'I'll listen.'

'Later, maybe?'

She thought about it. My heart thumped. Torture.

'Okay.'


I went straight from seeing Vicki, to the staff room where I'd arranged to brief the team. Thinking back, I wouldn't be surprised if they all thought I was high on something as I went through what I wanted them to do that night and over the weekend. I'm usually pretty laid-back when I brief. I prefer to keep things low-key, so people don't get the wrong idea. It's easy to get carried away when you talk about dealing with people in situations that may involve getting physical. It's not like you see on TV or films where the SWAT Team Leader works them all up to a frenzy of chest-thumping excitement before sending them out to deal with situations that, in reality, call for cold, precise judgement and clear thinking. Start talking about 'taking people out,' or, 'putting them down' and you're asking for trouble. But that evening, I kept having to rein myself in as I outlined the possibilities we might face and how I wanted them to deal with situations that could arise. As I spoke I kept seeing glances passing between them. Winston was there of course, but apart from welcoming him back I didn't pick him out for any special task. That would all come later. When I was finished I said 'Any questions?'

They all looked at each other, but all that came back was a chorus of 'No's and 'Okay's, apart from Eve who said, 'I s'pose its too late to put in for leave?' Then they all went off to their posts to wait and see what the night would bring.

The police turned up around nine, led by Carver, accompanied by Jess. By now everyone knew the drill and my team left them to do their thing, handing out appeal leaflets, speaking to customers, giving reassurance where it was needed. Not that there's much of that you can give when there's a nut-case killer on the loose and you've no idea where, when or how he'll strike next. Apart from a quick word with Carver when he first arrived we didn't speak much - we both had things to attend to - though his cryptic, 'I could do with a word later. Something I need to run past you,' left me wondering. I found out an hour later when he caught me in the office as I was changing a duff radio battery.

'That quick word?' he said.

'Go.'

'This theory of yours, about all the victims being good dancers.'

'What about it?'

'Jess and I have been giving it some thought. We think there may be something in it.'

'Okay.'

'We'd like to try something.'

'Such as?'

260

'Running bait.'

'What sort of bait?'

'So far the killer seems to be sticking with the bigger clubs. Stacy's, YoYo's, here.'

'Right.'

'We're thinking, if we could pick out one or two girls in each club who are known for their dancing, bring them in, give them a brief and let them do their thing. Then when they leave the club we put them under surveillance and follow them home to see what happens.'

'When you say, 'what happens' I take it you mean you hope the killer might have a go at them and you'll jump out and arrest him, right?'

'Something like that. What do you think?'

'I think it's a good idea. When are you thinking of starting?'

'Right away. The sooner the better.'

'I agree.'

'So. Who can you suggest for here?'

'Now you're asking, but I'm not sure that's my department. You're probably best speaking with the likes of Tony, or maybe Mickey, the DJ. They'd know better than me.'

Carver looked pained. 'I'd rather keep all this as tight as possible. The fewer who know about it the better. Can't you think of anyone?'

I gave it some thought. Truth was there were a couple of names I could have thrown at him, but though they had what was needed in the dancing department, I couldn't imagine either managing to keep their involvement with the police quiet for more than, oh, about thirty seconds.

'Anyone?' Carver prompted.

I was about to tell him I'd think abut it and get back to him when Vicki came in.

'Just who we need,' I said. 'Vicki will know. '

'What?' she said.

I let Carver outline his plan, though he went overboard giving me credit for coming up with the 'dancer' theory in the first place, I don't know why. When he finished I said, 'We were talking about who we could use here, but I'm struggling to come up with anyone off the top of my head.'

'No problem. I know the ideal person.'

We both brightened and together said, 'Who?'

She smiled. 'Me.'

I guess the way we both froze and said nothing for what must have seemed to her like an age, told her something was wrong.

When I looked at Carver he was looking at me in a way I had no trouble reading as, *Your shout.* He had seen how I was  when I thought she'd been taken. He wasn't about to say anything until he'd heard what I had to say. It probably came as no surprise when I shook my head.

'No.'

'WHOA,' Vicki said, grabbing my arm so I had to look at her. 'What do you mean, 'No'? What's wrong with me?'

I looked at Carver. I had no qualms about putting him in a bind on this one. Not after what I'd been through the last two days. Payback time. I glared at him. *Back me up on this, or...*

'There's nothing wrong with you, Vicki,' Carver said. 'And thanks for offering. But I think maybe we'd be better with one of the regular girls. It's less likely to arouse any suspicions.'

Not bad for spur of the moment, I thought.

But Vicki wasn't for having it. 'What's the difference? And why should the killer be suspicious just because it's me? If he's into dancers, he's into dancers. I work here and I'd prefer that I take any risk than you approach one of the girls. They're supposed to be our customers.'

I turned an imploring look on Carver. *Think of something for God's sake. Tell her you won't allow it.*

'We-ell,' he said. He glanced at me.

*Don't you fucking dare...*

'I don't know. What do you think Danny?'

I stared at him. *Bastard.* I turned to Vicki. I was remembering her reaction the last time we spoke about her dancing, knew I needed to be careful. I took a deep breath. 'I agree with him. If it's you, the killer may think something's going on and go elsewhere. Better you stay out of it. Besides, you've got your own work to do.'

'Bullshit. You just don't like the idea of me getting up on the podium.'

'It's not that. I just happen to think we'd be better off with someone else.'

'Like who? Go on, suggest someone.' She stood there, glaring at me, her face reddening. I was aware she was tapping a foot. I had to come up with a name.

'Jade what's-her-name. She's a good dancer.'

Vicki looked incredulous. '*Jade?*' She guffawed. 'You must be joking. Ask her to do something like this and before you know it, it'll be all over Facebook.'

'Okay, Maxine then.'

She didn't even reply to that one. She just stood

there, looking unimpressed. Eventually she shook her head. 'Get real Danny.'

'Well you suggest someone. There's got to be someone here can do the job.' I was beginning to feel desperate, probably sounded it.

'There is. I told you. Me.'

I turned away, chewing my lip and took a deep, calming breath. When I turned back, they were both staring at me, waiting. Carver said, 'I hate to say it Danny, but I think she may be right.'

I looked at the ceiling.

*FUCK.*

The conversation we'd arranged to have 'later' never materialised. Whether she was pissed at my objection to her volunteering, or whether we both sensed that maybe we needed to cool off before we spoke again I wasn't sure - both, probably. After Carver's less-than-helpful turn-around I had tried putting up a fight, but even as I groped for reasons why it was a bad idea to use Vicki - *Who'll cover the VIPs?* 'Miranda.' - *You're not paid to dance.* 'I'm sure Frank won't object.' - I sensed the ground sliding from under me. Eventually I had no choice but to cave. 'Fine,' I said. 'If it's what you want to do, then get on with it.' I turned to Carver one last time, and this time my finger was in his face. 'You better make sure this is done right, or so help me, I'll-' That was when I thought I better go and do my rounds, and left them to talk about what they needed to talk about.

I spent the rest of the night keeping busy with other things and trying to keep out of her way. Those times I did see her - when she came in with her VIPs, a local girl group that had done well on some TV talent show, and then later, having a coffee with Frank up in the lounge - I pretended I'd forgotten all about our little difference of opinion and had moved on. I suspect I wasn't particularly convincing.

Apart from our dispute, the rest of the first part of the night went more or less as planned. Numbers were still down but Carver got up and made his appeal again. Unlike the previous Saturday, it was met only with sombre silence. I was next to Frank when he did it. He wasn't happy.

'There's a limit to how much of this people will take. They come here looking for a good time, not to be scared shitless.'

And though I didn't like the sentiment behind his remark, I couldn't fault his reasoning.

As it happened, Yashin and his guys didn't show that night and despite me geeing my team up to stay alert, the night passed off without incident, apart from the usual bits and pieces. I did get to spend some time alone with Winston, talking things over, sounding him out. He said he would put out feelers and come back to me.

'We're on a really tight timescale with this, Winston,' I reminded him as he rose to get back on the door.

'Wit' you, Baasss. Leave it wit' me.'

I also kept an eye out for Elvis, intending to apologise for spoiling his fun. But he didn't come in that night. Strange.

By closing-up time, Vicki had already gone and, unusually for me, I could hardly wait to get off home. For once I went straight to bed, though I can't say I slept well.

## CHAPTER 38

*Friday*

The next morning, Laura and I finally managed to get down to Stoke to see Dad. Grant stayed at my house, working on his laptop.

As we walked up Dad's path, Alison-next-door made a point of coming to the window to adjust her curtains. I couldn't ignore her so I nodded and gave what I hoped was no more than a neighbourly smile. The way she didn't return it but just stared out at me made me wonder if she could be a bit of a stalker which, the way the week had gone so far, would be about par.

Dad was okay but I could tell he was anxious as to why we'd both come to see him.

'Is it about your Mother? Has something happened?'

'No, Dad,' Laura said. I could see she was shocked by the change in him in the three months since her last visit. 'Mum's been gone four years now, remember? I've just come to see how you are.'

'That's nice. I have to say, you're looking well, our Laura. Isn't she Dan? You married yet?'

'No Dad, I'm not married.'

'Engaged?'

'No, I'm-'

'Not even a boyfriend?'

'As I was about to-'

'You should have a boyfriend, a nice girl like you.' He nodded at the photographs on the wall. 'You've your mother's looks. You should be making the most of them. Clock's ticking if you're going to give us a grandson. How old are you now, our Laura? Twenty-four, five?'

'Thirty-six, Dad.'

'Thirty Six? You sure? You better get a move on. The way you're going you'll end up having to adopt, won't she Dan?'

'Dead right, Dad.'

As Laura turned to me, I gave her my sweetest smile. It said, *Now's your chance to ask him about putting the house in trust and him moving into a home.*

We stayed a couple of hours. He made a pot of tea and we ended up watching a recorded episode of CSI that I'd already seen half-a-dozen times. He used the oxygen a couple of times while we were there, but only after he made himself breathless by insisting he go out to the kitchen to get us some biscuits. On the way back, Laura barely spoke. An hour after arriving back home, she and Grant were packed and a taxi was at the end of the path.

As I bent down so she could kiss my cheek, I saw that her eyes were glassy. 'I'll call you twice a week,' she said. 'To see how he is.' I nodded. 'And I'll try and get up every other weekend and see him.'

'He'd like that.'

As the taxi disappeared I set myself a mental reminder to get something to give her the next time I saw her. For Christmas.

The Friday night was set to be much the same as Thursday, although Carver and his team weren't due as they were doing Stacey's that night. That afternoon I'd had a message off Carver confirming that Jess had met with Vicki and some girls from a couple of the other clubs and briefed them on the details of what would happen when they left to go home. I wasn't part of it and didn't want to be, though I couldn't stop thinking about the what-ifs. I just hoped to God that Carver had worked everything through properly. I knew that Vicki had already squared her dancing with Frank - and through him, Mickey the DJ. Her story was that seeing as her previous appearance had gone down so well, she wanted to keep it going for a while - in the interests of encouraging the punters. Frank had asked her how I was with it and when she told him I'd not objected, he was very much in favour.

One good thing. Eric showed up, right arm in plaster from wrist to elbow. Despite what I'd said in the hospital about getting back soon, I tried telling him he ought to be at home, but got nowhere.

'I can cover the cameras, if nothing else,' he said. Which suited me fine. Eric's a whizz on the CCTV.

During the early part of the evening, Vicki and I managed to not bump into each other any more than we had to. When we did, neither of us said much beyond mumbled words about, 'Having to speak sometime,' though neither of us tried to pin it down. Still, I asked her about her role in Carver's plan.

'You sure about all this?'

Her response was an impatient, 'I'm a grown woman Danny. If I wasn't sure, I wouldn't be doing it.' I didn't take it further.

Truth was, for all that I'd lain awake most of the previous night rehearsing what I'd say to her when we did eventually get together - as I hoped we still would - as the weekend loomed my focus was increasingly elsewhere. Specifically it was on Yashin. Where he was, what he was up to, what he was planning. And though looking back I hate to admit it, the fact that girls were being abducted, raped and murdered, wasn't at the forefront of my mind as much as it perhaps should have been.

That changed just after eleven o'clock when Vicki appeared for her first podium session. I tried not to look, but couldn't stop myself. Big mistake. As I watched her go through the routine she'd rehearsed with Mickey-the-DJ that afternoon, and saw the crowd responding as they had the previous Tuesday, I had a flashback. Suddenly all the worry and fear I'd gone through that night swooped back in and I found myself experiencing something close to another panic attack. I had to leave the floor and go outside for some fresh air and to slow my breathing. I remember thinking there was no way I was going to able to go through this night after night and that something better happen soon or I'll be a basket case.

I'd just returned inside when Eric radioed for me to come to the office. I found him and Winston staring at the main screen.

'Winston clocked these two at the door,' Eric said, pointing.

I came round to see the camera on the Dusk-Till-Dawn bar zoomed in on two men I'd never seen before. Swigging from bottles of Bud, they were tall, dark and swarthy. They had buzz-cuts and were wearing black leather jackets.

Winston said, 'It was da accents I picked up on, when dey was at the box office. One o' dem East-Europe places. Could be Russian, though they all sound the same to me.'

'What're they about?' I said.

'Not clubbing, that's for sure.' Eric said. 'See the way they're clocking everything? They've been doing that since they came in.'

As I peered in close, I could see them looking in all directions, heads turning first this way, then that, with each sweep.

'Where've they been so far?'

'Up to the Early Hours, then they did a circuit of the floor before coming back here. I think they're clocking the cameras. Probably doing a head count on us as well.'

'Hmm. Things are quiet at the moment. Tell the extra staff we put on to make their way to the staff room and stay there. Tell them to do it quietly, so no one notices.' I turned to Winston. 'Well spotted, Win.' Then to Eric, 'Let me know when they've gone.'

I made my way back to the front entrance and stayed there, backing up Eve and Chris. Less than twenty minutes had passed when Eric's voice in my ear called my name. 'Looks like our visitors have seen what they came to see. They're heading for the front. Out in about ten seconds.' Chris was across the lobby nearest the main entrance. I nodded to him, *Outside*. He returned the nod and went out.

It was the busiest time of the night on the door so I made sure I was paying attention to the entrance queue with Eve when the pair came through the doors and into the lobby. They didn't hang around but went straight out. I waited a minute then joined Chris. 'Where did they go?'

'Round the corner onto the car park. There was a black four-by-four waiting with its engine running. They jumped in and it went off towards Winwick.'

I nodded. 'Shout up if it, or they, come back.'


Ten minutes later, bang on midnight, I was still in the lobby when Yashin's black Mercedes limo pulled up out front. First out were Misha and Sasha - who I now saw in a different light since hearing Frank's story about Lily. Alexei was next, doing his Personal Protection thing, looking stern and checking around for ninja-assassins or whatever he looks out for, before leaning back into the car to tell his boss it was safe to come out. Then came Yashin himself. He paused only to link arms with the women either side before striding, confidently, towards the door. In the early days I'd tried pointing out that if he was worried about his personal security, a quiet entry through the back door was a safer bet, but he ignored it, preferring a big entrance that made people ask, 'Who's that?' I positioned myself just inside the front door, where I'd be the first person he'd see.

As he came in his gaze stopped wandering and fixed on me. The smile never wavered as he said, 'Good evening Mr Norton. Everything is well with you I trust?'

Since the attack on Eric, I'd thought of several super-cool things I could come out with at our next meeting. I'd even spent time imagining myself squaring up to him and either saying something so chilling he'd turn pale, or showing such a casual disregard over what had happened it would make him think that maybe this time he'd bitten off more than he could chew. Like James Bond does when he meets his arch adversary for the first time. But when the moment came, I settled, as I'd always known I would, for a rock-steady stare, and a pointed, 'I'm good, thanks.'

He waited a second, like he was expecting more. When it didn't come he turned towards the door leading up to the suites. 'Perhaps you wouldn't mind asking Mr Johnson to come up and see me, when he has a moment?'

He didn't wait for a reply and I didn't give one. But as Alexi went ahead of him I noted a large bruise on his right cheek and that he seemed to have suddenly developed a limp. I remembered the man on the bridge Gol had put down and who couldn't decide whether to hold his arm, leg or head.

As the party disappeared upstairs Eve materialised at my shoulder.

'One day, I'm going to have that bastard,' she snarled.

I turned to her. 'You'll have to wait in line.'

Her dark eyes sparkled under the lights. 'I can live with that.'

I went to tell Frank he'd been summoned.


Like the night before, the rest of the evening was routine. For the first time I could remember, the rest of Yashin's retinue didn't show and he spent the night up in his suite with only the two women and Alexei for company. I read it that after the thing on the bridge, he wanted to avoid exposing his usual party guests to possible trouble, though as far as Yashin himself was concerned and until next time it was, 'business as usual.' It was the 'next time' bit that was keeping me occupied.

Through Eric and the team, I kept in touch with what Vicki was doing and where she was at any given moment. I was aware that her dancing was the big talking point of the night, though it tended not to get mentioned when I was around. Even so I couldn't help picking up the odd passing remark, all complimentary, but usually couched in terms I preferred not to hear.

Later on I met with Frank in the office.

'What did Yashin want?' I said.

He gave a wary look. 'He's pressing. He talked about things getting worse and that I ought to think about getting rid of you.'

'What did you say?'

'I told him I had no reason to do that.'

'What did he say to that?'

'He said, I would, soon.'

After closing, I waited in the lobby to catch Vicki before she left for home. She'd arranged with her police observers that she'd walk into town and hail a taxi rather than using her car. It fitted better with the pattern of the victims, who had all been abducted after either leaving the club on foot or taking taxis. When she appeared and saw me waiting, she came over. She looked nervous.

'You okay?' I said.

'Yes.'

'I'm going to ask again. Are you sure you want to do this?'

Her lips tightened into a straight line and she took a deep breath as she nodded her reply. 'Yes.'

For all her previous confidence, I've seen fear enough times to recognise it. Dancing on a podium in front of a friendly crowd is one thing. Walking out into the night to put yourself up for grabs at the hands of a serial killer - police surveillance or not - is something else. As she turned for the door, I grabbed her arm firmly enough it would register.

'Anything. Anything at all. You call me.' I held her gaze for a long time.

Eventually she said, 'I will, ' then she was gone.

I remember how, watching her disappear out through the door that night, I was certain, absolutely cold-dead certain, that I was letting her go to her death. How I managed to stop myself from running after her, wrapping her up safe in my arms and taking her home with me right then, I'll never know.

# CHAPTER 39

The Man Who Likes To Watch knows he has to be careful. The first follow is always the most dangerous. Not knowing where they are headed, what their routine is, he has to be alert for anything untoward. Something that someone may remember, and which may later cause them to point in his direction. An unusual occurrence. An unexpected meeting. A sighting. Any of them, though innocent-seeming at the time, could stick in someone's memory enough that when later questioned, they may respond with, 'Come to think of it... there was something...'

He still remembers the near disaster with the black girl. What was her name, Donna? He is sure now she must have spotted him that very first night, trying to stay in the shadows as he followed her through the town. He can think of no other reason why, when he engineered the 'coincidental' encounter that is the oh-so-vital first step to what comes after, she rebuffed him so forcibly - and loudly. For days after, weeks even, he had worried that she may have thought the twin sightings of him suspicious enough to report it to the police. It was a long time before he stopped jumping every time the doorbell went. Even now, so long after, he has to be careful when ever he sees her, which he does fairly often around the clubs. There have been times when he has caught her looking at him with what seems to him open suspicion, as if she is placing him under the same sort of surveillance he once did her. His response on such occasions is to ignore her completely, in the hope that she will eventually be convinced that he has no real interest in her and that what happened was simply the coincidence it was supposed to be. He has, of course, thought about resolving the problem she represents another way. But he cannot be certain that she has not committed her suspicions to paper somewhere, or shared them with a friend. If she suddenly disappeared it could trigger an investigation which might lead to those suspicions coming to light, again putting him in the spotlight. Better just to leave her alone, and remember the lesson he took from that experience - if something does not go to plan, then walk away. There are after all, plenty of fish in the sea. Which brings him back to his present 'fishing' expedition.

He is surprised by the route the girl is taking, through the centre of town. He thought she normally comes to work by car, though that may be old information. He cannot even be sure she is heading home. For all he knows, she may be heading to another rendezvous. Maybe to meet someone, another club even. So he follows, quietly and waits to see where she will lead. As always at this time, Bridge Street is busy, thronged with clubbers either heading home or just lingering, seeking to stretch their night out as far as they can before their reserves of energy - and cash - deplete and they are forced to call it a night. He is conscious that many amongst them would recognise him if they saw him, so he keeps his hood pulled down low over his face as he matches his pace to hers.

But caution dictates he should not do so too long. People are alert for all sorts of things these days. A dark, hooded figure matching, exactly, the pace of a lone woman looking as she does, is the sort of thing someone may just notice. So he quickens his pace and, sticking to the side of the street furthest from her, passes her, making for the cross at the top of Bridge Street that marks the centre of town. It is a natural stopping place for many this time of night. There he can observe her approach and evaluate his options, depending on which course she takes from there. Forging ahead of her, he does not look back and resists the temptation to keep checking she has not diverted off somewhere, or changed her mind altogether about her chosen route and turned back.

Arriving at The Cross, he feigns interest in a men's clothing shop display window, before stepping into the recessed doorway where darkness enfolds him. From the shadows, he is free now to look through the shop's windows and down Bridge Street. She is still there, fifty yards away, marching along at the same pace she was before. As she comes, she ignores the whistles and occasional comments aimed at her by drink-fuelled groups of lads she passes and who hope in vain to grab her attention. Their amateurishness brings a smile to his face. If they only knew what he does, they would know how to grab a woman's attention in such a way that it stays grabbed.

He is wondering which way she may go when she arrives at the cross - there are four possible options, plus the taxis that wait in line, their 'for hire' signs lit - when something grabs his attention. As she passes Havana-

Fiestas, a couple who had seemed locked in the sort of passionate embrace many engage in towards the end of a good night out, break off suddenly to turn and follow her progress up Bridge Street in a way that is similar to what he is doing right now. After a short pause, they set off after her.

On the face of it there is nothing that marks the couple as different from any of the many others dotted around. A little older maybe than the average, but otherwise the same. Attractive, dressed in clubbers gear - him white shirt and black trousers; she, sparkly red dress and heels that add an extra three inches to her height. But what is noticeable, and what he focuses on is, that from having been clamped together like limpets moments before, now, as they follow in the girl's footsteps, they are not even holding hands. Also, their pace is now matching hers, the way his was before he decided it was time to move ahead. As he follows the couple's approach, ten yards or so behind her, he sees something that makes him take a further step back into the shadows. Lifting a hand, the man appears to press a finger to his ear. At the same time his lips move as if he is talking to someone other than his female companion.

Arriving at the cross, the girl stops, almost directly opposite him. If she were to look in his direction, she may even see him. But she does not. She seems to be waiting for something. Behind her, the couple have also stopped and are engaging in what seems a distinctly half-hearted imitation of their earlier embrace. After a minute or so, the girl sets off again, making her way towards the line of taxis to his left. Again, the couple behind part company. The girl approaches the taxi first in line, says something to the driver through the open window and gets in the back. Pausing only to check there is nothing coming up on his nearside, the driver pulls out and heads down Academy Way towards the Ring Road that is the route away from the Town Centre.

Now opposite the shop doorway, more or less where she stood moments earlier, the couple suddenly come to life again, he pressing a finger to his ear again while seeming to speak to some invisible party, she taking a mobile from her bag and making a call. Right now they look less like a loving couple, than a pair of professionals ringing into their office during a break in a meeting. For The Watcher, it is a telling moment. He waits, tense and alert for whatever will happen next. He does not have to wait long. A black Ford appears driving up Academy Way, towards the taxi rank. At The Cross it executes a U-turn and stops. A man sits next to the driver. Dressed casually, they nevertheless both have the clean-shaven look some still associate with police officers. The couple walk swiftly to it and get in the back, when it leaps forward and follows after in the wake of the taxi.

The Watcher waits to see if anything else happens that is out of kilter with what he regards as normal, early Saturday morning town centre activity. But there is nothing. Satisfied, he steps out of the doorway and crosses to where he can see down Academy Way, as far as where the road curves round to the left and he can see no more. Both the taxi and Ford are well-gone. He stands there for several moments, mulling over what he has just witnessed. To him, trained by having to research such things for his own ends, it had all the hallmarks of an organised surveillance. And he can think of only one reason why the girl might be the subject of something like that.

As he turns away to retrace his route up Bridge Street, he allows himself another smile - a knowing one this time. *Clever.* But he is not discouraged. In fact he is almost excited as he retraces his steps of earlier. His brain is already working away on how he should respond to this new development and what sort of change of strategy will be needed to lure her into his clutches at a time when her own watchers will not be around.

## CHAPTER 40

*Saturday Morning*

I spent the first half-hour after Vicki left, up in the Early Hours Bar with Eric, downing whiskey, though Eric insisted on taking my car keys before letting me have my first. The team would see me home.

At one stage my mobile buzzed and I grabbed at it like a drowning man grabbing a lifeline. But it was only a text from Laura telling me she had finally arrived home after a nightmare train journey. I didn't reply, and went back to the whiskey. Some time after three it buzzed again. This time it was from Vicki. The message read.

'Home ok. No probs.'

I let out a long breath, and downed the rest of my whiskey. I closed my eyes.

'You okay?' Eric said.

I stood up.

'Who's driving me?'

On the way home, with Eve driving, I replied to Vicki's text.

'Glad ur safe.'

I thought about adding an, 'x' but decided against.

When I woke, late Saturday morning, the first thing I did was ring Cliff Kehoe. Cliff's an old mate of mine. He and his brothers have contracts for doors all over Liverpool. They're a bigger outfit than we are, but we run things along similar lines and we've helped each other out the odd occasion we've needed a lift.

Cliff listened while I explained what I needed.

'How many?' he said when I'd finished.

'Six,' I said. He didn't hesitate, as I knew he wouldn't.

'Okay.'

Before I rang off I said, 'And Cliff?'

'What?'

'They need to be good.'

'If they work for me, they're good.'

As I hung up I gave a wry smile. It was what I'd said the last time we helped each other out.

Next, I thought to try and take my mind off things by catching up on my OU work. I needed to make some sort of effort 'cause earlier in the week I'd had an email off Angela, my personal tutor, pointing out I was falling well behind with assignments. But I was only an hour into it and still trying to get my head round what 'Heart of Darkness' was all about when Carver rang asking for a meet. I jumped at the chance. Being Saturday, the Tesco car park would be busy so we met out at The Swan With Two Nicks - an olde-worlde country pub the other side of Lymm.

I found Carver tucked away at a corner table with a bloke I'd never seen before. About Carver's age and with greying hair that flicked up off his collar at the back, his thick-framed glasses and brown cord jacket put me more in mind of a teacher than a cop. Carver introduced him as 'Will' and said he worked for the NCA, the National Crime Agency, which I'd heard much about but had no real idea what they did.

Carver told me Will 'had an interest' in Yashin, but didn't give any details. Over the next hour and a pub lunch that Carver paid for, Will listened mainly in silence as I told him what I knew of Yashin's present and intended involvement in Midnight's. I included the events of the past week and Frank's tale about what had happened to Lily. Will seemed particularly interested in Yashin's hangers-on - women and men - even going so far as to get me to describe each one as their names cropped up. The fact he wasn't taking notes made me wonder if the conversation was being recorded, which wasn't a problem as far as I was concerned.

As we talked, I had the impression Will was as concerned as Carver over the possibility that Yashin might get a foothold in the clubs. Every now and then I'd say something and a glance would pass between them. Will clearly knew more about Yashin than he was prepared to let on and a couple of times I was tempted to ask. But at the end of the day it was clear that, like Morris and his ilk, Yashin was just another gangster, though maybe nastier and therefore more dangerous than most. It didn't matter to me where he was from or how he'd got to be what he was, or what else he was into. My concern, plain and simple, was to keep him out of Midnight's by any means possible. Which brought us to Winston.

At this point Will smiled - the first since we'd shook hands. 'Ah yes. The famous, Winston.'

'You know Winston?'

'Let's just say I'm familiar with his brothers.'

The way he said it, I got the impression there was another story there as well. But again, none of my business. I turned to Carver. 'Have you told him what we talked about?'

It drew a pointed, 'Oh yes.' Will just nodded.

'So?' I said. 'What do you think?'

There was a silence during which the two of them looked at each other in a way that made me feel a bit like a marriage guidance counsellor - not that I've ever met one. I knew what was going on. Carver was waiting to see what Will thought about me. Eventually Will gave a nod, before leaning forward, elbows on the table. Carver and I did the same. It felt a bit like we were in some spy movie. I half expected him to look over his shoulder to see who may be listening, but all he did was take a long deep breath.

'These people of yours. What do you call them? The A-Team?'

'What about them?'

'How reliable are they?'

'They're the best.'

He looked sceptical. 'Really?'

'Really.'

He looked at Carver again, then back at me. 'Let's hope so.'

He began talking. This time I did most of the listening.


It was after six and I was at home getting ready to go to work when Carver rang back with two bits of information. The first was to confirm that Will had rung back to confirm his interest in what we'd talked about and would take it forward, which was good news. The second was to do with the murders.

'We've found a girl who lives over the field from where Naomi Wright's body was found. She says she was walking home in the early hours the night Naomi was killed and she heard music coming from that direction. She says she recognised it as something called the Adagio? Apparently it's popular around the clubs.'

'The Adagio For Strings,' I said. 'It's a remix of some classical music. It's become a bit of a dance anthem. It gets the crowd going. The kids love it.' Then I added, 'She's a bit late coming forward isn't she? Wasn't Naomi one of the early victims?'

'Second, actually. Apparently the girl mentioned it to a friend but has been scared to come forward in case her name ended up in the papers. Her friend's been trying to talk her into it and she finally rang us yesterday after all the publicity about Agnes.'

Agnes. Suddenly a mental image formed of her, surrounded by a crowd of fist-pumping clubbers as she lost herself in the piece's pounding electronic rhythms. 'I've just thought, 'I said. The Adagio was one of Agnes's favourites.'

'Is that right?

'Might it mean something?'

'I don't know. Maybe. I'll bear it in mind.'

'Anything else?'

'I didn't mention it in the pub earlier, but your girl did well last night. I've got to say she's bloody brave, putting herself forward like this.'

'I know, but do me a favour.'

'What's that?'

'Don't refer to her as My Girl.'

'Sorry. I thought-'

'Yeah, well... I just don't think she'd like it.'

'Okay. Anything I can do in that direction...?'

'If it's all the same to you, I'd rather not have the police trying to sort out my private life, if you know what I mean?'

'Point taken.'

'What's happening tonight?'

'Jess and I are going round the clubs. No doubt we'll see you some time.'

'Right.'

After he rang off, I rang Winston. He listened while I told him about my meeting with Carver and 'Will'.

'I need to speak with my brothers,' he said. 'I'll ring you back.'

Ten minutes later he came back on to say they'd come to the club that night, to talk, which was what I'd hoped would happen.

As I finished getting ready for work, I couldn't get the Adagio out of my head. When Carver first mentioned it, a thought, some connection, had flashed into my mind, but hadn't stayed. Now, the more I tried to retrieve it, to focus in on it, the further it seemed to drift away. Finally I gave up. Things like that tend to come once you stop thinking about them.

But I kept humming the damn tune all the way into work.

# CHAPTER 41

*Saturday Evening*

When I got to the club, Eric was already there, playing with the CCTV, checking the cameras. As I dumped my bag I said, 'Is it all working okay?'

'Fine, why?'

I explained what I'd arranged with Cliff Kehoe.

When I'd finished, he simply turned back to the screens. 'Better get practising then.' Then he added, 'By the way, Vicki's already in.'

'Right.' I left him to it and went about my business. For once it didn't include her.

I found Frank and Tony out on the dance floor, talking. They clammed up when I arrived. I played it like it was a normal Saturday night and stuck to the routine, numbers, guests, that sort of thing. None of us mentioned Russians, murders or Vicki's dancing, which suited me. Nor did I mention anything about the matters I'd discussed with Cliff and Eric.

I'd told my guys - A-Team and Rota - to come in early again to be briefed and I made sure I was in the staff room when they all arrived within ten minutes of each other. Before we started I made sure the door was locked. I didn't want Tony-the-Manager interrupting.

This wasn't for his ears. As the briefing went on and it became clear why, faces lit up with excitement.

'Let's not get carried away,' I said. 'If it happens we need to stay cool.'

There were several mutterings of the 'Roger Boss' variety, before I let them go off to do what they had to do.

Last thing before the doors opened, a few minutes before nine, I grabbed Chris and went out into the foyer and spoke with Amy and Perdita, the two girls working on Admissions that evening. I was particularly glad to see Perdita. She's sharp as a knife and as good as anyone I know at sussing people out. When I finished talking them through what I needed from them, I checked to make sure they understood. As if it were nothing unusual, they both nodded, light-heartedly, 'No probs,' before returning to what they'd been doing before I'd interrupted - dissing a girl who'd been sacked off the bar the week before after being caught with her hand in the till when it shouldn't have been.

As I was coming away, my mobile rang. It was Winston, asking if I could, 'Come to the back.' I made my way to the back door and out onto the car park. Winston was standing next to a big black Mercedes four-by-four. He waved to me and I joined him in the back where his brothers, Gabriel and Anthony, were waiting to give me the third degree.

As I expected, they were suspicious and wary. They were particularly interested in my meeting with Carver and 'Will', and I had to work at convincing them Carver could be trusted. After listening to what I had to say, Gabriel said. 'Give us two minutes.'

I got out and waited next to the car. I could hear the

brothers talking, not enough to make out the words but enough to tell there were matters on which they weren't entirely agreed. A minute later the door opened and Winston called me back in.

The moment I planted my backside on the cream leather seat, I found myself nose-to-nose with Gabriel.

'If you try to fuck wit us over this, in any way, then I don't care what your name is. It'll be the last thing you ever do.'

'I've given you my word Gabriel. I stand by it.'

'Alright then. Long as we knows where we stand,'

'We do.'

'Then me and Winston needs to speak. We'll see you aroun', Mr Norton.'

I left them to it.

As I headed back to the club, setting my shoulders against a cold night breeze I shook my head in wonder at the fact that after years of battling the dealers, here I was conspiring with two of the North's biggest. A case of the lesser between evils.

The next half-hour, I flitted between the door and the office. It was around ten and I'd just joined Eric, watching the cameras covering the foyer, when Perdita stood back and ran her hand back through her shining black hair in the way we'd agreed. A second later Chris came on the radio. 'Visitors, with Perdita, now.' But Eric was already zooming in on her. She was taking cash-notes from two men. Wearing open-neck shirts and without jackets, they looked lean, muscled and handy-looking. I didn't recall ever seeing them before, but checked with Eric just in case. Eric's got a photographic memory when it comes to faces.

He shook his head. 'New to me.'

As the pair turned away from the desk and headed for the doors to the dance floor, Eric switched cameras and caught them just as they were going in. He clicked on the mouse and took what he calls a 'screen-grab', showing them full-face. They were hard, lined and bore the odd scar. Not the usual, clubbers' faces. Another mouse-click and I heard the printer in the corner whir into action.

'I'm glad you know what you're doing,' I said.

'I've told you. If you'd bother to learn, it's not hard.'

I shook my head. 'Why have a dog and bark yourself?'

'Fuck off.'

Twenty minutes later I was checking on the queues out front with Gol when Chris shouted up again. 'Two more. With Amy.' By the time I returned to the office Eric had the print-outs laid alongside the previous pair. A couple more handy-looking lads I didn't recognise. I looked up to find Eric staring at me.

'I think you might've been right,' he said.

I nodded. 'I'm hoping I may still be wrong.'

From out in the corridor, I heard Tony's voice, approaching. 'Hide those,' I said to Eric. He slid the photos into a drawer just as Tony came into the office. Vicki was behind him and for all that my mind was focused on what I had to do next, I allowed myself a few seconds while I drank her in. If the mark on her face was still there it was even more well-disguised than the night previous. Her hair was done in a way that looked specially luscious, like she'd been to some swanky salon. She was wearing what I thought was a stylish off-the-shoulder dress. Silver-grey, it had a sparkly-satiny sheen, and though it wasn't as close-fitting as some I'd seen, it hugged enough curves to grab your interest.

Seeing me, Tony said, 'The very man. I've just been saying to Vicki that tonight perhaps we can-'

I held up a hand. 'Sorry, Tony. I'm in the middle of something. Speak with Eric.'

As I swerved around them to leave, I caught the look on Vicki's face - somewhere between suspicious and annoyed. Tony looked like he'd been snubbed.

Heading for the back door, I called Gol on the radio and told him to grab Eve and meet me in the staff room in two minutes. Then I dug out my mobile and rang a number. It answered at once and a man's voice said, 'Yo, Danny.'

'Looks like we're on. Back door.'

'One minute.'

The back door crash-bar was still playing up but I managed to get it open just as they arrived. There were six in all, as I'd agreed with Cliff. I recognised most of them. A tall and wiry chrome-dome by the name of Steve Welch was in front. I've known Steve a long time. He's one of Cliff's best. If he was mine, he'd be A-Team. No uniforms, they were all in their best clubbing gear.

As they filed through there was a chorus of, 'Awright Danny?'

I locked the door then led them through to the staff room where we met Gol and Eve and spent ten minutes going over things.

'Any questions?' I said as I finished.

There were a couple - mainly to do with 'disposal' - then I checked they all had earpieces that worked and told them to make their way out into the club in pairs. I returned to the office. Tony and Vicki were gone, thank God.

'We've four more,' Eric said. 'Just come in. A three and a one.' He thumbed behind him where the printer was whirring again. I went over and pulled off the images. The first showed three men entering together, the second, a man on his own. Four more faces, all with the same hard looks as the others. I wondered if they'd all served in the same unit some time.

'Eight in all,' Eric said as I returned to the screens. 'Enough to start a riot, don't you think?'

I nodded. 'More than enough.' I showed him the image of the one who'd arrived on his own. He seemed older than the others, heavier, thicker set. He had a calm, confident look about him that put me in mind of the likes of Cliff, or Eric, maybe even myself at times.

'Red Leader?' Eric said.

'I'd put money on it.' Red Leader is the designation we give to team leaders.

I checked the monitors. Three showed the two pairs and the three, now dispersed around different parts of the club. A fourth showed the team leader - if that was what he was - standing alone at the Dusk-Til-Dawn Bar. He was leaning back against the wall, scanning, not rushing to buy himself a drink.

'Can you track them all?'

'So long as they don't stray too far,' Eric said. He looked up at me. 'But it won't be easy.'

'No one said it was going to be easy.' I pointed to the fourth screen. 'If nothing else, stay on him.'

Eric nodded. 'I intend to.'

I gathered up all the print-outs. 'Do you need these?'

He tapped the side of his skull.

I left him playing with his controls and flicking between screens and returned to the main dance hall. Numbers seemed up compared to the night before. Not where they usually are on Saturdays, but not too far off. When all said and done, Saturday night is Saturday night. Gol and Winston were stood together just inside the doors, hands in front, watching as the floor filled up. I motioned them back out into the lobby where they could hear me. I showed them the photos and handed them to Gol.

'Clock these then pass them round to the others.'

Gol flicked through them, quickly. 'Eight? Bloody hell."

'Is that a problem?'

He showed his toothy grin. 'Nahhh.'

I went on patrol.

Because of her podium duties, Vicki had arranged for Miranda to be more involved looking after the VIPs. That night the guest DJ was a St Helen's lad who'd had a good run in the charts the last couple of years, though his star was starting to show signs it may be waning. Probably due to the tabloid reports about him smacking his Model girlfriend around. I caught him and Vicki just as they were about to enter the Green Room. Vicki saw me and hung back.

As I approached she said, 'Are you alright?'

'Fine,' I said. 'Why?'

'You look a bit.. serious. Is anything wrong?'

Given all that had happened I nearly gave a smart-Alec reply, but realised she was genuinely concerned. She doesn't miss much.

'No.' After a second I added, But-'

'But what?'

'If you see any signs of trouble tonight, anything at all, you get back in here right away and lock the door.'

She gave me an unconvinced look. 'You're expecting the killer might come after me here?'

'I'm not talking about that. I mean trouble on the dance floor.'

Her look changed. 'Oh.' Then, 'Is there anything I need to know?'

'Only that if you're on the podium, or anywhere around the floor and it kicks off, don't hang around. Get back here.'

This time she took it in. 'Okay.'

'And tell Miranda-'

'I will.'

'-But nobody else.'

She threw me a puzzled look. 'Why nobody else?'

'No reason. Just say you'll do it.'

'Okay.'

For a moment we stood there, looking at each other. I could feel myself bursting to tell her things. Lots of things. How gorgeous she looked, for one. That I was sorry for frightening her the way I'd done with Vincent - though I'd heard he was coming out of it. That I hated her being used as bait for a killer and that it was frightening me to death. That I needed, desperately, she should take care of herself. That how about we both take a week off and bugger off to Majorca.

Only now wasn't the time.

I headed back to the office to check in with Eric. He still had all the visitors within his sights, though one pair was tucked so far back in a corner, it was hard to see what they were up to.

'Not a problem,' Eric said. 'They can't go anywhere

from there. Besides, Steve and his crew are with them. Then he added. 'There's a lot of messaging going on, especially from this one.' He nodded at the screen showing the Red Leader. 'Like he's keeping tabs on them all.'

I leaned in for a clearer view. As before, the man at the bar was leaning back, relaxed, bottle in one hand, mobile in the other. Even as I watched he checked it, then started working his thumb. Seconds later there was activity on the other screens as the men responded to their phones' vibrations.

'They're all replying,' Eric said. 'This could be it.'

But after a minute or so of texting, they settled again.

'A bit early,' I said. 'And besides-'

'What?'

'The Russian isn't in yet.'

'You think he'll want to be here if, when, it happens?'

'Hell, yeah.'

For the next hour Eric kept me updated regarding the men's movements. By now all the team had seen the photographs. I'd also slipped copies to Cliff's man, Steve, to pass round his mates.

Yashin arrived with his usual fuss around half-eleven. As I followed his progress up to the suite on the screens, I turned to Eric. 'Where is everyone?'

He tapped the screen showing the pair tucked away in the corner. Behind them I could just make out Steve and some of his team behaving like normal punters. 'Steve's eye-balling these. Soon as they move they'll take them out and pass them onto our guys in the corridor.'

'I take it they've got ties?'

Eric nodded. 'Plenty.'

The official line is we don't use handcuffs. Strictly speaking, security staff aren't authorised to use them. Unofficially, most doormen usually make sure they've got some of those plastic zip-ties, the sort you can buy in DIY stores and garden centres. Easy to use and effective, you never know when they may come in handy.

'What about the others?'

Eric pointed to another screen, the one showing the three. 'Winston and Chris and a couple of our rota guys are keeping an eye on this lot. They'll delay them until Steve's done with the first pair, then they'll take them out as well.'

'Which will leave three-'

'Who we'll deal with ourselves.'

I threw him a look. 'We hope.'

He smiled. 'No problem.'

I turned to head back to the floor.

'Could be any time now. Stay sharp.'

'What? Like I was going to take a fucking nap?'

At the entrance to the dance floor I stopped to take in what was happening, starting with Eric's 'Red Leader.' I could still see him, over by the Dusk-Til-Dawn bar. He hadn't moved from there since he'd arrived. The area was crammed, mainly groups of lads but also punters - boys and girls - making their way to and from the bar. But while his body was facing the dance floor, his head was pointing away over his right shoulder, towards a huddle of four lads standing half way between the bar and the dance floor. Right now, they seemed to be taking all his attention. Swigging from bottles, they were doing what groups of lads in clubs do, checking out the talent, swapping laddish comments, voicing their fantasies in respect of whichever punter was, at that particular moment, pushing their buttons. I recognised two at least as regular Saturday-nighters, local lads in their twenties who, as far as I knew, had never caused trouble. Younger than our 'visitors', they would be easy meat for anyone wanting to start something.

Seconds later, I was proved right. Even as I watched, Red Leader stood up straight and turned away from the dance floor, towards the group of lads. Giving them one last look, he reached into his pocket, took out his phone and started thumbing.

I pressed my mic button. 'Eric? You with Red Leader?'

'Roger that,' Eric came back. 'Heads-up everyone. The Dusk-Til Dawn bar. We may be on.'

As Eric began issuing instructions and returning acknowledgements, I turned to scan the rest of the room. Across the other side of the floor Gol and Eve were finishing off giving the witch's warning to another couple of lads. On my way down, I'd heard over the radio that someone had reported some 'using' going on in the toilets. As I watched, Gol pressed his finger to his earpiece, listening in to Eric's commands. Turning, he saw me. The way he nodded at the two lads and shook his head, slowly, I knew they'd searched them and found they were clean, now. The policy is we look for supporting evidence before chucking people out. If we didn't, we'd never stop taking reports from pissed-off girlfriends trying to mix it for their wayward-eyed boyfriends. I gave a nod towards the bar. Gol nodded back and pulled at Eve's sleeve. They began to make their way round the edge of the floor. Descending the steps, I headed in the same direction.

## CHAPTER 42

By now, the place was bouncing like any other Saturday night. You'd never have guessed it was only a week since Agnes's murder. Mickey-the-DJ was in fine form and was doing a good job taking everyone's mind off the horrors they would be remembering a few hours from now. I wondered if it was because I was so focused that the music seemed even louder than usual, the dancing more frenetic. At that moment, the murders could have been happening in another town, another time.

As I watched, I remember having a weird feeling, almost like an out-of body experience. Suddenly I was as aware as I've ever been of how strange this job is. How it requires that you stay focused and calm in an environment geared towards scrambling your brain and making you as emotionally-charged as most people can stand. In that moment, and with a clarity I don't think I'd ever felt before, I saw how difficult - and dangerous - the job actually is.

Fuck me, I thought. I must be losing my bottle or something. But before I could worry about it further, Eric's voice sounded in my ear.

'They're all on the move, all heading for the D-T-D. Sierra One, can you stay on Red Leader?'

The reply came, 'Sierra One, Roger.'

Earlier, Eric and I had run possible scenarios. Assuming they were still unaware they'd been clocked - we'd seen nothing to suggest otherwise - our best guess was that they would rendezvous with their leader just in time to escalate whatever he was aiming to kick off. My plan was to be there and to deal with him directly. It all depended on timing. And ours needed to match theirs.

I was still about thirty yards away when Eric's voice sounded again. 'Crew Two striking.' Crew Two was Steve and his mates. At the same time I was aware of a sudden commotion in the crowd towards the back of the room, the area where they had been monitoring one pair of visitors. It lasted seconds then normality returned. A moment later Eric said, 'Pair One down and out.'

Okay, I thought. So far so good. At that moment the leader pushed himself away from the bar, picked up a glass of what looked like lager from the bar next to him and started towards the group of lads. As I headed for him, Gol and Eve joined from my right.

I was still yards away when the leader barged into the back of the lad nearest, hard enough to knock the bottle from his hand. It fell to the floor, spilling beer. I saw but couldn't hear his, 'What the fuck?' reaction. At the same time the leader dropped his glass, as if jarred by the impact. As the lad turned, still wearing an innocent expression, the leader shouted into his face. I still couldn't hear, but the way the leader was readying himself, his intention was clear enough. Behind the four lads I could see another pair of our visitors bearing down, arriving right on cue. The lad was saying something to the leader now, no threat as far as I could see, but more a, *'What're you about mate?'* query - the sort of response a lad not looking for trouble gives when first challenged. Red Leader was ready and came straight back with an angry tirade. This time I was close enough to catch the, '-FUCKING WANKER.' To my right I was conscious of bodies moving rapidly through the crowd, converging on the scene. I hoped it was Winston. If it was the other three, we could be in trouble.

As I neared, Red pulled his left arm back, fist balling, eyes focused on the lad he'd bumped. The spark that would ignite the fire. The lad's face changed as he realised he was in trouble. The fist shot forward, heading for the middle of the lad's face. It was six inches from its target when my fingers closed round the wrist behind it, pulling and diverting the blow into my chest. The attacker turned with it and just had time to register his surprise before my other hand closed on top of the first, pulling his fist even tighter into my chest and keeping it there. At the same time I took a step back with my right leg and bent forward from the waist. I felt the snap as something in his forearm gave, and he let out a scream of pain. I stood up again straight, bringing him up with me, then spun him round and away to where I hoped Gol and Eve were waiting to take him.

Looking through the group of lads - who were now spinning like tops, trying to keep abreast of what was happening all around them - I was relieved to see Winston's broad back. He, Chris and two rota-lads had formed themselves into a tight circle around the pair I'd last seen bearing down on the group. They must have got there just as I was dealing with the leader. The expressions on the pair's faces were of the, *'What the fuck's happening?'* variety. In my mind, an image formed as to what they'd have looked like a few short seconds earlier, about to launch themselves onto the group as their leader struck the first blow, only to find themselves suddenly surrounded by a group of doormen who'd appeared from nowhere. I turned to the lad who'd been the leader's intended victim. He was still spinning, looking from me, to his would-be attacker, to his mates and beyond them to the door staff who'd suddenly materialised next to them.

'What's going on?' he said.

'Nothing, now,' I said, giving him my best, Everything's-Under-Control smile. I turned to check Gol and Eve had the leader. They did. His face was racked in pain but, I could see his brain was still working enough that he was beginning to realise how his plan had come apart. I nodded to Gol, who turned to march him away, then did the same to Winston. Like a Roman Phalanx guarding the Legion's Eagle he, Chris and the others began shuffling the other pair towards the doors. I gave the lads one last nod. 'Have a great night lads,' and chuffed the arm of the one who'd nearly taken the hit, *You'll never know how close you came, sonny*. I walked away to the sound of their expressions of astonishment ringing in my ears.

'What was that all about?'

'Did you see what he just did?'

'Was that, *Danny Norton*?'

But for all that at that moment I was glad we'd managed to prevent some serious mayhem which would have seen blood on the dance floor and led to questions about DoorSec's competence - I wasn't about to crow. The man upstairs would not be happy to learn his plan had gone awry. It wasn't over yet.

I caught up with everyone in the staff room. We'd

arranged to take all the 'prisoners' there and, depending on how it had all gone, decide what to do with them. Sitting on their backsides, backs to the wall I found a line of pissed-off ex-militaries. But with their wrists cuffed behind and with Winston, Gol and Eve watching over them, they could be as pissed-off as they liked. They weren't a threat now. The only one on his feet was their leader, still wincing in pain and whose uninjured arm Gol had in his vice-like grip. The fly in the ointment was that Tony-the-Manager was there, looking like he was about to have a heart attack. Apparently he'd seen some of the commotion, wondered what was going on, and followed Steve's mob with some of the prisoners back there.

'What the fuck's going on, Danny?' he wailed as I came in. 'Who are they?' pointing at Steve and his crew. 'And who's this lot?' pointing at the Russians.

'I'll tell you later,' I said, not keen to get into the whys and wherefores when I still had things to do.

But Tony wasn't for having it. 'You're out of fucking control, Danny. Who do you think you are, the fucking SAS?'

At that point I nearly gave in to my instincts, but decided it would be undiplomatic. I turned to him and in the most even voice I could manage said, 'Tony, you may be able to tell that just at this moment we are dealing with a... situation. Perhaps you could come back later?'

For a moment he looked like he might explode, then turning, he stormed out through the door. His parting words were, 'Wait 'til Frank hears about this.'

I took a deep breath, turned to Gol. 'Right. Bring him.' Gol held up a mobile. It was buzzing like a bee.

'His?' I said, nodding at the leader. Gol nodded. I turned to Winston and the others, 'Wait quarter of an hour then let them out the back, in pairs. No rough stuff unless they piss about, then you can do as you like.' The way the prisoners responded, swapping wary looks, wherever they were from, most had no trouble understanding English.

As I made to leave with Gol and the leader, Eve said, 'Can I come?'

'Why not?' I said.

As we made our way towards the stairs, Vicki came into view, walking fast as her heels would allow.

'Tony's just collared Frank in the office. He looks well-pissed. What've you done now?' As she spoke, I could see her eyeing the man nestled between Gol and Eve, no doubt wondering why he was looking   so unhappy.

'We've just stopped a riot. Now I'm returning this one,' I thumbed behind me, 'To his boss,'

She didn't say anything but pointed up and let her face ask the question. I nodded.

Her response was a muttered, 'Oh, crap.'

'Do me a favour?' I said.

'What?'

'See if you can keep Frank in the office until I get back. If Tony winds him up, he'll want to do something. And whatever it is, it will be wrong.'

'I'll do my best.' She turned and headed back along the corridor. I loved her more than ever.

All the way up to the top corridor, the leader's mobile kept buzzing. Someone was ringing it, repeatedly. I could imagine who. Unusually, Alexei wasn't at his designated post. Crisis meeting, I thought.

At the door, I didn't knock or anything but went straight in. Yashin, Bergin and Alexei were in a huddle, all with phones to their ears. The women were over on the couch. The look on their faces, I could tell they were out of it. As the men looked round and saw us, the phones came down. A second later the mobile in Gol's hand stopped buzzing. I dragged the leader round to the front. Yashin's face was already turning puce.

'I believe this gentleman works for you.' I shoved him forwards. As he stumbled towards Yashin, he spat something back at me that I didn't understand. Making a last show of defiance I thought. So his boss may be minded to go more kindly on him. Fat chance.

Yashin gave the man just one derisory glance, before turning his attention on me. For once he seemed lost for words, but the way he was looking at me, I was glad he wasn't stupid enough to be carrying a gun. Though I was still wary in case that didn't apply to Bergin or Alexei. Yashin's silence wasn't a problem. I wasn't looking for conversation.

'As you've probably worked out, things haven't quite gone to plan.' I took a step forward, for emphasis. Our gazes locked. 'I'm not expecting this will put you off doing what you're trying to do. All I'll say is, if this keeps up, someone's going to get seriously hurt. And I mean, seriously. And I don't intend it'll be anyone from my side.' I could have added, 'You get my drift?' but didn't think I needed to. His eyes told me he got it.

The thin lips parted, his mouth opened. I waited to hear what his response was going to be. It never came.

From behind me came a bellow. 'WHAT THE FUCK'S GOING ON?'

I turned to see Frank Johnson coming through the

door, Tony behind him, Vicki following, looking desperate and face full of apology for having failed in her appointed task. Frank came between Yashin and me, looking from one to the other, but mainly at me. 'Speak to me, Danny.'

I nodded at the Russian. 'You may want to ask him.'

But Frank wasn't having any. 'I'm asking you.' He was as angry as I've ever seen him. Tony had done a good job. Vicki hadn't had a chance. I counted to three, knowing I needed to be careful.

'Our friend here thought that a riot on the dance floor might convince you I'm not doing my job properly. I was just telling him it wasn't a good idea.'

'Riot? What riot?' Frank looked to Tony, who shrugged his ignorance, then back at me. 'What're you talking about? I haven't seen any trouble?'

'That's because we stopped it happening.' Something was ringing in my gut. Frank wasn't calming down the way he should have been doing.

Frank turned to Yashin who said, 'I have no idea what he is talking about.' He turned to look at the man behind him whose wrists were still locked in the plastic cuffs. He said to Bergin, 'Who is this man? Do we know him?'

Bergin looked at Alexei, who shook his head, then spoke to the man in Russian. There was a brief conversation.

Bergin said, 'He says he is off a boat, from Runcorn. He was minding his own business when he,' - he nodded at me - 'grabbed him and broke his arm. He says he wishes to press charges and that we must call the police.'

I sighed.

Yashin turned to Frank. He tutted, like he was sorry about something. 'I think, Mr Johnson, your Security Manager does not like Russians perhaps?'

I sighed again. 'Go and look at the CCTV, Frank. Eric will show you-'

'I don't need to look at any fucking CCTV, Danny. I've had enough of this. You've gone too far this time. After tonight, you're off the door.' He turned to Tony. 'Get hold of Dave Charnley for me.' Eyes wide, Tony nodded, and disappeared. As he passed Vicki I saw panic start in her face.

'Hang on Frank,' I said. 'There's no need to-'

He whirled round on me, eyes like saucers. I wondered if he'd taken something. And he could barely get the words out quick enough.

'Don't start telling me how to run my fucking club again Danny. You've done that once too often. That's it. You're out.'

## CHAPTER 43

It was five o'clock in the morning. I was crashed on my living room couch, staring at the unlit gas fire. Apart from the tie, I was still in full uniform, jacket and all. The bottle of JD I opened when I got in was three quarters gone. I was fucked, in several senses of the word.

It's hard to remember the detail of the rest of the night. I knew from the moment of Frank's snap decision - which on reflection, may not have been that 'snap' - I was up against it trying to get him to see sense. But it didn't stop me trying. Apart from not wanting the business to go belly up, I had a responsibility, not just to the people who work for me but to the club and the people who use it regularly. As far as I was concerned, a change on the door would be disastrous for everyone. Not least I felt a huge responsibility towards Vicki. And while I couldn't have put into words exactly how a change on the door would be bad for her, I just knew it, instinctively.

So when the chance arose, after we'd all beaten a retreat from Yashin's suite and I'd gotten my guys to get rid of their prisoners, I tried to pin Frank down, in his office.

He didn't want to know.

'There's nothing you can say will make me change my mind,' he said, soon as he saw me. 'This has been brewing a long time, Danny. It's time for a change.'

I was conscious that since the confrontation upstairs, Tony-the-Manager had been hanging off Frank's shoulder like they were conjoined twins. So, as I have done in the past when I needed Frank to see some sense, I suggested that maybe we should speak, 'In private.'

'Tony's the Club Manager,' he said. 'Anything you want to say to me, you can say in front of him.'

Right then I knew I had my work cut out. I still gave it my best shot.

I tried explaining how, if we hadn't done what we did, there'd have been a riot. And that wouldn't only have reflected on me and my team, it could have affected his licence.

He said, 'If you knew something like that was brewing you should have told me, or Tony first.' I decided against mentioning that if I had, it would have likely got straight back to Yashin, who'd have postponed things to a day when we were less well prepared. 'Anyway, why go to these lengths? You've handled trouble on the floor loads of times.'

'With drunken clubbers. These were professionals. And sober.'

'So you say.'

As we'd already got rid of them, there was little more I could prove on that score.

I talked about my fears for the club if Charnley took over the door, who he would let in.

'All door guys have their favourites. You're no different.'

I pointed out - though I shouldn't have needed to -

our record. How over the past three years we'd done pretty well keeping organised dealing out of the club, which for a place like Midnight's is remarkable.

'So you say, but how do you know? How do you prove something like that?'

By now it was becoming clear that whatever I said, whatever argument I put forward, Frank was always going to have a comeback. His mind was made up. I thought I knew why.

'You're giving in to Yashin,' I said, finally. 'Letting him win.'

'Stop blaming Yashin. This has got fuck-all to do with him.' But the speed of his anger told me I'd hit the nail. Frank was scared.

I tried mentioning the contract, though I guessed what his response would be. 'You're required to give us one month's notice.'

He didn't disappoint. 'Don't worry, I'll pay you for the month. But as from Tuesday, you're off the door.'

Eventually there was only one thing left to say. Not an argument, just a statement of fact.

'I can't protect you if I'm not here, Frank.'

'I don't need protecting. I can look after myself.'

But as he said it, the look in his eyes, which Tony couldn't see but I could, gave the lie to it.

I shook my head. 'You've no idea how much I wish to God that were true.' I turned to leave. 'When you've seen sense, call me.'

I left him and Tony working out what to do next.

The hardest thing was seeing the night through. Word had spread like wildfire. Everywhere I went people were whispering. Not surprisingly, my team wanted to know what was happening. Their worries weren't only around Charnley taking over.

'They're saying we're sacked off the door. Is it true?'

'Does that mean we're all out of a job?'

'Where do we stand, money-wise?'

I couldn't blame them for a second. Most of them had other mouths to feed as well as their own. I gave them what reassurance I felt able. 'There's no need to panic. Give Frank a couple of days to calm down, then we'll see what comes out in the wash.' Inside, I wasn't holding out much hope for a change of heart.

At one stage I thought about ringing Mike. It was his business too. But then, what good can he do, I thought? If I can't talk Frank round, Mike sure as hell won't be able to. Through it all, I did manage to keep an eye on one thing. Vicki still had her podium duties to do. I was about to seek her out when she came looking for me. We spoke in the now-deserted staff room. She was still reeling, and feeling guilty.

'I'm sorry, Danny. I tried to stop him but he wouldn't listen.'

'It wasn't your fault. This isn't just about tonight.'

'What else is there?'

So far, I'd avoided telling her stuff I thought might unsettle her. That hadn't changed. 'I'll fill you in another time.' I checked my watch. 'Aren't you due on the podium?'

'What, with all this going on? No chance.'

I thought about it. 'There's nothing you, or I, can do about Frank tonight. I think you should carry on. Your guardian angels will be set up to see you home I take it?'

She nodded. 'But I thought you didn't like me dancing.'

I turned to face her. For all the strain in her face, she was still Vicki. God knows how, but I forced a smile. 'Maybe I'm getting used to seeing you strut your stuff.'

She looked doubtful. 'Yeah, right.'

'No, honestly. Maybe you'll do it for me... sometime.'

She stared at me, eyes narrowing, trying to weigh how far to believe it. 'Danny Norton... If I thought for one minute you were being serious, I'd-'

'You'd, what?'

She couldn't, or wouldn't finish it. 'Never mind. Another time maybe.'

I nodded. 'Another time.' As she turned to leave, I added, 'Message me.'

She threw me a glance over her shoulder, through her hair. Still sexy as hell. 'I will.'

After she'd gone, I let out a long breath. What I hadn't said was that after what had gone on with our visitors, I preferred that the police shadow her home rather than some Russian who might see her as the opportunity he needs to get his own back.

As for the rest of the team, to be fair to them, they were nothing less than professional, even if they were simply going through the motions while wondering how much longer they would have jobs. And I made sure I was in the lobby to see Vicki on her way when it was time to leave. We didn't say anything, but the look I gave her as she walked out the door was loaded, not least because underpinning it was a depressing thought. *Is this the last time I'll see her out?*

We closed up at the usual time. Before they went I told the team to keep what had happened, 'in house', until the storm settled. Some hope. Even Eric, who doesn't usually get wound up, was threatening to strangle someone. He didn't care who, just someone. After they'd gone I did what I normally do, then reported to Frank, as usual.

By then the talking was all done, so as I dropped the main set of keys on his desk all I said was, 'There are some things we'll need to talk about. Practical stuff. Handovers. That sort of things.'

'Right.' He didn't offer a time or place.

I thought, 'Fuck you, Frank,' and headed home.

When I got there I went straight to the kitchen cupboard and pulled out a new bottle. I didn't open it but just sat on the couch, staring into space, until I got Vicki's message.

*Home safe. Hope U R ok. x*

I sent back, *OK. And don't worry. Things will work out.*

I had no idea how they would work out but I thought I should at least try and give an impression I was still upbeat. That particular sentiment wasn't to last long. I waited a minute in case she came back. When she didn't, and knowing she was safe, I leaned back and settled in for some serious drinking.

I spent the next two hours, between refills, going over things. There was plenty to think on. Could I have handled the night's events differently? I didn't think so. Every alternative scenario I could think of still ended badly, one way or another. I thought about my guys, how many we might be able to hold onto, how many we'd have to let go. I thought about what might happen if Charnley had the door, though I probably knew the answer. Most of all there was Vicki, and how could I protect her if I wasn't there? The more I thought about things, the more I recognised the direction it was taking me. Everything led down the same road, to the same inescapable conclusion.

At one stage I got up and wandered the room, looking for a distraction from the slump that had me in its grip. Mistake. My gaze lit on the shelf where all my OU stuff lay, waiting. I stared down at it. Another dead end. 'And what a joke that is,' I said. Picking up the booklets, papers and study guides, I carried them out to the kitchen, trod on the pedal and dumped them in the bin. I went back to the couch.

Eventually, it must have been just before I passed out, I finally managed to give voice to what I was feeling. Turning my empty glass upside down so the last drop of forget-juice ran down to the rim where my probing finger captured it and directed it between my nearly-numb lips, I put my head back and shouted to the ceiling.

'You've fucked-up Norton.'

## CHAPTER 44

The Man Who Likes to Watch is staring out of the window of his bedroom. Across the surrounding fields, the first signs of the approaching dawn are seeping over the horizon, glimpses of glowing red already showing. It looks like it is going to be a nice day.

It has been a long night, not least because he has spent the last half of it lying on his bunk, thinking about what has happened, how it will affect his plans. When he first heard about what had happened, his reaction was he would have to ditch his new project altogether. But when it became clear that she was sticking to her plans - he'd been right, she is a cold bitch - he began to wonder if what had happened might not actually work in his favour. Later on, after things had calmed a little, he had managed to engage her in conversation, though casually, so she would not think anything of it.

At first it was difficult, she was tight-lipped and reluctant to talk about it. But bit by bit, as he probed for information, he began to see that, as far as she was concerned, it was business as usual, and that included her podium duties. Sure enough, at the allotted time she was there, looking fantastic and doing her thing as if nothing had happened and it was just another normal club night. It made him glad that his particular technique doesn't require that he spend time beforehand trying to foster any sort of 'relationship'. He is sure if he ever had to put up with her long-term, he would soon discover she is the sort whose main interest is herself. One of those who lacks the ability to empathise with the plight of others. And though the conversation was only brief, one especially good thing came out of it. The new strategy he was looking for.

It was only a chance remark, a reference to future intentions. Nevertheless, as soon as she mentioned it something clicked and he saw exactly how, if he could incorporate it into his plans, he could use it to achieve his aims - albeit in a way that was different to the others. It had cheered him to the point where he had actually got quite excited just thinking about it. By the time he left the club he could hardly wait to get home and indulge his imaginings in the way he did most nights. Only this time he had a whole new scenario to fantasise about.

It was this new 'scenario' that had kept him awake through the night, thinking on possibilities, options, adding layers the way a painter does with a blank canvas. Now, with the sun about to rise, he thinks he has it all worked out, and is pleased with himself.

The good thing is, he won't even have to wait long.

## CHAPTER 45

*Sunday*

I woke up thinking it was Remembrance Sunday. The Village Parade passes the end of my close and I always hear the Boys Brigade drummer banging out the pace. It was a few moments before I realised it wasn't the drummer, but my front door. I lay there waiting to see if it would stop, if whoever it was would go away. It didn't. They wouldn't.

I prised open an eye. When it focused, I was still looking at the fire, lying on the couch, still dressed.

'Fuuuck!'

I prised myself up into a sitting position. The banging moved from the front door to inside my head. I hadn't felt so bad in a long time. You get back into a regime, you tend to put a brake on the benders, even when you think you're giving yourself a night off. It hadn't applied the night just gone. I breathed slowly, gauging if I could stand without throwing up. I could, though it was close. After several more long breaths I stumbled to the door. It shows how bad I was that I didn't even bother trying to guess who it might be. I didn't care. I should have.

It was Vicki. All she said was, 'Oh. My. God.'

I turned and shuffled back inside. She followed me in, shut the door. I went back to the couch, collapsed onto it. My stomach started doing weird things so I shut my eyes and breathed slow again. When I opened them, she was staring down at me.

'Are you alright?' My face made some sort of non-committal response. I was still waiting for my brain to start processing information. She must have realised. 'Coffee.'

Ten minutes later the hot dark brown liquid was starting to do its stuff. I lifted my head to find her still staring. I thought I should say something. 'How are you?'

'I'm fine. It's you I'm worried about.'

'I'll be okay.'

'Hmmm.'

I went back to the coffee.

Eventually I made it up to the bathroom and into the shower. I dressed in my most comfortable sweats, then returned back downstairs. She was in the kitchen, doing clearing-up stuff. I poured myself another coffee, then went back to the couch. She finished running water in the sink then came and joined me, sitting in the chair opposite, mug of lemon tea - hers, not mine - in hand.

She gave me another couple of minutes before she started.

'What are you going to do?'

I decided to play dumb. 'About what?' She gave me the look she'd given me that first Saturday night only worse. Like, now I was being *really* stupid. I shrugged. 'What can I do? The job's fucked.'

She didn't say anything, just drank from her mug. But the look stayed, staring at me over the rim. It did it's

317

job.

'What?'

'You know what.'

'No, I don't.'

She sighed. 'If you're going to carry on being like this, I'll go. Shall I?'

I went back to my coffee, but held her gaze as I drank. Eventually I said, 'There's only so much I can do. If Frank wants us off the door, I can't stop him.'

'IF, he wants you off the door.'

'That's what he said. You heard him.'

'And you believe him?'

'What's the difference whether I believe him or not? It's done.'

'The difference is whether you walk away with your tail between your legs, or stand up and fight.'

'Fight? With what? As from Tuesday I won't even be able to get back in the club unless Charnley allows it. And that's not likely.'

'Maybe not. But if you need an in, I'm still there.'

'Thanks for the offer, but I think I've fucked up enough people's jobs without risking yours. Frank may love you to bits, but if he thinks I'm trying to use you in some way, you'll be down the road as fast as he can say it.'

'You may be right. But if I'm prepared to take that risk, then you should too.'

I thought on it. It was the same argument she'd used when we talked about her acting as bait for the killer. Her decision. I shook my head. It was time to enlighten her

'Yashin's putting pressure on Frank to buy him out. He's made threats against his family. But he wants me off the door first. That's why Frank was so adamant last night. He saw it as his chance.'

Her head went back and she nodded, slowly, the way someone does when the fog begins to clear. 'Right.'

'This murder charge the police are trying to pin on me is some of the same. They all want me out.'

'Who is all?'

'Frank, Yashin, Charnley. Whoever's setting me up for Ged Reilly's murder.'

'And that justifies you rolling over does it? What about Eric and the others? What about the club? What about everyone who goes there because they know that while Danny Norton's on the door, it's the safest place in town?'

'They'll manage. They did before. Besides, the way things are right now, they're probably better off without me.'

'I see.' She hesitated, then hit me with, 'And what about me?'

I looked up. 'What do you mean?'

She waited, holding my gaze. 'I mean what happens when I need my White Knight?' I stared at her. 'Dave Charnley doesn't exactly fit the bill.'

'I- I..' But I had no answer to that one. I went back to my coffee.

A minute later she went, 'Hmph.' I looked up at her again. She was giving me a sad look. She shook her head, 'Whatever happened to Danny Norton, the hardest man in Warrington? The man who's not afraid of anything?''

'He's a myth. He never existed.'

There was another moment's hesitation before she said, 'I think you're wrong. And I'm not alone.'

'Yeah, well. Like I said...'

Eventually she got up. I looked up at her. She pointed an accusing finger at me. 'You, need to get your shit together. And when you do, call me and tell me what I can do to help.' Seconds later the front door banged.

I sat on the couch a while longer, nursing my mug and staring down into the muddy coffee grains as I replayed our conversation. It worried me that for all her cajoling, I'd not even pretended to try and rally myself. I've always prided myself on my ability to remain positive, no matter how bad things may seem. But that particular quality seemed to have gone AWOL. I sat forward on the edge of the cushion. I ran a hand over my scalp, as if doing so might get my brain working again. But the only thoughts that came were of Vicki, and how I'd finally managed to reveal myself to her as the loser I am.

As I sat there, cringing inside, stomach churning and cursing myself for a stupid bastard, her words came back to me, 'What happens when I need my White Knight?'

I stopped rubbing my head. I sat up. *White Knight.* I thought back on all the conversations we'd had the past week. For all that I'd imagined myself playing that particular role to her damsel many times, fantasised about it even, I'd never mentioned the fact to her. I'd have been too embarrassed. But she had used the phrase without any prompting. I thought about what it said about her, her feelings towards me. Something stirred in my stomach, like it may not be dead after all. Was that how she saw me, her White Knight?

At that moment my stomach growled, calling for

food. It hadn't seen any for over sixteen hours. I stood up.

Heading for the kitchen, I passed the shelf where up to the night before I'd kept my OU stuff. As I passed something registered and I stopped to check it out, to make sure I wasn't mistaken. All the books, papers and guides were laid out as close as damn to the way they had been before. I peered closer, wondering if maybe I'd dreamed about dumping them in the bin. But as I saw the grease stains on a couple of the papers, the patch of damp on the cover of one of the guides - confirming evidence of their night in the bin - I realised. She must have come across them while tidying the kitchen and put them back where she had seen them the week before. Now, as I looked even closer, I could even see where she'd had to clean off some of the food waste which, if it had lain much longer, would have ruined it all completely.

'I'll be damned,' I said.

Then I saw it. On top of the Assignment Sheet, the one about Heart of Darkness that was giving me so much trouble, was a yellow post-it note. Written on it in red biro - not by my hand - was the instruction, *Finish me!*

I was still staring at it when my phone rang. Thinking it was her, I grabbed at it. But it was Winston.

'Yo doin' baazz?'

'If you're ringing to ask what's happen-'

'So'kay, baaaz. Jus' letting you know. Didn't get a chance to speak las' night. The Brothers. They did the deal. Jus' like you asked.'

'What?' With everything that had gone on the night before, I'd forgotten completely about the matter involving Winston and his brothers. 'When?' I added, trying to force my brain to kick into gear.

'Las' night. After your little trouble with the Russian and Mr Frank.'

'But-' I started again. 'I'm sorry Winston, I must have missed all this. Are you telling me your brothers met with Yashin?'

'That's what I'm ringin' for is'nit? You awake baaaz, or should I ring you another time. Like when you gotcha head on?'

'No, I'm with you.' I shook myself, took a breath, returned to the couch. 'Tell me what happened.' *Not that it's any good now.*

To begin with, I was only half listening as Winston gave his account. The arrangement with Winston's brothers depended on me having control of the door. Now that I didn't, the whole thing was dead in the water. And though what Winston had to say was interesting, the greater part of my brain was still occupied imagining Vicki, fishing around in the kitchen bin, writing her note. Part of me wanted to think about what other messages I could take from it all. But as the detail of what Winston was saying began to register, my thoughts began to turn. Winston had done well. More accurately, his brothers had. It was just a shame that it was all wasted. But then another slice of my conversation with Vicki jumped back out at me. My brain was beginning to kick in again, at long last. It was the bit where she'd said, '...If you need an in, I'm still there.'

I was on the phone to Winston for another twenty minutes.

# CHAPTER 46

On Sunday mornings, the lounge bar at Warrington Golf Club serves excellent bacon butties. I was halfway through one when my partner, Mike, came through the door above which the sign reads, 'To the Changing Rooms.' Seeing me, he headed across, pulling off his glove. As he dropped into the armchair opposite, he didn't look best-pleased.

'Whatever this is,' he said, 'It better be worth it. I was three-up at the twelfth when you rang.'

'Sorry. I didn't realise it was a competition.'

'You wouldn't, not being a golfer.' He decided to give me some of his attention. 'So what's so important?' It was then I noticed he was eyeing my breakfast like he had half a mind to order one himself.

'We've lost Midnight's.'

'WHAT? HOW THE FUCK-' He stopped, looked round, struggled to compose himself. A golf club lounge on a Sunday morning isn't the place or time you want to be seen throwing a fit, especially if you're manoeuvring for the next captaincy. But after a quick glance round, people were already returning to their papers and butties.

He pulled his chair closer, leaned in.

'What the hell happened? I thought you were sorting

it?'

'I was. Frank obviously didn't feel he could wait.'

'What changed his mind?'

I told him about everything we'd seen and heard the last few nights, ending up with the confrontation with Yashin, then Frank blowing his gasket. As he listened, Mike eased back into his chair. The concerned look stayed in his face, but I could see he was still eyeing my sandwich. At one stage a young waitress dressed in black wove between the tables.

'Get you anything, Mike?' she said as she passed.

He nodded at my plate. 'I'll have one of those, Evey. And a coffee, please.'

Evey looked at me. 'Something else, darlin?'

I ordered another coffee as well.

By the time I got to where I'd tried getting Frank to change his mind - without success - Mike had calmed a little. The bacon sandwich seemed to be helping in that regard.

'So that's it?' he said. 'We're out and Charnley's in?'

'That's the way it's shaping up.'

We talked over options. There were still a few. They ranged from calling a meeting with Frank, to consulting our lawyer, to seeing if Jamie Carver could have a word in Frank's ear and get him to see sense. But as we talked, I was surprised to find Mike more negative than I'd expected.

'This has been on the cards a while,' he said. 'I suppose it was only a matter of time.'

'I dunno about that,' I said. 'Another week and things may have changed in our favour.'

'What makes you say that?' So far I'd said nothing to Mike about my meeting with Carver's SOCA colleague, my discussions with Winston. My reasoning was, the less he knows the better. And while events had overtaken us, my view hadn't changed.

I shrugged. 'Something may have come up. It might still do.'

'You're living in cloud-cuckoo-land,' Mike said. 'Let's face it, as from today, DoorSecure's finished.'

'Whoa,' I said, putting down my coffee. 'Isn't that a little premature? The business is still viable, even without Midnight's.'

'But it's not just Midnight's. There's Frank's other clubs as well. With them gone what have we got? A dozen pubs and some clubs, none of which are close to the size of Midnight's? Plus, once word gets round we've been kicked out, no one will want to know us.'

I fidgeted in my chair. Truth was, Mike's negativity was beginning to get up my nose. 'You may be right in the end. But I've spent a long time building up my reputation in this town. I'm not ready to give up on all that just yet.'

Mike smirked into his coffee. 'Depends which reputation you're talking about.'

I stared at him. 'What's that supposed to mean?'

He backtracked. 'Nothing. I was joking.' He checked his watch. 'Look, let's talk about this in the morning, when we've both had a chance to think about things.' As he rose, he looked over to where the big bay window looks out over the eighteenth hole and the surrounding fairways. He checked his watch again. 'I'll see you in the office. Early. We'll work a out a plan, okay?' He seemed anxious to get away.

I nodded. 'Right.'

About to go, he stopped. 'Thanks for coming, Danny.

I appreciate you letting me know.'

As he disappeared through to the Changing Rooms to get back into his golf shoes, I thought about what it says about someone when they can't wait to get back to a golf match having just learned their business may be about to go tits-up.


Ricky Mason lives in a sixties-built semi-detached in the Orford area. It isn't much to look at from the outside and the area isn't the best, but Sharon is a good homemaker and keeps it clean and tidy, which isn't easy with four kids running around the place.

Ricky's VW Passat was parked outside so I knew he was in. As I passed it to walk up the path, I checked it out.

Sharon's smile when she opened the door was the brightest thing I'd seen in a while. It went a little way to cheering me up, but not much. I wondered if it would be there by the end of the day.

'Danny. Lovely to see you. Ricky's out back.'

She led me through the house to the back garden. As we went, I had to avoid stepping on toys or knocking over kids that came running up to wrap themselves round my legs. I responded as best I could to their raucous greetings, which was difficult considering the reason for my visit. In the back garden, Ricky was busy with a spade, turning over sods in the tiny vegetable patch.

'Look who's here,' Sharon said.

When Ricky turned and saw me, his face showed none of the enthusiasm it usually does when we bump into each other. Nevertheless he still effected a cheery, 'Aye-up Danny.'

'Hey Ricky.' I turned to Sharon. 'I'd love a coffee, Shaz, if the kettle's on.'

'Coming up. Like a biscuit?' I declined. Truth was I'd had my quota for the morning, but it got rid of her.

Ricky resumed his attack on a couple of sods. 'What brings you here, Captain?'

'Just called for a chat, mate.'

He paused long enough to throw me a wary look.

'Yeah? What about?'

I waited until he realised I was waiting for his full attention. He stopped digging and straightened up.

'You heard about my little problem with the police?'

'Uh-huh.'

'And you heard what it was about?'

'Someone said it was something to do with Ged Reilly?' In all the years I'd known Ricky, it was the first time he couldn't look me in the face.

'It was everything to do with Ged Reilly.'

'Yeah?'

I waited again. Eventually, he lifted his head and our eyes met. I could see he was having difficulty holding it together. Deep down, Ricky is as honest as the day's long.

Sharon arrived with the coffee. I looked at Ricky. His face said, *Not here.*

'Sorry Shaz,' I said. 'We've decided to go to the pub. It's time I bought my mate a pint.'


I took him to The Albion. Neither of us are particularly known there. I sat Ricky at the most out-of-the-way table we could find while I went to the bar. As I made my way back with two pints of bitter in hand, I could see Ricky's knees jigging under the table, his hands twiddling in his lap.

Taking my seat I said, 'I noticed your Passat's got a nice new set of wheels.'

He looked at me across the table and, just for a second, I saw him grappling over whether to try to bluff it out. Then his face caved, he dropped his head and his shoulders shook as the tears came.

'Christ Danny. I'm sorry. I'm so sorry.'

I pushed his glass towards him. 'Have a drink.'

He supped long and slow, gathering himself. I waited, saying nothing. Eventually he put his glass down. 'I needed the money. I was desperate.'

'You could have asked me.'

He shook his head. 'The car needed tyres. The gas board's insisting we replace the boiler and the kids all need uniforms for the new school year. You've been good to us Danny, but I couldn't ask you again.'

'So you dropped me to the police for Ged Reilly.'

He looked horrified. 'God no, Danny. I'd never do that.'

I gave him an even stare. Like I say, Ricky's not into deceit.

'How much?'

'A grand.'

I shook my head. The going rate for treachery these days.

I said, 'Tell me about Ged.'

He picked up his pint, drank it straight down, then went to the bar and came back with two more. Then he began. He told me how, two weeks after the night I went looking for Ged Reilly but missed him, Ricky heard Ged was lying low at his brother-in-law's. 'He was shitting himself,' he said. 'Apparently he was convinced you were going to take him out for fingering me in Havana's.' Ged's plan, Ricky said, was to wait until he knew I was out of town then do a runner. He'd been heard talking about going to Thailand where there was a woman he'd been stringing along for a couple of years. Ricky never said a word to anybody but staked the house out for three days and nights, eating and sleeping in his car. Eventually, at one o'clock in the morning, Ged came out, got into his car and drove off. Ricky followed and managed to force him off the road just outside Winwick. At first Ged thought I was with him, and when he realised Ricky was on his own, tried buying him off. But Ricky wasn't interested in money. Ged had ruined his career, his whole life at that time. There was only one thing on Ricky's mind - giving Ged some of what his Liverpool connections had meted out to him. Only things didn't go as planned. In the process of giving Ged the hiding he richly deserved, Ged tried to get away by jumping across a ditch. He misjudged it and fell onto an old tree branch that was sticking up. It penetrated deep into his chest. He must have died at once. Ricky panicked. He buried him in the woods just outside Winwick and got rid of his car through Eddie Meers's scrap yard.

I waited while Ricky took another long swig. Nothing he'd told me so far had come as any great surprise. As soon as DCI Welbeck mentioned about my phone being found with Ged's body, I knew Ricky had to have been involved, though I hadn't known the detail of course. Now he was saying that Ged died because of an accident. I believed him. Ricky may be daft, but he's not into wasting people.

'Tell me about my phone.'

The look of shame in Ricky's face as his head went down confirmed my worst suspicions, though I still needed to hear it from him.

He shook his head. 'During the days Ged was laying low, people were already beginning to say you'd aced him. Not me of course. I know you better than that. I visited you in your office. Your phone was on the desk and I slipped it into my pocket. I don't know what I was thinking. My head was all messed up. I guess I'd already made my mind up that if I got the chance, I was going to sort Ged out.'

'And you took my phone so you could frame me.'

'I know it looks that way now, Danny, but honest to God. It wasn't like I planned it or anything.'

'But when you buried Ged you still managed to throw my phone in with the body.'

'Like I said, I was panicking. I wasn't thinking straight. I thought that if I could make the police look somewhere else, then they wouldn't look at me. I thought there was no-way they could pin Ged's death on you just on the basis of finding your phone so I knew you'd be okay.'

'You couldn't know that for sure. And it hasn't stopped them trying.'

He started crying again. 'I know. I'm sorry Danny.'

I supped my pint. 'We were best mates Ricky. I was looking out for you.'

'I know.' The tears were flowing now, like a river. And I still hadn't asked the sixty-thousand dollar question. I did so now.

'How did the police come to find the body?'

He squeezed his eyes tight. Forcing back tears.

'A couple of weeks ago someone asked me if I knew

anything about Ged's disappearance, if you were involved. They said there was big money in it. I didn't say anything about you, I just told them where the body was. They must have passed it onto the police. Honest to God Danny if I'd known, I'd never have told him.'

'Who is this someone you keep talking about. Is it the Russian?'

'No.' As he shook his head, a strange look came into his face. It took me a moment to recognise it as fear. In fact, he was terrified.

'So who was it?' I said.

Ricky looked up from his pint. 'You're not going to like it.'

As I stared at Ricky waiting for me to tell him to give me the name, a feeling like nothing I'd experienced before came over me. I guess you could say it was a bit like a, 'feeling of impending doom.' And it was at that moment I realised that by confronting Ricky, I'd let a Genie out of the bottle, and it was going to change everything. I swallowed and said, 'Tell me.'

Seconds later, I knew I was right.

# CHAPTER 47

*Monday*

The next morning I woke early, nursing a feeling like jet-lag. It had been another of those nights where sleep had taken its time coming. On top of the alcohol-fuelled stupor of the night before, I could feel it all building up. At least, my body could.

It was a real cocktail that kept me awake. The events of Saturday night. My depressing meeting with Mike. The even more depressing discoveries that came out of my meeting with Ricky. They all kept running through my mind, as if battling over the right to stay longest. Top of them all, there was the phone call to Vicki.

After showing her my ability to wallow in self-pity the previous morning, not to mention my complete lack of anything that could be called a backbone, I felt I owed her an apology, as well as some explanations. My mistake was choosing to broach it over the phone. With hindsight, I should have just gotten in my truck, driven over to her flat and rung the bell. But it was the fear thing that stopped me. Like I've said before, Vicki scares me to death. Then there was the embarrassment factor. I guess I was worried she would laugh in my face, having discovered that far from being 'the hardest man in Warrington', I was, in fact, a complete wimp.

The conversation ended up being stilted. Full of misunderstandings, badly-expressed thoughts and feelings, long pauses during which we both struggled to work out what the other was trying to say. At least, that was my take on it. She was probably thinking, how do I get rid of this lemon? I suppose I'd hoped she would invite me over, in which case I'd have been out the door like a shot. Only she didn't. The reasons why she didn't had contributed to all the tossing and turning.

For once I was ready and waiting for Mike in the office when he arrived. Over the first coffee of the day we picked up on the discussion we'd started the day before. But Mike seemed even less inclined to get into exploring the options that might keep us in business than he was over the Golf Club's bacon butties. I didn't push it, and was happy when Mike made vague noises about letting things ride for a couple of days while we 'see what comes out in the wash'. In truth, that suited me. I wasn't yet ready to challenge Mike over the reasons for his lack of concern that DoorSecure might be in trouble. Besides, other matters needed my attention.

The first was ringing Jamie Carver, which I did soon as I left Mike - I had no intention of sharing my plans with him - and got back to my truck. Normally I wouldn't bother Carver first thing on a Monday morning. He's told me before it's the busiest time of the week for him, but that morning he seemed happy to give me his time.

'I heard what happened.,' he said. 'Any signs of Frank changing his mind?'

'No. And I don't think he will unless someone

changes it for him.'

'This thing with Winston you mean?'

'And his brothers.'

'Them too. But how will it work if you've not got the door?'

'Leave that with me. I've got a couple of ideas.'

'You still want me to ring Will?' I still only knew Carver's NCA mate as, 'Will.'

'Yes.'

'In that case you better tell me how you see it panning out. He'll want to know.'

Over the next fifteen minutes we talked through the details. There were a couple of points where Carver expressed doubts. But when I reminded him of the alternative, and Yashin's ambitions, his resistance lessened. Eventually he said, 'I'll speak with Will and get back to you.'

'One other thing.'

'Go on.'

I took a deep breath. 'I know what happened to Ged Reilly.'

There was a pause. 'Do you want to tell me?'

'Not sure yet. Depends how things turn out. I can tell you he wasn't deliberately murdered.'

'Hmm. My advice?'

It was my turn to say, 'Go on.'

'When you're in the frame for murder, don't piss about. If you know something, you've got to share it.'

'It's complicated.'

'It always is. My advice sticks.'

'I'll bear it in mind.'

'Do.' He rang off.

Next, I rang Winston. It was a shorter call. I only had

one question.

'When can I meet your brothers?'

## CHAPTER 48

I can still remember the first time I called on Lucy Maddocks. I was fourteen and it was my first attempt at a proper date. I'd arranged to take her to the pictures. As I stood there, waiting for her dad to come to the door - it was always the dad in those days - I discovered for the first time what it was like to suffer from nerves. And I mean real nerves, as in pounding heart, dry throat, sweaty palms, a hot/cold thing going on, the works. I still see Lucy occasionally. She works on the tills at Tesco. Let's just say the years haven't been kind. Six kids before turning thirty probably had something to do with it.

The nervousness I experienced on Lucy's doorstep that night returned the moment I pressed my thumb to Vicki's doorbell, having decided to call in on my way back from meeting with Gabriel and Anthony. When a patch of ground to my left lit up, I knew she had opened the blinds above to see who it was. I didn't look up or make a point of showing myself. My truck was parked under a street lamp in one of the bays out front. She would either come to the door, or not. The two minutes that passed before I heard her descending the stairs were the longest I've ever experienced.

The door opened and she stood there, looking

straight at me. She was wearing a white v-neck top, black leggings and slip-on trainers. The sheen on her skin and the flush in her face made me wonder if she'd been watching some fitness DVD.

'Hi,' I said.

'Hi,' she came back. Nothing else. And I mean, *nothing*.

'I think maybe it's time we talked. Properly.'

She seemed to consider it, then gave a slow nod. She stepped back and swung the door open.

Fifteen minutes later, I was sitting on her couch holding a glass tumbler containing a reassuring measure of JD. She was in the chair opposite, nursing her wine. The way she'd tucked her legs under as she'd listened, looking at me through narrowed eyes, had made me think of a cat, waiting in long grass for a mouse to make its move. But the expression on her face at that moment was the sort a parent might adopt when trying to decide whether to buy their teenage son's/daughter's excuse as to how they came to be excluded from school.

She sipped from her glass then said, 'I've never heard of something called, 'A Lone Ranger Complex.'

'That's how the psychologist described it. I don't think it's a medical term.'

'Really?'

It was a second before I realised. I'd just been thick again. I continued.

'Whatever it's called, it's part of me. Like I said, I thought it had gone away, until last Wednesday.'

She looked thoughtful. 'People say you got in trouble years ago for nearly killing someone.' I nodded. 'Was that this... complex thing?'

I nodded again, told her about Kevin Campbell.

337

When I'd finished she sat there, watching the wine swirl in her glass as she twirled the stem.

'So you're saying this only happens when you're trying to protect someone, especially if they're close?'

'Yes.'

'And that's what happened with Vincent?'

'I know it sounds like I'm making excuses, but believe me, it's the truth.'

She gave another slow nod. 'I believe you.'

I started. 'You do?'

She took another drink. 'It explains a couple of things. A lot of things, actually.'

'Such as?'

'Such as how you can be so...' She wafted a hand, 'Scary, one moment, and... nice, the next.'

'I'm scary?'

'Only sometimes.'

'That's alright then.'

She smiled. 'Don't shoot the messenger. I'm only telling you how others see you.'

'What about you? Do you think I'm scary?'

She weighed it. 'I used to.'

'And now?'

She hesitated in a way I wasn't entirely comfortable with. 'Not so much.' But she must have read my face because then she said, 'I'll re-phrase that. No. Now that you've told me about your condition, I'm not scared of you at all.'

'Good.'

'But it doesn't really matter what I think.'

'It does to me.'

'What I mean is, what matters is doing something that will stop what you did to Vincent ever happening again.'

'Something like what?'

'I don't know, but it should probably start with you talking to someone who knows about these things.'

'A psychiatrist, you mean?'

'Not a psychiatrist. You're not mentally ill. I mean someone like this woman from Chester. A psychologist.'

I thought about it. If I'm honest, I'd thought about it before. But not for a long time.

After I was acquitted of trying to kill Kevin, there were recommendations - from the sorts of people who know about these things - that I should undergo counselling, to try and get to the root of my problem. Mary Oakley even offered to take me on again, for free and in her own time. I think she felt a bit guilty that she hadn't sorted my problem out for good the first time. But I was twenty-two, arrogant, like a lot of lads that age, and I'd just got off at Crown Court. I made the right noises about following all the advice, but once I got back to work I soon forgot about it, sure that what I did to Kevin was a 'one off' and would never happen again. Within hours of me beating Vincent up, I knew I'd been wrong. Now, talking to Vicki, I finally realised what my real problem was.

I make a good part of my living putting myself in the way of people who intend violence, either to me or someone else. Ever since Kevin, I've worked to show I can be relied upon to deal with those sorts of people in a way that is in line with how doormen are supposed to work. Firm, fair, always in control. Admitting to someone - even myself maybe - that there are circumstances where I might lose that control and hurt someone, maybe badly, is no small matter. In short, I was scared to do so.

Vicki must have been reading my mind.

'There's no shame in seeking help, you know.'

'I know. It's just- uhh,'

'What? Hard guys like you don't do counselling? Opening yourself up to others is for wimps?'

She was spot on. 'No, it's just...' But I couldn't think what to say.

'Listen, Danny, if it was good enough for Tony Soprano, it's good enough for you.'

I didn't know what she meant, though I'd heard of The Sopranos and knew it was a TV series about gangsters. When it comes to watching TV, a good action movie and sports are about my limit. David Attenborough as well sometimes. When I told her I'd never watched it, she shook her head.

'I can see I'm going to have to educate you in a few areas.'

I liked the sound of that. 'What sort of areas?'

The way she looked at me over her wine glass, with her hair falling forward and what I hoped was a sexy smile playing about her lips, the heart-thumping started up again.

'If you'd like to get us both another drink, I might tell you.' I wasn't about to refuse.

When I returned, she'd moved to the couch. I wasn't sure where everything was going, so before it did I said, 'There's something else I need to speak to you about.'

'Like what?'

I hesitated, worried in case she thought it was the only thing I'd come for. 'Yesterday you mentioned that If I still needed an in to the club, you would help.'

She gave me a suspicious look. 'Ye-s?'

'I might need one.'

She took another drink. 'Tell me.'

I did.

When we'd finished talking she said. 'Anything else?'

The way she said it, abruptly, caught me off guard. 'Uh- No, I don't think so.'

'Good.' She stood up, suddenly. My stomach fell, certain she was about to ask me to leave. But instead she simply held out her glass. 'You see to the refills and I'll change out of my training togs. Then we'll talk about what areas I might be able to educate you in.'

I stood up and took the glass. By then all I could manage was a hoarse, 'Okay.'

It was while I was in the kitchen pouring her wine that my phone rang. The caller ID said 'Alison'. My first thought was Dad, but then I pictured her the last time we'd met, that day, at her house.

'Alison?'

'You need to come down here, Danny.'

'Is he alright? What's happened?'

'He went missing this evening, but he's ok now. He's here with us.'

'Missing? How?'

'He went out, to the corner shop we think, but must have got confused and couldn't remember where he lived. The police found him and brought him home. Lucky he had his wallet with his old driving licence still in it.'

'Oh, Jesus. I'll come right away. Be there in an hour.'

'Okay.'

'And Alison?'

'Yes?'

'Thanks.'

'No problem.'

I hung up. *Shit.*

A noise behind made me turn.

Vicki was standing in the doorway. She'd changed into a different outfit. One I'd never seen before, but imagined many times.

It was the absolute worst timing. *Ever.*

## CHAPTER 49

'Right,' I said. 'Now you know where you are?'

Sitting up in bed in his striped pyjamas, Dad nodded. 'I'm at your place. In- Warrington.'

'Whitely, actually. But close enough. So if you wake in the night just remember. I'm only next door so you can call me if you need anything, okay?'

'Yes, okay. Don't fuss.'

*Don't fuss? That's rich.* But all I said as I rose from the side of the bed was, 'Get a good night's sleep.'

At the door I was about to switch out the light, when he called, 'Danny?'

I turned. The sad look was back again.

'I'm sorry.'

I gave him a big smile. 'What for? I was only thinking yesterday that a change of scenery would do you good.'

He returned the smile, or tried to. I pulled the door to, but didn't close it fully.

Downstairs, I rang Laura. She likes her early nights during the week but as it wasn't much past ten o'clock, I took a chance.

'I'm just in bed,' she said. *Good guess.* 'What's up?' .

I told her what had happened. How Dad had gone walkabout and got lost. About the police finding him and bringing him home. That Alison had seen the police car and come out and taken charge of him before ringing me.

'Thank God. That woman's a saint. You'd better send her a bunch of flowers or something tomorrow, as a thank you.'

'I intend to.' Though not too big, I thought. I didn't want to risk anything being misinterpreted.

'How was he when you got there?'

'According to Alison, a lot better than when the police brought him home, though he was still a bit agitated. He settled down after a while and by the time he'd had another cup of tea he seemed to have got over it.'

'I take it he hadn't?'

'When I took him back into his house, he became confused again. He didn't seem to recognise it. He kept saying it wasn't his house and he wanted me to take him to his proper home, in Warrington. Which is how I ended up having to bring him back here.'

'Oh my God, it doesn't sound good. How is he now?'

'That's what's so damn frustrating. He seems more or less normal again now. He's just asked me how long he's staying because he was planning on clearing out his shed and he wants to do it while the evenings are still light.'

'Oh, Danny.' To be fair to her, she sounded sympathetic. I'd been half-expecting she would start on the, 'told-you-sos' about putting him in care. 'What are you going to do tomorrow?'

'I'm going to take him to the Medical Centre in the morning and get him assessed. But I wouldn't be surprised if they say he's fine. It's obviously something that comes and goes. The trouble is, it looks like it might be happening more often.'

'Is there anything I can do?'

I hesitated. I'd anticipated she would ask. I took a deep breath. I was hoping straight out honesty would hit the spot. 'Yes.'

'What?'

'Right now there are some things I'm working on. Important things that affect my business, as well as this thing the police arrested me for. I can't do them if I can't go out.'

The silence on the other end lasted several seconds. Eventually she said, 'You want me to come up there and look after him.'

'Only until Friday. It'll all be over by then.'

'You make it sound like a showdown.'

'It is, of sorts. Can you do it?'

For once, it only a took a couple of seconds for her to say, 'Yes.'

## CHAPTER 50

*Tuesday*

After the previous two lousy nights, my sleep must have been deep enough that when I heard the crash, my brain played one of those tricks where it instantly translated it into a dream involving a car crash. A split second later my eyes shot open and I was wide awake. I leaped out of bed and got to the window just in time to see a dark figure disappear out of sight round to the left. Somewhere, a car engine revved, loudly. I was straining to see it when I noticed the flickers of orange directly below, where the living room window looks out over the garden.

I turned and bounded across the bed and out into the hallway. I smelled the smoke at once. Looking over the rail, I could see more flickering, red and yellow as well as orange now. As I watched, a tongue of flame leaped across the kitchen floor.

I dived into the other bedroom. The bed was empty. He wasn't in the room.

'DAD?'

I raced down the stairs and stopped a couple of steps from the bottom. The heat was already intense. A good part of the front living room was ablaze, carpet, curtains, the couch. There was a strong smell of petrol, glass fragments visible here and there. And a big hole in the window.

'DAD?'

Leaning round and into the room, I searched for him through the smoke, frantic in case he was lying amongst the flames. Then I saw him, standing like a statue in the corner at the far end of the room furthest away from the flames. *Thank Christ.*

'DAD?' But I knew he couldn't hear me. His gaze was locked on the fire in such a way I could actually feel his terror.

I swung, two-handed, round the newel-post so I landed in the back half of the room and ran over to him. As I did so I trod on a piece of glass and knew it had broken the skin. When I got to him one look was enough to tell me he was out of it. I didn't try talking to him but just scooped him up in my arms and turned back towards the fire. My back door is actually a side door off the kitchen, where I'd just come from. Where I was, there was nowhere I could go. I had no options. Even as I watched, flames reached out across my route licking up the walls. Bloody footprints marked my path back. The smoke was billowing now, becoming thicker. Before I set off I sank to one knee, bent as low as I could and filled my lungs with the clearest air I could find.

As I stood up I shouted, 'HANG ON, DAD,' but doubted he heard me.

I ran back to the kitchen, feeling the heat of the flames against my bare legs, arms and back as I went. Just as I got there, Dad started shaking, violently, in my arms. God knows what was going through his mind.

'WE'RE OKAY, DAD. WE'RE NEARLY THERE.'

Caroline always used to complain that for someone who runs a security business, I was the least security-minded person she'd ever met. Right now I was glad I always leave the key in the lock when I lock up at night. I guess that somewhere deep down I've always thought that one day, something bad might happen. In which case-

Ten seconds later we were out in the cool, night air. I didn't want to get trapped in the back garden - it's only small - so I carried him down the side and out into the close and away from the house. By now Tom and Liz from next door were out. I could hear someone shouting. I was aware of lights going on in upstairs windows. Someone shouted, 'I've rung the Fire Brigade. They're on their way.' But my focus was on Dad. After the shaking he'd gone limp in my arms and as I laid him down on someone's lawn a coat appeared in front of me. I threw it over him. Someone draped a jacket over my shoulders.

I shouted to him, 'DAD? DAD?' and slapped his cheek, though gently. There was no response. I put two fingers to the side of his neck - my concern right then was he'd had a heart attack - and I've never felt so grateful as when I felt the faint throb that told me his heart was still beating.

'SOMEONE CALL AN AMBULANCE,' I shouted.

# CHAPTER 51

At four o'clock in the morning, Warrington General's Intensive Care Unit can be quite unsettling. For a start everyone talks in whispers, which immediately sets you in mind of a church, or somewhere else associated with spirituality and death. Then there's the subdued lighting. Subtle shades of greens, blues and yellows lend the place a sense of drama, as if to emphasise that it's a place where Bad Things sometimes happen. The sounds of the machines that monitor the patients, or pump air into their lungs and medicines into their compliant bodies, serve as reminders that the people there are living, literally in some cases, on the 'edge'. To me, there's something deeply creepy, about all the beeping and artificial breathing noises. I think it comes from watching too many horror movies and scary thrillers set in hospitals where the noise suddenly cuts off and someone either dies, or they sit up suddenly in their cot and sink their teeth into someone's neck.

How much of this I was conscious of as I looked down on Dad lying in his Assisted Breathing Unit, I couldn't now say. I do know that during the hour I'd waited for word from one of the team who'd met us when we arrived and rushed him straight through A&E and into one of the treatment rooms, I'd pondered on all of it more than once.

This was my third - or was it fourth? - visit to the ICU in the space of a week. By now I was on nodding terms with a couple of the night nurses. I'm not religious or anything, but I couldn't help wondering if I was being prepared in some way for when something happened that would put me in there, and that's assuming I survived what some people clearly had in store for me, if tonight's incident was anything to go by.

The irony of it all was that right now, Dad was looking about as good as he had in a while, apart from the yellowish tinge to his skin. The doctor had said he'd given him something to make him sleep so that the ventilator could do its work without interference. The peaceful look on his face made me wonder - hope? - he was having happy dreams about Mum or family holidays long-past.

It was clear now that the fact he was still alive was pretty miraculous. According to the medics, what he'd been through could easily have seen off any man his age, never mind one whose lungs were only operating at half capacity. Apart from all the smoke he'd inhaled, there was the shock of being in the room when the petrol bomb crashed through. So far I'd managed to not dwell on what would have happened if he'd been near the window, instead of the other end of the room. I still had no idea what he was doing there, probably never would.

For myself, I'd finally managed to stop the shaking and get my brain functioning at something close to normal. Even so, some part of me was still back on my neighbour's lawn giving the limp figure on the grass CPR while shouting, 'DON'T YOU DIE ON ME,

YOU BASTARD. DON'T YOU DARE DIE.' I think I was still shouting at him when the paramedics shoved me out of the way, clamped a mask over his face and did whatever it was they did that the doctor said saved his life.

Amongst everything I was experiencing in those moments, one thought stood out. What had happened to Dad was my fault. I couldn't believe I'd been so stupid as to bring him back to mine. Ever since the night I'd gone nose-to-nose with Yashin over Bergin enticing Agnes upstairs, the same night she was taken, I'd been expecting some sort of come-back. The white van on the Brigadoon's car park and the attack on Eric, were just them putting out feelers. And far from my being sacked off the door removing the danger, my foiling of the intended riot would have only strengthened Yashin's determination to demonstrate to the world that you fuck with him at your peril. I should have been thinking about that every moment since, rather than carrying on like I was Captain Invincible. The only good thing was that so far they hadn't linked me with Vicki or any-

HELL. *Vicki.*

The thought hit me like a hammer. For all I knew, they could have followed me to her flat the night before. They might even have been outside, pouring petrol into milk bottles when I got the call from Alison.

My hand went, instinctively, to my pocket, only to remember that my phone was still on the table, next to my bed. So far I'd neither called nor told anyone about what had happened. The only ones who knew were me, my neighbours, the emergency services, and the bastards responsible. Which was where my thoughts went next.

I cast a final glance down, struck by the way he now seemed only half the size of the father I remembered from my youth. I gritted my teeth and fought against the feeling that threatened to engulf me and which I'd been resisting ever since I'd seen him disappear into the examination room. I took a long, deep breath. 'I'm sorry, Dad.' Then I turned away, quickly, and headed for the exit.

Jamie Carver and DS Jess were still waiting for me in the corridor outside. They'd arrived just as I'd been about to go in and see Dad and I'd only had time to speak with them briefly. It was Carver who had told me that the Fire Brigade had managed to get the fire under control before the whole house went up. He also said he needed to speak with me, 'Urgently,' and, 'Before someone gets killed.' I gave them the bare story - not that there was much more I could give - then left them talking on their phones to whoever was working the scene with the Fire Investigation guys. I guess a Fire Bomb is still a rare enough event to warrant the call-outs you see with any major crime investigation.

As I came out, they both stood up, showing genuine concern. I was conscious I probably looked ridiculous in the way-too-small tracksuit and slip-ons one of my neighbours had given me.

'How is he?' Jess said.

'He's holding his own, for now. They're saying the next twenty four hours are critical. If he can get through that, then he's in with a good chance.'

Carver nodded, but didn't attempt any of the forced optimism many show in such circumstances. He'd have heard similar many times before, and would know the odds.

'We need to talk,' Carver said.

'Okay. But can we make it short? There's stuff I need to do.'

He gave me a warning look. 'That's part of what we need to talk about. You need to calm down and let us deal with this.'

'I am calm.'

'Sure you are.'

I turned to Jess. 'Do I look like I'm about to run off and do something stupid?'

'You look like you always do.'

I wasn't sure how to take that so I let it ride. 'Right, but two things before we start.'

'What?'

I told them about my concerns about Vicki. Carver understood at once and told Jess to arrange for a team to go to her flat and stay there until further notice. As Jess made the calls he turned back to me. 'What's the second thing?'

'I need some coffee and you'll have to pay for it because I've no money. Then one of you can run me home.'

As I led them off in the direction of the cafeteria, I saw their reflections in the glass lining the corridor and saw them exchange looks and shake their heads.

Fuck them, I thought.

## CHAPTER 52

As always when I ring him at odd hours, Eric answered with, 'What's up?' I knew Margarita starts her cleaning job at six so wasn't surprised he sounded wide awake and alert.

'I need you to meet me at our offices, now.'

'At five-fucking-thirty in the fucking morning? You're having a fucking laugh.'

'They petrol-bombed my house.'

'WHAT?'

'Dad was there.'

'FUCK. Is he okay?'

I gave him the story, the short version.

'I'll be there in twenty minutes.'

The first thing I did when I arrived at the office was put the kettle on. Then I switched on the computers, and waited for Eric. I knew exactly what he would say when he walked in and he didn't disappoint.

'If you'd been fucking listening when I showed you how all this works, you wouldn't need me.'

As I spooned sugar into his coffee I said, 'But then I wouldn't have the pleasure of your company. Besides, all you do after you've dropped Margarita off is study the racing pages so I'm saving you money.'

'Fuck off.'

I gave him his coffee and as he booted up the system on the main office computer and logged in to whatever he needed to log into, I filled him in on the night's events. His responses didn't go much beyond, 'Fucking hell,' and, 'Jesus Christ.' After a few minutes playing with the mouse he said, 'Okay, we're in. What time was it, roughly?'

'Around two, I think.'

'Let's try from one-thirty. Front, rear or both?'

'Front. It looked like a straight approach. Hit and run.'

I checked the screen and saw that he'd split it in two, a video player showing a dark grainy image in each. After bringing up and clicking on several menus, the images lightened and became sharper, almost like daylight. One of the videos showed the view from the camera fitted to the side wall of my house. It covered most of the driveway, front path, garden and that part of the close outside my front door. The other was the view from the camera fitted to the gable end of the house two doors round from mine and which faces straight down the close. I made a mental note to pass another bottle of Jura in to Arthur. He's never asked for ground rent or anything, but I liked to keep him sweet. That said, the system benefits him and the close as a whole, as well as myself.

It was Eric who'd convinced me, a couple of years before, that it was probably a good idea to invest in some sort of CCTV monitoring. It wasn't long after the last, 'Door Wars' when feelings were still running high and threats had been thrown around like confetti. Eric pointed out that apart from my protection, as the boss of a security company it made sense that I should be seen to be using the technology that is available these days. We arranged it through a company we knew, Samson, that specialises in remote CCTV surveillance. From their site in Kirkby, just outside Liverpool, they monitor something like two-hundred-and-fifty sites around the country, industrial, commercial and residential. Most of it is automatic and the camera operators only have to respond when an alarm or sensor activates. I sat through the very professional presentation their representative gave at our office but when he started talking about, 'terrabytes of stored data', and 'remote servers', he lost me. The only things I needed to know were the costs - it was surprisingly cheap - and the installation timescale - 'Tomorrow, if you're ready.' And while I was seen as the highest risk, Mike decided that we could afford to have it put in at his and Eric's houses as well. In the end we opted for a passive system, one that simply records, but keeps the stored data for three months. What I was clear about was, if the time ever came when I needed to access the recordings, I would need Eric.

To begin with, the only activity on the screens were a couple of cats and a fox scavenging for open bins. The video time-stamp read 01:56 when that all changed. The camera mounted on Arthur's gable-end picked it up first. A four-by-four, driving slowly, passed across the end of the close. Seconds later it reversed in, at speed, stopping when it was still a few houses down from mine. The front passenger door opened and a dark figure, clearly a man, got out. He was holding something in his right hand. He jogged down towards my house, coming in to view now on the other camera as well. Stopping a few yards from the front window, he brought his hands together in front. There was a spark, a cigarette lighter I assumed, then the object in his hand flared alight, like a roman candle. Taking his arm back, he launched the bottle at the front of the house. The camera on Arthur's house showed it go straight through the front window, followed immediately by the explosion of flame as it did what petrol bombs are supposed to do. I imagined Dad, in the room right at that moment, and a chill ran through me, making me shiver.

'Bugger me,' Eric said.

'Bastard,' I said, though it was more of a growl. As we'd watched I'd been aware of the burning rage that had been growing inside me from the moment the four-by-four appeared, and I was glad I'd anticipated it. Even so, I had to make a conscious effort not to flip-out. Pains in the palms of my hands and wrists reminded me to unclench my fists.

Almost before the bottle hit, the figure was racing back to the waiting four-by-four which was already moving as he scrambled into the passenger seat. The door closed, the car turned left out of the close and disappeared. By now, flames were leaping out of my front room.

'Stop it there,' I said. I didn't need to see any more and wasn't interested in seeing me carry Dad out, or reliving the minutes leading up to the paramedics arriving.. They were memories that could stay where they were for now. But at that moment, I was conscious of a feeling of disappointment. Even with Eric's adjustments to the settings, the pictures on both screens had been too indistinct to pick up detail. It hadn't given me what I'd hoped for. I said so.

Eric was nodding and clicking his mouse even before I finished. He half turned in his chair and jerked a thumb at a shelf containing several ring-binders. 'Pass me the one marked, 'Samson.' I did so and he started flicking through it.

'What are you looking for?' I said.

'I'm looking to see if all that System Enhancement Software we didn't tell Mike he was paying for when we had it installed is as good as your mate in Samson said it is.'

I nodded as a vague memory surfaced. It was of Eric, looking pleased with himself as he explained to me one night how he'd got Samson to bury the costs of something he seemed to think was important within the overall system installation costs. And that if Mike ever asked, I was to say I'd done it so Mike wouldn't sack him. After a minute flicking back and forth through the manual, Eric found what he was looking for then spent another couple of minutes refreshing himself on the technicalities. Then he put the binder aside and started bringing up menus again and clicking. And clicking. All I could do was watch. Used to being in charge of things and telling others what to do, I felt about as useful as a chocolate fireguard.

Eventually I said, 'Is there anything I can be doing?'

'Yeah. Make us another coffee.'

As I reached across for his now empty mug I said, 'A please would be nice.'

Ignoring it he added, 'And when Ladbrokes opens across the road, go over and put fifty quid on Sandy's Double in the two-fifty at Wetherby. On the nose.'

# CHAPTER 53

The next few days passed in a blur. There were meetings, and more meetings. With Winston. With his brothers. With my team. With Carver and his NCA mate, Will. The last was a strange one. They wanted to know everything, but made clear right at the start there were some things they didn't want to hear me say, which quite honestly I thought was a bit ridiculous but went along with because that was the game we were playing.

I saw a fair bit of Vicki, but only because I was sleeping in her second bedroom - a weird reversal of where we'd been the week before. It was only ever going to be a temporary arrangement, while I waited to hear back from the insurance before sending Harry Shankley in to get on with the repairs. Any other time I'd probably have thought that me sharing a flat with Vicki would be like all my Christmases coming at once. But the attack on my house affected her - and me - far more than I expected.

She was jumpy from the moment I landed at her flat after getting away from Carver and Jess at the hospital. Earlier, the arrival of the police team, who only knew they were to protect her but little else, had sent her into a panic and it was only when they reassured her that no one had died, she started to calm down. Even so, when I walked into her lounge I was shocked by what I saw. She was nervous to the point of shaking and was wearing a haunted expression that made me ache inside. When she came over and threw herself on me - I judged it as a need to feel safe, rather than a show of affection - I was surprised to find she smelled of cigarettes. Looking down at the coffee table I saw an ashtray containing several stubs, next to it a packet of cigarettes and a lighter. I'd never seen Vicki smoke, ever.

She stayed that way through most of the week. I was out quite a bit but when I was there, I lost count of the number of times she went to the window to check what was happening outside. We spent a fair bit of time cuddled up next to each other on the couch, though it wasn't as nice as it sounds. The last thing on her mind was reawakening the sort of feelings we'd explored, occasionally, the previous week. I did wonder if she might feel safer if I went and stayed somewhere else, but when I mentioned it, she wouldn't hear of it. 'You're going nowhere. Besides, you can put some shelves up while you're here,' which I did.

The one good thing was that once she'd had a couple of glasses of wine, I was able to talk to her about the part I needed her to play on the Friday without her freaking out. That first night, when I came in from the hospital, her first instinct was to never go near Midnight's again.

'I've had it with that place,' she'd said. 'I'd have to be fucking mad to go back there. They're all fucking crazy.' Her cussing came as another surprise. I put it down to stress. But once I'd had the chance to talk to her, to lay it all out, describe how, if it all worked, it would remove the very dangers she was worrying about, she began to come round. After I explained that it was important she was seen to be acting normally, she finally agreed to go into work on the Tuesday evening - though she was adamant she wouldn't be doing any dancing. I didn't argue, though I knew I might have to later. If she didn't dance on Thursday and Friday someone might start wondering what had spooked her. But right then her involvement in trying to help the police draw out the Club Killer had fallen way down my list of priorities. It was a mistake I'll always regret.

Then of course, there was Dad. He got through the Tuesday and into the Wednesday alright, but he still wasn't good and they kept him on the respirator. Laura came up as we'd arranged anyway - on her own this time - and managed to bunk up with an old, now-married, school friend. It meant we could split the visiting, though she took on most of it, which I was grateful for. That week I wouldn't have heard a word said against my sister, even if she did still seem to have difficulty recognising that others as well as herself, were being inconvenienced. Once she confirmed that her brainless brother had actually managed to remember to keep up the insurance on the house, and that I had a place to stay, - *'Is she attractive?... Knew it.'* - she promptly forgot that your house burning down is a pretty shitty thing to have to go through. The fact it could have seen me off as well, seemed to fly by her completely.

There were other things I could have given my time to that week, if I'd chosen to do so. Ricky Mason for one. My partner Mike, the business, and what we were going to do about it, for others. But I made the decision to leave all of that until after Friday. My hope was that things might be clearer then. Besides, thinking about it only got me upset, and there's only so much upset I can stand at once. Worrying about Vicki, and Dad and Friday was enough for now. One interesting thing. After speaking to Mike on the telephone, when he was relieved to hear I was okay, I hardly heard from him that week. As far as the office was concerned, he kept an even lower profile than usual, which wound Julie up no-end. 'I know you've got a lot on your plate right now, Danny, with your house and your Dad and everything. But someone still needs to sign letters and cheques and get back to people when they leave messages. Can't you have a word with him?' I said I would, but ended up sending messages and emails - 'RING JULIE' - when I couldn't get a response on his phone.

And during those rare times when I wasn't seeing to all this, there was one matter I kept having to deal with and which made sure my mind was always fully occupied. Controlling the urges that made me want to go out and kill some bastard.

## CHAPTER 54

*Friday*

The Man Who Likes To Watch can barely contain his excitement. After the disappointments of earlier in the week, when it looked like events over which he had no control were conspiring to rob him of the opportunity he had engineered so cleverly, he is back on track.

Tonight, assuming all goes well, he will go to bed looking forward to the promise of something wholly new the next day. A change in the routine which, the more he thinks about it, the more he wonders if he ought to include it in his repertoire again sometime. The trouble with sticking to one particular system, he now thinks, is the danger it may become predictable. That the police may find a way of working out when or where he may strike next - though he can't see how. After all, even he finds it difficult to predict these things.

Take Vicki Lamont for instance. Ordinarily, he would never have considered another so soon after the last. But the way things have happened, the opportunity that has been presented to him, out of the blue so to speak, is simply too good to pass up. It amazes him how, in the space of two short weeks, she has gone from not even being on his radar, to perhaps becoming the pinnacle of his achievements to date. They have all been attractive of course, that goes without saying. And talented - though some more than others. But if he is honest, none of them measure up to her. What he saw last night - Tuesday's rest must have done her good - was way better than anything he has seen so far. A reminder of how special she is. How special she WILL be, when the time comes. Which is not far away now.

Leaning back on his bed, he puts on the earphones that are never far away, presses the 'play' button and lets the music that is now so familiar he knows every beat, take him to that place where he takes pleasure in reliving what has gone before, whilst also imagining what is yet to come.

# CHAPTER 55

By eleven o'clock that Friday evening, I'd realised my mistake. When we first piled into Harry Shankley's van, I'd noticed it didn't seem as roomy as I remembered. But, 'Hey,' I thought. 'It's only a couple of hours. What's the problem?' Three hours later I knew what the problem was. Rather, problems.

For a start, eight bodies - mostly hefty - packed into a van with no windows and only two small grilles to let in air, generates a hell of a lot of heat. Also, it was a builder's van, which meant no seats. With only a mattress and several cushions to spread out on, it meant that by ten o'clock we were all suffering from various forms of cramp, back-ache and associated discomforts. Even Jamie Carver, with all his experience of sitting in the backs of vans on police operations, and who at the start had made light of the crowded conditions, was looking decidedly pissed off. I won't even mention the smells, though I suspected it would be a long time before Eve would forgive Chris and Winston - or me for that matter - though I could claim, with honesty, that my only crime was the planning. What grown guys do in small places when they're keyed-up is beyond my control.

Discomforts apart, Eric and I were doing our best to

follow the reports being fed to Carver and Will from their sources inside the club. As far as I'd picked up, all of Will's team - around twelve I believed - were now inside, having turned up as regular punters and paid their admissions. The pair designated to keep eyeball on Winston's brothers when they arrived were in place and ready. The others were spread around the club in twos and threes, waiting for the, 'Go' word.

But by now everyone was getting impatient, even Gol.

'Any sign of Yashin yet?' he said, trying for the umpteenth time to find a position that offered his squat bulk some degree of comfort, a mission which was doomed to failure, I thought.

Carver shook his head, but stayed focused on listening to his earpiece. 'We're assuming it'll be his usual time.' He turned to me. 'What? Midnight-ish?'

'Give or take quarter of an hour,' I said. In the run up, I'd told The Brothers to make sure they didn't try to push Yashin into breaking his routine. For him, as with everyone, it was important that the night seemed no different from any other Friday. We didn't want to scare anyone off.

'Any more from Vicki?' Eve said.

I checked my phone. There'd been no new messages since the last telling me that everything seemed as normal, apart from Frank spending a lot of time holed up in his office with Charnley, which was understandable. It was still only Charnley's third night in charge of the door. There was a lot to take in. It had taken me a couple of weeks, at least.

I shook my head. 'She's due to do one podium stint before half-eleven, then another an hour later. Hopefully it'll all be over by then.'

'It better be.' Eve's snarl was accompanied by the dirty look she threw at Winston and Chris. Neither offered any defence or denial. They just exchanged smirks and high-fives.

A minute later, Winston's phone rang and he rushed to answer it. 'Hey, Bro.' He listened intently, 'Uh-huhing' and nodding at intervals, before ending the call and turning to me. 'They're here. They've parked over on the Trading Estate and are walking in. They've rung Bergin and he said they'll be here in ten minutes. When Yashin's settled upstairs he'll come down and let them in the side door.'

The news seemed to excite Carver. 'Excellent.' He passed the information out to Jess and warned her to be ready with the camera. Jess had opted - wisely - to work the Obs Van with another DC. Marked to look like a private hire minibus but with blacked-out windows, it was parked up in the small drop-off car park at the front. From there they had a view of both the front and side entrances. Armed with night-scopes, cameras and video, their job was to capture anything that might come in useful later, as well as give a running commentary on comings and goings.

'How are things in there?' I heard her ask through Carver's ear-piece.

He turned to give me a wry look as he replied, 'Hot. And whiffy.'

'Tee-hee-hee,' she said, though not loud enough for Eve to hear, thankfully.

I settled back. Ten minutes to Yashin's arrival meant at least a further thirty or more of sweating.

Reaching into the ice-bag I took out another can of

coke. Pulling the tab, I raised it towards Eve. 'Cheers.'

'Piss off.' she said, as if she'd had lessons from Eric.

Bergin was as good as his word. Ten minutes later, Carver held a hand up, listened then said, 'Yashin's limo's just pulled up out front.'

It got everyone stirring and prompted bursts of, 'About frigging time,' and 'Thank fuck.'

After another minute, Carver said, 'They're in. Yashin, Bergin, Alexei and the two women.'

Sitting next to Carver, Will had been quieter than most throughout, which made me realise how he probably had as much riding on the next hour as I did. Now he came alive as one of his inside team relayed Yashin's progress. 'They're heading upstairs. Bergin's carrying a black sports bag.' Then he smiled as he added, 'Looks like there's some weight in it.'

I raised an eyebrow at Carver. I'd never seen Eighty-thousand-quid cash, but had tried imagining it. A sports bag seemed about right.

My phone beeped a text from Vicki. 'She's about to go on the podium,' I said. 'Fifteen minutes then she'll be free.' I turned to Winston. 'Tell Anthony he can be at the side door in five.'

'Right, Baaaz.'

Exactly five minutes later, Winston confirmed his brothers were at the side door. 'They've rung Bergin. He's coming down to let them in.' Carver passed it to Jess. The next few minutes saw a stream of messages confirming the brothers were in and being escorted upstairs, one of them carrying a briefcase. Will was on his radio almost constantly now, marshaling his team. Through all of it, I was conscious that for all the police's readiness, everything still depended on us doing our bit.

Then everything went quiet.

The next thirty minutes felt like as many hours. During that time several people's nails got bitten even further down than they were. At one point my phone beeped and everyone jumped, but it was only Vicki letting me know she was off the podium and ready. I messaged back, 'Thnx.'

It was Will who got the first update. 'The brothers are in the lobby. Bergin's showing them out. Gabriel's carrying a sports bag.'

'Hot damn,' Winston said, and smacked Gol's knee.

I brought up Vicki's number, ready.

Two minutes passed. Winston's phone rang just as Carver was receiving Jess's confirmation that The Brothers were heading away from the club. He held the phone, tight, to his ear. The call lasted only seconds. 'Uh-huh. Right. Love you, Bro.' He rang off, then lifted his head to look at me. His eyes were wide with excitement. 'It's done.'

I checked with Carver and Will. They both nodded. I pressed my phone's green 'ring' button. Vicki answered at once. 'Soon as you can.'

'Two minutes,' she said, and rang off.

Carver and Will began speaking on their radios. They were using different channels so as not to cut across each other. Everyone eased themselves up, stretching cramped limbs. My phone rang. As I lifted it to my ear I noticed the time. Midnight.

'Ready,' Vicki said.

I nodded to Gol. He pulled the handle on the back door.

We all jumped out, and started running.

## CHAPTER 56

Harry had parked the van on a spare piece of land just off Bold Street, less than a hundred metres from the club's back door. Twenty seconds later, we were lined up in the shadow to the right of it. I knocked, twice, then twice more. It opened. Vicki stood back as we all trooped inside.

'Okay?' I said to her and felt for her hand. It was clammy. She nodded, quickly, and tried a smile. I gave her hand a squeeze. Then I turned to the others, who were waiting for my lead. 'Let's go,' I said. I remember thinking how it felt a bit like we were in some SAS movie, about to take out a bunch of terrorists.

We jogged down the corridor. The busiest time of the night, I'd have been surprised if we'd come across anyone in that part of the club and we didn't. As we approached the main office I made sure Carver and Will were at the back, just in case there was any 'resistance' when we went in.' At the end of the day they were police and I didn't want to compromise them any more than necessary, especially considering what might happen later.

As we turned through the door, two of Charnley's guys were behind the desk. They were peering hard at the screens and playing about with the controls. Still trying to get their heads round the system's configuration, I guessed. We got to within a couple of yards of them before they even looked round, by which time it was too late. Not the best, I thought.

'What the fuck?' one of them managed before my team closed around them.

As the youngest's gaze flicked, just for a second, to the radio, Eric jabbed his finger in their faces. 'No fuss, and not a fucking word.' The look on Eric's face, they weren't about to argue. Zip ties and duct tape appeared. A few seconds later, they were tied, mouth-taped and sitting on the floor at the back of the office, Chris standing watch.

Eric sat at the desk and pulled the screens round to him. 'Right. Let's see where everyone is.'

But even as he rotated the cameras, Vicki popped her head round the door with what we needed. 'Charnley's in with Frank.' If the others hadn't been there I'd have gone over and kissed her. I looked at Will. 'Is your team ready?'

'All within striking distance of the stairs.'

'Right. Come with me.'

We left the office and made our way round to Frank's. The door was closed, I didn't knock.

As he saw me come in, Frank leaped out of his seat as if it was wired to the mains and someone had thrown a switch. Charnley was in the easy chair next to the desk but facing towards Frank. By the time he reacted and started to rise my hand was on his shoulder, pressing him back down into the cushion.

'Evening gents. Sorry to disturb.'

'DANNY, What the hell are you-?

Charnley said nothing, concentrating on weighing

what was happening, like I'd have done.

'Easy Frank,' I said. These gentlemen just need a word.'

As I stepped back, Carver came forward. Reaching inside his jacket, he produced several sheets of paper. He put his 'official' face on.

'This is a Search Warrant issued to me under the Misuse of Drugs Act, Frank. It authorises us to search your premises for illegal substances that are banned under the act. Are you, or any persons on these premises in possession of any such substances?'

Frank's head was turning from Carver, to me, to Charnley and back again. He looked like he wasn't sure if he was dreaming. 'You've got to be joking. This is a nightclub.' He turned to me again. 'What the fuck's going on Danny? What is all this?'

I said, 'You'll see,' and wondered how many more times I'd hear the same question before the night was over.

Carver said, 'I'll interpret that as a, 'Not to my knowledge." He turned to Will, and nodded. Will turned away and I heard him say into his radio, 'All Sierras, it's a golf-lima, repeat, a golf-lima.'

I hid a smile. Earlier I'd worked it out. G and L. Green Light. Cops love their code words.

Frank was becoming more agitated. I could imagine what he was thinking and, in truth, I felt for him. I hoped his heart was okay. He said to Carver. 'You're not going to search the whole fucking club. There's close to a thousand people out there.'

Carver said, 'Technically, we could. But I don't think that will be necessary.'

I could see Frank getting ready to try again. There

wasn't time. I leaned forward and grabbed his arm and locked eyes on him. 'It'll be alright Frank. Stay calm and let them do their job.' His Adam's apple bobbed, like a cork on the tide.

Two minutes later, we were all back in the main office, Charnley on the floor next to his guys and Frank planted in one of the chairs where Eric could keep an eye on him.

The part of the script we'd played so far had been pretty tight, time-wise. The next part would be even tighter. I turned to find Chris and Gol by the door, waiting for the nod. I gave it. They disappeared.

As we waited, Frank said, 'What's happening now?'

'Just bear with us Frank.'

He lifted his head and gave me a hard look. Then he said. 'I hope you know what the fuck you're doing.'

I leaned down to whisper in his ear. 'So do I.'

Eric said, 'They're there.'

I moved round to the screens. One of them showed the main entrance. I could see Chris and Gol just outside the front doors. They'd already attracted the attention of one of the door team, his hand behind his back, signalling to his mates. Even as we watched, two more came into view, alerted to the danger. Can't fault their response, I thought. Charnley would have drummed into them what they were to do if I, or any of my team, showed up.

I turned to Carver. 'Now's the time.'

He nodded and turned to Frank. 'Come with us Frank.' Taking him by the upper arm, he eased him out of the chair. Frank looked scared to death.

'Where are we going?'

'We need you there,' Carver said.

As they dragged him out of the office I heard Frank squeak, 'Where's there?'

By now Eve had left to get ready. We were down to Eric, myself and Winston, keeping an eye on Charnley and his staff.

Eric brought up the camera covering the door that led upstairs to the private suites. Half a minute or so later, there was a sudden commotion out front as Chris and Gol kicked off right on cue, launching themselves at the two doormen they'd been talking to. Immediately several black shirted figures flashed across the cameras as every door supervisor in the vicinity responded to help deal with the incident. At the same time, the radio burst into life as those responding radioed 'control' to let Charnley know. As Eric pressed the mic button and gave out an acknowledgement in a way that was sufficiently garbled to disguise his voice, I held my breath and focused on the door to upstairs. Even at this point, if someone twigged and made a warning phone call, it could still ruin everything. There was a gap of only seconds, then bodies appeared from all directions, converging on the door and filing rapidly through. I just caught sight of the women going in front, followed closely by Will and his team, with Carver, towing Frank, bringing up the rear. I kept my eye on what I could see of the melee taking place in the foyer. No one broke off to deal with what was a significant breach of security. As the doors closed and stayed shut and there was still no response from any of Charnley's crew, I heaved a sigh of relief. Eric switched the cameras to seven and nine, which cover the top corridor from both ends.

Outside the Ten-To-Midnight Suite, Alexei stood,

erect and relaxed. He was playing with his phone, either checking messages or playing some game. As Vicki, Eve and Eve's partner, Colleen appeared from round the top of the stairs, it disappeared into his pocket and he turned to meet them. Even knowing it was Eve, I was hard-pushed to recognise her in the long blond wig she was wearing. And I couldn't recall ever having seen her in a dress and heels before, certainly not like the one she had on now, with a split up the side that went nearly up to her waist. Colleen was dressed in similar, spectacular fashion, only hers was designed so that it pushed her ample bosoms up and out like twin Mount Vesuviuses. With Vicki in the middle, the three women approached Alexei like girls in nightclubs sometimes do when they bear down on doormen, all giggles, wiggles and sharing supposedly            hidden-behind-the-back-of-a-hand comments about something that seemed to be catching their eye. Eve and Colleen were showing just enough wobble as they leaned into Vicki to suggest they were enjoying a really good night out. As Alexei drew himself up to his full height and clasped his hands behind his back, I even thought, 'You poor sap.'

Stopping far enough away to draw him a few feet further away from the door he was guarding, Vicki went through the motions of introducing him to her companions. At the same time she made sure he had plenty of time to note their respective attributes.

It happened regularly, though not often, that certain types of girls would ask about the possibility of being introduced to the, 'Rich Russian Upstairs.' And though these things were usually negotiated by way of calling Bergin down to peruse the merchandise and report back to his boss, there had been the odd occasion where Vicki had found herself getting involved, much to her distaste I knew. My hope was, therefore, that Alexei would see nothing alarming about her bringing up two, 'new girls' for an, 'on the spot' inspection.

But as Vicki had indicated when I first broached it with her, she wasn't going to stay to witness the second act. Having facilitated introductions, she made her excuses and headed back the way she had come, leaving Alexei to decide on whether or how to take things a stage further. There followed a short play-act during which Eve and Colleen flirted away, making sure Alexei was properly disarmed, before making their move. For his part, Alexei played along. He seemed to be enjoying the attention. When he reached into his pocket and brought out his phone, I imagined him explaining how he, 'just needed to check if it was okay to show them in.'

As he turned away for the scrap of privacy he needed to make the call, Eve reached into the bag that had been hanging off her shoulder all the while, took out the Taser, pointed it at Alexei's broad back and pressed the button. As the barbs hit him square between the shoulders, he went instantly rigid, before collapsing to his knees.

I know from demonstrations I've seen that Tasers affect people in different ways. Some collapse at once into deep unconsciousness. Others seem able to resist the voltage for a short while, though it may only be for a few seconds. Very rarely, an individual will manage to shrug off the effects altogether, though it's usually where the subject is high on something.

Alexei was a big guy. By dropping to his knees, he showed he wasn't in the first category of Taser responder. And Eve and Colleen weren't about to wait to find out which of the others he might fall into. Like a pair of ballet dancers who had spent weeks choreographing it, Eve spun round and raised her right leg up and out between the split in her skirt. Then, in a twisting martial arts manoeuvre, swung her right foot round so it connected with the side of Alexei's head. At the exact same time as Eve's kick landed, Colleen drove her knuckles into the area just above his right kidney. He went down, and stayed down.

The moment he hit the floor, Will and his team appeared from round the top of the stairs and raced down to where Eve already had a pass-key in the door lock, just in case. Then, throwing the door to the suite open, she stood back as they all rushed passed her into the room and out of our view. Coming immediately after, though at a more leisurely pace, Carver dragged Frank around Alexei's prone figure, and followed through the door, which slammed shut behind them.

I put my head back and let out a long breath. We'd done as much as we could. It was a police matter now. Eric and I turned to each other, and slapped palms.

Behind us Winston called out, 'Fuckin' A.'

But Eve wasn't quite finished. As she bent to put her shoe back on, she twisted the barbs free from Alexei's back and stowed them and the taser back in her bag. Then, as she and Colleen turned away to return downstairs, she planted a kick, short but vicious, into Alexei's side. There was no sign he felt it.


I'd had some long waits recently. The next ten minutes were as long as any. I didn't dare move from the screens. Behind me, Charnley and his mates were

377

beginning to get worked up. I left them to Winston, along with Chris and Gol, who had rejoined us. At one stage I turned and found Vicki at my elbow, also looking at the screens. My hand found hers and I gave her another squeeze, 'Well done,' I said. She just nodded.

Eventually the door opened and Carver stepped out. He didn't look up at the camera but took out his phone and punched a number. My phone rang and I snatched it up.

'Well?' I said, trying to keep my voice even.

It was only then that Carver turned to the camera, raised a fist so I could see his thumb, and said, 'Bingo.'

I was surprised. I'd never have credited Carver with a sense of drama.

## CHAPTER 57

Alexei was beginning to stir just as Will's team started to bring out Yashin and the others - the women, Bergin, and two more of Yashin's goons. Two of the team helped Alexei up, cuffed him, like the rest, and added him onto the end of the line. I noticed that one of Will's men was carrying something square-shaped, wrapped in a black bin bag. They marched them down the corridor, round the corner to the stairs and out. By then Carver had radioed up for the uniforms and police vans he'd had on stand-by at Warrington Nick and they were all waiting, outside.

If I'd had my way, I'd have been there to see Yashin off the premises. But Carver didn't want to give him anything that might make him think he'd been victim of anything other than a tip-off. If he saw me he might start wondering about all sorts of things - some of which hadn't happened yet.

So I watched it all on the screens, then, when Carver and Frank returned, we went to Frank's office and shut the door. When I asked Carver how it had gone upstairs he said, 'Like a dream.'

It turned out that after The Brothers left, Yashin must have decided they needed to sample their recent purchase. When the police burst in, they were all gathered round the glass table, cutting the powder in lines with cards. There were twenty and fifty-pound notes, rolled-up and ready, lying around. The briefcase was on the bar with its lid up, one bag slit up the middle. I could see Carver was pleased. 'I don't think he's going to be able to claim he didn't know it was there.'

'So what happens now?' Frank said. 'Am I in trouble?'

Carver gave a sneaky smile. 'Oh, I think we should be able to keep you out of it, Frank-' A huge look of relief came into Frank's face. 'Provided one thing.'

Frank looked suddenly wary. 'What's that?'

Carver pointed to me. 'We need to keep Danny and his team's role in all of this, under wraps. No one must ever know.'

'Why's that?' Frank said.

'Let's just say that my colleague who you just met, is interested in Yashin for all sorts of reasons. He's hoping to play him in various different ways. I don't know the details, but apparently it'll help if Yashin doesn't know about Danny's involvement.'

'But- Does that mean he might not be charged?'

'Oh, he'll be charged alright. He'll appear in court tomorrow in fact. After that- Well let's see.'

Frank looked worried again. 'But what if he comes- Will he be able to come back here?'

Carver stood up. He had things to do. 'I think you'll find that after tonight, Yashin will no longer have any interest in getting into the club business. Besides, he'd never get a licence. For anything.'

'Thank fuck.'

'And speaking of licences.'

'Yes?'

'I believe yours is due up for renewal soon.'

Frank hesitated, looking at me. 'Yes it is.'

I made sure to quash the smile that kept threatening. Carver was playing him like a fish on a hook.

'I'm sure the licensing authority will be pleased to receive the confidential letter from my Chief Constable making them aware of how cooperative you were during a recent police operation. You and your Security Manager, of course.'

Carver threw me a look and a wink then left, shutting the door behind him. I turned to see Frank looking at me. The expression on his face was the sort he might wear if he'd just discovered I wasn't actually a security guy, but third-in-line to the throne. After several seconds, he collapsed into his chair. His hand went to his forehead, and he rubbed at it, vigorously.

'Holy mother of God. I need a drink.'

Turning the chair, he grabbed the bottle of Macallan and two glasses off the cabinet behind him. He poured one, showed me the bottle. I nodded. His went straight down and he poured himself another.

We drank in silence. I watched Frank as he stared at the top of his desk, taking stock of everything. Eventually he looked up at me and we stared at each other.

I finished my whisky. 'Well?' We both knew what I meant.

He nodded. 'Where's Dave Charnley?'

'Gone.'

Gone? What do you mean gone? I thought you had him tied up, in the office?'

I played it straight. 'I'm told he escaped. He's gone.'

Frank stared at me. He dropped it. He took a deep breath. 'So...'

'Yes?'

He looked at me, swallowing pride. 'So, can you take over?'

I smiled at him.


I found Vicki sitting on the couch, alone, in the Green Room. Her podium duties done and with no VIPs that night, she was working her way through the bottle of Vodka next to her. When I told her we were back on the door, she said, 'Thank God,' filled her glass up, and offered me one. I shook my head. I couldn't afford to get too relaxed just yet.

I sat down next to her. She'd kicked off her shoes and her legs were tucked under her. Her skirt had risen up, showing lots of thigh. 'You were terrific tonight,' I said. 'Thanks.'

'You weren't too bad yourself.' She raised her glass in a toast, kept her eyes on me as she drank.

When I'm alone with Vicki, my stomach had always done this strange thing. That week, staying in her flat, I'd noticed it had stopped doing it. Now it started up again. I reached over and with one finger, pushed back the lock of hair that had fallen across her face. As I did so I said, 'We make a good team.'

As I drew my hand back hers came up to take it and she held it in front of her face. Her eyes bored into mine. 'Yes,' she said. 'We do.'

She guided my hand to her cheek. As I caressed it the way I might a delicate flower, she closed her eyes and leaned into it. For the first time in what seemed a long time, I noticed the fragrance I'd first become familiar with long ago. I don't know why, but I felt the urge to ask. 'What's that perfume you wear?'

She opened her eyes to give me a puzzled look. 'Guess.'

'I haven't a clue.'

'No, that's what it's called, "Guess".

'Oh, I see.'

'Why do you ask?'

I stroked her cheek some more. 'No reason.'

She seemed to remember something and sat up 'By the way. After tomorrow I'm coming off the podium.'

'Yeah? Why's that?'

She shook her head. 'After this week, I think I could do with a break.'

I nodded. 'I understand.' Then I added, 'Shame though.'

She started. 'What do you mean?'

'I was just getting used to it. You do know you're an amazing dancer, don't you?'

She beamed. 'I know some people have said that, but I never believed them.'

'No?'

'But I do now that I've heard it from you.'

'Good.'

She gave me a conspiratorial kind of look. 'Just make sure you're watching. I'll be going out on a high.'

'Oh, yeah? Planning something special, are we?'

'Let's just say I'm working on it. Which reminds me, you'll have to look after yourself tomorrow afternoon.'

'Why? Not rehearsing, surely? Hellfire, you must be taking it seriously.'

She punched my ribs. 'Just be there.'

'I wouldn't miss it for the world.'

We fell silent and she sipped her drink. When the glass was empty, she reached behind her and put it down, all very slow, very leisurely. I still had things to do, but, hey, no rush. Besides, I had this weird feeling going on inside and wanted to see what it meant.

Vicki turned back and looked up at me. The lock of hair had fallen forward again. This time I didn't bother to push it back. Slowly, gracefully, she unwound herself from the position she'd been in since I arrived, then seemed to fold herself, almost naturally, into me, as if we were a matched pair.

I felt the warmth of her body in my arms, pressing against me.

It was the best feeling in the world.

# CHAPTER 58

As I approached Harry's van, the two Crime Agency guys from Will's team saw me coming. Flicking their cigarettes away, they nodded their farewells to Chris and Gol and headed towards me. But as we passed, there was no eye contact or acknowledging nods of recognition and they carried on as if they were just two punters, making their way to the club.

I stopped at the back of the van, just as Chris dropped his butt and ground it into the dirt. 'Where've you been?' he said. 'We was beginning to think you'd got tied up.'

'I was, kind of.' I held my hand out. He handed me the keys.

'You need us to come with you?' Gol said.

I shook my head. 'You better get back. Eric's in charge.'

'See you tomorrow, then?' Chris said.

I nodded. 'Come in early. I want to run all the checks. Just in case those idiots have buggered anything up.'

'Will do.'

I waited until they'd gone then got in, started the engine, and drove off.

The track was one I knew from long ago, during my fishing days. It leads off the main road at Glazebrook and meanders for about a mile down towards the old McAlpine site, next to the River Mersey. There's nothing there now but wasteland. The fishing pool we used to use as kids is actually half way down, but I carried on past, driving slowly and watching out for anything sticking up that might do a tyre. Apart from anything else, Harry wouldn't be pleased.

Not far from the river side, I stopped the van so it was facing a brick wall that looked like it used to be part of an old factory. I needed some light, but didn't want to sit there with the van's headlamps shining out across the river in case someone over that side rang the police to complain.

I got out and wandered round to the back and had a quick look round. As far as I could tell in the dark, nothing seemed to have changed since when I'd scouted the location the day before to make sure it was suitable for my purpose. Satisfied, I unlocked the back doors and swung them open.

The two figures were lying, back-to-back, on the mattress. They were hooded and zip-cuffed together at the wrists and ankles. I climbed in, took out my lock-knife and cut the ties that were holding them together, making sure I didn't cut their individual cuffs by mistake. Then I lifted them up and manoeuvred them into sitting positions, backs against the van wall. I pulled some of the cushions into a pile, took out my torch, and sat in front of them.

With my torch in my mouth, I reached forward with both hands and pulled both hoods off, together. The light from the torch must have hurt to begin with as they both squinted and tried to squirm away from it. I gave them a while to get used it. Then I leaned forward and tore the duct tape off their mouths, the one on my left, Charnley, first, then Bergin.

'Hi Guys,' I said.

Charnley spoke up first, his voice shrill and containing more than a note of panic. 'What the fuck, Danny?' The way he blurted it out, I could tell he was scared shitless. 'What the fuck are you doing?' I guess that, tied up in the back of a van, and feeling it rocking and rolling down a country track at night, the old imagination starts working.

Bergin was calmer, but breathing heavily, staring at me with eyes full of hate. 'You're fucking DEAD Norton, ' he spat. 'They will come for you and gut you like a pig.'

'You think so?' I said. 'Well tomorrow morning, when your boss realises you're not standing next to him in court and begins to wonder why and who set him up, I'd be interested to know who he thinks of gutting first, you or me.'

It was enough to shut him up, for the time being at least. But I saw the way his gaze kept drifting to out the back of the van. Even tied up as he was, he was weighing his chances, checking to see who else was around. I decided to enlighten him.

'There's no one there,' I said. 'It's just the three of us.'

The possible significance of that must have struck them both at the same time as they suddenly stopped squirming to stare at me. I knew they would each be trying to gauge how well they knew me - very well in Dave's case - and what they believed I may be capable of.

Eventually Charnley stopped gauging to stammer, 'Wh- Why have you bought us here?'

'I thought you'd never ask,' I said. 'I brought you here because it's a nice, quiet place for a chat. And if neither of you want to chat, well then, it's nice and quiet for other things.'

'What… things?'

I gave him my most meaningful stare. 'Things like- Well, what sort of things can you imagine, Dave?'

There was more staring, and heavy breathing. The adrenalin - fight or flight - would be coursing through them now. The trouble was, neither option was available.

I reached behind to my jeans pocket and produced Eric's print-outs. After a quick look to check which was which, I turned to show them to them, shining the torch so they could see them, clearly. I held out the one in my right hand towards Bergin, making sure he could see it. Then I held it up, briefly, next to his face so I could compare. I nodded.

The man in the photograph was in the forward arc of this throw, just before he released the flaming bottle in his right hand. It meant that his face was three-quarters on to the camera fixed to the side of my house. Ironically, but sadly for him, it was the light from the flaming rag stuffed into the top of the bottle, shining directly onto his face, that had enabled Eric's cunningly-purchased, System Enhancement Software, to do its stuff so efficiently. The dark, hard features, the low forehead, the short, black hair. There was no mistaking it was Bergin. He didn't even try to argue. Which was fine with me. I wasn't looking to debate it.

I turned to the other photograph. Charnley was

looking from it, to me, and back again. I turned it round to look at it. A still from the camera on Arthur's gable end, It showed a dark coloured four-by-four, stopped a few doors down from mine, a shadowy figure stepping from the front passenger seat.

'Not bad eh, Dave?' I tapped the roof of the car, where the light was reflecting off the bullet-shaped silver-grey roof box. 'Two o'clock in the morning, and only one streetlight still on in the whole close. And you just happen to stop right under it. Marvellous.'

He tried shaking his head. In fact his whole body was shaking now.

'No- Not- Not mi-' He tried. Couldn't get the words out.

'Oh, come on, Dave. How many people do you know drive a Range Rover with a bloody roof box like that? What is it you use it for, golf clubs?' I tapped lower down on the picture. 'And the number plate. What can we see there? Is that an S? And that looks like what, a 6? And that, I think, is a J. Yes, definitely a J. Clear enough I would say. And what's your reg Dave? SU68MJL? A bit of coincidence if it's not yours, wouldn't you say? What are the odds you reckon of someone else with a grudge against me having a car like that, with those numbers? Thousand to one? Hundred thousand to one? A million?'

It was then I noticed the wet patch that was spreading, slowly out across the mattress under Charnley's legs. I didn't mention it. I wasn't looking for outright humiliation.

He went for broke. 'Believe me, Danny. We didn't know your Dad was there. We wouldn't have done it if we'd known.'

It didn't surprise me he'd heard about Dad. By now all of Warrington probably knew. Which thinking about it, was the reason we were there, partly. I leaned in towards him, but made sure I was speaking to both of them.

'I know you didn't know he was there, Dave. Either of you. But that's not the point. He was.' I paused, then added. 'And the thing is, you see. I've a reputation to maintain.'

For a moment no one said anything. But when Charnley realised what I was referring to, he lost it. He started struggling and screaming and rolling about the back of the van. It took me a while, but eventually I managed to get the duct tape I'd ripped off his mouth back on so all he could manage were muffled squeaks and moans. Bergin wasn't so theatrical, but concentrated on trying to break out of the zip-tie round his wrists. No chance. They make that stuff tough. The blood I had to clean off the van floor later showed just how hard he tried. And when I replaced his tape-gag, he didn't move a muscle, just kept staring at me with his dark Russian eyes. To be fair, he's a brave guy that Bergin. Not one for pissing his pants.

I picked up the printouts I'd dropped during the struggle with Charnley, folded them over and put them back in my jeans pocket. Then I backed out of the van and checked around once more. There were heavy-industry sounds from somewhere further along the river, but they were far away. Where we were, all was quiet. No one close enough to hear anything.

'Okay,' I said 'I think its time you both had a bit of fresh air.'

Reaching back into the van I grabbed hold of the ties

round both men's ankles and pulled them towards the open doorway so that their legs dangled over the drop. Charnley started moaning into his gag again.

'Give it a rest, Dave,' I said. 'You're getting on my nerves.'

# CHAPTER 59

*Saturday*

It was a good two weeks since I'd been to Sammy's Gym in Stockton Heath. I stopped going to Joe's years ago. It was never the same after he left. Sammy's has got everything I need. Weights, machines, treadmills, and those cross-trainer things which I really like. And it's closer to home, by which I mean Whitely.

After the night before, which ended later than I'd planned, I woke up in Vicki's flat feeling I could do with a good work-out. Vicki, wasn't there - her note said she would be back around three - so with no more meetings or arrangements to put in place, I decided a few hours pumping iron and running off the cramps and tensions of the last few days would do the trick.

I was half-way through my weights routine when my phone rang. It was Jamie Carver. I'd been expecting he would call. Before he could say anything, I said, 'How'd it go this morning?'

'No problem,' he said. 'The court remanded Yashin to custody for seven days. It'll give Will time to work on him.'

By now I was aware that Will was hoping to explore some options with Yashin that could result in him not ending up in prison. I'd heard him mention a couple to Carver in passing - some drugs stuff going on in London, something about sex trafficking through Belgium - but stuff like that is all above my head. Where I come from, you get caught with fifty-thousand pound's worth of coke, you do time. Not that I was overly-bothered. The aim had been to scupper his plans. Between us, we'd succeeded. If he eventually went down, fine. If not, then so long as he was out of Midnight's - which he was - that was all I cared about.

Carver and I talked a bit about the night's events, and he thanked me for our help, several times. I told him it was nothing. He asked how Vicki was, and I said she was great.

'So... are you two getting along alright again now?' he said.

I sighed. 'Move on, Jamie.' He laughed.

After some more aimless chat there was a pause in the conversation. I'd been expecting there might be.

'There's just one problem.'

'What's that?' I said.

'In all the confusion last night, it seems one of Yashin's guys, Bergin I think his name is, managed to slip the net.'

'Is that right?'

'Yes. Does that worry you?'

'Bergin? Nah. If he comes near me I'll be surprised.'

'Any idea where he might be?'

'Not that I can think of. Have you tried Runcorn docks? There was a Russian boat in there last week.'

'Someone made an enquiry there this morning. They say they haven't seen anyone fitting his description.'

'His looks may have altered.'

'In eight hours?'

'You never know.'

'Hmm. Well if you happen to see him, you will let me know, won't you?'

'Of course.'

'Same goes for Dave Charnley. Apparently he's not been seen since last night either.'

'Really? I did hear he was talking about heading off to Thailand.'

During the silence that followed, I tried to imagine what sort of expression Carver was wearing.

'Take care of yourself, Danny.'

'And you.'

About to ring off he added. 'By the way, we may see you again tonight. There's still the other problem to sort out yet.'

A shadow fell. I'd all but forgotten. 'Of course.'

After, I stood staring out the window onto the car park for a while, thinking about what Carver might be thinking. I was still there when a voice said, 'Hello stranger.'

I turned. A tall black girl smiled back at me. 'Donna,' I said. 'Long-time no-see. How are you?'

'Great. How are you?'

'Not bad, what're you up to?'

Donna Parkiss is what some would call, a looker. A keen athlete - distance runner and javelin - she is, in every sense of the word, fit. Once a regular at Midnight's and maybe the best podium dancer we've ever had - before Vicki that is - I hadn't seen her for months. She was sweating buckets and had obviously just come off one of the treadmills.

'You look like you might need to replace some

liquid,' I said.

'I do.'

'Me too,' I said. 'Come on.'

We retrieved our formulas and went out to the small courtyard at the back where Sammy has put out some tables. The sun was out, but it wasn't particularly warm, which is okay when you're working out. As we supped at the spouts on our flasks, we caught up. It turned out that the reason I hadn't seen Donna for a while was, she'd taken some sort of Medical-Sales Rep job near Cambridge and only got back to visit family once every few months. And though her membership had lapsed, Sammy had told her she was free to use the gym, anytime. He isn't daft, our Sammy.

'How are things at the club? You still running things?'

I thought she didn't need to know about anything that had happened since we last saw each other. 'Yep. Same-old, same-old.'

'And the team? They all still okay?'

I knew she meant Winston. Donna was Abi's predecessor, long ago. I told her the team was fine. The way she hesitated, I guessed what was coming next.

'I heard about Agnes. And the others. Isn't it awful?'

I nodded. 'Very sad. And yes, it's bloody terrible.'

We spoke a bit about the murders. She asked if the police had any ideas and I told her I wasn't aware of any. After our nice conversation, it was bit of a downer.

She finished with, 'I hope they catch the bastard soon,'

'That's what we're all hoping.'

She stood up. 'I've got another five thousand metres to do, so I'd better be getting back to it.' She bent to pick up her flask and towel off the chair next to me. While she was there, she gave me a peck on the cheek. 'Nice to see you again, Gladiator.'

I smiled. 'And you, Princess Marigold.' Private joke.

As she was about to disappear back inside, I turned in my chair. 'As you're around, why don't you and whoever come to the club tonight? I'll sort some admissions if you like, for old times' sake.'

She looked back at me, hesitating. 'I, er-'

There was something there, but I wasn't sure what. I wondered if she'd maybe thought I was trying to hit on her, and I worried in case I'd embarrassed her. I thought to try and retrieve it.

'Don't worry if you can't. Just thought I'd offer, that's all.'

'No, it's good of you to offer. It's just that- I, We, er-' She seemed to make a decision. 'To be honest, Danny. I am out tonight. But I'll be doing Stacy's.'

I started. 'Oh.' In fact I was stunned. I'd always thought of Donna as Midnight's through and through. Stacy's is hardly the same.

She must have read my reaction, as she turned round and slid back to the table, as if she thought she ought to explain. She didn't have to, but I understood.

'Its just that- Well, its just that Hayley and me, and some of the others. We don't do Midnight's any more. It's just- It was-' The way she was skirting round it, my thoughts were heading towards a problem with Winston. I asked her outright if it was.

'Oh God, no. Me and Winston, we're fine.'

'So what then?' More hesitation. 'Come on, you can confide in Uncle Danny. I won't tell anyone.'

She sat down again, looked around, not that anyone was there to listen.

'I began having a bit of a problem. It put me off. Eventually I'd had enough and stopped coming.'

I was intrigued. 'What sort of problem. You mean with someone, or what?'

She thought about it. Made another decision. 'Oh, Hell. If you must know, it was Mickey.'

'Which Mickey?' I could think of several.

'You know, DJ Mickey.'

She'd caught me again. 'You mean, Micky Midnight?'

'Mickey Creep-Me-Out more like.'

'Why do you say that? What happened?'

'It was silly really. And it was probably as much my fault as his.'

'I leaned forward and rested my hand, lightly and only briefly, on hers.

'Tell me what happened.'

She told me it all went back to when she was dancing the podium regularly. She described how she'd sometimes look up and she would see Mickey looking down at her, 'strangely.'

'Strange like how?' I asked.

'Like-' The embarrassment again. 'Like he was doing something... naughty.'

I almost smiled. Donna comes from a good background. 'A well-brought-up young lady,' is how my Mum would have described her .

'Naughty..?'

'You know, playing with himself.'

Supping on my spout, I almost choked. 'WHAT? Up there? In the club?' She nodded. 'That's not all.'

She described how, one Saturday night, she was making her way home - her family live on Callands -

when she thought someone might be following her. She slowed down to check and saw someone dive behind a wall. She went round a corner, then ran and hid behind a car up someone's driveway. A few minutes later the man she thought she'd seen came past. 'It was Mickey.'

'Are you sure?'

'Defo.'

She waited until she was satisfied he was gone, then went home and thought no more about it. It had always been obvious to her that Mickey fancied the pants off her. So did lots of men. She just put it down to Mickey being, 'maybe a bit creepier than most.'

'What happened after that?'

'A couple of weeks later, I was walking home again, in the same area, when I heard this music coming up behind me. A car came past with its windows down, then stopped and reversed back. It was Mickey. He made out it was a coincidence, that he was on his way to some party in the area, and asked if I wanted a lift.'

'And you said?'

'Well, I knew it was no coincidence. He'd bloody-well set up to just, 'happen' to bump into me. I told him thanks, but no thanks. Mickey's charms never did work on me. Unlike some of the girls.'

I sat back, beginning to work on it. 'So that's when you stopped coming to Midnight's?'

'Oh no. I kept coming. For quite a while after, I think. But over time, I began to notice that every time I was around the dance floor, if I happened to look at Mickey, I would catch him watching me.'

'Playing with himself again?'

'No, different to that. It was like he was-'

'What?'

'I can't really say. He used to have this weird look on his face. You know, like a stalker-type look?'

I didn't know what a stalker-type look looks like, but I could imagine something close. Donna continued.

'It was really creepy. In fact, it got to the point where he was freaking me out and I became quite scared. That's when Hayley and I stopped going to Midnight's and started doing Stacy's instead.'

'Did Hayley-'

'Hayley used to go to school with Mickey. She said he'd always creeped her out back then as well and was happy to try somewhere else. So now, we just do Stacy's, and sometimes one of the other clubs.'

'Have you seen Mickey since?'

She shook her head. 'It wasn't long after that I got the job in Cambridge, so the problem solved itself I suppose.' She leaned back in her chair. 'That's why I'm not really that bothered about coming back to Midnight's. Not while Mickey's there at least.'

I nodded. 'I'm not surprised. It can't have been very nice.'

'It wasn't.'

She stood up again. 'I hope you didn't mind me telling you all this. I feel like I'm being, like, disloyal.'

I stood with her. 'Don't be daft. And of course I don't mind. I'm glad you did.'

'You won't tell anyone else will you? I don't want to cause any embarrassment.'

'Like I said. Don't worry.'

'Thanks Danny. Say 'hello' to Winston for me.' She gave me another peck.

'I will.'

She disappeared back inside.

I sank back down into my chair, thinking about her story, while supping from my flask. Mickey? 'Good-old', Mickey? I'd always known he liked to put himself about a bit, and over the time I'd been coming to Midnight's I'd heard how he sometimes doesn't always take 'no' for an answer. But a stalker-type? Mickey? Or even worse..? I thought about it some more. If I'd ever imagined Mickey having a problem with women, I'd have put him in the 'nuisance' category, not someone who was any sort of danger to women. But then, what did I know? Mickey was tallish, but by no means heavily built. I'd always imagined him as a bit a wimp, actually. But that could be down to my prejudice about guys who prance about like loons while wearing stupid outfits. I'd come across plenty of guys whose slight build belied both strength, and a taste for violence. But Mickey...?

Mickey had worked at the club since long before the murders ever started. I thought about the girls who had fallen victim to the killer. Only one other, apart from Agnes, had come from Midnight's, and they'd both been taken on a Saturday, when Mickey would have been there. But I seemed to recall that some of the others had died on other nights. Tuesday and Thursday came to mind. Then I remembered, and sat up straight. Occasionally, Mickey would do a 'guest DJ' spot at another club. All the established DJs do it. Something to do with showing they're 'in demand.' But never on a Saturday, which is always 'Home-Club' night.

I stood up.

I'd never heard Vicki say anything bad about Micky. But then it was only the past week or so she'd begun to spend time around the dance floor and podiums. As far as I could tell they'd been getting on fairly well. Hell, she'd even mentioned about him giving her some of his time to rehearse some routines. I froze. Something she'd mentioned the night before, in the Green Room, had suddenly popped into my head. Something about planning something 'special'. for tonight. What was it she'd said? *I'm working on it..? You'll have to look after yourself tomorrow...?*

A prickly feeling started at the back of my neck. I remembered her note. 'Back about three...' It was then I realised. Right now I didn't know where she was. Or what she was doing. My heart started thumping. I thought about something Donna had said. I looked for her through the window. She was pounding away on the treadmill. I went back inside. I must have been showing something in my face as she saw me approaching, fast, as she pulled her ear buds out, ready. But the treadmill was whining loudly, her shoes thumping on the rubber.

'THE MUSIC,' I shouted.

'WHAT?'

'THE MUSIC.'

'WAIT.'

She put her thumb on the 'minus' button. The machine slowed, her footfalls became less noisy. 'Say again?'

'The music.'

'What music?'

'You said you heard music coming up behind you, the night Mickey pulled up in his car.'

'Oh, yeah, that. What about it?'

'What was it?'

She looked at me, blankly. 'I've no idea. It was months ago.'

'Try.'

She thought again, shook her head. 'I'm sorry, I can't remember. Why do you want to know anyway?'

I shook my head. 'Nothing. It was just-' I turned away, looking for my phone. It was with my bag, over by the weights. I ran over, grabbed it, then hit Vicki's speed-dial. It rang for the usual few seconds, then dropped into voicemail. 'It's me,' I said. 'If you pick this up, ring me. Right away.' I cut off.

*Shit.*

'Danny?'

I turned. Donna was waving at me. 'It just came to me. The music. It was the Adagio. For Strings. He always used to play it. If you ask me, I think he's got a thing about it.'

It was then I remembered what I'd been trying all week to think of, off and on, ever since Carver first mentioned it. It was Mickey, the morning after Agnes disappeared, telling me how he'd always loved watching her dancing… to the Adagio.

That was the moment I went into full-on panic mode.

## CHAPTER 60

I don't ever remember leaving Sammy's. I do recall the frustration I experienced trying to battle my way back into town through the Saturday-shopper traffic along Wilderspool Causeway while trying to get hold of people. It wasn't just Vicki not answering. I couldn't raise Carver, or Eric either. I'd also tried my font of all knowledge, Greta, but struck out there as well. I imagined her in the middle of some noisy shop somewhere, oblivious that her phone was ringing. There were moments when, if I'd got my hands on whoever invented voicemail, I'd have strangled 'em.

Nor can I remember what my plan was. I don't think I had one. My only thought was that if I got back into town, I might see or meet someone, or be jogged into thinking of something, that might help me find her.

It was after ringing her phone six times on the trot, getting voicemail and ringing again immediately, like some obsessive nutcase, that I realised I was close to losing it. I pulled over to the side of the road and stopped the engine. I took a long, deep breath, closed my eyes and said out loud, 'Calm down and THINK, you stupid bastard.'

I did. Nothing came.

'FUCK.'

I thought that maybe I could logic it out. My fear was that she was somewhere with Mickey, rehearsing, and that he might be the killer. I couldn't know for sure of course, but with what I'd heard from Donna and what I already knew, I wasn't about to be giving him the benefit of any doubts. So, where would they go to rehearse? It was early Saturday afternoon, so the club wouldn't be open and Mickey wouldn't have keys or the alarm codes anyway so they couldn't be there. They could be at Mickey's, but I didn't know where he lived - which was why I'd tried Greta. I seemed to recall someone once mentioning that they thought he lived on a boat somewhere. It made me think of the canal, which in turn made me think about the fact that at least two, or was it three? of the bodies had been found somewhere close to canals.

'Oh, Christ.'

But then I thought, even if he did live on the canal, a narrow-boat isn't the sort of place you can rehearse podium dancing, so they wouldn't be there anyway. Which left a room somewhere big enough to dance in and where you could play music. My heart sank as I realised. They could be anywhere. The thought of waiting around until three o'clock to see if she arrived home safe, terrified me. She might need me, NOW.

My phone rang. It was Eric. 'Sorry I missed your call,' he began. 'I'm just at B&Q loading up-'

'I'm trying to find Vicki, have you any idea where she is? Did she say anything last night?'

'WHOA,' Eric said. 'Slow down. What's the emergency?'

I took a breath. 'I think she may be with Mickey the DJ and he may be the guy who's killing the girls.

404

They're supposed to be rehearsing somewhere and I need to know where.' There was the briefest hesitation at the other end and I knew why. 'Before you say anything, this isn't like it was with Elvis.'

'Go on.'

'He stalked Donna Parkiss a few months back. Scared her enough to stop her coming to the club.'

'Mickey the DJ?' I could hear the disbelief.

'ERIC,' I shouted. 'I've no time to talk about it. Do you know where they might be?'

Silence, then, 'Have you tried the club?'

'They won't be there. It's closed and anyway they've no-'

'I gave her some keys.'

'What?'

'Last night. She asked me if I'd lend her the spare set of keys and give her the alarm code. Something about needing to get in today to prepare some sort of surprise. I thought she was talking about one of the girls' birthdays or something.'

'When was this?'

'Last night. Just before she left.'

'Shit. Gotta go Eric.'

'Danny I need to tell-'

But I'd already cut him off. I started the engine and put my foot down. I was less than a mile from the club, but traffic was a nightmare. It always is through Bridge Foot on a Saturday. As I got to the main traffic lights before the bridge - they were on red - I could see the club across the river. My heart was racing faster than ever. There was a line of traffic in front of me. 'Fuck this,' I said, and went for it.

Weaving out of line, I swung up onto the central

reservation, then skipped in and out through the gaps until I reached the front of the queue. I paid no attention to the horns and shouted obscenities coming from behind. The lights were still on red, a bus coming in from my right. I floored the accelerator, shot forward. I didn't look to see the expression on the bus driver's face, but had no trouble imagining it. There was a long, loud blast behind but by then I was already heading over the bridge. The left turn off the bridge into Arpley Road is where the traffic slows the worst. The club is only two hundred metres up on the left, where the road snakes right, then left again. I wasn't going to waste any more time. I pulled over onto the narrow pavement lining the bridge, got out, and ran.

The steel shutters over the front doors were down and locked. Normally, if someone is inside they would leave them up, but they can be locked from the inside. I keep a set of keys but they were back at Vicki's. For security reasons, I don't take them out unless I'm planning on calling in. I banged on the shutters, hard, several times. No one came. I put my ear to the metal but heard nothing, which didn't mean anything because if the doors behind were closed, it would stop noise getting through anyway. I banged on the shutters one last time, more a blow of frustration than anything, then legged it round the back.

As I expected, both the side door and the back fire exit door were closed and locked. They looked secure, but a sliver of hope was burning in my brain. Over the past couple of weeks, we'd been having trouble with the rear fire exit locking-bar sticking. I'd noticed it getting worse the week before and had told Eric to ring the maintenance company. As far as I knew they hadn't been yet. There'd been a couple of occasions when whoever did the last checks at night had missed the fact that the door wasn't properly locked. Closed enough for the alarm sensors to make contact, but not locked. It had led to a couple of bollockings being handed out, one to Chris the other, a rota-guy. I wondered who'd done the checks last night?

I stood in front of the door. It looked secure and when I pushed against it, it didn't budge. But I knew it would take more than a push. I took a step back, lifted my right leg then kicked at the door, as hard as I could. A crack appeared between the door edge and the jamb. As the other times it had happened, the bar hadn't been properly engaged. I didn't worry about who hadn't done their job properly but got my fingers in and pulled the door open. I stepped inside. The first thing I heard was music. I recognised it at once. The Adagio For Strings.

## CHAPTER 61

I raced round the corridor towards the front. The emergency lights stay on all the time so there was just enough light to see. The music was playing as loud as it would be on a club night. It wasn't some cleaner with a radio. With the shutters down, the lobby was in semi-darkness, but one of the doors to the dance floor was standing open, flashing light spilling out.

I ran through and followed the wall until I reached the point where I could see the dance floor and stopped. The scene will stay with me the rest of my life.

Vicki was lying on the floor, Mickey straddled across her chest, facing more or less towards me. He was leaning forwards, straining to pull at something. At first I couldn't see what it was, then I realised. He had something round her throat. I was vaguely aware of what may have been a video camera on a tripod close by, and that he'd set spots so they were shining on them - a bit different to a canal tow-path at night. But all this barely registered, because there was only one thing I was focusing on - Vicki - and the fact that she wasn't moving.

I launched myself down the steps shouting, 'MICKEY,' hoping to distract him enough he would stop pulling on what looked to me like a scarf.

It worked.

He must have caught my movement because as I reached the bottom of the steps he looked up and saw me coming. He reacted at once, rolling off Vicki to scramble towards a small, black object lying near the edge of the floor. I was less than twenty feet away and focused more on Vicki than him now - I could see her face looked purple in the light - when he reached it. He rolled again and came up in a sitting position and pointed it at me. I was thinking, Mickey wouldn't own a gun, when there was a flash of bright light and something hit me with the force of an express train. Pain like nothing I'd ever felt before racked my whole body and I went down. I knew at once what it was. Taser.

I came to sitting in a chair in the middle of the dance floor. The music had finished but the floor was still lit. As my vision cleared and focused, I saw Mickey in front of me. He was adjusting the camcorder on the tripod. I followed the way it was pointing and saw Vicki. She was lying across one of the square tables he must have brought down from the Early Hours Bar. Her head was hanging over one edge so that her hair trailed down, her legs dangling over the one opposite. Her dress was pulled up, exposing her lower half. Her knickers were gone. The fact she wasn't moving - at all - sent my stomach into free-fall.

I made to get out of the chair, but found I couldn't. It was only then I realised, my arms were pinned behind and over the back of one of the tubular-steel chairs that are standard around the club. I tried to move my legs, but they were stuck to the chair legs. I tested what was pinning my wrists and realised it was a zip-tie, already digging in tight enough that my hands were tingling. I tried to shout out but couldn't do that either. There was something soft stuffed in my mouth - I was conscious there was no sign of her knickers - held in place by duct tape. I thought of last night. Charnley and Bergin, in the back of Harry's van, and knew what they'd felt like.

'Welcome back, Danny.' I looked up. Mickey was smiling at me as he made his final adjustments to the camera and straightened up. 'Bloody effective these Taser things. I wish I'd got hold of one sooner. I'll have to thank Eve when I see her next for running me through how it works last night. I'm not sure if she's missed it yet. I'm sure I'll find out later.' He pointed at the table, and Vicki. 'Shame you didn't get here in time for the main part of the show, I think you'd have liked it.' I wasn't sure what he meant but didn't like the sound of it. I hardly dared look at her but had to. There was something, horribly *final* about the way she was just lying there. *Vicki*...

I exploded into action, pulling at my ties - and got nowhere. But I could see that my sudden attempt to break loose had spooked Mickey enough to wipe the smile off his face. He'd taken a step back and his hand had gone to his waistband where a large knife, like a hunting knife, was lodged in his belt. I remember thinking, you may kill women, but you're still a wimp.

Satisfied I wasn't going anywhere, it seemed, Mickey, became active.

'Now I can't hang around Danny, because Tony will be here about six to open up. But that still gives us enough time to do what we have to do.' He nodded at Vicki. 'Beautiful like that, isn't she? You should have seen her Danny. She was *sooo* good. She told me it was supposed to be something special, for you, tonight. I never realised you and her were- Ah well, never mind. At least I got to see it.' He pointed at the camera. 'And I'm sure I'll enjoy seeing it many more times to come.'

I tried to shout, 'YOU FUCKING BASTARD,' but it just came out as series of mmmphhs.

He continued, 'But you're here now, so at least you'll get to see what I do to them, after, so to speak.' He stopped, as if he'd thought of something. 'In fact, that gives me an idea. Hang on.' He went back to the camera, checked the viewfinder, adjusted it. Then he approached the table and dragged it a few feet across the floor, nearer to me. He's putting me in the shot, I thought. He went back to the camera. 'There, that's good. Now you're both in.' The smile came back. 'Ever done any dogging, Danny? No? I have. It's a blast. Watching someone shagging your girlfriend, or wife. It's becoming very popular they tell me. You'll have to try it sometime. Oh, hang on. No, you won't be able to. Never mind. You'll get the idea in a minute.' He lifted a hand and I saw he was holding something small and black. He pointed it at the camera. There was a soft 'whirr' and a green light came on. 'Right, let's go.'

He approached the table. He turned to me one last time, winked, and said, 'Enjoy the show,' Then he stepped between her legs, and began to unbuckle his belt.

I screamed into my gag. 'NOOOO.' I pulled again, hard, at my wrists and ankles. They stayed tight. I strained back against the chair itself. But tubular steel isn't designed to break. I looked up. Although he was facing away from me, the way his shoulders were hunched and his right arm - the one furthest from me -

411

was making rapid movements, I knew what he was doing. Then I saw it, in his left hand. The knife. His head started to come back, a strangled groan starting in the back of his throat. He swapped the knife into his right hand, lifted it, high, above him. I screamed again.

That was when everything went black.

## CHAPTER 62

I remember it all so clearly now. I'll never need the video. Not that I'd ever watch it, even if they'd let me.

It starts with a strange buzzing in my head. A voice, far away, calling to me,

'Danny, Danny.'

I open my eyes. Everything is red. Blood red. Suddenly I remember. Vicki, the knife hanging over her. Oh Christ, it's hers. It's Vicki's blood. On my hands, the floor, everywhere. The voice comes again, becoming louder.

'Danny. DANNY.'

I look down. Her face is covered in blood, so much I can't even make her out clearly. In fact, I can't make *anything* out clearly.

'Fucking *JESUS. DANNY.*'

I feel something, on my face. A pain, and I realise. I've just been punched, hard. I turn to where I think my attacker is. A man stands there. It takes me a moment to recognise him.

'Eric?'

'Thank FUCK.'

I start to turn back to her.

'NO. Stay with me, Danny. You've got to stop.'

I turn back to him, slowly. Why must I stay with

him? What must I stop?

'IT'S OVER,' Eric shouts, but I don't understand.

'Wha- What's over?'

'THIS. HIM.'

I see he is looking down at something at my feet. I look down as well, at Vicki..

Only it's not Vicki. It's... someone else. A man. But I can't tell who, not through all the blood. Then I realise. It's Mickey. And he isn't moving. At all.

It's happened. Again.

In a rush that makes me suck at air like a drowning man surfacing for the last time, it all comes back to me.

*VICKI.*

I look around. We're not on the main dance floor, where I last remember us being. We're way over, on the upper dance floor. I look back down to where we were. The table is still there, only now it's been tipped over onto its side, like someone banged into it. Vicki is lying next to it, not moving. 'OH, GOD NO. JESUS NO. PLEASE' I look at my hands, my wrists. My hands are grazed and bloody. My wrists are cut and bleeding, with deep, livid-red burns. I'm kneeling over Mickey. His face is a bloody pulp. I realise what's happened. After breaking free of the zip-tie - is such a thing even possible? - I must have chased and caught him up here.

I get to my feet, a little unsteadily, then turn and race back down to where she is lying. Behind me, Eric calls. 'DANNY, WAIT.' But I can't wait. I need to get to her. To save her, like I always promised her I would.

I stop, standing over her. She is lying face down. I bend to her. Eric is still shouting,

'DANNY.'

I turn her over. I see her clearly now, for the first

time since I'd arrived. I see the hole in her dress over her stomach, from which dark red blood is oozing.

'OH MY GOD.'

## CHAPTER 63

*A Sunday*

I think I've mentioned it before, but Warrington Golf Club does nice bacon butties on a Sunday morning. I was half way through one when Mike showed up. I didn't see him come in, he just appeared, standing over my table. I'd been about to take another bite, but I stopped, my butty six inches from my mouth. I looked up at him.

He said, 'Holy shit, Danny. Are you alright?'

I looked at him for a few seconds, then finished my bite. Between chews I said, 'What do you think?'

I saw him look round, at everyone who had put down their butties and coffees to look at us, or more accurately, me. Everyone in that room would have heard about it all by then. I didn't give a fuck. I took another bite.

Mike was becoming agitated. He reached down and grabbed at my arm. 'You shouldn't be here, Danny. Not in your condition.' He tried to pull me up out of the chair but I shrugged him off, more violently than I'd intended and the force of it sent him off balance so he nearly fell. Around the room, there were sharp intakes of breath. I looked round at them.

'What're you all staring at?'

'Danny,' Mike pleaded.

'Tossers,' I threw out.

'Danny. Please.' I could see he was desperate for me to stop. He sat down. I took the last bite of my sandwich, licked my fingers, then met his gaze.

'Can we not do this here? Please?'

'Where then? I don't seem able to find you anywhere else. I've been trying all week.'

He looked around again. Everyone pretended to go back to their own business.

'Come with me.'

As I stood up, I shouted across to the lad behind the bar. 'Great butty. I'll come again.' I followed Mike as he hurried out of the lounge.

The plate on the door of the office upstairs read, 'Club Secretary.' Mike led me in. There was a round table under the window. We sat down. He looked at me, sadly.

'I- I'm sorry about what happened,' he said.

'Me too,' I said.

He hesitated. 'I'm talking about-'

'I know what you're talking about. Skip it. Let's talk business.'

'You don't have to be like this, Danny. It wasn't me who-'

He stopped as my head snapped up. He'd seen what was in my eyes. He lowered his head, and sighed.

'What do you want me to do?'

I reached into my jacket and took out the sheaf of documents, spread them out in front of him. Then I took out a pen, and laid it alongside.

'What's this?'

'An agreement.'

'What sort of agreement?'

'The sort where you agree to sign over your half of the business to me.'

He looked at me like I was crazy. 'You're fucking crazy. Why would I do that?'

'Because if you don't, I'll have to take some other action.'

'What sort of other action?'

I made sure he was looking at me when I said, 'The sort a nutter like me might take against the man who sold his partner out to a Russian crook for fifty thousand quid so he could pay off his gambling debts.'

As I watched the colour - all of it - drain from Mike's face, I knew I had him.

'Wh- What are you talking about?'

'I'm talking about you taking a bung from Yashin in return for setting me up for Ged Reilly's murder, so that Frank would have a reason for sacking us off the door.'

'Set you up? What makes you think I set you up?' Even as he said it, his Adam's apple was doing a little jig. 'And why would I want us sacked off the door? It's my business as well isn't it?'

'It is, but let me come back to that point. You got Ricky Mason to tell you what happened between him and Ged and where Ged's body was buried, then made an anonymous phone call to the police, saying I was responsible. But then you panicked and tried to cover your tracks and confuse the issue by paying Stevie B another thou to ring me and tell me he'd found Ged in Thailand. How's all that for starters?'

I stopped and waited. He didn't answer, but I saw

him swallow.

'And the why is because you needed more spare cash than the business is pulling in because you've landed yourself in trouble again with the gambling. You had an agreement with Dave Charnley that if he got the door, he was going to pay you a retainer for three years. With the bung from Yashin you'd put yourself in the clear, and still make an income from your IT involvements.'

He made one last, feeble attempt. 'Where've you got all this crap fro-'

'Ricky Mason for one, Stevie B for another.'

He stared at me. 'But what about the Russian? We never-'

'Bergin. His number two.'

'Bergin? He'd never blow out his boss.'

'Oh believe me, Mike, he would. He did. Amazing what a bit of gentle persuasion can do.'

'What sort of, gentle persuasion?'

'Oh I don't think you need to know that Mike. Let's just say that guys like Bergin sometimes need to have things explained to them in ways that are really easy to understand. And I got the last bit from Dave Charnley himself.'

'Charnley? People are saying he's gone missing. Do you know where he is?'

I gave a shrug. 'I believe he's taking a sabbatical from the Security business for a while. My understanding is he's left town.'

He gave me a strange look. 'A, *sabbatical?*'

I pointed at the papers. 'Sign.'

He stared at me for a while. Then he started to read. He scanned down the first page.

'It says here you're paying me ten thousand.'

'Yeah, so?'

'Have you got ten thousand?'

'Not to give you I haven't.'

'So why should I sign?'

I looked down at the floor. Clasped my hands together. Then I looked up. Stared into his face, and let him look deep, deep into my eyes. 'Would you prefer the alternative?'

After about ten seconds thinking about it, he picked up the pen. His hand was shaking as he signed. He dropped the pen on the table. 'Is that it?'

'Yes, Mike. That's it.'

He stood up and stared out of the window. There was a lovely view out over the eighteenth green. As he turned he said, 'You do know, Danny. It was never personal.'

I already had the door open, but I stopped to turn and look at him. 'Who do you think you are, Mike? The fucking Godfather?'

As I headed back downstairs, I wondered if he'd got the reference. He was never into films wasn't Mike.

## CHAPTER 64

*Saturday night*

The floor was bouncing as much as I'd seen it in a long time.

'What do you think?' Eric said.

I finished my scan, turned to him. 'Tell Winston that's it. No more tonight.'

Eric checked his watch. 'Jeez. And it isn't even midnight yet.'

'As the saying goes, there's no such thing as bad publicity.'

I watched as Eric weaved his way through the crowd. For a big guy, Eric can be surprisingly light on his feet. As he passed by a gang of four lads, one of them nodded to me and raised his bottle in salute. I recognised him as the one the Russian had tried to pick a fight with that night, and nodded back. I turned towards the Dusk-til-Dawn bar. Babs and Carmen were perched on their usual stools. They did the girly-wave thing and flashed me their big smiles, other things too. I returned the smile, but didn't go over. After everything that had happened, I'd decided to try and adopt a lower profile for a while.

When I first mentioned doing so to Eric, in the

office, he was sceptical.

'Yeah, right.' he said.

'I mean it,' I said.

I felt his gaze on me so I met it. 'What because of...'

'And other things.'

Eric nodded. Of everyone, he understood most. He'd been there.

Now, as I watched Babs and Carmen going through the routine with a couple of lads from the Tiger's rugby team I couldn't help but notice the two empty stools next to them. Bernadette has never been back. I doubt she ever will be.

My earpiece crackled. 'Sierra One, over.'

'Yes Chris?'

'Can you make the office? Visitors.'

'Two minutes.'

As I made my way off the dance floor, I wondered how much Frank was paying the new DJ for taking over a killer's job.

Skirting away from the lobby, I bumped into Elvis coming out of the Gents.

'Sorry Elvis,' I said.

About to move on, he grabbed at my sleeve. 'Word, Danny?'

'Wassup?'

'That little episode you witnessed at mine, with Gloria?' I nodded. 'You, er, you never mentioned it to anyone, did you?'

I smiled at him. 'Not a soul. Why?'

He gave me his jack-the-lad look. 'Oh you know. Just checking.' Then he became suddenly conspiratorial and leaned into me. 'Actually, I think I may be in with Babs, and I just wanted to make sure there was nothing that might, you know, put her off.'

I leaned back into him. 'Actually, Elvis.' I looked around. 'I can tell you for a fact, Babs is right into that sort of thing.'

His head snapped up, eyes wide with excitement. 'Is that right?' I nodded again, solemnly. 'Well-well. Who'd have thought.' He pulled his tie straight, stretched his neck to ease it from the collar and as he headed off on his mission said, 'Owe you one, Danny.'

As I watched him disappear back into the disco, I wondered if I was being maybe a bit too cruel. At the end of the day Elvis is harmless. Weird, but harmless. I decided to have a word with Babs later. She'd enjoy making the most of the opportunity.

My visitor was Carver. DS Jess was with him. We shook hands and I led them to the back of the room away from the CCTV where we could talk.

'How're things?' Carver said.

I nodded. 'Settling down, bit by bit.'

'How's the wrists?'

Instinctively, I held them up. The white bandages blended well with the white shirt I'd taken to wearing now that I was the sole 'boss' as it were. 'A lot better thanks. The stiches are coming out next Thursday.'

Jess said, 'In case you're interested, we did a test in the office. On those zip-ties.'

'Yeah?'

'It took four DC's, two pulling on each side to snap it.'

'Yeah, well I guess you could say I had some motivation.'

They looked at each other, changed the subject. I didn't tell them Eric and Gol had tried the same experiment and managed it between them.

'We also wanted to make sure you're aware. Mickey's up in court tomorrow.'

I nodded, but then thought I ought to say something. 'I'm just glad he's alive to get what's due.'

'Really?' Jess said.

I looked at her. 'Really.'

Carver said. 'I'm not sure everyone thinks that way.'

'They might if they thought they'd killed him.'

'But you didn't.'

'I know, but that week he was hovering, I thought I had. And I can tell you, it wasn't a nice place to be. I think I may have taken it out on a few people, that week.'

'Like your ex-business partner you mean?'

I looked at him. 'You heard about that?'

'Our Area Superintendent's a member of the golf club. He was there.'

'Give him my apologies.'

'I think he enjoyed it. Shook the place up a bit he said.'

'Yeah, well it wasn't my intention.'

'Danny?' I turned. Chris was holding up the office phone. 'Miranda's asking if you can come to the Green Room. She says one of the Boy Band needs speaking to.'

'Tell her I'll be right there.' I turned back to Carver and Jess. 'As you can see, I'm needed. Thanks for coming by.'

'That's okay.' About to turn away, Carver put his hand on my arm. In a quiet voice he said, 'How are things... otherwise?'

I looked at him. Then at Jess. The looks on their

faces, I could see they weren't just being polite. I said. 'Rough at times, but getting there.'

They nodded, like they understood. I wasn't sure they did, but I wasn't about to enlighten them. They can be nosey bastards at the best of times.

When I got to the Green Room, Miranda was outside, waiting for me.

'It's the blonde one, Warren. He's had too much to drink. He's getting stroppy. and they're due on in ten minutes.'

'Like me to have a word with him?'

'Would you?'

'No problem.'

I put my hand on the door lever then stopped. I looked at Miranda. 'Is...?' I pointed through the door. She nodded.

I took a deep breath. 'Right.'

I opened the door and walked in. The five lads were stood at the bar. I could see that four were trying to stop the fifth necking a bottle of vodka. I didn't know much about them, but I'd heard that the baby-faced one, Warren, had been getting a bit above himself lately. As I approached, baby-face had his back to me. The others saw me coming and fell quiet. It was a moment before Warren noticed. Then he spun round and found himself looking at the middle of my chest. His head went back and our eyes met. He swallowed.

'Hi,' I said. A whisper passed among the others and I heard, '..*Danny Norton.*'

'Hi,' Warren said.

'You alright, mate?'

He nodded, quickly, 'Yeah. We're just- Just getting ready to go on.'

I made a point of looking at the vodka bottle in his hand.

He followed my gaze, then showed it to me. 'Like a drink?' He tried to make a big joke out of it and started to laugh. He was on his own. As he turned back from his mates and saw my face, the laugh died in his throat.

'Miranda?' I called without turning.

'Yes, Danny.'

'Are you ready to take these fine young lads out to show them to their screaming fans?'

'I am, Danny.'

I looked at each in turn, Warren last. 'And are you lads ready to do as Miranda tells you?' They all nodded, rapidly. 'Right then. Off you go.' They all rushed to obey. But as Warren made to follow his fellow band-members, I grabbed his arm and pulled him back, close. I put my head down and whispered in his ear. His head snapped round and he looked up at me, shocked, and just a little scared, which was what I'd aimed for. I smiled at him and let go his arm. He couldn't get away from me quick enough and I listened without turning as they all left the room. The last I heard was Miranda's, 'Thanks Danny,' then she closed the door and everything went quiet.

I stayed like that for a while, looking at the bar, remembering. I took a deep breath. I remembered all the times I'd been here, watching her do her stuff, looking at her, in awe of her, though secretly. There were no secrets to keep any more, well, not many. I remembered the smell of her perfume, Guess. I'd wondered a few times where she bought it, but had never got round to asking.

I ought to, I thought.

Because I wasn't just remembering it. I was smelling it. I turned round.

She was over on the couch, staring at me, a wry smile playing about her lips. I was pleased to see that the spotted silk scarf I'd brought her to hide the mark round her throat went as well with the pale yellow dress as I'd hoped it would. I was learning, slowly. And the dress showed off her eternally tanned legs, not that I'd ever give her secrets away. Her hair was as sleek and shiny as ever. Considering how she'd looked two weeks before, lying on the dance floor, she looked amazing.

'Hey,' I said.

'Hey, yourself. Where have you been all night?' Her voice was still hoarse and croaky, though not as bad as the week before. But at least her 'light duties' stint was giving Miranda her chance to shine for a while, which would do her good.

'We've been busy since I got here.' I said. 'We've had to put up the 'Full' signs.'

'Wow. Don't things get back to normal fast?'

I went and stood next to her. She looked up at me.

'Thanks for the scarf. It's nice.'

'Glad you like it.'

'You slept better last night?'

'A bit. I'm getting there.'

Out of her view, I shut my eyes, tight, for a second, trying to shut out the memory. To be fair, the nightmare hadn't seemed as vivid the last few nights. Not like the first few days, when I worried, quite seriously, that I was going to spend every night for the rest of my life reliving the moment when I turned her over, saw the stab wound in her stomach and thought she was dead. And while everyone knows one stab wound can be fatal,

I know now that Mickey liked to take his time and that he always made sure his first cut was fairly superficial - twisted bastard that he is.

'How did your visit go?' She was talking about my trip to Chester, to see Mary Oakley.

'Okay, I think. She's fixing me up to see a bloke she knows. She says he's the best there is outside London.'

'And does she think he will be able to help you?'

'She seemed pretty positive. She reckons the science has moved on a lot since I was lad. Still might take a bit of time, though.'

'Well you've got plenty of that.'

'True, I have.'

'It's strange though, isn't it?'

'What is?'

'Well-' She hesitated, though I knew what she was about to say. I'd thought the same every day since. 'If it hadn't been for your, 'condition', I'd be dead.'

'If it's all the same to you. I'd rather not think about that.'

Suddenly she stood up, turning to face me.

'But it's true. You'd never have found the strength to snap the tie if you hadn't been in one of your rages.'

'Maybe, but I'm not going to not have treatment on the off-chance that my 'condition' might get me out of trouble again one day.'

She smiled, and sidled round to me. 'I'm not saying that. I just think it's strange, that's all.' She was close to me now, looking up at me.

I said, 'You're the strange one.'

'Why am I strange?'

'Having anything to do with a nutter like me.'

'You're not a nutter. You'll be an OU graduate soon.'

I gave her a look. About to reach for her, my earpiece crackled. 'Sierra one. Trouble at the front door.'

I jumped to it. 'On my way.'

Leaving her standing by the couch, I headed for the door. About to shut it behind me, I remembered something and opened it again. She was still standing there. Angelic came to mind.

'Remind me to speak to you tomorrow about something before I go down to see Dad and Laura.'

'Give me a clue.'

'I need to know if you've ever read any Joseph Conrad.'

'Who?'

I didn't answer, but closed the door and went to help my team.

The end

Enjoyed this book and want more of the same? Visit my Amazon Author Page where you will find details of my other books or read on for a preview of my next, *Death In Mind.*

**Coming next in the DCI Jamie Carver Series**

**DEATH IN MIND**

*How do you catch someone who kills through others,
when the others don't even know they've done it?*

A busy railway station. A young woman walks to the
edge of the platform, waits, then steps out in front of the
oncoming train.

A lonely road at night. A man deliberately steers his car
into a tree at speed.

Tragic suicides, clearly. Or are they?

When evidence shows that neither victim were
contemplating suicide, DCI Jamie Carver faces a
conundrum. Is it possible to programme someone into
taking their own life? And if it is, then can they also be
programmed to murder?

These are the questions Carver must answer, and
quickly, before more die. But how do you do that when
the person you suspect is pulling the strings may also be
pulling yours? And how do you stay safe when someone
is targeting you for murder, and even they don't know
it?

The next in the DCI Jamie Carver Series sees the
detective charting new territory as he grapples with the
possibility of 'unconscious murder' - and comes up
against not just a killer whose methods are unique, but
one who knows what the questions will be before they
are even asked. Read on for a preview of the opening
chapters of, Death In Mind.

# Death In Mind

## Chapter One


Five minutes before she killed herself, Sarah Brooke had never had a suicidal thought in her life. In fact as she waited for her train home that evening the only thing on her mind apart from the cold, was what to do about dinner.

Gary's call saying he'd been dragged into an urgent meeting and may not be home until, 'Ten, at the earliest,' had blown her plans for a surprise three-year-anniversary supper. Both working for the same bank - she, Accounts, him Lending – the resurgent banking crisis was still playing havoc with their home life. The alternative supper option was yet another delve in the freezer for a ready-meal. And while it didn't hold much appeal, the way her journey home was shaping up *and* the way she was beginning to feel, it was rapidly becoming the most likely.

Turning her face to the screen above the platform, she read the latest update.

The next train through Crewe Station's Platform 3, due in four minutes, was the Glasgow to Euston Inter-City express. Her own, Stafford train, showed another three behind. Which would make it over a quarter of an hour late. The third such delay this week. And it was still only Thursday.

As the chill wind that haunts railway halls in winter wafted down the platform, Sarah folded across the lapel of her Camel-wool coat and resolved to wear a thicker scarf tomorrow; maybe even the multi-coloured horror Gary had brought her last Christmas - part of a gift-set. With no sign of the late cold snap that had gripped the country the past week disappearing, style may just have to go on hold for a while. *Better than bloody freezing.*

She thought about making her way back to the American-Style Coffee House the other end of the platform and grabbing a cappuccino. At least it would take her away from the annoying cacophony she'd been subjected to the last few minutes.

When she'd first arrived at her usual waiting spot, three-quarters of the way down the platform, she didn't give the middle-aged man in the full-length Crombie and quirky Fedora pulled low a second glance. But after a few minutes, as the sound of some vaguely-familiar tune she couldn't quite make out intruded more and more into her consciousness, she turned to see where it was coming from. She was mildly surprised when she saw the wires emerging from within the man's coat's depths and running up to disappear under the hat's brim. For some reason, he didn't strike her as the sort who would listen through earbuds, not unless they were Bose. But the way she and others close by were being forced to listen along, the ear-buds were definitely not Bose, not the way they were allowing the sound to leak to the annoyance of those around.

Thinking of him again prompted her to glance over her shoulder, which when she realised he was standing much closer than before, barely a metre away and still all-but hidden behind the newspaper he was holding up. The page facing showed a headline above a report with an accompanying photograph. Sarah paid it scant regard yet still gleaned it was something to do with a lighthouse; some dramatic rescue. For some reason the image it evoked, like the music, seemed strangely familiar.

*Deja-vu or what?*

For his part, the man in the hat seemed oblivious to the annoyance he was causing – especially to Sarah. The thought came as to what the thumping beat must be doing to his eardrums if she could hear it so clearly. It also made her wonder again what it was. It irked more than she knew it should, that she couldn't place it.

Thrusting her gloved hands deeper into her pockets, she decided. Though the cappuccino down the platform wasn't up to much, it was preferable to having to listen to some weirdo's idea of music.

But as she made to turn to where the café's leaded windows cast a spider's web of yellow light across the platform, she was surprised to discover she was reluctant to tear herself away. It felt almost like she was in the grip of some compulsion by which she couldn't leave until she had identified what the music was, where she had heard it before. The deep bass tones had a curiously affecting quality.

And now there was something else.

Though she couldn't say why, her brain seemed to be making a connection between the music and the story she had glimpsed in the newspaper. The one about the lighthouse rescue. An image of a cheering light, growing brighter, came to her. A feeling like none she had felt before but seemed to be at least part apprehension, rose inside her.

At that moment a voice, melodious and silky smooth, sounded close to her ear.

'Make ready, Sarah. Your salvation draws near.'

She knew at once it was him, though how, she couldn't say. And there was something about the words that made her feel lethargic, like she had suddenly been drained of energy. More than that, they brought with them an overwhelming feeling of *sadness*.

*What's happening to me*, she thought?

Close to that time of the month, Sarah's first thought was she was about to experience one of her debilitating migraines. But as her vision stayed clear and the nauseous pain didn't come, she dismissed it. This was something else. Confused and becoming just a little concerned, Sarah glanced behind.

At first all she could see was the newspaper, still hiding his features. But then it began to lower, slowly. At the same time the head and hat behind lifted so that, bit-by-bit, a pair of eyes, dark and staring behind thick-framed glasses, appeared over the top to meet hers.

Something happened.

# Chapter Two

Across the tracks on Platform 4, the young man in the worn anorak lowered his new Fuji to stare across at the face that was so familiar, worried about the sudden change he'd seen come over her.

Throughout their relationship, such as it was, the thing Wayne Clarke had always liked most about Sarah was her self-assurance. Whether sitting at one of the Coffee House's round tables sipping cappuccino, talking animatedly into her mobile or just waiting for her train, Sarah always showed herself as the sort he liked best. Businesslike, oozing confidence and with beautiful blond hair - his favourite, though he had been known to stretch to redheads and, once even, a brunette.

Wayne was twenty-four. Unusually in one so young, his work-life balance was everything he wanted it to be. The reason was simple. Wayne had but two interests, attractive young women and trains. The first came from nature, the second from a time-served British Rail Signalman-grandfather who went out of his way to make sure his only grandson shared his life-long passion for railways. In this regard, Crewe Station's Signal box Number Three had substituted well for pre-school. Through luck or judgement, by the time Wayne was twenty and working as a Station Booking clerk, he had hit on a strategy through which he could indulge both interests at once. And while many would have regarded it at the very least, distasteful, it involved nothing more than doing what like-minded people do day-in, day-out at railway venues up and down the country. Taking photographs.

Wayne had learned long ago that provided he remembered to focus first on those quirks of railway architecture, rolling stock and platform furniture that are only visible to the enthusiast, no one ever noticed when he shifted his attention - and camera - to his other interest.

Work-shifts allowing, Wayne had been 'seeing' Sarah for almost three months now. In that time he had taken hundreds of pictures of her. For that reason, he noticed immediately when the face that was so attractive he sometimes ached, suddenly began to crumble, as if she had just received the most awful, shocking news.

Lowering the Fuji, he swung his gaze around the platform, checking to see what has happening that would explain her distress. But there was nothing. Everyone was just stood around waiting, quiet as usual, reading, sipping from cardboard cups, staring into space.

He lifted the camera again and zoomed in, checking he wasn't mistaken. But now she'd turned away and for seconds all he could see was the back of her head – a beautiful curtain of shimmering gold. As he waited, he wondered what she was looking at, if she was speaking to someone, though he couldn't see who. The nearest was an older man bundled up in a dark coat and hat pulled low, but he was engrossed in his paper. Eventually she started to turn. The camera's mode was set to 'continuous' as he pressed and held the 'shoot' button. What he saw as her face came into view sent Wayne's stomach into free-fall.

Tears streamed her cheeks. The look on her face was one of utter hopelessness. Yet less than a minute before she had seemed at ease, happy even, if maybe a little distracted.

What the hell's happened, he thought? He wondered if perhaps she had received some tragic news on her mobile. But he'd witnessed the moment the change began and was sure she wasn't using it. He zoomed in on the face he knew so well, but at that moment she turned again to look over her shoulder. But not all the way this time. He could still see her, three quarters-profile.

Her lips moved.

She *was* talking to someone.

Using the viewfinder he checked those around. But the only person close was the man in the hat, and he was still reading his paper, paying no attention. Wayne wondered how he could be so near, yet not notice her distress.

About to move back onto Sarah, he stopped, suddenly. Though the hat shielded most of the man's face, the camera was focused in close. And as Wayne started to swing away the man's lips moved, as if he was talking, but without looking up or shifting his gaze from the paper.

*What the Hell?*

Returning to Sarah, Wayne saw the vacant look was even more pronounced than before.

'What's wrong, Sarah?' The words sprang unbidden from his lips, driven by the illusion she was right before him. A few feet to Wayne's right, a woman in a green Macintosh and with a stash of plastic shopping bags at her feet turned to look at him. Nudging the bags with her foot, she shuffled further away, but still keeping him in her field of vision.

As Sarah turned suddenly to loom large in the lens, Wayne rocked back, tricked into thinking she was about to bump into him. Panning out a couple of stops he saw she was swaying slightly from side to side as if she was dazed, or even drunk. She lowered her head and he followed her gaze, tracking down until he came to the mobile in her hand. She stared at it for some while, before going through the rapid finger-thumb thing young women are so expert at. Finished, the hand dropped, loosely, back to her side.

About her, people stirred, beginning to pick up cases, shifting their positions. Wayne swung the camera onto the monitor above where Sarah was stood. It still gave the ETA of the Stafford train as three minutes, but showed the next train through Platform 3, the Inter-City Glasgow to Euston Express, as due in one. Something crawled in Wayne's gut. He returned to Sarah. She wasn't there.

Lowering the camera, he swept his gaze over the platform. He picked her up thirty yards away, walking stiffly, arms at her side, staring straight ahead. He brought the camera to bear just as something bright and shiny fell from her hand. Her mobile. She didn't stop to pick it up.

*Where's she going?* He followed her progress away from the main body of commuters.

The public address system blared. An man's voice, echoey, ethnic, heavily accented, warned of the imminent approach of the Glasgow to Euston Express. Passengers on Platform 3 should stay well behind the yellow line. Sarah carried on several yards then stopped, close to the North end of the platform. She stood there, not moving. Away to his right, through the station and beyond, Wayne could see the express approaching, its bright light piercing through the evening dark. At the same time a rushing noise began to fill the station, growing louder.

'Sarah-' Wayne tried, but stopped. There was no way she could hear him. He watched her turn ninety degrees right to face the tracks. Even without the camera, he could see her cheeks streaked by tears.

The approaching light grew stronger.

This time he shouted, 'SARAH'. Those nearest cast wary glances in his direction. He started jogging down the platform just as she took three zombie-like paces forward, taking her over the yellow line. She stopped at the platform's edge. Wayne quickened his pace.

'SARAH!'

The bright white light from the approaching express cast her shadow behind her. She turned towards it, as if gauging the right moment. Wayne broke into a sprint.

'SARAHHHHH!'

The noise grew to a crescendo as the Glasgow to Euston Intercity Express rushed into the station.

At the same time, Sarah Brooke stepped out into space.

From the middle of the three oak benches to the left of the witness box, Carver tried not to think about the time-bomb that had just landed in his lap. It wasn't easy. His mind kept flipping back to the challenging look in Jess's face as they parted and the question it inevitably raised. How much did she know about Helen Flatterly? Then again, how much *could* she know? No more than him, surely? Thrusting it aside, he tried to focus on the here and now.

To his left, the five men and seven women were filing back into their two rows of leather-backed seats. Though the last time they would be together, the order of seating was as it had been throughout. Beside him, in his Crown-Court-best blue-pin-stripe, Detective Superintendent Andy Gray, the man who had led Operation Golan from start to finish, leaned in to mutter a redundant, 'Here we go.'

Mind not yet where it should be, Carver managed only a nod.

Their position next to the witness box was where Case Officers usually gather at the conclusion of proceedings before the City of Chester's imposing Crown Court Number One. Carver had been there more times than he could remember, though few had felt so personal. From here he had an unobstructed view of the key players, Judge, both sets of Counsel, Jury and, most of all, The Accused. Directly facing across the other side of the court, the dock was some thirty metres away. Nevertheless, as Carver's gaze settled on the burly figure waiting quietly, head down, he still caught the feint whiff of aniseed. Once thought to mark either an unfortunate choice of cologne or an over-fondness for some culinary staple of his homeland, it was now known to be simply a by-product of Kisic's embarrassing but otherwise harmless hormonal condition.

As he waited for things to settle, Carver let his gaze roam, drinking in the sights and sounds he looked forward to later recalling. Apart from anything, they marked the end to a difficult and sometimes dangerous operation.

All things considered Carver thought, the trial had gone as well as they could have hoped, better even. Considering the case's complexities, the credentials of some of the witnesses and the reputation of the man now waiting to hear how and where he may spend the rest of his life, there had been no shortage of predictions that it would never get this far. To Carver's relief, they'd all been proved wrong. Even the evidence they had worried most about not getting in, such as the accused's penchant for violence, had been laid before the men and women now settling into their seats for the final time. Carver's experience told him, *never take anything for granted.* Deep down he thought things looked pretty good.

That this was the case was in no-small-part due to the be-wigged figure in the purple robe now waiting for the Jury Foreman to signal they were ready so he could get on with wrapping things up. Gaunt to the point of cadaverousness, it was his Honour Judge Henry Willard who'd allowed Alike Mikolas's damning evidence. A former Nigerian beauty queen and one of Jadranko Kisic's many ex-lovers, she'd been present during the lead-up to Bernie Grucott's brutal slaying. Her account threatened to leave in tatters the carefully worked-up alibi the defence had spent the best part of the past three weeks drip-feeding the Jury. The Judges' decision triggered uproar in the Kisic camp.

Like a row of jack-in-the-boxes, his legal team had jumped to their feet, appealing, loudly, for a recess so they could take, 'Instructions.' By then as fed up with the defence's convoluted shenanigans as everyone, the Judge refused.

On witnessing the disarray that followed, Carver couldn't help indulge a moment of weakness. Usually scrupulous about staying professional in sight of the jury, he let the smile that crept into his face linger enough so Kisic would see, though it wasn't really necessary. By then the Croatian knew it was Carver who had traced Alike Mikolas back to Lagos where Kisic had assumed, wrongly, she would be beyond the reach of Golan's investigators. And as soon as Kisic saw the smile, Carver wiped it. In the event things weren't as cut and dried as everyone thought, he didn't want the Jury to think he was cock-sure. Rock-solid trials had been lost for less.

And on top of Alike's evidence of course, there'd been His Honour's summing-up.

The law demands that the Judge's closing statement be impartial, confined to matters already put before the jury. But it is the Judge's prerogative which parts of the evidence to take his time over, as well as when and where to introduce a meaning-laden, 'Hmmph.' Long critical of the jury system, Carver was nevertheless glad that the tradition of the Judge's Summing-Up had resisted calls for its abandonment. Had any of the jurors been harbouring doubts, it was clear enough which side of the fence Henry Willard thought they should lean.

Now, as the Judge and the retired-banker-type Foreman exchanged bows – the signal for everyone to sit – Carver hid another smile. He'd seen the look that passed between the young man behind the foreman's left shoulder and the somewhat older woman to his right.

Lengthy trials impact on Jurors' private lives in unexpected ways. Most often they take the form of changing attitudes towards, the Law, *'Crazy'*: the Courts, *'Can't believe the amount of time and money that's wasted'* and, occasionally, the Police, *'Sincere, but woeful'*. But sometimes the enforced confinement affects people in other ways. Having witnessed the pair's body language change over the past few weeks - she was old enough to be his mother - Carver suspected that today would not be the last time they would be together, even if the Judge did discharge them, their civic duty done. It wasn't even that rare. Carver's ex-sister-in-law and her husband had met on Jury Service.

As the Judge leaned forward to check some point of procedure with his clerk, Carver turned his full attention on the man now staring across at him.

Jadranko Kisic's beefy arms were folded across his body-builder frame; the face that bore marks of conflicts never reported to the police, impassive as ever. The impression,- as no doubt intended, was of a rough-but-equable sort. Someone whose confidence in the system of justice about to determine how he may spend the rest of his life remained undimmed. A man who, having done nothing wrong, had nothing to fear, certain that the protestations of innocence he had maintained throughout would soon be vindicated.

It was the image Kisic had made a point of presenting to the court the past five weeks.

It was also the one Carver wasn't alone in recognising as a sham. For though the Croatian-born Crime-Master was known to have several sides to his character, none could be described as 'equable'. In fact any attempt to classify Kisic's various personality traits would more likely make use of words such as manic, obsessive, and psychotic. Several times during the past weeks, Carver had found himself wondering what cocktail of suppressants his resourceful legal team had managed to get some tame GP to prescribe.

Whatever it was, it had worked. Kisic's conduct throughout was in stark contrast to that Carver had witnessed the last time they faced each other across a courtroom. On that occasion as the trial neared its conclusion, the several angry outbursts the court had already witnessed gave rise to concern that, if convicted, Kisic might have a go at any official he could lay his hands on - including the Judge. It led to the courtroom being surrounded by a full Police Support Unit, shields and all. With someone like Kisic, no one was willing to take chances, not even the burly young PCs who long for the sort of hot summer and undercurrents of social unrest that spark riots on Britain's streets every decade or so. Carver had even overheard the Court Security Manager, an ex-Police Custody Sergeant, ask the PSU Inspector if he could arrange, surreptitiously, an armed presence so that, 'You can at least take him out before he reaches the Judge.' As it turned out, quarter-inch-thick steel cuffs and three Dock Security Officers who would have done justice to a rugby-scrum second row were enough. Between them they ensured that, despite the Croatian's oaths and curses to the effect that everyone from the ushers to the Judge himself could, 'Rot in Hell' - and which began as soon as the words, 'Six years,' passed the Judge's lips, the PSU was able to stand down without being called to action - much to their collective disappointment.

But during this trial so far, Kisic's behaviour had been exemplary. Presumably for that reason, the only obvious restriction upon his ability to have a go if he felt like it was the pair of flanking security guards. Heavier-built than Kisic and taller by inches, Carver suspected - hoped - they had been specially chosen. Before the case began, he was concerned to hear that the Judge had accepted the defence team's argument that the sort of Security Contingency the police had recommended – and which the jury could not have failed to notice - would be seriously prejudicial to their client's interests. Carver hoped that the judge wouldn't live to regret his decision - no reverse pun intended.

As the Court Clerk stood to utter the time-honoured phrase, 'Will the foreman of the Jury please stand,' Carver sat forward. He didn't want to miss a word of the exchange about to take place, especially not what would follow. Earlier in the day he had seen the Clerk return to the court where he retrieved several thick texts from the Judge's table, amongst them the Lord Chief Justice's Recommendations On Sentencing and the Home Office Guidelines on Tariffs. During the hours the jury had been out, Carver suspected that Henry Willard had been refreshing his memory regarding the copious advice contained within them. Carver was looking forward to one thing in particular. Seeing the change in Kisic that would mark the moment when realisation finally hit. The moment when Kisic would know that his brutal reign was over. That no longer would he be free to engage in the sort of activities that had seen him rise from mere former-Crime Squad, 'Target', to one of the National Crime Agency's 'Top Twenty'. Only then would Carver, SMIU, and the other agencies who made up Operation Golan be able to mark their files on Jadranko Kisic, 'Closed' - something they had not been able to do even when he was doing time in Belmarsh. Two and three quarter years counting parole wasn't that long. Rigorous though the regime within The Bell's Maximum Security Wing is, even it wasn't enough to loosen Kisic's grip on those parts of England's north where his influence reigned supreme; sex-trafficking, drug-dealing, armed robbery and the sort of protection rackets more often associated with larger American cities.

Now, as the man upon whose words Kisic's fate rested unfolded the piece of paper containing the Jury's verdicts, Carver held his breath. Across the court and behind the cadre of three Barristers who made up the Crown's Prosecuting Team – QC, Lead and Junior - Carver just caught the confident nod and wink that Darius Hook, the CPS Solicitor in the case, threw his way.

As the Clerk to the Court made ready to read through the list of indictments, he reached back over his shoulder to adjust the black cloak that hung on his bony frame so it looked less like an ill-fitting curtain.

'Count One,' he began. 'That on or about the twenty-fifth of April, two-thousand-and-twelve he did murder Bernard Thomas Grucott. Do you find the accused

Guilty or Not Guilty?'

The silence that filled the short gap before the foreman gave his response marked it as The Big One. Next to it the others on the indictment barely mattered. Not that conspiracy to murder and GBH weren't serious. But this, the charge relating to Bernie's grisly slaying was the one that counted. It was also the one Carver was most confident about. It wouldn't bother him a jot if the Judge ruled that the others should, 'Lie on file.'

The eagerly awaited response came. '- guilty.'

*Yes.*

But wait. A commotion about the room. Murmurings, growing louder, of the 'What did he say?' variety. There was a collective holding of breath.

'I'm sorry, Mr Foreman,' the Clerk spoke up. Again, for the record, if you please.' He made a half-turn towards the young stenographer sat below the Judge. Her ring-bedecked fingers still hovered over the keys. Confusion showed in the pretty face.

The foreman cleared his throat, loudly. 'S-sorry,' he stammered, as if realising that his badly-timed Colonel Blimp impression had just cocked up what should have been his Big Moment.

For Carver, everything seemed suddenly to happen in slow motion. *God no! Surely not...*

The foreman repeated the words only those nearest had heard clearly and which they had scarcely believed.

'Our verdict is, Not Guilty.'

Carver barely heard the clamour that erupted, the whoops from Kisic's entourage in the gallery, the clapping, the gasps of outraged astonishment from everyone except the Jury, Lawyers and Judge - too busy calling, 'Order.' Nor did he hear the Clerk's gallant attempts to continue in his appointed duty despite the chaos. Instead it seemed as if all of Carver's visual and auditory faculties focused in on one thing - the face of the man in the dock. For several seconds it stayed impassive. Then it turned, slowly, on the thick bull neck. Only when their eyes met did the killer's rough-hewn features give way to the leering smile Carver had seen many times, though not during this trial. And Carver never knew if he actually heard Kisic's words above the tumult or merely read his lips and imagined he had, so clear was the message.

'FUCK. RIGHT. OFF. CARVER.'

As the two men's gazes remained locked on each other and the Clerk went through the rest of the indictment, the repeated phrase, 'Not Guilty,' barely registered in Carver. By then their import was lost and he had but one thought.

*What the Hell just happened?*

# FREE DOWNLOAD

Get the inside
story on what
started it all...

Get a free copy of, *THE CARVER PAPERS,* - The inside story of the hunt for a Serial Killer, - as featured in LAST GASP

Click on the link below to find out more and get started

http://robertfbarker.co.uk/

## About The Author

Robert F Barker was born in Liverpool, England. During a thirty-year police career, he worked in and around some of the Northwest's grittiest towns and cities. As a senior detective, he led investigations into all kinds of major crime including, murder, armed robbery, serious sex crime and people/drug trafficking. Whilst commanding firearms and disorder incidents, he learned what it means to have to make life-and-death decisions in the heat of live operations. His stories are grounded in the reality of police work, but remain exciting, suspenseful, and with the sort of twists and turns crime-fiction readers love.

For updates about new releases, as well as information about promotions and special offers, visit the author's website and sign up for the VIP Mailing List at:-

http://robertfbarker.co.uk/

Printed in Great Britain
by Amazon

21211760R00263